Doctor Tyrant
Mercy Emergency Medical

A Novel

by:
Grace Maxwell

Mercy Emergency Medical: Doctor Tyrant/Grace Maxwell — 1st edition

CHAPTER 1

Christian

The first rays of dawn slip through the blinds, casting a warm glow on Lillian's bare skin as she eases out from under the sheet. Her silhouette is a familiar dance of curves and grace, a performance I never tire of watching. She doesn't look back as she pads softly toward the bathroom, confident and unhurried. The sound of the shower is a subtle reminder of our uncomplicated arrangement. Lillian Bryant, no strings attached. It's exactly what I need — no emotional entanglements to muddy my already chaotic life.

With the bed now empty beside me, I prop myself up against the headboard. I find my phone on the nightstand, its screen lighting up to reveal a barrage of emails. Each one demands attention, but it's the calendar reminders that weigh heaviest — a triple bypass at ten sharp, followed by implanting a heart monitor in the late afternoon. A marathon run in scrubs and sterile gloves. I can almost feel the dull ache that will settle into my feet by evening. Running a hand down my face, I suppress a groan. Surgery requires precision, control, qualities I've honed over countless hours in the OR. But today, anticipation claws at me.

There's no time for distraction. I swipe through my inbox, mentally preparing for the long day ahead. I am Vancouver's most sought-after cardiac surgeon. And I'm not a narcissist. I just know I'm the best.

The doorbell chimes, and I click over to look at the security camera feed on my phone. A woman stands at my doorstep, a stranger. Probably lost. I ignore the persistent ringing. She'll figure out her mistake soon enough.

Shifting my attention back to my messages, a smirk forms as a spicy text from Cinnamon pops up — an image of her perfect breasts. They're a little more than a handful, round, with small, light pink nipples.

Cinnamon: Something to look forward to after your surgeries.

Me: See you tonight.

We're fire together, and she always knows exactly what I need — a distraction, a release without commitment.

Cinnamon: See you at the club at eight. Don't be late.

That's followed by a string of emojis — handcuffs, blindfold, paddle, and a red kiss. It looks like tonight's menu will be particularly hot. Kinky even. *Good.* I need something to clear the cobwebs and keep the shadows at bay.

The doorbell intrudes once more. An irritated sigh escapes as I tap the intercom button. "What do you want?"

"Delivery for Christian Bradford." The woman's voice is assertive and unwavering.

I frown. "I'm not expecting any deliveries," I respond.

"Sir, you need to accept this personally. I can't leave until you do." Her tone brooks no argument, but I'm not one to bend easily.

"Look, I'm busy," I insist. "You must be mistaken."

"Dr. Bradford, I am not leaving this doorstep until you come down," she fires back.

The determination in her voice irks me.

"Fine," I snap. I toss the covers aside and swing my legs over the bed. But then I watch as Lillian emerges from the steam-filled bathroom, swirling the lingering mist. She's a vision of composed elegance in her business attire, a stark contrast to the disarray of bed linens we've left behind. Her dress — a tailored navy number — hugs her figure with an understated sophistication that suits her no-nonsense disposition.

Just as she's fastening the clasp on her pearl necklace, that incessant doorbell chimes again.

"Can you get that?" I ask, gesturing vaguely downstairs. "I should start getting ready." My tone is casual, but mentally, I'm running through the day's surgeries again.

"Sure," Lillian replies with an easy smile. "It's probably your summons to court. Maybe someone's suing the miracle-working heart surgeon." Her laughter tinkles in the air, a playful jab at my expense.

"Ha-ha," I respond dryly. "There's nothing going on that could lead to that." Although I am smiling now. Her jokes are part of what makes this arrangement so refreshing.

"See you next time, Christian." She leans in, pressing her lips to mine.

"Next time," I confirm, breaking away. She's already a distant second to the meticulous rhythm of surgery that awaits me.

With a final glance at her retreating figure, I step into the shower, letting the hot water cascade over me, washing away traces of perfume and passion. Steam rises, fogging up the glass, enclosing me in a world where there's only the steady beat of water against tile.

The shower door slides open abruptly, jolting me back.

"Christian, you need to hurry up." Lillian's voice cuts through the mist. "There's a package, and it's kind of insistent."

"Insistent?" I frown, raking a hand through my hair. "Just

leave it on the bed, Lillian. I'll be out soon."

"No, really," she says. "I've got to head out, and it seems…important."

"Fine, almost done," I call, though I take a moment longer than necessary. The steady pulse of water calms my pre-surgery nerves, and I'm not ready to face whatever awaits outside this sanctuary.

Finally, I shut off the faucet, droplets trailing off as I wrap a towel around my waist. A clean shave is next, the razor gliding in familiar strokes over my jawline, methodical and calming.

Eventually, I emerge from the bathroom, and my gaze lands on the bed—and freezes. There, nestled in a car seat atop my scattered bedding, is a baby. A soft pink bonnet crowns her tiny head, and a plush brown teddy bear stands guard at her side. She slumbers peacefully, oblivious to the turmoil her presence stirs within me.

"Six months, maybe?" I murmur, trying to gauge her age as I inch closer. She's so small, so vulnerable. I stand there, uncertain, my mind grappling with questions I can't begin to answer. A bag sits beside the car seat, its contents undoubtedly tied to the child before me.

I stare down at her, feeling the weight of responsibility press upon me like never before. This wasn't part of today's plan—or any plan, for that matter. And yet here she is, breathing softly, a new life in my stark bachelor's world.

I pace back and forth, feeling the thud of my heart against my ribcage. "Lillian?" I call. The silence that greets me is as heavy as the air before a storm. I fumble for my phone, and in moments, her number is ringing through the speaker.

"Hey," Lillian answers, her tone breezy, nonchalant.

"Did you see this…this baby?" My words trip over each other, hoping this is some kind of elaborate prank.

"Congratulations. It's a girl." She chuckles, but there's no humor in her voice. "The woman who left her said there's a letter for you in the bag."

"Can you come back? Please, I need help with this."

"Sorry, Christian, but no way. I don't do kids. They're too

much work." Her finality stings more than the dead connection that follows.

I hang up, my hands shaking as they reach for the bag and find an envelope inside. I tear it open, and papers spill onto the bed. I snatch the first one I see—a birth certificate. Addison Hearst Bradford. My name is printed, bold and accusing, on the father's line. Born September 30. That's…five months ago. The mother is Taylor Tull Hearst.

Christian,

This will no doubt come as a great shock, but I must ask you to read through this letter in its entirety.

My name is Erica Hearst, and Taylor Hearst is my sister. Taylor and I have always been close, and I was as surprised as she was when she got pregnant after a one-night stand. But she was committed to being a mother, and I was there to help her. When she asked me to babysit Addison this last time, I didn't hesitate. I'd done it many times before. Taylor got an audition for a movie in Los Angeles and was only supposed to be gone for a few days, but she never returned. Despite my efforts, I can't locate her.

You are Addison's father. Taylor always intended to tell you, but life and circumstances got in the way. Addison is a beautiful baby girl who deserves to know her dad. Enclosed with this letter, you will find her birth certificate, a list of her doctors, and a picture of her with Taylor.

Caring for Addison has been an immense joy, but also an overwhelming responsibility. I have a job and a life that makes it difficult for me to provide the care and attention Addison needs and deserves. I cannot do this any longer. I want you to know that Taylor loves Addison very much, and she always wanted you to be a part of Addison's life. I know this is a lot to take in, but I believe Addison needs you. She needs her father.

Please, take care of her. She is an amazing little girl, full of life and potential. She deserves to grow up knowing that both of her parents love her deeply.

I understand that this is sudden and difficult, but I hope you can find it in your heart to step up and be the father Addison needs.

Sincerely,
Erica Hearst

The room is spinning.

"Taylor..." I whisper the name, trying to summon a face, any memory from the haze of my past relationships. No, that's too strong a word. *Encounters.* Nothing comes.

There is no way this baby is mine. I always wrap it up. Always.

No. This is some sick joke this Taylor woman is trying to pull on me.

Addison stirs in her car seat, her cry a sharp contrast to the numbness spreading through me. I'm anchored to the spot, clutching the letter and the birth certificate. This can't be real, yet here she is—my daughter.

That word is foreign on my tongue, and it tastes bitter.

My hand trembles as I dial my mother's number. The phone rings twice before she picks up. "Christian, darling, what a surprise. What can I do for you?" Her words are like silk, smooth and unruffled.

"Mom, I need you to come over. Now," I say, struggling to keep my voice steady.

There's a pause, and then a sigh. "It's Thursday. You know I have my spa day, sweetheart. Massage, facial, mani-pedi...then my hair appointment. It's my regular Thursday."

"Mom, please. This is important. I never ask for your help, you know that. But I need you here, quickly." My words rush out, pleading.

Another sigh, heavier this time, resonates through the

phone. "All right, Christian. I'll be there as soon as I can."

"Thank you." I breathe out, relief momentarily easing the tightness in my chest.

As I end the call with my mother, my thoughts race to the hospital. Today is supposed to be a marathon of surgeries, responsibilities I cannot simply abandon. With shaky fingers, I dial Joanne Kim, my practice manager and scheduler.

I look around the room. I know I can't just leave this baby behind, but this is not how my day was supposed to work out. Joanne answers.

Thank goodness for a small miracle.

"Joanne? It's me. Listen, I need you to get the on-call doctor to start the triple bypass at ten. I'll be there as fast as I can, but I don't know when that's going to be."

"Is everything okay?" Joanne asks.

"Something's come up. Just handle it, please," I say, trying to maintain composure.

"Understood. I'll take care of it," she responds efficiently.

"Thanks, Joanne." I hang up and glance at Addison, back to sleeping innocently in her car seat. She's still there. At least she's asleep.

I need to figure this out. And fast.

I think back to my Christmas or New Years — not this past one, but the year before that — that's generally when this baby would have been conceived. Nothing stands out for me.

I stand frozen, my gaze locked on the tiny figure. Addison's delicate features tell a story all of their own, one I struggle to comprehend. Her eyes, although shut, slant gently upwards. I study her, noting the single crease across her palm and — after I dare remove her sock — the pronounced gap between her toes. She has Down syndrome.

A surge of confusion washes over me again. Taking a deep breath, I force myself to calm down, to focus on what lies before me. My fingers, steady now, pick up the note again. A photo flutters out, landing softly on the bedspread. *Taylor and Addison* reads the elegant script on the back of the photo. The woman radiates a familiarity — the kind I'm drawn to — yet her face

13

evokes no spark of recognition.

I scrutinize the details in the letter, a trail of Addison's short history. She was born at Mercy Hospital, my own workplace, a detail that adds a surreal edge to the unfolding drama. Michael Khalili was the OB, and his name implies a complicated birth. Cordelia Johns is her pediatrician, and Davis Martin her pediatric cardiologist—all names synonymous with excellent care within the hospital's walls. All people I know. Have I walked past this child and her mother in the halls of the hospital?

Relief flickers briefly, knowing Addison has been in capable hands, but it's quickly chased away by a stubborn certainty. She can't be my child. This must be a mistake, an error that brought her to my doorstep. I need to confirm this somehow. I have no time to be in a relationship, let alone be a parent.

Yet as I look down at the sleeping baby, I feel a strange pull, a connection that defies logic and precaution. Who is this little girl, and how has she found her way into my life?

A whimper cuts through the silence, and I freeze. In an instant, Addison's cries escalate, ripping at my composure. She's loud, insistent, and I'm out of my depth. My hands shake as I reach for the car seat, rocking it in a desperate attempt to soothe her. It's futile. Her distress grows, and with it, my panic. I don't know what to do.

"Christian!"

I barely register the door swinging open or the click of high heels across the hardwood floor. My mother, Madeline, strides in, a vision of composed luxury. I can't make out her words over Addison's cries. With an exasperated sigh, she scoops Addison up, giving her a pinkie to suck on. I stand there, useless, as she expertly changes the baby on my bed. I can't bring myself to step any closer.

"Christian, you must have formula or breast milk somewhere," my mother says.

"Uh, right." I fumble with the bag, tipping its contents onto the bed. Two cans of formula and a bottle emerge among a jumble of baby items. She takes charge, instructing me on the mixture — two scoops, six ounces of water. "All I've got is tap," I mumble.

"Tap water will do just fine," she says, and I can hear her patience thinning. When I return with the bottle, I hand it to Mom. She takes it from me but shoves Addison into my arms before handing it back. "You've got to learn."

Addison squirms against me, her small form a foreign weight in my arms. I tip the prepared bottle toward her, but it crashes to the floor.

"Christian!" There's more than a hint of reprimand in her voice now. She retrieves the bottle and thrusts it back into my hands. "Hold it properly."

I want to tell her I don't know how, that this isn't my life, but the words won't come. So I just nod, my throat tight, and tentatively hold the bottle to Addison's lips, praying she'll be quiet, praying I can somehow manage.

My hands shake as she latches on, drawing from it with a ferocity that belies her small size. My mother, with deft fingers, unfurls a clean diaper.

"Once she's done eating, you may need to change her again," she says.

I can't even begin to process the thought of changing a diaper. "I — I don't know how," I admit, feeling the weight of my helplessness.

"Life is full of surprises," she replies with a wry smile. "Now, tell me, where did this little one come from?"

I recount the morning — the persistent doorbell, Lillian's departure, the package left behind. With a sigh, I point to the letter resting on the nightstand, its words still echoing in my head.

Mom picks up the letter, scanning it. Her brow furrows slightly as she reads. After a moment, she looks up at me, her expression unreadable. "Christian, do you recognize the girl? Taylor Hearst?"

I hesitate, again searching the archives of my memory, but still, no clear image forms. "I'm not sure," I confess.

She offers me a knowing smile. "You should get a DNA

test, just to be certain," she advises. "But honestly, look at her... She has your coloring, and your hair was the same when you were born. I'm quite sure she's yours."

I stand there, the bottle still in my hand, looking down at Addison's peaceful face and wondering how my life has shifted so suddenly. There's a vulnerability in her that tugs at something deep within me, something I hadn't known was there.

"Get a DNA test," my mother repeats gently.

"Mom, what am I supposed to do if she's mine?" My voice cracks as the weight of potential fatherhood bears down on me.

She looks at me, her gaze piercing. "Christian, you'll be her father, and you'll have to care for her." Her voice has an edge of iron, a reminder that some things in life can't be shrugged off or sent to voicemail.

I reach out, trying to pass Addison into her arms, so I can escape to work, to normalcy. "Can't you just watch her for today? I've got surgeries—"

She steps back, hands raised in refusal, shaking her head. "No, Christian. This is your child. You need to be responsible for your actions. We had this conversation when you were fifteen."

Her words sting, but I know she's right. "Then what am I supposed to do?"

"Find a nanny, and quickly," she says, already moving toward the door, her presence receding like the tide pulling away from the shore. "You have room here for Addison and her nanny."

"Mom!" But she doesn't turn back. After a moment, I hear the front door open and close.

I'm alone now, save for the tiny human being who has finished the bottle and gone back to sleep. Her steady breathing fills the suddenly cavernous room. With trembling hands, I lift Addison, swaddled in her pink blanket, and settle her back into the car seat. She stirs slightly, a soft sigh escaping her lips as she nestles in.

"Okay, Addison," I whisper, more to myself than to her. "We're going to figure this out together."

The quiet is profound. My heart clenches, a strange mix of

fear and something else. But I can't place what it is.

I pull out my phone, the screen lighting up with unread emails and messages, all ignored for now. I do a search for local nanny services, my fingers clumsy and uncertain. There's a whole world I need to navigate now, and it's one I never prepared for. *What am I going to do?*

CHAPTER 2

Hailey

I rush through the door of Steaming Mugs, the bell above jingling a frantic tune. I'm late, as usual. Dana's already here, seated at a table near the window, her expression a mix of annoyance and concern.

Dana Stewart is my best friend. We were assigned as roommates our first year at the University of British Columbia, and we just clicked. She now has my dream job working for a marketing company because she finished university while I dropped out. But I'm not going to dwell on that now.

"Sorry," I pant, sliding into the seat across from her. "Time got away from me."

Dana raises an eyebrow, her crimson lips parting for the question I've been dreading. "Why couldn't we meet at our regular spot?" The Steaming Mugs we usually frequent is cozy and familiar, but this alternate location is farther away.

I tuck a strand of hair behind my ear, avoiding her gaze. "Well, I was working there…as a barista." My fingers fiddle with the edge of the menu. "I got fired."

Her eyes widen. "Why didn't you tell me?"

"Didn't want to make a big deal out of it," I mumble, tracing the floral pattern on the ceramic mug already waiting for me — hot chocolate, as always.

We drink our beverages and take in the same-but-different location. I can feel Dana studying me, trying to read between the lines I'm drawing in the condensation on my water glass. "So, how's everything else?" she asks. "How's Franklin?"

"Franklin's great," I lie smoothly, the words slipping out like practiced lines from a script. "Probably home right now, watching whatever game is on." I don't let on about the doubts swirling in my head, the ones that keep me up at night while he snores beside me, oblivious to our financial problems.

"Sorry about the job, though. What happened exactly?" she asks, sipping her coffee.

"I wasn't fast enough. Kept getting orders wrong." My laugh is hollow. "Fast-paced work isn't really my jam."

As Dana nods sympathetically, the weight of untold truths sits heavy on my chest. But I can't burden her with all that — not yet. For now, I let the warmth of the mug seep into my hands, hoping it might thaw the cold knot of anxiety within me.

"Any word on your parents?" she asks, steering the conversation to safer waters, or so she thinks.

"Nothing since they checked in a few months ago," I say. "They're touring somewhere, though I can't remember exactly where." The admission tastes like guilt on my tongue. I should know where my own parents are, and I wrote down when they thought they'd be where. But they don't have a cell phone for me to call them, and they prefer living off the grid.

"You seem...off," Dana says after a moment. "Is everything okay with the rent and stuff, now that you lost your job?"

"Honestly, I'm not sure how I'm going to make rent this month." The words come out in a rush, a relief to confess. "Unemployment won't cover it."

"Can't Franklin help out?" Her brow furrows.

Franklin Richards. My live-in boyfriend of nearly two

years now. When we met, I was still in school, and he drew me in, showering me with flowers and gifts. He was the first guy who'd ever seemed to love me, and we were together when my grandmother passed. He was my rock as I dealt with the loss of the one person who had always been there for me.

To repay him, I gave him some money so he could start his dream. But within two months, his dream became his nightmare, and he's never recovered. I'm trying hard to support him and believe in him, but it's been hard with him not looking for work. "He's applying all over town," I lie.

"You still have the money in your European vacation account for our trip year, right? You don't have to dip into that…"

Dana and I both want to go exploring, and we planned to give ourselves a gap year after we finished university before we became adults. But I got more involved with Franklin and left school, and then my grandmother passed away, so we pushed back our departure date.

A bitter laugh escapes me. "I didn't want to tell you, but I used my savings for last month's rent."

"When were you going to tell me you can't go to Europe?" Dana's face floods with hurt, and I can't blame her, but I'm not giving up yet.

"I figured once Franklin found another job, I could make it back." I reach for her. "Going to Paris and London and exploring for a year is still my plan."

"What kind of work is Franklin looking for?"

I fiddle with the frayed edge of a napkin, avoiding her eyes. "Franklin hasn't really found solid footing since the food truck went under. He applies for work all the time but never gets calls."

"What is he applying for?" she asks again. "I mean, you've had several jobs this year."

"He's looking for something he can do long term."

"And? The food truck went under nearly eight months ago," she presses. "Maybe he needs to settle for paying his part of the bills. Vancouver is expensive."

"He knows that," I again lie smoothly.

Dana reaches across the table, her hand warm over mine. "I'm sorry, Hailey. That's really tough."

I nod, unable to trust my voice. My dreams of eating baguette by the Seine—replaced by the stark reality of overdue bills and a future eviction notice—flutter through my mind.

I take a shaky breath, trying to compose myself. "Franklin wanted to cut costs wherever possible..." I trace the rim of my mug with my fingertip as I tell her what she already knows. "He bought this old truck that seemed like a bargain at first." I force a half-smile. "But it was more duct tape than metal by the end, always breaking down."

"Sounds like a money pit," Dana comments.

"It was," I admit. "The food costs didn't help either. We started serving breakfast and lunch, but then egg prices tripled from eleven cents each to thirty-three. All within one month. You can only hike up the price of a breakfast sandwich so much before people stop coming. And the parts..." I sigh, letting my eyes drift to the window. "Every other day, something else would snap or fizz out. Replacing them cost a fortune, and poof—my grandmother's life insurance money was gone."

"All in less than two months." I hear the edge in her voice, the unspoken accusation.

"Spent," I reply, feeling the weight of every penny. "We took a chance on the food truck, and now, it's gone." My heart throbs painfully. Franklin's dream of being his own boss, serving up comfort food on city streets, is over.

"What did he do with the money when he sold the truck?" she asks.

"We almost had to pay the scrap yard to take it. We were unlucky."

Dana leans forward, her gaze intense. "Be honest with me. Do you think Franklin used you? Did he take your money without considering you at all?"

My throat tightens, and for a moment, I can barely swallow. I know what she wants me to say, what part of me screams is true, but love is a stubborn thing. "I can't think that way," I murmur, almost to myself. "I love him, Dana. And when we get married—because we will—he'll make it right. What's mine is his, isn't it?"

Dana's frown deepens, but she doesn't push further, just squeezes my hand once more before withdrawing into her own thoughts. We sit in silence, surrounded by espresso machines whistling and a low hum of conversation.

After a minute, she turns back toward me, and I take a deep breath, bracing myself for her next volley of well-intentioned concern. "He should cover the rent, especially now that you're out of work," she says. "It's your turn to take a break while he earns money. Maybe go back to school. There are lots of jobs that don't require a university degree."

"Franklin does pay rent." I hear myself lie again, betraying no hint of the truth that it's been months since he's contributed anything more than empty promises. The falsehood tastes bitter on my tongue, yet I convince myself it's just another little white lie to keep the peace.

"Well, I hope he's at least fantastic in bed."

"I can't remember," I joke.

"What?"

I take a deep breath. I might as well be honest. "These days he goes over to his friends' in the evenings to play video games, and I'm asleep when he gets home."

"I'm sorry. It will all work itself out," she promises.

I hope she's right.

She doesn't need to know I'm the one juggling bills and dodging calls from bill collectors. That's my burden to bear, not hers.

The clock above us ticks away the minutes until it's time to wrap up our liquid breakfast of confessions and half-truths. We part with a hug, the kind that's meant to transfer strength, but all I feel is the weight of everything left unsaid.

Dana returns to her apartment, where she works from home, and I walk back the way I came, looking for help-wanted signs in windows. I stop at the IGA and apply to be a grocery checker.

I brace myself as I push through the door of our apartment. My hope is for silence, but the familiar sound of a cheering crowd on the TV greets me. Franklin is sprawled on the couch, his attention riveted to the screen. I watch him for a moment.

"Hey," I say softly, trying to hide the worry in my voice. He grunts in acknowledgment, never taking his eyes away from the game.

"How's the job hunt going?" I ask as I hang my coat and take off my rain boots.

"Nothing new out there," he mumbles.

He's reclining there, in nothing but his underwear, the very picture of relaxation, and I find myself making excuses for him in my mind. His last job nearly ground him down with its demands, and then he poured himself into the food truck venture. It wasn't just money he spent. It was hope, effort, and dreams too.

"Everyone deserves a break after working so hard," I whisper, though a small, insidious voice questions why I don't seem to deserve the same. I shake the thought away and head to the kitchen to fix myself something to eat, leaving Franklin to his game.

With a cheese sandwich in hand, I wander back to Franklin. The scent of pot hits me the moment I step into the living room, heavy and unmistakable. My eyes narrow as I look over at him, lounging like a lord on his makeshift throne of cushions.

"Franklin, you know we're not supposed to smoke inside." My voice is firmer than I feel, but I know what our rental agreement says.

He laughs, a short burst. "They'll never find out," he says with dismissive certainty.

For a moment, I envy his carefree attitude. I chew on my lip. "I lost my job."

Franklin finally tears his eyes from the TV, looking at me like I'm a minor character in his show. "Again? What kind of severance are you getting?"

"Nothing." The word feels like a stone in my throat. "They fired me because…I wasn't fast enough."

"Shocker," he replies, the snide tone cutting through the smoky air and straight into my chest.

For a second, I'm speechless, wounded by his lack of empathy. But then the fear of what comes next propels me forward. "Rent is due in two weeks, Franklin. We need to figure something out."

He shifts, the couch creaking under him. He doesn't look at me, and I wonder if he's even heard.

"I mean, you could get any job, just until things pick up." My voice wobbles with unshed tears. I see so much potential in him if only he'd set aside his pride. But he clings to an image of himself as a big shot running a company, expense account and minions at his disposal — a dream far removed from our harsh reality.

"Right," he says flatly. "Because that's what I went to school for."

My heart sinks. Arguing about this is useless. I nod silently, knowing the conversation is over before it truly began. I glance around our small apartment — our life encapsulated by these four walls — and I feel utterly trapped. "Okay," I whisper, more to myself than to him. I retreat to the tiny bedroom we share, leaving Franklin to his televised sports and the fantasy he refuses to wake up from.

My phone rings, and I can see it's a bill collector by the toll-free number. I walk back to him in the living room. "They're starting to call again."

"Who?"

"Could be any one of the people we owe money to — the store where we bought the couch you're sitting on, BC Hydro for the electric, your car —"

"You better not miss my car payment."

I look at him. How did we get here? "I have forty dollars in my checking account. Last month, I emptied my savings. Unemployment is only going to pay me two hundred dollars a week. I applied to work at the IGA today. I'm trying to find work."

"What do you expect me to do?"

The words hang between us, charged and heavy. "You could get a job," I repeat. It's an act of desperation, goading Franklin into action, but the moment it leaves my lips, I know it's a mistake.

He rises abruptly, his body taut with anger. "Me? Get a job?" His voice is incredulous, a crescendo of disbelief. "I won't go work in some hourly job and put that on my resume. I'm a mid-level manager. I've owned my own business. I'm not going to degrade myself for just any job."

My heart thuds painfully against my ribcage. "But I can't—"

"Can't what? Can't pay the rent? That's your problem." He steps into his worn joggers with a swift, jerky motion and slips into a T-shirt. "Figure it out. Borrow from your parents or someone else. Just don't expect anything from me."

Tears well in my eyes as I shake my head. "Franklin, you know I don't talk to them. I have no one to borrow from. We've spent all my savings, and my grandmother's life insurance."

"Then that's on you!" he snaps, his face contorted with frustration. Without another word, he storms out, slamming the door behind him.

Alone, the tears break free, streaming down my cheeks. I collapse onto the couch, burying my face in the cushions that still hold the faint scent of Franklin's cologne. It's a cold comfort.

Gradually, my sobbing subsides, leaving me empty and exhausted. I reach for the remote control and flick through the channels until I stumble upon the familiar opening credits of the first Jason Bourne movie. There's an odd solace in watching a hero who knows exactly what to do, who moves with purpose and certainty. If only life came with a script, clear antagonists, and choreographed fights where the good guy always wins in the end.

I watch all three movies in the trilogy and then another, eating instant ramen for dinner—still no Franklin and no solution to our problem.

As the action unfolds on screen, my eyelids grow heavy, despite the day's events and the uncertainty of tomorrow. Eventually, sleep takes over, offering a temporary reprieve from reality.

CHAPTER 3

Christian

I guide the scalpel with a steady hand, each movement meticulous and measured. The heart beneath my fingers is a battlefield, riddled with blockages I have to navigate.

"Clamp," I order without looking up, my voice even despite the crescendo of beeps from the surrounding monitors. The assisting nurse places the instrument in my hand, and I redirect the flow of blood.

"Let's do it," I tell her as we prepare to turn off the bypass machine, which has made sure the patient's blood continued circulating while I repaired the damage to his heart caused by years of use and abuse.

The machine shuts down, and the heart monitor screams its solid line.

"Come on..." I murmur. I administer open-heart CPR, reminding the heart how to beat. I won't lose this one. Not today. With a jolt, the heart beats. It's a battle of wills, mine against the silent reaper hovering at the edge of the operating table, and I'll be damned if I won't win.

I nod after a moment. "Okay, let's close him up." With the final suture tied, the heart steadies into a strong, reliable rhythm. *Victory*. Relief floods me. "Dr. Morgan, you can finish here," I say to my resident.

"Dr. Bradford, you're needed outside," a nurse tells me as I peel off my bloodied gloves.

"Can't it wait?" My question is rhetorical. They wouldn't interrupt unless it was necessary. I stride through the double doors, ready to confront whatever crisis awaits while keeping one eye on Dr. Morgan.

"Here, she needs you." A nurse practically thrusts the familiar car seat into my arms. Addison gazes up at me, her wide grin revealing the first hints of baby teeth.

"Where's Anya?" I ask, scanning the hall for the latest nanny. This one's actually been a fixture in Addison's life for a few weeks now. I thought things were sorted. *I don't have time to deal with this!*

"She quit," the nurse replies, her tone disapproving.

"Quit?" The word feels foreign on my tongue. "Why?"

"Because you haven't been home in three days. She said she couldn't do it alone."

"Three days? She's exaggerating," I counter, annoyance flaring. It's been two nights, and those were spent here, at the hospital, the on-call room serving as a makeshift bedroom, though I wasn't exactly lonely during those nights.

"Two nights, then," the nurse corrects, still unimpressed. "Doesn't make much difference to a six month old or the person taking care of her."

I bite back further comment. No one understands the demands of my job, the lifesaving work I do. They see it as an excuse, but they would feel differently if it was their loved one or themselves on my table.

I don't have time to do this father thing, and I don't have the bandwidth to learn. So I pay a nanny to care for my daughter. *Or at least I did.*

"Thanks," I mutter, though gratitude is far from what I

feel. As the nurse walks away, I look down at Addison, her innocence a stark contrast to the complexity of my world. I need to find her a new nanny, one who won't bail so easily, one who understands that my job is demanding and requires long hours.

Why is dependable childcare so difficult? How dare Anya just quit! Her job is to be there for Addison, all day, every day. I roll my neck to release the tension building.

I look back at Dr. Morgan, and he's just finishing the final stitches.

"Can you keep an eye on her for a minute while I talk to the family?" I ask the person standing closest to me.

"Yes, doctor," the tech says.

I hand him the car seat and walk outside to the waiting family. "Good news. He tried to give up, but I wouldn't let him."

My patient's wife sits on a chair and fans herself. "Thank you so much."

"I'll be by again tomorrow. He'll be here a few days, but things are on the right track."

I answer a few questions and return to Addison, who hasn't much charmed the tech I left her with. I thank him before picking up the car seat.

"Let's go to my office," I tell her softly, hoping the day's battles are behind me.

The rhythmic beep of monitors from the adjacent recovery bay sounds in my ears as I carry Addison down the hall.

"Joanne, can you watch her for just a moment?" I ask, depositing Addison on my practice manager's desk as I continue toward mine.

Joanne's eyes soften. "Of course, Dr. Bradford," she says with a smile, already reaching in to remove the strap and scoop Addison out of the seat.

I retreat to my desk, dialing the nanny service, a number I know too well. They pick up on the second ring.

"I need a replacement immediately," I inform the woman sharply. "Anya quit on me without notice."

There's a brief pause, a shuffling of papers, a muted sigh. "Dr. Bradford, we're not certain we can provide someone on such short notice—"

"Your employee has left me without any notice," I cut in. "We have a contract."

"Perhaps," the voice ventures cautiously, "it might be beneficial for you to take some time off to—"

"Impossible," I interject, my grip tightening around the phone. "Do you understand that I am the top cardiologist in this city? If I step away, lives are at risk. People will actually die."

"Dr. Bradford—"

"Two days," I insist, and then I end the call, leaving no room for further discussion.

A soft coo pulls me from my reverie, and I turn to see Joanne approaching, Addison cradled against her shoulder. "I have to head out, Dr. Bradford," she says apologetically, passing Addison back.

"Right. Thank you, Joanne." I look down at my daughter, whose bright eyes are fixed on mine. She's oblivious.

"Do you have someone for her tomorrow? I don't think Charles Johns is too crazy about having her here."

I roll my eyes. Dr. Charles Johns is the head of medicine for the hospital—my boss's boss and a pain in every doctor's ass. "I'll find someone."

"Goodnight." Joanne waves as she leaves us.

"Addison," I begin, my voice a whisper as I secure her into the car seat. "You won't believe how important your daddy is." She gurgles in response, a bubble of drool forming at the corner of her mouth. I chuckle despite myself. "Yeah, I didn't think you'd understand. But one day you will."

She smiles, a toothless grin that lights up the room, and kicks her legs in delight.

"Don't worry. We'll find someone to hang out with you all day."

I pull out my phone and scroll through my contacts. Dana's name pops up, and I hesitate for only a second before tapping the screen. My stepsister works from home and has a lot of flexibility.

She picks up after the third ring, a lot of noise in the

background. "Hey, Christian, what's up?" she asks.

"Hey, I'm in a bind here. Can you take Addison for a couple of days? I'm on call, and the nanny quit," I confess.

She sighs heavily on the other end. "I can help out for a bit, but Christian, you need something long term. You can't keep doing this."

"I know," I reply, rubbing my forehead. "I'm working on it. Thanks, Dana. I need to be at the hospital tomorrow by five thirty."

"In the morning?" she screeches.

"Sorry. Medicine is a twenty-four/seven job."

"Whatever. But seriously, find someone permanent. I have a job, you know."

"Tomorrow morning at five, and don't be late."

She groans. "You're going to owe me big for this."

"Whatever. Just be here."

"Aren't you forgetting something?" she sneers.

I run through my brain and don't come up with anything. "I don't think so."

"How about a thank you for bailing your ass out again?"

Oh. "Thank you. I'll see you in the morning, and don't be late."

She hangs up, leaving me staring at the phone. She'd understand if my father, the stepfather who raised her, needed my surgical skills. This is all on Anya. Why is everyone upset with me? It's not my fault.

Shaking off the frustration, I carry Addison down to the locker room. I place her outside the showers so I can see her while I wash off the sweat and the smell that comes from all the antiseptic in a hospital. I emerge refreshed and relaxed, and I quickly dress in casual clothes suitable for the outside world.

Addison gurgles happily as I carry her to my Porsche. I love this car, and I'll never give it up. I settle Addison into the front passenger side, aware of the eyes on us. I fasten her seatbelt with extra care.

"Dr. Bradford, can she sit in the front seat?" a passing nurses asks, her eyebrows knitting together.

I force a smile, feeling the judgment like a physical blow. "It's perfectly safe. There is no backseat, and I've deactivated the airbags."

Her gaze softens slightly, but as she walks away, she whispers to another colleague. I ignore them, sliding behind the wheel. Starting the engine, I glance at Addison once more. Her eyelids are heavy. Then I smell her, and I can't get the car windows down fast enough. *Oh gawd. Great. Now, I've got that to deal with.*

"Let's go home," I say, the engine's purr drowning out the hospital's whispers as we leave it all behind — for now.

Back at home, I park in the garage, next to the minivan I bought for the nanny but no one has driven. I push open the back door, only to stand aghast at the sight before me. My usually immaculate living room looks as though a cyclone has swept through it — toys scattered like confetti, cushions upturned. I step over a building block and nearly turn my ankle.

"Unbelievable," I mutter, balancing Addison on one arm as I navigate through the debris. A sinking feeling settles in my stomach as I approach the nanny's room, ready to unleash a torrent of frustration. But I turn the handle and find the room…empty.

The closet doors hang open, gaping voids where there should be clothes. The shelves are bare, photos and personal trinkets gone. The bed is stripped to its mattress, a single piece of paper left behind.

I set Addison down in her seat gently before picking up the note, scanning the words that deliver blow after blow.

I can no longer do this. You are a tyrant. I know you don't want to admit that Addison is not perfect, but having her in all the classes gives us no free time to do anything, and she hates them. You don't come home at night, and I'm alone to take care of your daughter. I'm not her mother. I've told you many times that I needed a break, as my contract stipulates, but rather than listen, you left me alone for three days straight. I quit. This is what I have to do for myself and my mental health.

My hands tremble slightly, crumpling the edges of the paper. Me? A tyrant? My gaze flickers to Addison, who is oblivious to the gravity of the situation.

"Addison doesn't hate her classes," I whisper defensively to the empty room. "And, of course, she's not perfect, but —"

I cut myself off, forcing my focus back to the letter. The nanny's plea for a break echoes in my mind, a nagging guilt that I quickly suppress. Why would she need a break? Being a nanny is a privilege. *You live in my home rent free, and I feed you on top of a very generous salary.* She can read all day. Addison isn't that demanding. She doesn't know stress or what it's like to have one thing go wrong and end someone's life. Forever.

I move Addison to her room, and with surgical gloves and a mask, I change her diaper and put her in her bed, checking to be sure the monitor is on.

"Her job is being a nanny," I say aloud. "Addison doesn't do a lot. Break time is ample."

I refuse to let the nanny's departure disrupt our lives. She's wrong, I know it. The activities, the classes — they're not just for Addison; they benefit both of them. Structure. Growth. Socialization.

"Isn't that right, Addie?" I ask, turning to face my daughter, lying peacefully in her crib. "Daddy knows best."

We'll be fine. Just another obstacle to overcome. We'll get a real nanny in here soon. Not some complainer.

CHAPTER 4

Hailey

Panting and slick with sweat, I push open the door to the apartment, ready for a cool shower and some breakfast. Silence hits me as I enter—no sports playing on the television, no clatter of dishes. It's been like this for a week, and for a while, it was a welcome relief. But this time, something feels different. A shiver runs down my spine as my gaze sweeps over the empty space where Franklin's stereo once sat. My chest tightens. *Where is his stuff? And why?*

Rent looms in my mind—due in three days—and suddenly, I'm drowning in dread.

I rush down the hall. The closet is empty. There's nothing that belongs to him in the bathroom, not even a toothbrush. It's like he was never here.

"Franklin?" My call echoes unanswered. I check my phone, but there's nothing. No note, text, or missed calls. He's just…gone.

What am I going to do?

34

I thumb the screen frantically, pulling up Dana's contact and tapping a message with shaking fingers.

Me: Franklin moved out. Didn't say anything. Help.

I hit send before I can second-guess myself.

The reply comes as a call, and Dana's voice is soothing even through my phone's tinny speaker. "Breathe. It's going to be okay," she assures me. "Let's grab lunch, my treat. Coal Harbor Cactus Club?"

"I shouldn't—"

"Yes, you should. I'll expense it to Tate. I promise it will be okay."

Tate Rutherford is her boss, and he's pretty easygoing.

"Okay," I say, though I feel far from it. "Just need to shower. And dress."

"I'll meet you in an hour."

I hang up and drop the phone on the counter, letting out a long breath. One foot in front of the other, I force myself to the bathroom, peeling off my damp running clothes along the way. The hot water scalds my skin in the best way, washing off the sweat and maybe a bit of the shock. I scrub my face fiercely, trying to erase the morning's events.

Once done, I twist my hair up into a messy bun that sits lopsided atop my head. It's not chic, but it'll do. I pull on jeans and a soft sweater, hoping comfort can somehow translate to confidence—or at least the appearance of it.

The bus ride to Coal Harbor is a blur. My thoughts ricochet between Franklin's disappearance and the impending rent. I stare out the window, unseeing, until the bus hisses to a stop and jolts me back to reality.

Stepping into the Cactus Club, I scan for Dana, my heart skipping when I spot her waving from a booth. There's a baby in her arms.

"Who is this cutie?" I ask as I slide into the seat across from them.

Dana smiles. "Meet Addison, my stepbrother's daughter.

Her mom kinda…left her with him. Long story."

Addison gurgles happily before yawning wide, her eyelids fluttering closed as she succumbs to sleep. Dana slides her expertly into her car seat. Despite the chaos of my morning, I have to smile at this baby's peaceful face. Maybe that innocence and joy are precisely what I need right now.

We order our usual—mixed greens with dried fruit, goat cheese, and chicken with a raspberry vinaigrette. But when the salads arrive, I pick at mine, the greens limp against the fork. My appetite has taken flight, much like Franklin did with all his belongings. Dana listens, concern present in her features as I recount the morning's discovery.

"Franklin left the day we grabbed coffee at Steaming Mugs," I finally confess. "We had an argument when I got home, and I haven't seen him since. I thought he was going to come back, but then all his stuff was gone when I got back from my run today."

Dana reaches across the table, covering my hand with hers. "You're better off without him," she says firmly. "You've got dreams bigger than what he could offer—like our European adventure and finding something…meaningful."

Her words are meant to be comforting, but they pry open the box of doubts I've kept sealed tight. "He told me he loved me. I don't know why I stayed so long," I mutter, avoiding her gaze. "He always made it clear he wanted someone more…fit. Not someone like me."

"Stop that," Dana chides gently. "You're perfect the way you are. You've got curves most women envy. You're like Marilyn Monroe. Fuck him. You deserve someone who loves you for you, someone who doesn't make you feel like you have to change."

Tears pool in my eyes, blurring the vibrant colors of the restaurant. I blink hard, but they overflow. "I can't find a job, and I don't even have the money for rent now," I choke out between sobs. "I've got nowhere to go."

"I can help you," she offers.

I shake my head. She still doesn't have the whole story. I

take a deep breath and tell her about the credit card bills, Franklin disappearing at night, the empty fridge, and how I have nowhere to go when I am evicted.

"You're not alone." Dana squeezes my hand again, her thumb stroking soothing circles on my skin. "What do you want to do for work?"

The question stirs a whirlpool of thoughts and fears, leaving me unable to form coherent words. All I can manage is a helpless shake of my head, an admission of my utter cluelessness.

I'm staring at my salad, feeling every ounce of the world's weight on my shoulders when Dana reaches across the table, her eyes earnest and caring. "I can loan you the money for rent this month," she offers.

A tiny spark of hope flickers in my chest before guilt douses it. Dana isn't swimming in cash either, and we're both saving for our trip.

"I can't. That could ruin our friendship." My voice is barely a whisper.

"No, it won't. This way you can give notice about moving out, and if you haven't found a job by next month, you can sleep on my couch until you're back on your feet." She leans over as Addison fusses in her car seat. With motherly grace, Dana lifts the little bundle, who immediately snuggles into her shoulder, making contented baby noises.

"Addison rarely cries," Dana notes, bouncing her gently. "She's such a happy baby."

As if on cue, Addison turns her head, grinning at me with drool-coated gums. My heart does a strange flip-flop, a smile spreading across my face despite the turmoil inside.

This baby belongs to Dana's stepbrother, Christian—all towering height, sandy hair with just the right amount of wave, and an easy smile. I met him once, and the image of his broad shoulders filling a doorway is seared into my brain. He's the kind of hot that disrupts a girl's thought process.

"Actually, there might be a job for you," Dana says, tilting her head as Addison shifts position. "Would you consider being Addison's nanny?"

"Me? A nanny?" I stammer, taken aback. The idea is ludicrous, and yet... The image of Christian crosses my mind again, and I force it away, afraid of where my lady bits want it to lead. *That would be bad. No. I can't.*

"Think about it. You'd have room and board included, and you could save up for our European trip next year."

Addison has wriggled her tiny hand out of her blanket and is reaching for my finger, her touch feather-light. Despite myself, I'm charmed, playing peekaboo with her until she giggles, and laughter bubbles up from within me for the first time in days. "I don't know anything about kids," I protest. "I was raised by my grandmother, and I'm an only child. I didn't even babysit as a teenager."

"Maybe just for a year?" Dana presses. "It'll give you some financial stability, and you can give notice to your landlord and still have a good reference when you need it."

"Reference?" I echo, my brain trying to juggle the numbers, the possibilities.

"Yes, I'll cover this month's rent," Dana reminds me. "That way, you can try nannying without giving up your security deposit."

"What is Christian going to say? I think this is a bad idea."

"Look, I didn't grow up with brothers and sisters, and I do just fine. Plus, you were a lifeguard. That's practically babysitting."

I sit back in my seat and chew on my lip, considering. There's a warmth growing in my chest — gratitude, affection for the baby, and maybe a small sliver of excitement at the prospect of a fresh start. But uncertainty still lurks at the edges of my decision. I look back at Addison, her tiny fingers wrapped around mine. Could this be the safety net I need? "What happens if there's an emergency?"

"You call nine-one-one. And I can always be your backup."

"I don't know how to change a diaper."

Dana snorts. "It's not that hard. Look, it doesn't have to be your profession for the rest of your life. This is a chance to make some money and dig out of the debt your dickhead boyfriend put you in."

I know she's right, but I don't have the first clue what a nanny does. When I started university, I was going to go into marketing. I thought maybe I'd work for a large company to get experience, and then run my own agency. But my grandmother got sick, and my world changed. Now, here I am with nothing — no boyfriend, no degree, no plan. I'm unemployed and drowning in debt with only my friend to hold my hand. And I'm going to live in someone else's house and take care of a child?

Dana holds Addison's head as she places her back into her car seat. Then she fills a bottle with two scoops of formula powder, shakes it, and holds it for Addison as she eats.

I can do that. And what do I have to lose? I twirl the stem of my water glass, watching the light play on the liquid's surface. "I'll try it," I murmur.

"Really?" Dana's eyebrows lift, a spark in her eyes.

"Really," I confirm with a nod, even though my stomach knots with uncertainty. The thought of moving into Christian's house — playing house, really — sends a shiver down my spine. "Are you sure he's going to be okay with this?"

"His last nanny left him high and dry. He's a little desperate, which is why I get to hang out with this cutie."

Addison gurgles.

"As long as he's okay with it…"

"He'll be thrilled," Dana says, reaching over to squeeze my hand. "This is perfect. It could be exactly what you both need right now."

"Maybe," I concede. I take a deep breath, letting the reality settle in. A change of pace could be good. This could be my chance, at least temporarily. "Christian's going to wonder what hit him," I say, trying to mask the tremble of nerves behind humor.

Dana laughs. "Once he sees how good you are with her…" She trails off, giving me a knowing look.

"Right," I reply, not fully convinced. But for Addison's sake — and my own fragile peace of mind — I have to believe this could work out. I finish my water and set the glass down with resolve. There's no turning back now. I'll be stepping into a new world, one with baby giggles and diaper changes—and a towering, distractingly attractive boss.

"Let's do this," I finally say. "Tell me everything I need to know about her."

CHAPTER 5

Hailey

Dana takes me home so I can pack an overnight bag, and then she drives us to a waterfront townhouse on False Creek, not far from the hospital. As we enter, my senses are nearly overwhelmed by the sleek lines of modern furniture and the scent of lemon polish. The afternoon sun pours through the floor-to-ceiling windows, and Dana guides me to the kitchen counter, where laminated sheets are spread out like some bizarre menu.

"Here's the drill," she says, tapping the papers. "When Addison eats—all bottles right now—when she naps... You know, all the essentials." Her fingers skim over a list so detailed it makes my head spin. Nutritional charts, nap schedules, even preferred toy rotations. It's all there, micromanaged to the minute.

"Wow," I mutter, taking in the color-coded timetable. "This is...intense."

"Tell me about it," Dana replies with a chuckle, her eyes rolling slightly. She points to another sheet. "And these

41

activities..." She waves dismissively at the baby yoga, music therapy, and sensory playgroups. "It's no wonder he can't keep a nanny around. It's like running a mini-preschool for one."

I nod, sympathizing with the unseen procession of nannies who couldn't keep up with this regimen. My gaze drifts over the rest of the papers — the appointments, the play dates, the developmental milestones to tick off. It's daunting.

"Anyway, I skip most of this fluff," Dana confesses, leaning against the counter. "Just stick to the doctor and therapy appointments. Addison enjoys hanging out more than structured play, anyway."

"Sounds like a plan," I reply, trying to sound confident.

"You're going to be great," Dana assures me.

"Thanks," I say with a half-smile. I hope she's right, but I'm not ready for her to abandon me to it just yet. "How are things going at BrandFusion?"

Dana smiles. "It's good. Tate lets me get away with murder because I bust my ass for him. He knows I'm good."

Tate Rutherford is Vancouver's *it* man for company branding. He's also going through a very messy and public divorce.

"Must be nice to have that kind of trust from your boss," I muse.

"Trust, ha!" Dana snorts. "More like mutual exploitation. I work hard, and he pays me well. But we've got a good thing going."

"Sounds like a perfect setup," I agree.

She nods and then gestures for me to follow as she heads down a hallway. "Here's the nursery," she announces, gesturing to a room decked out in pastel hues and plush toys. There's a comforting vibe to it, a sense of calm that contrasts with the chaos of that schedule I just saw. "And here's your room," she adds, stepping down to the next doorway.

I move closer to take in the modest bed, clean lines, and lack of personal touches. This space isn't meant for someone to live in; it's just functional, temporary. And the proximity to Addison's room highlights the reality of my new role — constant, vigilant caretaker.

"Guess I have little choice," I whisper. Dana gives me a sympathetic look but says nothing. I let out a resigned sigh and nod. "Okay. This will work."

Dana's fingers dance across her screen, and then my phone chimes. "There," she says, showing me the transaction confirmation. "Rent's taken care of."

"Thank you," I tell her, a little emotional at her generosity. "I'll pay you back, I promise."

"I know you're good for it." She goes back to her screen. "I just let Christian know you were here. He's in surgery today, but you can call Joanne in his office if you need to get to him or there's some kind of emergency. Her information is on the card in the kitchen."

"Sure, uh, okay. No pressure or anything."

"You got this," she assures me. "You're doing Christian a huge favor!" She slings her purse over her shoulder, and for a moment, her silhouette is framed by the doorway. Then, with a final wave, she's gone, leaving behind silence.

My heart flutters. *Addison.* A living, breathing little soul, now under my hesitant guardianship. I swallow hard. She needs someone—constantly. Fear grips me. This isn't just a gig. I'm the lifeline for a tiny human who depends on me for everything. *What did I just agree to do?*

I pick up my overnight bag and put away the few clothes I brought. I never imagined this would be where I am.

Addison starts to fuss. I pull out the formula and realize I don't know how many scoops belong in the bottle. I look frantically for the sheet that details this as Addison's irritation grows. "I'm working on it."

I quickly read two scoops—should have remembered that from watching Dana at lunch—and add cold filtered water from the fridge. I shake the bottle while bouncing Addison, but her fussing moves to a full-fledged cry. Her face is beet red. I put the bottle in her mouth, but she pushes it away and cries harder.

What am I doing wrong? Why did I think I could do this?

Suddenly, my T-shirt is wet. I look down, and there's

formula everywhere. *No!*

I hold her away from me as tears streak down her face. She's furious. I put her down in her car seat, whip off my shirt, and try my best to focus as I again read the directions on the laminated card. I need to use warm water, or put the bottle in the warmer.

I sigh and get the bottle going in the warmer. While we wait, I carry her into her room and the changing table. She's still screaming, and I look at the diaper, but for a moment, I can't figure out how to take it off of her. I stare stupidly, feeling my own tears well up, and finally realize I put the tabs backward. Now, I'm crying right along with Addison, but I get the diaper off, and after a few clumsy minutes, I finally have her changed. When we return to the kitchen, both still crying, the bottle is warm. I offer it to her, and she almost immediately settles.

Cradling Addison, I pull in some deep breaths and sit us in the glider in her room. After a minute, she smiles at me, and I realize she's not holding a grudge. "It's going to take some trial and error," I tell her. "But we'll get this."

I find myself some snacks when it's dinner time. Doesn't feel right to whip up a meal in Christian's kitchen when I haven't even spoken to him yet. Then I put Addison to bed—those instruction cards are actually useful, in some cases—and night creeps over the townhouse. The shadows grow long, and my fears multiply as I sit out in the living room. Christian hasn't come home yet, and I'm alone with Addison. What am I supposed to do? The baby monitor crackles softly from time to time.

Midnight ticks by, and I let out a defeated sigh, abandoning my vigil. I'm allowed to sleep, right? The sheets are cool as I slip between them, but sleep eludes me, my thoughts knotted around the day's events and jumping at every noise from the monitor.

Then, sometime later, a faint sound stirs me from my restless doze. I lie still, listening as Christian's voice drifts through the baby monitor.

"Hey there," he murmurs, and I picture him leaning over

Addison's crib. He begins to sing, soft and sure, telling her she's his sunshine, a lullaby that threads through the static and wraps around my heart.

I feel myself smile, and something inside me shifts, a flutter of something tender, vulnerable. *He really cares about her.* My heart swells. *That doesn't mean he cares about you,* I chide myself. Good grief, Franklin has left me a mess. But here in the quiet of two o'clock in the morning, with Christian's voice floating through the monitor, it's impossible not to feel drawn to him, the nurturing father he is.

Addison's crying cuts through my sleep, jolting me awake. I fumble for my phone on the nightstand, bleary-eyed. It's six o'clock. I set my alarm for six thirty, but it seems Addison is ready for her feeding now. I shuffle out of bed, clad in the grubby T-shirt and men's boxer shorts that are my pajamas.

With Addison in one arm, I hustle to the kitchen. I'm scooping formula into a bottle when Christian strides in, dressed for the hospital.

He stops dead in his tracks, his eyes narrowing. "Who the hell are you?" His voice is sharp, as if ready to tackle an intruder at dawn.

I jump, nearly spilling the formula. "I—I'm Hailey," I stammer. "Dana's friend? We met once at your father's surprise party." His gaze doesn't soften, so I hurry on. "Dana asked me to step in as the nanny, just for a while."

His lips press into a thin line, and I can tell he's not pleased. At all. "She didn't tell me about this," he accuses, crossing his arms over his chest.

"Actually, she did," I reply a bit more confidently. My fingers are tight around the bottle as I shake it hard and nod toward his pocket. "She texted you. Check again."

Christian fishes his phone from his pocket with a huff. He taps and swipes impatiently, and then his eyes flicker back to me. "Right," he says curtly, though I don't hear any apology in his tone. "I see it now."

"Okay, beautiful," I say to Addison as I offer her the bottle. She latches on and begins to drain it.

"I don't have time for this. Dana promised she'd be here."

My heart races. What will I do if he kicks me out? I've never been fired before I was actually hired. I square my shoulders, meeting Christian's gaze. "Dana has a job. So she showed me Addison's schedule and explained what to do," I tell him. "For the time being, I can help you out. But we're taking a European trip in a year."

Christian paces the length of the kitchen, his hands raking through his hair. "Heaven knows Dana has never been the epitome of responsibility," he mutters. "Fine. You'll do...until I find a replacement."

His words sting, even though I know I'm not particularly qualified, nor is this anything I'm interested in doing for the long term. I just need a job.

He turns to face me again. "Have you ever been a nanny before?"

I shake my head. "No."

He pinches the bridge of his nose and looks up at the ceiling. "Did you grow up in a house with a lot of kids?"

I shake my head. "I'm an only child, raised by my grandmother."

"Why the hell did Dana think this was a good idea?"

"Because I need a job, and you need a nanny," I say.

His face morphs into horror, but it's the truth. We're both desperate.

"You haven't been background checked."

I nod. "That's true," I reply softly. "I'll stay until you find someone qualified."

"Can you at least drive a car?" He raises an eyebrow, as if this is some sort of litmus test for my competence.

I suppress a scoff. "Of course I can drive." I don't have a car right now, but I know how to operate one. "I grew up in Langley. The SkyTrain didn't exactly stretch to our doorstep."

There's a flicker of something in his eyes—surprise, maybe respect?—but it's gone before I can read it properly. He nods briefly, as if filing away this information. "Many nannies can't drive," he informs me.

"Maybe that's why you're having trouble keeping one," I mumble.

But he hears me, his gaze snapping back to mine. "If I didn't have to get to the hospital right now, I'd kick you out for talking to me that way."

The threat hangs in the air between us, and for a moment, I almost wish he would. It would save me from the sinking feeling that taking care of Addison is going to be way more complicated than I expect.

But then something shifts in his stance. He leans against the doorframe, arms crossed over his chest. "Do you know CPR?" he asks.

"Yes," I answer, grateful for something solid in this whirlwind. "I was a lifeguard at the rec center during the summers when I was growing up."

He seems surprised by my response, but he's quick to recover. "And why do you want to be a nanny? Really."

"Dana offered it at the right time," I explain. "I'm looking for something to tide me over for a year, so I can save up to travel through Europe with her."

"Uh-huh." I can tell he's weighing my words. "How long have you known Dana?"

"Since university. We were roommates our first year."

His hands ball into white fists, and his jaw clenches. I'm ready for him to kick me out. I will pay my month of rent and give notice and try to figure out what to do with my furniture. But I am still holding his daughter. He hasn't once tried to take her from me, so how serious can he be about this concern?

He grills me further. "Your full name?"

"Hailey Phipps Spencer."

"Proof."

My hands are surprisingly steady as I balance Addison, find my wallet in my purse, and hand over my driver's license. He examines it, then pulls out his phone to snap a picture. "This isn't a regular nanny job where you clock out at the end of the day. My schedule is very demanding and often unpredictable. You'll be staying here at the house because I expect you to be available for Addison whenever she needs you."

I swallow hard, nodding, as he hands back my license.

"If you pull any stunts," he warns, "I'll have the entire Vancouver PD on your tail." He points to a set of keys on the kitchen counter. "Those are for the minivan. And here—" He pulls two hundred-dollar bills from his wallet, placing them on the table. "In case you need anything for Addison."

With that, he grabs his coat and strides toward the door. I watch as he slips into his coat, then turns back to me with a pointed look. "One last thing," he says, and something in his tone makes me stiffen. "There are nanny cams all over this house. So don't do anything stupid."

The words hit me like a slap. For a moment, I'm too stunned to respond, feeling like some petty criminal under his scrutiny. Then my irritation flares, and my eyes roll dramatically.

"Excuse me?" Christian's sharp voice slices through the room. I've clearly just flipped a switch I didn't know was there. He strides back toward me, his presence suddenly towering.

"Sorry," I mutter, though I'm not, particularly. "It's just a bit much, you know? I'm not here to rob you."

"Maybe not, but I can't take any chances," he snaps, his blue eyes cold and hard. He's close enough now that I can smell the faint scent of his cologne, something clean and spicy. "You're a stranger in my house. My daughter's safety comes first, always."

"Understood." *Though you haven't picked her up once this morning.* I keep that last bit to myself, though, caught between wanting to lash out and needing this job more than I care to admit. His need for control is unnerving. He seems to think he can dictate every move within these walls.

He holds my gaze a moment longer, then backs away, the tension easing as he puts distance between us. But the warning hangs in the air, a command from a man used to being obeyed. "Good," he says at last. "I have rounds at the hospital, and I'm in my office today. I don't know when I'll be back."

"We'll be here." I watch him leave and shake my head. This just keeps getting weirder and weirder.

"But I was right about one thing," I tell Addison as I lay her on a blanket on the floor. "Control freak or not, your daddy is as attractive as I remembered."

CHAPTER 6

Christian

I clench the steering wheel, my knuckles whitening with the effort of suppressing my frustration. I can't believe Dana passed Addison off to her friend like she's a hot potato instead of my daughter.

The image of Hailey, all sun-kissed skin and youthful exuberance in that bikini at my father's surprise birthday bash last summer, flits through my mind. I can't deny the visual appeal, but it's followed swiftly by a mental admonishment. *This is about care for your daughter!* And anyway, she's too young.

Though as I navigate the morning traffic, my thoughts drift to Dana. She and Hailey must be the same age. How old is she again? Twenty-five, twenty-six? But what does it matter? Why am I even considering entrusting Addison's care to someone who's only planning on sticking around for a year? But then reality intrudes. The other nannies didn't make it anywhere close to that long. Anya was the longest, and she only lasted three weeks. They couldn't handle Addison.

"Damn it," I mutter, weighing the pros and cons as the car hums beneath me. A fleeting presence has to be better than no presence at all, yet the thought leaves a sour taste in my mouth. There's an unsettling feeling about this whole arrangement. I've got this nagging feeling about Hailey, like an itch I can't scratch.

Pulling into the staff parking area, I grab my phone, and hit Dana's number.

"Hello?" Her voice is groggy, thick with sleep.

I picture her, probably still wrapped in her sheets, caught in the land of dreams.

"How old is Hailey?" I cut straight to the chase. There's no time for pleasantries with rounds awaiting.

"Same age as me. Twenty-three." Dana yawns into the phone. "We met during our first year at UBC."

"Right." Okay, so *young*, I remind myself again. "And why does she want to be a nanny?"

There's a heavy sigh on the other end. "We went to lunch, and Addison really liked her..." She sighs. "Look, her grandmother left her a bit of money a few years back, enough to get her through UBC. But things went south for her. She had this boyfriend — a real piece of work — who convinced her to drop out. He's a guy with big ideas and little ability."

"Sounds like a solid person to take care of my daughter," I retort.

"She's a great person," Dana counters immediately. "She's on her own now. Her parents are off the grid in a Winnebago, and the boyfriend turned out to be a giant mooch. Blew through her inheritance on some ridiculous food truck idea and then took off. She's broke. She needs a job. And you need a nanny."

I kill the engine, my hands gripping the steering wheel. All this still sits uneasy with me.

"It's only for a year," Dana adds, as if reading my mind.

"I don't think that improves the situation any," I snap.

"Treat her nicely, be fair, and she'll do a good job for you. That will make things more stable, and you'll have some time to figure out a longer-term solution."

I suppose that does make sense. "I just don't know if she's right for the job. The way she looks — "

"Christian, don't even think about sleeping with her," Dana's warning is stern.

"Please," I scoff. "As if I would. That's not what I was going to say, and Hailey's not my type anyway."

"Good. I know she's not, and that's my point. She's kind and sweet, and I won't let you or anyone else break her heart. I know you have quite a recreational life, but keep it separate from this."

"Obviously," I snap. The image of Hailey in my kitchen this morning flashes, unbidden. I shove it aside. *Focus, Bradford.* "I have to go. I have rounds." I end the call without waiting for a response.

Before I step into the hospital, I call the nanny service and ask for an update on where they are with finding me someone new. "It's been over a week," I say through clenched teeth.

"I'm sorry, Dr. Bradford," the receptionist says once she's pulls up my file. "We've refunded your deposit. We don't have any nannies who can work nonstop for weeks at a time."

"Isn't that a nanny's job?" I fume.

"No, it's not. Your contract was clear. They get a break every day for at least four hours."

I look up at the sky. "I'm on call for forty-eight hours every three weeks. I've taken the two-a.m. feeding so they can sleep. That's more than a four-hour break."

She sighs. "That's a sleep break. The break we require is four *daytime* hours, so that they can leave your premises and do something they choose without having to care for your child. I'm sorry, but that's the law, and we have to follow it. We can't provide you with what you want."

She disconnects the call. So there's the decision. I don't have a choice about Hailey now. She's the only one who didn't balk when I told her what my schedule requires. She'd better be responsible. *If she screws up, Dana, you're going to hear about it nonstop.*

As I stride into the hospital, I remind myself that I'm the best at my job, better than anyone else in this province and all of

Canada. People beg to get on my schedule. I'm doing what I have to do, and there has to be a way to make this work. "*Addison liked Hailey*," Dana's words echo in my mind, a feeble attempt to soothe my nerves. Maybe if the agency isn't involved, things can be a little more flexible to suit this particular situation.

I don't have surgeries today, but that doesn't mean my schedule is any less packed. At least I can monitor Hailey through those nanny cams. That's just due diligence.

My first stop on my rounds is my patient from yesterday. I almost lost him on the table. When I enter the room, Ronald Jenkins is out like a light, his chest rising and falling with the steady rhythm of sleep. But something's off. A cardboard box sits on the bedside table, reeking of grease and poor choices.

"Is that your breakfast?" I ask, pointing at the takeout container as I move to stand beside his wife.

She wrings her hands, her eyes darting between me and her husband. "He hates the food here," she admits, sheepishly.

"Mrs. Jenkins," I start, my voice firm yet not unkind, "your husband's body can't handle this anymore. He needs fresh, heart-healthy meals. Low salt, no grease."

"He doesn't like that." Her eyes well up, brimming with fear. "I don't want to lose him," she whispers.

"Then it's time to make some changes," I insist. "Be strong for him. His life literally depends on it." Scribbling a note, I call for a nutritionist consultation before moving on, another life nudged back on track, another crisis averted.

But as I leave behind the scent of saturated fats and step back into the cool, antiseptic air of the corridor, my thoughts drift involuntarily home—to Addison, to Hailey, and to all the ways this could go wrong.

I stride back to my office, the echo of my footsteps mingling with the mental checklist of tasks for the day. As I take a seat behind the desk, my hand instinctively goes to the mouse, flicking open the nanny-cam feed on my monitor. The livestream from home fills the screen.

And there she is—Hailey, splattered in an abstract painting of baby food, yet wearing a smile. It reaches through the pixels and tugs at something inside me. Addison is giggling, her cherubic face lit up in joy as Hailey makes a fool of herself just to entertain her. That makes me smile too, but then a visceral reaction stirs in my pants, unbidden. *What the hell is wrong with me? She's the temporary nanny. Keep it together.*

With a deep breath, I shake off the unwelcome arousal and bury myself in work. Charts, referrals, follow-ups—they're the distractions I need, the kind that don't have legs I shouldn't be noticing. Hours blur together until my watch beeps, a reminder of Addison's schedule, which I've practically memorized.

I pause, considering. Then I pull up the app that tracks Hailey's movements via the Air Tag on the mini van's keychain. Still at the house. Frowning, I check the time again. They should be at swimming lessons now, not… I switch back to the nanny cam.

There they are, curled up together in the soft fortress of the bed in Addison's room. Both asleep, peaceful. A wave of irritation crashes over me. The sight is not nearly as endearing as it should be. I grab my phone, ready to unleash a torrent of pent-up frustration. My thumb hammers her number before I can second-guess the impulse. *She can't just ignore the schedule!*

It rings. And rings. No answer.

"Damn it," I mutter, concern I refuse to acknowledge battling my annoyance. She'd better have a good explanation for this. *She can't just ignore me!* I press redial, my impatience mounting with each unanswered ring.

Finally, I drop the call and, on impulse, dial my mother instead. "Mom," I say as soon as she picks up, "I think I lost another nanny."

"Christian, you need to pay them more," she replies without missing a beat.

I clench my jaw. I don't want her money solutions. I need to vent. "It's not about the money, Mom. It's—"

"Money solves a lot of things, darling. Maybe you're not offering enough to keep them around." She speaks like we're discussing the weather, not my personal crisis.

"Hailey's different." I defend the girl I'm currently

frustrated with. "She's Dana's friend. It's complicated."

"Everything with you is complicated." Her sigh crackles over the line.

"Never mind," I say tersely, ready to end the conversation I shouldn't have started.

"Remember what your time is worth," she advises before I can hang up.

Her words are meant to be comforting, but they scrape against my nerves. "Thanks," I reply flatly and disconnect.

As soon as I've put the phone down, Joanne appears at the door. Concern wrinkles her brow. "Dr. Bradford, you have patients in all four exam rooms. You're running behind schedule."

"Right, sorry." I stand so quickly that my chair rolls back and bumps the wall. "Let's get to it." Professional mode clicks into place, but not before I stab out Hailey's number one last time. Nothing. Not even voicemail this time.

Frustration coils within me as I pocket the silent phone. They should be transitioning from swimming lessons to the playgroup now, part of the carefully structured routine I've created for Addison. Instead, they're napping, off schedule and unreachable.

"Joanne, give me two minutes," I say, trying to shake off my annoyance as I stride toward the first exam room.

"Of course, Dr. Bradford," she replies.

Behind each door, patients wait, trusting me to have answers, to be in control. If only they knew how little control I have over a simple thing like a nanny following a baby's schedule.

I check over the patient in the first room quickly and answer their questions, perhaps a bit more briefly than I should. But everything is fine here.

Then I slip back out of the exam room, my white coat a shield against the chaos blooming inside me. I pull my phone out as I walk to the next door. Hailey's number stares back at me from the screen. I dial again, and each unanswered ring increases my frustration.

"Dr. Bradford, is everything okay?" Joanne catches my eye.

"Fine," I lie and press call again. It beeps into the void.

I see patient after patient, but my mind is elsewhere, caught in the web of Addison's failed schedule. Each minute that ticks by is a missed opportunity for my daughter's growth, her happiness.

"Dr. Bradford?" A nurse's voice brings me back as I step out of exam four. "Frances Chow is asking for you."

She's a patient. She can wait. But then I stop myself. "Right away," I reply, each word measured, precise. I can't let my personal life bleed into my professional one — not here. Not when these people need me.

But between heartbeats, between diagnoses, I dial again. And again, silence answers.

Finally, I steal a moment in my office to cancel my evening plans. I text the woman I was supposed to meet.

Me: Sorry, something came up.

When my patients have all been seen, I check my phone again. My date has sent back a pouting emoji and a picture of her bare breasts. It feels trivial. I mean, the plastic surgeon did a nice job, but there's a fire I need to put out at home. The moment I'm able, I shut off my computer and race back to the house.

I don't bother taking off my coat as I march through my front door. "Hailey!" My voice echoes off the walls, a commanding presence that brooks no disobedience. I find her in the living room, not packing, not flustered, just…there with Addison in her lap and a book open.

"Pack your things. You're not following the schedule. This isn't working. You didn't answer any of my calls today." My words are like bullets, meant to pierce any defense she might muster.

But she doesn't falter, doesn't crumple under the weight of my authority. "The phone didn't ring. Not once." Her eyes lock onto mine, steady and sure. "And Addison," she continues, her voice softening as she speaks of my daughter, "is getting a cold. The pediatrician advised us to take it easy today."

I blink, taken aback. "A cold?"

"Yes," Hailey confirms. "Dr. Cordelia explained that her immune system isn't that strong. We have to be careful."

There's conviction in her eyes, a steeliness that says she believes she did the right thing. It's jarring, this unexpected resistance.

"Careful," I repeat, though the fight slips away as the doctor in me acknowledges the sense of her actions. My shoulders slump slightly. "Okay. Just…keep me updated next time."

"Of course," she responds.

I turn away, emotions churning inside me. As much as I hate to admit it, maybe Hailey's judgment was better than my schedule. I look back at my smiling daughter. *Maybe she's what Addison needs.* "Where's your phone?" I command, my voice betraying a hint of desperation.

Hailey reaches for it, the sleek device in her hand looking utterly benign, yet it's at the center of my frustration.

Pulling out my phone, I dial the number I've been trying all day, watching Hailey's screen for any sign of life. Nothing. No vibration, no ringtone, just silence hanging between us like an accusation. "What's your number?" I demand.

She recites her number as if it's something sacred.

A chill runs down my spine as the digits fall into place. I've been calling the wrong number. I inverted the last two digits. A cold knot forms in my stomach. My anger has been entirely misdirected.

Without a word, I turn and leave, a silent apology hanging in the air, too late to be uttered. The need for escape is overwhelming. I don't want to call my canceled date, so instead I flee to Joe Fortes, seeking my friends. Maybe they can help me calm down.

My drive across town is a torrent of emotion. *How can I agree to this? What other choice do I have?*

When I enter the bar, I spot my friends, their laughter a

beacon in the dim lighting, and I weave through the crowd to join them.

"Christian!" They greet me, slapping my back, pulling up a chair.

"Rough day?" Griffin Martin asks.

"You could say that," I reply, mustering a tight smile.

"A drink will help," Kent Johns chimes in, signaling the bartender.

Before long, a beautiful blonde sidles up to our group. "I'm Candy," she purrs, introducing herself with a twinkle in her eyes, "and I like to be licked."

We flirt, the banter light and meaningless, and it's exactly what I need — a temporary soother for my bruised ego. Laughter comes easy, drinks go down smoothly, and when the night grows late, I find myself leaving with Candy, chasing the promise of forgetfulness.

But when we arrive at her place, I leave Candy at her apartment door. This is suddenly not what I want, so I return home.

The house is quiet, and my shadow long in the moonlight. There's a note on the counter, written in Hailey's neat script, informing me of dinner covered in the fridge. I hesitate before peeking inside, finding a simple ham sandwich. Hunger, unacknowledged until now, springs to life, and I take a bite. It's pretty good — better than anything I would have managed. This is a welcome change.

Time slips away as I eat, and suddenly, it's two o'clock, time for Addison's feeding. I lift her gently from the crib, bottle ready, and as she suckles contentedly, I find myself humming a lullaby, soft and soothing. Her tiny hand wraps around my finger, a trust so complete it steals my breath.

"Everything's okay, Addison," I whisper. And in this moment, it truly seems it is.

CHAPTER 7

Hailey

The rarely broken silence serves as a constant reminder of Christian's ghostly presence in our lives. My first month with Addison is quickly passing, yet, he remains an elusive shadow that flits through the edges of our days. He eats the dinner I leave behind, though not at any regular dinner hour, and I think he reads my notes, but he's gone when we get up. When he's not on call, his whispers and gentle songs to Addison during her two o'clock feedings weave through the baby monitor, a nocturnal lullaby that tells me he's been home. It's strange, feeling both connected and disconnected from him at the same time.

He did leave me an employment contract to sign today, though. I guess that means my trial period is over. I flip through, but there isn't much to it. I live here, my hours are Addison's hours—whatever that means—and other duties include light housekeeping. Time off needs to be arranged in advance with him, and he'll pay me quite a generous sum as long as I give him my direct deposit information. I do some quick math in my head, and I shouldn't have any problems digging out of debt and affording Europe in a year. I guess that means I should sign.

I do so with a flourish, and then head up to check on Addison during her nap. She has plenty of time for that these days. Dropping most of her activities was a choice made of necessity, and I have no regrets. She still has a packed schedule of occupational, and physical therapy sessions, each twice weekly, not to mention her regular heart doctor and pediatrician appointments. Those fill our calendar with plenty of structure and purpose. I'll need to get her up soon so she can sleep tonight.

There's a knock at the door, and I rise to answer it. Dana's on the other side, holding a bag from Harvest Deli.

"Hi!" She steps into the warmth of Christian's living room. "Brought your favorite for dinner, a turkey club with extra pickles."

"You're a godsend," I reply with a grin, relieved to have both company and comfort food.

Addison fusses, so we walk back to get her from her crib and change her while Dana launches into a tale about her latest dating escapade.

"So, this guy — tall, dark, definitely handsome — he does this double-take as he walks past me, right? Comes back, follows me into the Steaming Mugs on Commercial," Dana explains, her hands animated as she speaks.

We return to the kitchen, and after we get Addison set up with a mobile she enjoys, we settle at the kitchen table and unpack the sandwiches.

I take a bite of mine. "And?"

"And he's Greek, works in banking. But get this, his only interest? Well, you know…" She rolls her eyes.

Sex. "Really?" I probe, swallowing a mouthful of sandwich. "Did he expect you to say, 'Let's go back to my place'?"

She chuckles. "I was flattered, but there was something off."

"Like maybe he was married?"

"Claimed he was single." Dana shrugs and sighs

dramatically. "But all he could talk about was what he wanted to do to me in bed. I started having second thoughts, made an excuse, and left."

"Smart move leaving him there," I say with a nod.

"Trust me, it wasn't worth the drama." Dana takes a sip of her iced tea, and we share a knowing look. We've both had more than our fair share of drama lately.

"Thanks for bringing dinner," I tell her.

"Anytime. When Christian gives you a day off, let's do something fun, just the two of us." Dana smiles.

I nod, as that sounds wonderful, but I realize Christian and I haven't talked about days off. I don't know how that works, but I'll need one soon for my move. I don't really have a backup, though, and I don't want to ask Dana to help. It's embarrassing to be such a mess, and she's already found me a job and a place to live.

I crumple the sandwich wrapper, tossing it into the bin before turning back to Dana. Her eyebrows arch in question, and I know what's coming next.

"Have you heard from Franklin lately?" she asks.

I shake my head. "No, and to be honest, I don't miss him." The words feel liberating.

"Good for you," Dana says, her approval clear. "I saw on Facebook he's shacked up with some new girl."

"Really?" I feign surprise, though I've also been tracking his movements online — masochism in digital form.

"Yep. Looks like a messy situation. He still doesn't have a job, and she's constantly posting about needing 'a man who can step up.'" Dana's lips twist into a wry smile.

"Sounds familiar," I mutter, thinking back to all the promises Franklin made, none of which he kept. "He always talked big but never followed through."

"His ambition couldn't fill a thimble." Dana stands, collecting her trash. We laugh, but it feels hollow, tinged with the bitterness of wasted time.

I feel rejuvenated now that I've spent some time with someone who speaks in return, but Dana can't stay forever. She has an early morning tomorrow, and I've got to get this kid to bed.

She waves goodbye, and as the door closes behind her, it's as if she took my energy with her. Addison is wonderful, but her constant care with no backup or breaks is a lot. Sometimes, it hits me all at once.

I force my feet to move through Addison's bedtime and bath routine, but once she's asleep again, I stare at the pile of laundry, knowing I should fold it, but my limbs feel like lead. "I'll do it later," I mutter, letting myself sink into the couch.

Later never comes. I close my eyes for just a second, but then the baby monitor crackles to life, jolting me awake. Christian's whispers drift through it, a lullaby for Addison. He's home. He's always here when it's too late to matter.

Over the last few days, I've spent a few hours each afternoon at my old place, packing up my things and preparing to move this weekend. Addison happily watches from her car seat or lying on a blanket close by. My old apartment feels empty and musty without someone living in it. I look around and inhale deeply, and there it is — the faintest trace of Franklin's cologne lingering in the air. That ghost of a scent transports me back to better days, though that was a long time ago.

I've been transferring my life to my new home, one or two boxes at a time. I'm supposed to be moved out and have everything here cleaned by the end of this weekend. Franklin hasn't called or shown any sign he intends to return. I've reached out to him a few times, but each unreturned call is a brick added to the wall I'm building around my heart.

"Shouldn't have expected anything different," I whisper as I pack another kitchen box. It's easier this way. Every item I move out takes me one step farther from him.

"Let's go home, Addie," I say once the box is full. How could he just walk away from everything and move in with someone else?

The answer is simple: Franklin used me. And it took me too long to stand up for myself. I can't let anyone do that to me again. I've read about love bombing — a man showers you with love and affection and you fall hard for him, and he gets what he wants and moves on to the next woman. I'm not proud of what happened, and I can't believe I didn't see it, but I won't allow that to define me.

I secure Addie in her car seat and close the last of the cardboard boxes, the tape dispenser making a satisfying screech as it seals my past inside. I'm moving everything but my clothes and a few items into storage, but I need help getting the bigger items there. My old neighbor, Ray James, stopped by earlier with my mail and offered to help me with the furniture this weekend — thank goodness. By Monday, strangers will start their story where mine ended.

I glance around the almost-empty apartment. So much still to do.

"Need a hand with that?" Ray's voice floats in from the hallway.

"Hey, Ray," I greet him with a smile. "Yeah, thanks. It's just these last few boxes. I should be ready to move all that's left on Saturday." My grandmother's china cabinet stands against the far wall. That's going to be the hardest to move.

"I've cleared my calendar for you," he says, a bit too eagerly. His crush is obvious, but he's a good guy, and right now, I need all the help I can get.

"Thank you so much, Ray," I say as we load the last box. "I don't know what I would do without you."

"Always happy to help," he replies, his gaze lingering. "I should get your new address for any of your mail that winds up here after you're gone."

"Sure." I grab an old receipt in my purse and write it down for him. We don't know why the postal worker often puts my mail in his box, but Ray's always been kind about it.

I load Addison into the car and wave goodbye. We stop to drop the boxes in my storage unit and return to the townhouse with enough time to feed Addison and put her down before Dana stops by with dinner.

My stomach grumbles in anticipation. Today, she's bringing bento boxes with sushi and chicken teriyaki.

I get Addison down just as I see her pull up.

"That smells so good," I announce as I open the door. The sweet tang of teriyaki sauce fills the air.

We head for the kitchen, and she pushes a plastic bento box over to me.

"Oh!" I remember as we eat. "Thank you for the loan." I e-transfer the money she lent me back to her as we sit at the kitchen counter, munching on dinner. "One year, and I should have enough saved to travel Europe. Can't wait to bum around with you."

"That was fast," Dana replies. "And how's work going? You've been at it almost a month now."

"Addison is great," I tell her, savoring a bite of California roll. "Nannying is a lot of work, but it pays the bills, and it's building my escape fund, so I can't complain. What about you?"

"Work is fine," Dana begins, her tone shifting, "Tate's ex-wife… She's a piece of work. Makes his life hell, poor guy. He's started sharing things with me. He hasn't really gone out since she left. She was so sure he was dating someone."

"Wow. Tate's telling you about his divorce?" I ask.

Dana nods, her expression clouded for a moment. "I don't want to talk about Tate. I'll get mad at his ex-wife. Let's focus on our Europe trip. We'll make it epic."

"Definitely," I agree. "I've started a list of things I want to do and see."

"Oh, me too."

We talk for a while about Paris and London and riding the Eurostar.

Eventually, I push a stray lock of hair behind my ear and lean back against the cool kitchen counter, watching Dana's face soften with concern. "Are you okay?" she asks, closing the lid on her salad container.

I don't want to sound ungrateful to the person who has helped me pull my life together. But sometimes, it's hard. "I think things are going fine, but Christian is practically a ghost. It often feels like it's just me and Addison here. If he hadn't left a credit card for me to use for food and baby supplies, and if he didn't eat the food I leave for him, I'd never know he came home. I mean, he clearly loves Addison, but serenading her with lullabies at two in the morning while changing diapers can't be enough daddy-daughter time."

A tiny wrinkle forms between her brows. "Dad says he's struggling with the Addison surprise."

"I can only imagine." I sigh, pressing my fingers to the bridge of my nose. "He's not on call this weekend, and he's supposed to be home. I need him here so I can move. I've plastered the house with notes, drowned his inbox with emails, made sure Joanne put it on his schedule, and my texts must be creating a digital pileup on his phone." I force myself to laugh.

It's not the lack of sleep that's getting me. It's the emptiness of doing it all alone. Christian floats in and out, leaving nothing behind but dirty dishes. I don't mind taking care of Addison — she's the only thing grounding me — but the loneliness is ever-present. And the interactions at her appointments don't make a difference. I'm not Addison's mother; I'm the nanny. Each time I hear Christian's car pulling away before I've even had the chance to talk to him, my resentment rises a little higher. Is this what my life has become? A series of endless days watching someone's daughter? I need a break now and then, but I have no idea how to get that.

Dana chuckles, shaking her head as she collects her things. "At this rate, I'd better keep my weekend open. You know, just in case you need help with Addison when Christian pulls another Houdini."

"Wouldn't dream of bothering you with this," I reply with a forced grin, though I fear I might have to take her up on the offer.

We stand, and our hug is brief but tight, a silent exchange of strength. Dana steps back, slinging her purse over her shoulder. "You're looking better, Hailey. I know what Franklin did was awful, but you're excelling at this."

"Thanks, Dana." I feel a little warmth seep into my cheeks.

"Stay strong," she calls over her shoulder as she heads for the door, leaving me alone in the silent townhouse.

For a moment, I let myself indulge in the quiet, imagining a different kind of weekend, one that doesn't hang by the precarious thread of someone else's whims. Then I square my shoulders and turn toward Addison's bedroom. When I check on her, she's sleeping peacefully, blissfully unaware of any turmoil. My heart swells with determination. I can do this.

The house alarm beeps when the back door opens in the dead of night, rousing me from restless sleep. I listen, half-dreaming. Christian is home. I can feel it. My eyes open, and for a moment, I consider getting up to remind him about tomorrow — or maybe it's today by now. But I don't want to nag. He knows. I'm relieved he's home as exhaustion pins me to the bed, and I drift back to sleep.

Next thing I know, morning light spills across my face — too bright, too harsh. Addison is fussing, and I don't hear Christian. My alarm clock's red digits mock me. Panic needles at my chest. *Where is he?* I scramble out of bed, heart pounding, and rush to Addison's room. She smiles when she sees me.

I check every room — empty. His car is gone. He didn't stay. *Again.* My mind races with theories about where he could be as I dial his number with shaking fingers. Wind whips at the phone as he answers, and his voice, casual and distant, floats through the receiver.

"Hey, what's up?" he asks.

"When are you coming home?" My words are clipped with urgency.

There's a pause, filled with the sounds of water and laughter in the background. "I'm on my sailboat, heading to Victoria with some friends. Why?"

"Because I need to move out of my old apartment today," I say, clenching the phone. "Addison needs you to watch her."

"You should have told me." His tone is flat, dismissive.

A bitter laugh escapes me. "I did tell you. I've texted, left notes, Joanne put it on your calendar and sent emails… How do you not know this?" Frustration scorches my throat, each word tinged with disbelief.

"Look, I must've missed them. Call Dana or something," he counters, seeming unbothered by my growing desperation.

"Christian, I—"

"Sorry, I gotta go. We're docking soon. Talk later." The call ends with a click.

Is he kidding me? I haven't asked for any time off, and I work essentially all day every day. I stand there, phone still pressed to my ear, the surrounding silence suddenly suffocating. I want to scream, to release this mounting pressure inside me, but I swallow it. Addison doesn't need to see me like this.

Christian let me down, just like Franklin and every man before him. I can't expect anyone to come through for me. I should know better by now.

"Great," I mutter to the empty room. "Just great."

Taking a deep breath, I gather what little composure I have left and dial Dana's number. She picks up after a few rings.

"Hey, Dana, it's me," I say, trying to keep the tremble out of my voice. "I—I need your help with Addison today."

"I knew he'd do this," she replies without missing a beat. "I'll be right there."

"Thank you," I whisper, fighting back tears.

As I end the call, I glance at Addison, peacefully drinking her bottle. She's the reason I stay.

Dana's car pulls up just as I finish strapping Addison into

her swing. I wipe my hands on my jeans. "Hey, Dana," I call as she steps inside. "Everything you need is on the counter." I motion to the neatly arranged baby supplies.

"Go, Hailey. Don't worry about us," Dana insists, her eyes soft but firm. "But I have to meet Tate at three, and I can't take Addison with me."

I nod. I don't have all day to get this done. "I'll be back." I slip out the door, feeling the weight of responsibility momentarily lifted from my shoulders. I make all the green lights as I drive the minivan over to my old building.

Ray spots me as I approach, already waiting. "Are you ready?" he asks as I exit the car.

"I hope so," I manage, my voice tight. We work in silence, an assembly line of furniture and memories boxed and bagged, each stashed into the vehicle until there's no more room. Sweat beads along my forehead.

"Storage unit next?" Ray queries, closing the door with a thud.

"Yes. I really appreciate this."

"Happy to help."

The drive to the storage unit is a blur, my thoughts a cyclone of anger and desperation. It takes four trips to deposit my past into the dimly lit space, piles of history haphazardly stacked against cold metal walls. The unit is a disaster, but I don't have time to straighten it. I'll have to come back later.

"Thank you, Ray. I couldn't have done this without you. I owe you drinks and dinner. Let me know when you're available," I tell him as I drop him back off at my old building. Though it occurs to me that I have no idea when *I'm* available.

"Great. I look forward to that."

We wave goodbye, and I drive as fast as I can back to the townhouse, screeching into the garage just after two thirty.

Dana greets me at the door with Addison cooing in her arms. "She was perfect," she says, but her eyes stray to the clock, and I can tell she's itching to leave.

"Thank you," I say, settling Addison's warm weight into the crook of my arm.

Dana slips away with a wave, leaving me alone again, and my anger resurfaces. It's all directed at Christian.

My apartment still needs cleaning. But I can't do it all, not with Addison needing me, not with my energy sapped by anger and betrayal. I pull out Christian's credit card, and with a few taps on my phone, the cleaning service is booked—a petty victory, perhaps, but a necessary one.

"Sorry," I whisper, even though I'm not. Not really. He should be here, helping, being a father. Instead, he's sailing away from his responsibilities.

I sit down heavily on the couch, Addison nestled against me. I stroke her cheek, vowing silently to keep her world steady, even as mine threatens to spin off its axis.

The garage door creaks open, and the security system alert sounds. Christian strides in, casual, as if it's just another Sunday evening, not the tail end of a weekend that's left me frayed and frantic.

"Finally," I exhale, the word heavy with exhaustion.

"Hey," he says, his glance across the room fleeting. "Sorry, got caught up."

I look down at myself—spit-up stains on my shoulder, sweet potato smeared into my hair. I just finally got Addison down. "Caught up?" My voice cracks, but I keep it low, mindful of the baby who has only recently gotten to sleep. "Did you even see the notes I left? The texts?"

"Oh, those," he mutters, scratching his head as if trying to dredge up a minor detail from the depths of his memory. "Yeah, saw something about that."

"Something?" I gesture toward the fridge, where a bright yellow sticky note waits, then to the counter where his empty plate from Friday night still sits—crumbs and all. "I said I needed you here this weekend."

"Right." He doesn't meet my eyes, just shuffles his feet and shrugs. "Looks like you managed, though."

"Managed?" A brittle laugh escapes me. "I used your credit card to pay for cleaners at my apartment because I couldn't do it myself."

"Fine by me." Another shrug. "Anyway, looks like you could use a break. You can have tonight off."

"Off?" I echo, incredulous. The digital clock on the microwave confirms it's past nine. "Offering me 'time off' when there's nowhere I can go, nothing I can do—that's not…" *Generosity? Thoughtfulness? Legal?* a small voice chimes in. It's none of those things, and a part of me wants to scream at him.

"Never mind," I say, tamping down the anger. I need to keep working here. "Thanks."

"Sure," he replies, seemingly oblivious to the sarcasm in my gratitude. "I'm gonna grab a shower."

And just like that, he's gone again, leaving me wondering how much longer I can keep doing this, how much longer I can balance on this razor's edge without falling off.

I head for my bathroom and peel off my dirty clothes with the kind of carelessness that comes from sheer exhaustion, dropping them into a neglected corner. The tub beckons, and with a few twists of the taps, steam begins to rise.

I sink into the bath, hot water enveloping me, seeping into my pores, untying the knots of stress. My mind wanders. It's been months since Franklin's touch, months since I've allowed myself the luxury of acknowledging desire.

But tonight, the quiet of the house and a fatigue that's both physical and emotional strips away the layers of my resolve. I close my eyes, letting the memories surface, memories of closeness, of shared breaths, I suppose of Franklin, though that doesn't seem quite right. I don't miss him or want him. Not really. A sigh escapes my lips, unwilled and unchecked.

Still, my hand moves almost of its own accord, fingers trailing along the water's edge, over the softness of my skin.

Soon, I'm all worked up, a knot of longing in my belly, an ache that's gone ignored for too long. There's that drawer, just within reach, where I keep a small, discreet vibrator.

I hesitate, but only for a heartbeat. Then I lean over the edge of the tub, water lapping against my skin as I retrieve the waterproof vibe. It's cool to the touch at first but quickly warms in my hand. The faint buzz, once activated, is a promise whispered against my flesh.

I give myself over to sensation, to the humming vibration that seeks out the core of my need. It's a floodgate opening, and I arch into the touch. For these precious moments, there's nothing else—no dirty diapers, no strained conversations, no unanswered messages. Just me, the water, and my little friend.

The last vestiges of tension melt away as the vibrations and my fingers work hard to find my release. I'm angry with Christian, but suddenly, my mind wanders to him and his bare chest. Only he's not the aloof man I know. This is my fantasy, so he can be anything I want. I think of his hard pecs and imagine he's here with me, pushing me closer and closer to the cliff's edge. I close my eyes, carried away by the sensations, by the wave building inside me. My breath quickens, the thrum of the device building pleasure deep inside me. And then, with a gasp that echoes off the tiled walls, I let go.

CHAPTER 8

Christian

Long after Hailey has disappeared into her room for the night, my hands remain fisted, tension coiling in my chest. I don't understand what's happening, why I feel this way.

It's not guilt exactly… But she almost has me convinced I missed something by not being here this weekend. Maybe I should be spending more time with Addison, and maybe I—Dammit, maybe I should have been here when she needed time off. I don't like how that makes me feel. It's like I'm losing control of something, and I'm not even sure what it is.

Of course, she's attractive, and I can't deny that as part of my issue, but I have more self-restraint than that. I guess I just resent that the situation requires it. I'm not that guy. I don't lose control. Not over this. Not over her. But every time I hear her voice, every time she looks at me with those eyes, it gets harder to hold back.

I lounge on the couch and make sure the baby monitor is on. It's been a hell of a week—scalpels and sutures I've placed weigh heavy on my mind. I lost a patient in surgery on Friday, which still gnaws at me, though I've been down that road before. I'm a doctor. Saving lives is woven into the fabric of my being. But sometimes, the burden of those I can't save feels almost suffocating.

And that gets me right back where I started. I know Hailey's upset. She thinks I'm running from responsibilities, and maybe from her. But this work, it's not just a job. It defines me. And I'm damn good at it. Just sometimes not good enough.

I remind myself that I'd earned the break this weekend. I have to stay sharp for work. Anyway, with the erratic hours I keep, sleep is more of an acquaintance than a friend, so I should make the most of this evening at home. There's something serene about the stillness of the house at night, quiet moments when I can set aside the weight of being a cardiac surgeon.

Only when I set that weight aside now, my thoughts turn yet again to Hailey. I want to touch her. I want to feel her skin under my hands, to pull her close and breathe her in. But I can't. I won't. Hailey is here for Addison, and that's essential. Anything else... It's dangerous. I'm already too close to the edge. One wrong move, and I'll ruin everything.

My stomach reminds me of its neglected state with a low grumble. In the kitchen, Hailey's culinary peace offering waits for me — sausage and peppers baked with pasta. I take a bite, appreciating the way the tangy tomato sauce complements the savory sausage, the peppers adding just the right amount of bite. It's fantastic. Even cold, the flavors meld together perfectly, comfort in a dish.

Perhaps she made this to show me what I miss when I'm gone too long. Or perhaps I'm overthinking it. Maybe there were just leftovers, and she's a thoughtful person. Regardless, these small acts are a pattern of care and domesticity that I'm still learning to navigate. Maybe that's what's gotten under my skin.

I should have told her why I slept on my boat Friday night and left at sunrise with my friends. She might have understood the need to be away. I'm just not used to sharing my choices and reasoning with anyone. I shouldn't have to.

I take my meal to my room and flip the pages of the latest Michael Connelly thriller that's been collecting dust on my nightstand. As much as I try to lose myself in the fictional drama of Harry Bosch, the weight of Friday's loss still presses against my chest. Sailing to Victoria with Griffin and Tori this weekend was a respite for a time, but nothing has really changed.

The ping of my phone cuts through the quiet. I glance at the screen — a saucy email from one of the nurses who occasionally enjoys blurring the lines between professional and personal. It's flirty, teetering on inappropriate, but it's also familiar territory. A diversion. I'm about to craft a witty reply when a sound from the baby monitor snatches my attention.

Heavy breathing, uneven and ragged. My heart kicks up a notch. *Addison.* I toss the book aside, adrenaline flooding my system as if I'm back in the OR. In moments, I'm down the hall at her door, pushing it open with a surge of protective urgency.

"Addison?" My voice is tight as I scan her crib, expecting the worst. But she's there, peaceful in slumber, utterly relaxed.

Confusion knots my brow. The noise… It's still coming through the monitor. An unmistakable moan follows, and realization dawns. It's not Addison. It's Hailey. She must have accidentally nudged the microphone in the bathroom.

I should give her privacy, but instead, I find myself rooted to the spot, listening. The sounds sketch an intimate picture, and despite my better judgment, I imagine what she's doing in there. The curve of her neck, the tilt of her head, the fall of water over her skin…

"Damn it," I mutter under my breath, a mixture of self-reproach and unwanted arousal. I return to my room, but the sound follows me over the monitor. This isn't me — I'm not the voyeuristic type — but Hailey is unraveling the threads of my self-control.

With a deep breath, I force myself to turn off the monitor, though the echo of her moans lingers in my ears like a siren's call. I refuse to answer. She's not actually calling me anyway.

I pace the length of my bedroom, my mind a restless sea of churning thoughts. Last week, I kept my hands steady as I performed an aneurysm repair. I do those often enough that my mind occasionally wanders, and that day, images of Hailey kept flashing through my mind—her laughter, the warmth of her smile. Why does she command my attention this way? I've had so many nannies and never had a problem before. My distraction could have been catastrophic.

"Get a grip," I chastise myself, raking a hand through my hair. The answer seems obvious. She needs to go. It's the only way to regain the balance I've lost. Hailey is replaceable. There are dozens of services dedicated to nannies. I just need to contact a new one.

But then there's Addison. Hailey is more than her nanny, or at the very least, she's a better nanny than any of the others were. She's nurturing and patient, like a mother would be. Addison has lost so much already. How can I justify taking something else away from my little girl?

I squeeze my eyes closed. The solution isn't to push Hailey out. It's for me to wall up my feelings. Cold turkey. Stop this madness before I do something stupid.

But then I flip the monitor back on—for safety, I tell myself—and my resolve crumbles as I hear her again. She's breathing in soft, airy moans that shouldn't be for my ears. Yet here I am, dick in hand, hot and hard as I succumb to an urge far stronger than my willpower. I stroke myself, each pull a silent plea for release, yet I hold back, timing my pleasure with hers. The knowledge that she's so close, yet untouchable, tears at me. I'm furious for being weak and, suddenly, for being a bastard to her. I know that's the truth.

But even as regret consumes me, my hunger doesn't wane. I groan low, a sound swallowed by the darkness of my room, and we find our release together, separated by walls but united in this secret act.

Not long after, exhaustion claims me, pulling me under. I fall into a fitful sleep, haunted by her image and my desire for her. I'm desperate, and I hate myself for that, all the more because I don't understand it in the least.

Sometime later, I wake to the unfamiliar sensation of a full night's rest, a luxury so rare it feels alien. The baby monitor is silent, its small green light steady. Addison must have slept through the night. I tiptoe to her room. A quiet relief eases through me as I push open the door and see her in her crib, but it's quickly overtaken by my reaction to what I find as I scan the room.

Hailey stands in the soft morning light, wearing sleep shorts and a tank top. Her hair, a chaotic tumble of chestnut waves, is piled high on her head, a few strands framing her face. She's looking down at Addison, and it's an intimate, unguarded moment that tugs at something primal within me. Love for my daughter, yes, but something intensely protective of her caregiver as well. I want to weave my fingers through Hailey's messy locks, pull her close, and hear those breathy moans from last night, this time for my ears alone.

Silently, I withdraw and pad across the cool hardwood floor to the kitchen. The action is mechanical, a distraction from the turmoil churning inside me. Breakfast — a futile attempt to regain some semblance of normalcy. But even as I crack eggs into the sizzling pan, my mind isn't on the task. It's on Hailey.

The soft patter of her footsteps announces her approach before she rounds the corner into the kitchen with Addison. My chest tightens as I watch them, a reminder of what I've been trying to ignore.

"Are you going to be around for a while?" Hailey's voice is casual, and she's likely assessing my mood.

"What are you planning on doing?" The demand leaves my lips sharply, my grip tightening on the spatula.

She pauses. "Just wanted to go for a quick run if that's okay."

"Sure," I manage, though nothing feels sure at all. Not anymore.

She nods and offers me Addison. This takes me by surprise, though I suppose it shouldn't. Our hands graze as I take her, and it's electric. I wonder if she felt it too.

"I cut some strawberries, and they're in the fridge. You can also give her Cheerios." Hailey disappears down the hall to her room, and I force myself to look away, jaw clenched. Hailey is supposed to be here for Addison, not...me. But damn it, every time I see her, it's like something in me shifts. I want to please her, to get along. To work together toward a common goal. There's this low hum under my skin, growing louder, harder to ignore. She makes everything seem lighter. Easier.

I put Addison in her highchair and turn off the stove, the eggs forgotten and overcooked. I lean heavily against the counter, my hands bracing the edge. I'm out of control. This is not like me.

I hear the door open and close. Hailey's gone for her run, leaving me with Addison. I don't know what to do with her. I spread too many Cheerios on the tray of the highchair, and she reaches for them eagerly, chasing them around the tray.

The minutes crawl by. Hailey said something about strawberries, so I find the small container in the fridge and add them on the tray in front of Addison. She just looks at them. I pick up a piece and put it in her mouth. After a moment, she breaks into a smile. I feed her one piece at a time, and she happily enjoys them.

Forty minutes is beginning to feel like an eternity, and then an eyelash-curling smell wafts from Addison. She giggles. *Oh no.* I can't. Thankfully, just then I hear the front door open and close, heralding Hailey's return. My attention moves to the entryway as she steps into the kitchen. She looks different somehow — more alive. Her skin glistens with the sheen of exertion, and her cheeks are flushed with the morning chill outside.

Wordlessly, she moves to the sink and fills a glass with water, downing it in swift gulps before refilling it for a second round. Her silence is loud and clear. I've screwed up, and she's not ready to forget it. My throat tightens with a cocktail of frustration and guilt.

"I smell the need for a diaper change," she says as she eyes me.

I nod. "It happened just before you walked in."

She scoops Addison from her highchair. "Did you like

your strawberries? I think you have more on your face than in your belly."

Addison giggles, and they disappear.

I should feel like an ass for making Hailey change the diaper. And I don't *not* feel like an ass... But I'm a doctor, and I'm not sure there's anything worse than what came out of my child.

It doesn't take long before Hailey is back with Addison in her arms, all clean and smelling fresh. She heads for the living room where the toys are.

"What's on the agenda for you and Addison today?" I ask.

She turns to face me. The air between us charges. "We're planning to walk around VanDusen Gardens. They have an orchid exhibit, and I love orchids. I want to take advantage of the dry weather while we can."

Suddenly, her plan strikes me as perfect. Perhaps it would even be a respite from the turmoil inside me. I hesitate, then decide to take the leap. "Can I join you?"

She keeps her expression carefully neutral, guarded. But after a moment she nods, offering a tentative smile. "Sure. Addison would like that."

My chest eases with something akin to relief, though the underlying current of tension remains.

After she takes a quick shower, we pile into the minivan, and I drive us across town to the gardens.

"This thing is terrible." I navigate through the city streets with Addison babbling in her car seat. The vehicle is clunky, its engine groans, and it lacks the visceral thrill and power of my Porsche. I bought this car for safety, but now I wonder if it's safe at all.

"Maybe it's time for you to trade in speed for space," Hailey teases, casting a sidelong glance my way.

I suspect she's enjoying my discomfort. "Never thought I'd be the one driving this vehicle," I mutter.

She shakes her head, and I realize how ridiculous that sounds. But it's true. I don't have a long-term parenting strategy. I just need to get by, keep my daughter safe and happy, and keep my life functioning.

We pull up at VanDusen Gardens as the morning dew begins to lift, ushering in the warmth of the sun. I park the minivan and practically leap out, stretching my limbs before heading straight to the bistro. "Need coffee," I grumble. "You want anything?" I ask over my shoulder.

"Hot chocolate, please," Hailey responds, her voice soft but without the chill from earlier.

The queue at the bistro is short, just early birds so far, and I order a double shot of espresso for myself and a hot chocolate for Hailey. We take our beverages to go, stepping out into the fresh air, laden with floral scents.

As we wander along the winding paths, Addison coos from her stroller, and I find myself unwinding with each step. The flowers are a riot of colors.

"Tell me about your family," I say, trying to make this experience feel more normal with conversation.

She shrugs. "I'm an only child, and I was raised by my grandmother. She died a little over two years ago. What about you?"

"My parents divorced when I was very young. I grew up with my mother and grandfather, and my father... Well, he's more like a buddy, I guess. He's busy with his new family — Dana's family."

"Seems we're both a little untethered," she remarks. There's no sadness in her tone, just acceptance.

"Untethered," I repeat, tasting the word. It feels right, fitting for this moment, for us. For me lately, that's for sure.

We wander for a while, and as lunchtime approaches, my stomach growls. "What's your plan for lunch?"

"I brought a bottle for Addison, and I usually just wait and grab something back at the house."

"Any interest in one of the box lunches from the bistro?"

She looks over at the Welcome Center and then back at me. "Sure. Why not? I have a blanket we use for tummy time, and then we can feed Addison before her nap."

She requests a roast beef and cheddar sandwich box and a sparkling water, and I head off to pick up our lunch.

I watch her from the bistro's line. She and Addison are all smiles. They find a nice spot next to the pond, and Addison sits on Hailey's lap while she's doused in sunscreen, followed by a hat and baby sunglasses. Hailey sets her on the blanket and takes her picture. My heart swells — with what, I'm not sure. But I owe Dana for Hailey. None of the other nannies were nearly as good for Addison. I have to keep that at the forefront of my mind. Certain parts of me really seem to think she could be good for me too, but she is in no way meant to be my plaything.

When I finally have our order, I make my way back. "Sorry that took so long," I apologize.

"That's okay. Addison likes watching the ducks on the pond."

I settle on the blanket, feeling the softness of the grass beneath it. Hailey gently sets Addison down on her tummy, and her face scrunches up in protest before she bravely pushes herself up with tiny arms.

"I got to know your dad through Dana," Hailey says as she opens her lunch. "They would come over to campus and take us out for dinner, and they often included my grandma. It's great that you're friends with your dad."

I look down at Addison. "I don't know that we're really friends. They have me over for dinner a few times a year. And he calls and checks when he hasn't heard from me." I shrug and take out my sandwich.

"That sounds like a friend. That's what Dana and I do. Except we go out a little more often, and we each buy our own meals."

I busy myself with my lunch and keep my distance from Addison. It's strange to spend this much time around her. *Should I pick her up? Should I be doing something?* I don't know.

"What did your parents say when Addison arrived?" Hailey asks.

"She was dropped on my doorstep when she was about six months old. My mom said to hire a nanny, and my dad said they would help out."

"Have you asked him for help?"

"No," I admit, watching Addison's determined movements. "I haven't needed his help."

"What about Dana?" Hailey turns to me now, curiosity on her features. "How's your relationship with her?"

"Better...closer these past few years. We're definitely more like brother and sister." It feels odd to talk about Dana this way, but what I say is true. "When she needs advice or help with something, she calls."

"And you do the same with her?" she presses.

"Not really."

Hailey looks at me over her sunglasses. "Why not? How did I end up here?"

I look away. She's right. And why is that so awkward? "Yes, she was my lifesaver when my last nanny walked out."

Hailey nods and returns her attention to Addison. "You're doing great, sweetie." Addison grunts with effort and finally rolls onto her back. "Soon you'll be sitting up by yourself, and then crawling."

"Who told you that?" I ask, a touch of skepticism in my voice. I'm not doubting her, but I want to understand where she's getting this information.

"From a book." Hailey's gaze doesn't waver from Addison. "On developmental milestones for children with Down syndrome. According to what I've read, she's right on track."

"Right on track," I repeat softly, the phrase bringing an unexpected comfort. A surge of pride swells within me. I'm providing for her. I'm doing this. Maybe we're both learning, both growing, in ways I didn't expect.

We finish our lunches, and for some reason, I tell Hailey about losing my patient on Friday. "I knew the repair was going to be tough. An aortic aneurysm is a bulge in the wall of the body's main artery."

Hailey listens, and when Addison fusses, she pulls her into her lap and feeds her a bottle.

"This one was fairly large, but women's heart problems present differently," I explain. "The patient showed up at the emergency department having trouble breathing. They treated

81

her for asthma and sent her home. It got worse, so she came back, and they ran a CT. She didn't have any heart pain, but the bulge was as big as my thumb." I shake my head, still remembering my shock when I saw her images. "We rushed her in for surgery, and I hoped we'd gotten to it in time, but we didn't."

Hailey shakes her head. "I couldn't do what you do."

"I love it." I pick some grass and let it blow in the breeze. "I love saving lives. I make a difference."

"I understand that. I'm thinking I might get my real estate license," Hailey says after a moment. "I can make a difference by helping families find a home to buy."

An alarm sounds in my head. "When are you going to do that? I thought you were staying for a year?"

She looks at me strangely. "I am. But after Dana and I explore Europe for a while, I need to come back and get a real job."

Addison has finished her bottle and is drifting toward sleep. I watch as Hailey makes quick work of her diaper and tucks her into her car seat. She's good at this.

We collect our things and walk back to the minivan. "Would you like me to drive?" she offers.

"No. I've got it."

"It's not the horsepower you're used to."

I narrow my eyes. This hunk of metal isn't even close to what I drive. But I can see she's making fun of me. "That's okay."

I navigate back to my townhouse and pull into the garage.

Hailey's already unfastening Addison from her car seat, cooing gently to calm any stirrings of discontent. "Let's get you down in your crib," she whispers to Addison, her voice soothing, and Addison's eyes slide closed again.

I watch them, noting the ease with which Hailey manages my daughter. It leaves me feeling strangely adrift. "I'm going to catch up with some friends," I announce, more to fill the silence than anything else. The truth is, I don't know what to do with myself. I've never spent this much time with Addison, but being alone with Hailey seems even more daunting. It's like standing on a precipice, knowing I'm going to fall. The only way I know how to resist is to leave.

"This was fun," Hailey says suddenly, turning to face me as she heads down the hall, her expression apologetic. "Sorry for all the chatter… I'm used to talking to Addison all day."

"No need to apologize." My words are genuine. "I enjoyed it."

She smiles, and it's disarming.

"Let me know when she talks back," I tell her, the idea bringing a grin to my face. I imagine Addison's voice, the things she might say, and it's a future I look forward to.

"Will do," Hailey promises, continuing down the hall to Addison's crib.

I head back out, to the Porsche this time, the sleek lines of the car promising a different kind of journey than the minivan. I let the road take me, each turn distancing me from the house, from Hailey, and from the confusing emotions swirling inside me.

But despite my attempts at detachment, my mind replays the day—the laughter, the wonder of Addison, the shared conversation with Hailey. It was a great outing, a day filled with unexpected joys and simple pleasures.

I'm surprised to admit it, but I enjoyed myself—in a way I haven't for a very long time.

CHAPTER 9

Hailey

I can hear Addison fussing as I rise, the digital clock blaring just after six a.m. in red digits. I listen for Christian, but I don't hear him. I haven't seen him since we went to VanDusen several days ago. I push off the covers and shuffle to Addison's room. She's stirring, little fists flailing for attention. I lift her, feeling the dampness of her diaper through the onesie.

"Let's get you changed," I whisper, and she coos as if she understands. After a fresh diaper and a warm bottle of formula, I rock her gently, talking to her about our garden visit, the way Daddy made her giggle with his silly faces. But even after she's burped and back to sleep, my mind races.

I need something to do with this wakefulness. A calendar, I decide, rummaging through the drawers until I find a simple desk one. Settling at the kitchen table, I find yesterday's date and write, *First time on the swing at the park*! My heart swells, thinking of how Addison's eyes lit up. I add our visit to VanDusen.

Photos. Yes, those moments need preserving. I pull out my

phone, scrolling through the snapshots of laughter and sunlight, then connect to Christian's printer. As each photo slides out, I arrange them in a growing collage of memories.

Christian's credit card lies next to a pile of bills. He said I could use it for things with Addison. I navigate to an online craft store and lose myself in selecting scrapbooking supplies and an actual photo printer. This will be my gift to Addison. Eventually, I'll be long gone, but this will be something tangible to hold on to, documenting all her firsts.

My phone buzzes. Suddenly, it's not so early anymore.

Dana: Hi!

Me: Hey, what's up?

Dana: Are you and Addison up for brunch today? Maybe Homer St. Café? Say, in an hour?

I narrow my eyes. Something's up.

Me: Sure, we'll be there.

I smile despite the fluttering in my stomach. What could be going on?

When Addison wakes up again, I put her in a warm onesie and dress myself in a flowy blouse and jeans. I pack us into the minivan, and in a few minutes, we arrive at the café. There's Dana at our usual spot, but she's wringing her hands, mascara threatening to streak down her cheeks.

"Hey, what's wrong?" I ask, sliding into the booth, positioning Addison's carrier beside me.

She gulps back her emotions. "I think I'm about to lose my job."

"What? Tate adores you. Tell me everything." I reach across, covering her hand with mine.

"It was supposed to be just drinks after work, to discuss the Henderson account..." Her voice trails off.

85

"Okay," I prompt.

"Turns out, it was a date. A date, Hailey! With my boss!" She throws her hands up, disbelief in her eyes.

"And…it was fun?" I hazard a guess, piecing together her erratic energy.

"More fun than I've had in years." Dana slumps, conflict on her face.

"Then let's focus on that. The fun." I nudge her, hoping to bring some lightness to her mood.

The server arrives, and I order oatmeal. Dana decides on avocado toast.

When the server leaves, Dana reaches for me. "Thanks, Hailey. I needed this." She manages a weak smile, sipping her coffee as we wait for our food.

After a moment, Dana's face lights up. "He surprised me with a ride on a floatplane," she says, her hands fluttering. "We flew over to Vancouver Island and had lunch in Nanaimo. I kept waiting for him to bring up work, but he never did. We just…talked."

"Sounds amazing," I respond, trying not to let my envy color my voice. I have to wonder what that must be like, soaring over the water, going somewhere fun for lunch.

Dana sighs, the struggle clear in her furrowed brow. "It was fun, but I feel so conflicted."

I lean in. "Why?"

"Because I'm not supposed to fall for my boss," she confesses, looking down.

"Why not?" I ask, genuinely puzzled. "You're both adults, right?"

"Sure, but…" She hesitates, biting her lip. "He already has a family, and he doesn't want more kids. That kills me." The words spill out, each one heavier than the last. "Plus, his ex is a monster."

I shake my head, pausing as our food arrives.

"Dana, if it's great now, why worry about all that?" I ask as we dig in. "Don't focus on the finish line. Just enjoy the race."

Her eyes meet mine, a spark of mischief replacing the

worry for a moment. "Maybe you're right."

Addison giggles from her carrier, drawing our attention. Her joy is infectious, and even Dana can't resist breaking into laughter.

We finish our brunch, and I confirm that Dana is *not*, in fact, about to lose her job. That's just a worst-case scenario her mind had conjured. She hugs me goodbye, promises to take things one step at a time, and we walk out of the restaurant. I load up Addison to drive back to the townhouse, and Dana heads home to work. We didn't solve all the problems, but we did give her permission to date her boss.

For a moment, my brain flashes to what it might be like to date mine.

When we return to the townhouse, I carefully lay Addison in her crib. Soon, her tiny chest rises and falls with peaceful breaths, and I take a moment to marvel at the serenity of her sleep. Pulling the door closed, I gather the scattered toys and bits of life that have made their way to the living room floor.

A knock at the door pulls me from my domestic whirlwind. I peek through the peephole before opening it to find Ray, my old neighbor, standing there with a sheepish smile and a small stack of mail in his hand.

"Sorry to drop by unannounced," he says, handing me the misdirected envelopes. "These found their way into my box by mistake, and I thought I'd bring them by. Maybe we could figure out a time for that dinner and drinks?"

"Thank you, Ray. Come in," I reply, stepping aside. "Can I get you something to drink? Maybe some lemonade?"

I've barely finished the offer when my cellphone rings. Christian's name flashes across the screen, and a knot tightens in my stomach. Ray steps into the living room as I answer, pressing the phone to my ear while I work.

"Christian," I greet, trying to keep my voice steady.

"Who's there with you?" comes his immediate demand. "You know the rules about overnight guests."

My grip on the phone tightens, and a flare of indignation courses through me. "It's the middle of the afternoon, and it's just Ray, my old neighbor. He brought over some mail. There's no need to—"

"He's got a thing for you," Christian interrupts. "I don't want him around."

"He's just a friend. And who I spend time with is none of your business," I counter, struggling to maintain my composure.

There's a brief silence on the other end before the line goes dead. Christian has hung up on me. So much for the rapport I thought we were building. How can this man trust me with his child, yet refuse to see me as a functioning human being?

I lock eyes with the camera tucked in the kitchen's corner. Blowing a kiss directly at the lens, I pull the lemonade from the fridge and pour a glass. "Watch all you want," I whisper, though Christian can't hear.

I exhale slowly, trying to shake off the experience. Returning to Ray, I apologize for the interruption and hand him his drink, determined not to let Christian's weirdness overshadow the rest of my day.

But once we're seated, my cheeks flame as I find Ray's wide-eyed gaze fixed on my chest. Does Christian know something I don't about Ray? Why is everyone weird all of a sudden? My phone rings again, and I grab it, mumbling, "Excuse me," as I head for the balcony. It's Christian again, but I won't give him the satisfaction of answering. It rings through to voicemail as I take a moment to breathe. Dinner with Ray is the last thing that seems appealing now, but there's no way I'll let Christian think he can dictate my choices.

As I step back into the house, I hear Addison begin to fuss through the monitor. That's it. This has to be a sign. I return to the living room to find Ray. I gesture to the monitor. "I'm sorry.

I think you should go. Evidently, there's a lot going on here at the moment, and I need to get the baby."

"Of course." His face is flushed with embarrassment, but he stands promptly, setting down his lemonade. "Let me know when you can meet for that drink and dinner."

"I will," I manage, ushering him to the door.

Once he's gone, I rush in to Addison, cradling her softly, murmuring apologies for the delay. I bring her out for her dinner, and the stillness of the impending evening wraps around us.

We do our routine — bath, bedtime, stories — and it's not a huge surprise that Christian doesn't come home before Addison's in bed. I guess he can see everything he needs to from the cameras. I sigh as I sink into the couch. Maybe I overreacted. He only wants Addison to be safe, and he doesn't know Ray is harmless. But still, he doesn't have to speak to me that way.

I consider what I might eat for dinner, but then I pick up my phone, hesitating only a moment before I send a message to Dana.

Me: Rom-com and chill?

I crave the company more than I care to admit.

Dana: Be there in 20.

Relief washes over me as I open Netflix, scrolling through endless options before settling on something light and funny.

The knock on the door comes sooner than expected, and Dana breezes in. She studies my face a moment. "Girl, you need this more than I do." She laughs, sinking down beside me and pushing play.

We lose ourselves in the predictable plot twists and easy laughter of the movie, but when the credits roll, the reality of life nudges back in. Dana's gaze meets mine, inquisitive and concerned. "So, how are things going?" she asks. "Did something happen?"

I shrug, picking at a loose thread on the throw pillow. "It's hard."

Dana nods, her expression earnest. "I know you have to be a little lonely with only you and Addison around most of the time. I don't know what to tell you about Christian. I don't entirely understand how he operates." She sighs. "He has a reputation for thinking he's God's gift to women — and the world at large. Perhaps you've noticed," she says with a laugh.

I nod. "That does ring a bell. And perhaps that's part of why he's almost never here. Off saving the world, you know…" I force a laugh. I don't want to go into all the weirdness of this afternoon.

"Well, and don't get me started on him being a man-whore," Dana adds.

Ah. Of course. I'm sure that keeps him very busy as well. Perhaps that's why he assumed Ray had nefarious intentions. Although I guess Ray did…

A sigh escapes my lips, and I nod. "I can see that as well," I tell her. "But I don't think that's an issue for me."

"Well, I'd hope he has more sense than that, but he might be a bit shameless." She rolls her eyes. "Anyway, you're too good for him." She stands and stretches, pulling on her coat before giving me a quick hug. "You're doing a great job here, Hailey. Even if it's hard. And you can call me anytime, day or night."

"Thanks. Really," I reply, walking her to the door. As it closes behind her, the silence of the townhouse presses in again, heavier now that I'm alone.

I head to bed, the sheets cool against my skin as I slip under them. Despite feeling unsettled, sleep soon tugs at my consciousness.

The door alarm jolts me awake, and I squint at the glowing red numbers on the alarm clock. Two o'clock. I hear the soft murmur of Christian's voice in Addison's nursery. Pushing back the sheets, I go to her room.

In the nursery doorway, I watch Christian, his back to me as he cradles Addison close, the bottle's nipple disappearing into her eager mouth. He hasn't noticed me, but a waft of something hits me — stale cigars and a floral perfume.

"Where have you been?" I ask softly, but still, my voice cuts sharply through the quiet.

Christian turns, his expression is unreadable in the semi-dark. "What business of that is yours? Are you forgetting I'm your boss?" he asks, setting the empty bottle down with more force than necessary.

"Addison needs you," I insist, stepping closer. "She's starting to think you're a stranger."

Christian steps forward, and suddenly, he's too close. I can feel the heat of his body, and it makes my heart race. His gaze flickers down to my lips, and for a second, I wonder if he's going to kiss me. In the moment, the pull between us is undeniable, but I force myself to step back.

Addison fusses, and he turns away. "Go to bed, Hailey. I've got this." His dismissal is curt, final.

Nonetheless, I stand there a moment longer, watching him put Addison back in her crib. Why is this so complicated? Though I've gotten much better at handling a baby over these last five weeks, I still feel entirely out of my depth.

Without a sound, I slip out of the room and return to my bed.

CHAPTER 10

Christian

It's Saturday morning, and I should be doing something better with my time, but I find myself pacing the length of my living room, each step a metronome tap of frustration. Hailey and Addison are out for their walk, and I'm climbing the walls. Last night, instead of coming home, I found myself at a hotel bar, nursing a scotch, replaying the way Hailey had smiled at her old neighbor the night before.

Their exchange sent me into a panic, though not for any valid reasons. I trust her enough to know she wouldn't endanger Addison, but I'll be damned if I'll watch her flirt with another man in my very own home. Yet clearly, I need to stay away from her as well, since I can't stop thinking about what she might be beyond my child's caregiver.

My phone rings, my mother's name flashing on the screen. I consider ignoring it but swipe to answer instead.

"Darling, you will join me for brunch at the Botanist this morning?" This is a command more than a request, her voice brimming with authority as always.

"Mother..." I press my fingers to my temples, as if I could massage away the inevitable.

"None of that now," she counters. "Eleven sharp. Don't be late." And with that, she hangs up.

It occurs to me that Hailey is perhaps the polar opposite of my mother. Is that what draws me to her? Wait, am I drawn to her? Or does she just seem like an inviting lay? Frustration flames within me again. I can't reduce her to a warm body — unattached, effortless fun. She's too important to Addison. I've seen them connect in ways I can barely fathom.

Which is all the more reason I should *stop thinking about her at all.*

My pacing continues. I'm usually good at keeping people at arm's length. Hell, I've been doing it my whole life. It's what I know, what my mother taught me. Growing up, warmth wasn't something we shared in our house. Everything was measured, calculated. Even affection felt like a transaction. If I did well, if I kept up appearances, I earned her approval. But love? That was never part of the deal.

This brunch is a prime example. I'm not going because I want to. I don't. I'll do it for her approval, and she does it to show her "friends" that her son is loving and doting. Ha! If they only knew.

And now, here I am with Addison. I'm keeping her at a distance, the way I always do. It's instinct, thanks to Mother. I've spent years building walls, keeping control, because that's the only way I know how to survive. But does that work with a baby? It certainly doesn't work without Hailey... But then I'm back to square one. The one person I shouldn't be trying to connect with seems to make me wish I could. Truly, I don't know if I can handle this.

I think about telling my mother how things are spiraling out of control. But I already know what she'd say. "*Don't let your emotions cloud your judgment. Stay the course. She's just the nanny.*" Mother wouldn't understand. She never does.

The Botanist is the last place I want to be in a few hours,

stuck amidst the chatter of the well-heeled elite, their conversations as curated as the exotic plants lining the walls. Yet the thought of escaping the mess my home life has become, even just for a little while, offers a reprieve I'm desperate to take. Maybe a few hours surrounded by the familiar pretenses of my upbringing will help me regain control, remind me of who I am and who I'm supposed to be.

Right on time, I sit across from my mother at The Botanist, and her friends float by our table like perfumed specters.

"Christian!" Mrs. Pemberton appears, as if summoned by my most cynical thoughts, her smile brittle. "You remember my daughter, Clarissa?" She gestures to the willowy figure next to her. "She's just returned from abroad."

"Of course," I say with the noncommittal politeness I've mastered over the years, standing to offer a handshake.

Clarissa, now a polished echo of the gangly girl I vaguely recall, extends her hand, her grip surprisingly firm. "Nice to see you again," she offers with a rehearsed tilt of her head.

Likely story. I manage a half-smile. "Welcome back, Clarissa."

"Isn't it wonderful? Two old school friends getting together after all this time," Mrs. Pemberton coos, nudging us closer in a maneuver as subtle as a sledgehammer.

"Must be fate," I quip.

Clarissa's eyes flicker with shared understanding. At least there's mutual disinterest to spare us both the ordeal of pretense.

"Let's catch up soon," she says after a moment, a polite dismissal. I agree, knowing *soon* translates to *never*, and with grace, they retreat.

My mother watches them go before turning her gaze on

me, hawk-like and probing. "Addison," she says, slicing through the veil of trivial conversation. "How is she?"

"She's doing well," I reply, my defenses already rising against the scrutiny I know is coming. "Growing fast."

"Too fast for Hailey to keep carrying her around like a favorite doll," she retorts. "She needs structure, discipline. A German nanny would provide that."

I can almost hear the click of boots on polished floors, the stern voice issuing orders. That was my childhood. My mother's idea of child-rearing is outdated and regimented, a means to sculpt a Bradford heir, not nurture a child.

"Perhaps," I concede, hating how timid I sound, how timid I feel, actually. "But Hailey seems to have a good handle on things."

"Hailey," she scoffs, her lip curling. "That girl doesn't understand the value of firm guidance. Addison will thank us later for providing someone who does."

"Maybe," I say again, but the thought tightens my chest. Getting rid of Hailey would likely simplify my life, but that doesn't make it right. The idea of replacing her stirs a protective instinct for Addison I didn't ever expect to have. One day Addison will look back on the choices I made for her. And so will I.

"Consider it," my mother presses, but I sense her attention drifting to her next target. Another friend approaches our table with the gleam of social conquest in her eyes.

I nod, beginning the routine again, as the ghost of my childhood governess looms over the conversation. The woman was a bully in sensible shoes, her voice a sword of discipline that seemed to chip away my youth. I'd longed for a mother's touch, not the cold efficiency of a hired enforcer. The memory alone is enough to solidify my resolve.

I know Hailey has been good for Addison. My gut twists at the thought of shaking up the small patch of stability she's managed to create. No, displacing Hailey isn't an option—not yet, not until I can guarantee it's the best move for my daughter. That's what matters.

Eventually, we finish eating, and there's a break in the line of visitors to our table. Escaping the brunch feels like breaking free from a vise. The Botanist's chic decor and clinking glasses fade into the background as I head for the Vancouver Country Club, a refuge of green lawns and casual camaraderie. Here, at least, I can lose myself in the swing of a club and the chase of a little white ball.

"Hey, Christian!" Davis Martin, my friend and fellow doctor at the hospital, waves from where he's leaning on his golf bag, an all-too-familiar smirk on his lips. "Ready to have your ass handed to you?"

"Keep dreaming," I shoot back, but there's no heat in it. These guys, they're part of a world I understand, one where the rules are clear cut, and the only thing that needs nurturing is my handicap.

We play, we jest, we revel in the simple pleasure of the game until the shadows stretch long across the fairway and the clubhouse beckons us with the promise of a cold drink. Here it's easy to forget the complexities of a life that now demands more of me than I ever expected.

"By the way," Davis says as we settle in with our drinks. "How's Addison's temperature tracking going?"

The inquiry catches me off guard. I'm her father, I should know. But the truth is, I barely know what he's talking about. I recall something about children with Down syndrome having a hard time regulating body temperature, but I rely on Hailey to manage that. She's the one with the charts and the apps, the careful observations, and I suppose I trust that she'll let me know if there's a problem. A surge of something unpleasant—guilt, maybe? embarrassment?—worms its way through my chest.

"Hailey's got it covered," I deflect, hoping my nonchalance passes muster. Davis nods, but I see the flicker of surprise in his eyes.

One by one, the guys leave for homes filled with partners, the noise of children, and warmth. I've never pictured that life for myself, but oddly, I'm struck by a pang of…what? Envy? Longing?

"See you, man," Davis finally says, and I wave, suddenly solitary in the dimming light of the clubhouse.

I guess it's time to go home. I push away from the bar. *Home*, where Hailey and Addison wait.

As I drive, I think back to when I was three. It's my earliest memory. I'm clutching the hem of a dress that's too fine for chubby, uncertain fingers. There's been an argument. My father — a silhouette against the door — fades into nothingness, leaving my mother, cold and distant. She's always elegant, composed, her affection parceled out in public appearances where I am less son, more an ornament to her tailored image.

"Christian, smile," she would command, her own lips curving just so, engineered for the camera flash rather than warmth.

I push the memory away with a shake of my head, hoping something will wash it all clean. It doesn't. It never does.

My phone vibrates. I don't want to look, but curiosity is a persistent itch, and when I reach a red light, I swipe to bring the screen to life with a video, Addison's bright eyes wide and sparkling with joy, Taylor Swift's latest hit playing in the background.

"Are you dancing, Addie?" Hailey's voice, teasing and tender, floats through the speaker.

Addison's response is a gurgle of laughter, pure and unfettered. She lifts her arm, a tiny conductor orchestrating her delight, and something inside me shifts, a tectonic plate of emotion grinding against the bedrock of my guarded heart. It's a strange sensation, this mixture of pride and something softer, warmer as I watch my daughter discover rhythm in her little bouncing body.

A grin I can't suppress pulls at my mouth as Addison bobs and weaves, her movements jerky yet earnest. "God, I hope I get this right," I murmur, returning my focus to the road.

Before the traffic starts to move, I thumb a message into my phone, a decision that surprises me. *Heading home*, it reads, and I hit send before I can second-guess myself. Maybe it's Addison's laughter in the video, or maybe it's the realization that

I'm at a crossroads between repeating history and forging a new path. I need to make this work. I need to do what's right.

My car hums and weaves through the city streets, guiding me back to where I need to be. When I push open the door to my house, quiet greets me, punctuated by soft murmurs from the living room.

Hailey looks up, her expression a mix of surprise and something unreadable as she lifts Addison from the floor. "You're back early," she says.

I can smell that fresh baby scent. "Couldn't stay away," I admit, feeling the truth of it settle in my chest. I extend my arms toward them. "Let me."

Without hesitation, Hailey passes Addison my way, the warmth of my daughter's body flooding my senses. Her small head finds the crook of my arm, as if she's always belonged there. Perhaps she has. Hailey gives us a small, knowing smile before slipping off to her room.

Addison squirms in my arms, her little fists rubbing her eyes as I carry her to her nursery. It's bedtime, or at least I think it is. I'm still getting the hang of her routine, but for the moment, I feel like I'm doing something right.

"You ready for bed, Addie?" I whisper, lowering her into the crib. She lets out a tiny yawn. Her stuffed bunny, the one Hailey gave her, is waiting at her side, and Addison immediately reaches for it, clutching it close to her chest.

I dim the lights, and her tiny breaths slow to a rhythm that's both calming and unnervingly foreign. I suppose I adore this little being, but where is the visceral pull, the primal bond that seems to tug relentlessly at the hearts of other fathers? Am I not capable of that?

I linger for a moment, watching as she settles. I sing softly under my breath — something I never thought I'd do — but the melody seems to calm her. Her eyelids droop, and a wave of contentment washes over me. She needs me. I'm not used to acknowledging that so literally. In this moment, we are truly connected.

"Sweet dreams, baby girl," I whisper, brushing a hand

over her soft hair. I stand in the dim light, watching her drift toward sleep, and for the first time, I realize being her dad isn't something I need to control or perfect. It's just...being here. Being present. That's the heart of it.

Am I broken? my mind asks again. But that's absurd, isn't it? I feel the protectiveness, the love for Addison, but it's not all-consuming. I have a lot of other things in my life, a lot of other people who need me, count on me. I brush my lips across her forehead, hoping she understands that I'm trying, that I'm here even if I have to learn how to fully be her dad.

When I turn, Hailey is waiting in the doorway, a question in her eyes.

"She's out," I say, feeling the beginning of something new, something warm and capable, threading its way through my old fears and reservations.

I walk out to slouch into the cushions of the living room sofa, still feeling Addison's weight in my arms.

Hailey busies herself in the kitchen, but after a moment, her voice cuts through the silence. "Working tomorrow?"

"No," I answer, shifting to sit up straighter. "I'll stay with Addison. You can take the day off."

She leans against the doorframe, a shadow of a smile on her lips. "That's not why I asked, but thanks. I meant do you want a drink?" Her offer hangs between us, simple yet impossibly complex in its implications.

"Sure." I nod, looking for the company more than the alcohol. I appreciate Hailey's way of taking care of things, even me, without making a big deal about it. I'm just not at all sure it's wise.

Moments later, we're both nursing glasses of whiskey. Music floats from the speakers, a soft melody that's familiar yet distant. "So, are you into Taylor Swift?" I ask. "Addison sure seems to like her."

Hailey nods. "She does. This album is so good. It takes listening a few times to absorb the lyrics. Taylor can sing, but her brilliance as a songwriter is melodic. And she tells a story better than any writer."

The whiskey burns pleasantly as it goes down. "I've always been more into grunge. Pearl Jam, Nirvana…"

"Kurt Cobain was legendary," Hailey agrees, swirling the liquid in her glass. "I read somewhere that he was the first to make the expression of anger and depression in music mainstream. Do you think he'd still be a music god if he were alive?"

"Hard to say…" I ponder that, staring out the window to where the lights of False Creek dance like fireflies. "Some legends grow larger in death. But Cobain had raw talent. He'd probably still be shaking things up."

She smiles and hums a tune under her breath, one I recognize as a Swiftie anthem. I smile despite myself.

We fall into a comfortable silence, sipping our drinks and watching the world outside. *I can handle this, right?* Reflections ripple across the surface of the creek, reminding me how life's patterns can be disrupted by the smallest stone—or person—thrown into their midst. "Thanks for this," I say after a while, lifting my glass in toast. "It's nice…just talking." I can hardly believe it, but that's true.

"Anytime," Hailey replies, her eyes warm. "Music, drinks, or stubborn babies—I'm here."

And I believe her. I feel the need to reciprocate somehow. I want her to know I'm trying, that I want to do this better, though even I'm not sure what I mean. I shift in my seat, the leather creaking under me as I meet her gaze, deep and questioning.

"Addison's mother… I don't actually remember sleeping with her." The words feel like stones in my mouth. "She's definitely my type—dark hair, enigmatic eyes—but it's all a blur. What I know for certain is that Addison has my DNA."

She nods, waiting for me to continue.

"I hired a private investigator," I confess, feeling the twist of anxiety in my gut. "Taylor, Addison's mother, is in LA now, chasing her acting dreams. She hasn't tried to contact Addison or me, not even once. I'm not even sure she knows her sister dropped her off."

"How could she not know?" Hailey asks. "She must have

checked in with her sister."

"I sent paperwork." I shrug. "I've asked her to relinquish her parental rights, but she hasn't signed anything. It makes me nervous, the uncertainty of it all." I look away, focusing on a spot where the light catches the rim of my glass. "She's been absent for over three months now. Sometimes, I tell myself she's just sorting out her life. But there's a clock ticking on her chance to be a part of Addison's world."

"Christian..." Hailey begins but trails off, perhaps unsure what to say.

"Let's not dwell on it," I interject, eager to escape the tightness in my chest. *Why did I start this conversation anyway?* "You look like you could use some relaxation." Without waiting for an answer, I lift her feet onto my lap and start to massage them.

I look down at my hands, feeling like I'm on autopilot. Count on my gut to return to what's familiar when I'm alone with a woman, I suppose. For a moment I worry Hailey will withdraw, though that would undoubtedly be for the best, but instead, she lets out a low moan.

Something inside me stirs, a primal response I can't control. My hands move over her feet, thumbs pressing into the arches, eliciting another quiet sound of pleasure from her lips. A wave of heat rolls through me, desire building at the sounds of her satisfaction.

I feel myself hardening. "You can take tonight off too." My fingers knead her heels, slowly, deliberately. "I'll be on call later this week, so there won't be much time for breaks."

"Thank you," she breathes, her voice tinged with drowsy contentment.

Then the monitor crackles, and Addison fusses. Her timing is perfect.

"Go on, get some rest," I say, sliding her feet off my lap before standing carefully, to avoid any embarrassing revelations. "I've got Addison. Goodnight."

"Goodnight," she replies, her smile lingering as I retreat toward Addison's room.

When I open the nursery door, Addison has already settled on her own, leaving me alone with the memory of Hailey's moans and the faint scent of her skin on my palms. But as I linger a few minutes, waiting until Hailey retreats to her room, my thoughts refocus on my daughter. Once again, warmth swells within me.

I return to the kitchen to pour myself another drink and resume my place on the couch, focusing on the burn as I swallow, rather than the thoughts that now threaten to consume me.

What is this strange tightness in my chest, the way my throat constricts when I look at Addison? Is that what love feels like? It's not the fierce rush of passion or the sharp pangs of jealousy I'm accustomed to. It's something more enduring, more terrifying in its quiet intensity. I think I must love her, this small creature who depends on me, yet I'm not entirely sure. I certainly resented her at first, and love has never been a tangible quality in my life. It just seems like one more part of this that's impossible to understand.

But none of that matters to Addison. She asks for nothing more than to be held, fed, and kept safe. And though I've outsourced even those simple needs, I find myself more and more willing to do anything, spend any amount, fight any battle, but also forge a connection. I want to keep her as part of my life, away from Taylor, the mother who hasn't bothered to claim her. Surely, it's my duty to protect this innocent life from becoming a pawn in an adult game.

CHAPTER 11

Hailey

Sunlight pierces the gap between my curtains, pricking at the edge of my consciousness. I roll over and squint at the clock. It's after nine. My eyes pop wide. That can't be right. Confusion tugs at my sleep-fogged brain. I never sleep this late. The house is always awake by seven, stirred into motion by Addison's chirpy summons on the baby monitor. Speaking of which... Why is it so silent?

I sit up, heart hammering, and notice the monitor's dark screen. Off? It's never off. Panic coils in my stomach as I throw back the covers and bound across the room. I race to Addison's room. *Empty.*

The scent of coffee drifts up the stairs, a bright spot in my dread. I follow it downstairs, and then I hear it—Christian's voice, gentle and melodic, singing the "Itsy Bitsy Spider." Relief washes over me in an overwhelming wave, followed closely by embarrassment at my overreaction. She does have a parent. Could it be that he actually wants to be one? Rounding the corner to the kitchen, I find Addison snuggled into the swing, giggling with delight as Christian makes exaggerated gestures with his long fingers climbing up an invisible waterspout.

"Good morning," I say, my voice sounding too loud in the cheerful domestic scene. "I'm sorry. I didn't mean to oversleep."

Christian turns, offering a smile. "Don't worry about it," he says. "I turned the monitor off. You looked like you could use the sleep."

Surprise widens my eyes, but I'll take it. "Thank you," I mumble.

"Everyone deserves a break now and then," he replies, rising to pour himself a cup of coffee.

Who is this guy, and what did he do with Christian Bradford?

He gestures to the coffee carafe, asking if I want one too, and I nod. "Besides, we've got plans today," he continues as he hands me a mug. "We're heading to Stanley Park and the aquarium. You can take the day off if you want. Or…" he trails off for a moment. "You're welcome to join us."

The offer hangs in the air between us, surprising yet sincere. A day off sounds tempting, a chance to recharge, but the thought of spending some less-pressure time with Addison—and yes, with Christian too—pulls at me. And it's not like I could come up with something to do on the fly. Dana is swamped with a big work project.

"Thanks," I say. "I'd love to come along if that's really okay."

"Of course it is," Christian says, and there's a warmth there I rarely see. "We'd like having you there." Addison beams up at me.

"Then it's settled," I reply, unable to contain a small smile of my own. I run my fingers through my hair, still tousled from sleep. "Do I have time for a shower?"

"Sure," he says. "The aquarium doesn't open for members for another hour."

I nod and hurry upstairs. I don't know what any of this means, but it feels good. The hot water is a welcome shock, washing away my lingering drowsiness. I dress hastily, nerves prickling at the thought of spending an entire day with Christian. For once, my day won't be just about watching Addison, but about being with both of them.

By the time we're all loaded into the minivan, I'm a bundle of quiet anticipation. Christian navigates the streets while Addison's laughter fills the space between us. Soon we arrive at the Vancouver Aquarium, a place that's become almost as familiar as home.

We wander to the jellyfish exhibit first, and Addison's eyes widen at the ethereal creatures pulsing gently behind the glass. This is her favorite exhibit. I can't blame her. The room is lit with blacklights, and the jellyfish glow as they float in floor-to-ceiling aquariums.

When Addison grows restless, we move toward the next exhibit. A high-pitched screech cuts through the crowd as we approach the tank of sea life from local waters.

"Mommy, it's wet!" a young girl cries, soaked from head to toe. An octopus, its tentacles waving wildly, has somehow escaped its enclosure and splashed her. Staff members are already converging on the scene, but the poor girl is inconsolable.

"Stay back," Christian instructs, placing himself between us and the commotion.

In the ensuing confusion, the little girl slips on a puddle, her small body hitting the floor with a thud that sends a collective gasp through the bystanders. Without hesitation, Christian is at her side, shifting into clinical focus.

"Hey there," he says softly, checking her over. "Can you tell me your name?"

"Mimi," she whimpers, clinging to her mother.

"Okay, Mimi, you're doing great." He runs his fingers over a bump on the back of her head. Then he turns to her anxious parents. "She has a pretty big bump, but I think she'll be fine. Keep an eye on her. If she vomits or becomes unusually sleepy, take her to Mercy's emergency room immediately. Do you know where that is?"

They nod. "Thank you..." The mother trails off expectantly, seeking a name.

"Dr. Christian Bradford," he supplies, helping Mimi to her feet. Her parents thank him again, gathering their daughter in their arms.

The aquarium staff have the wayward octopus contained and are repairing the aquarium so the other octopi don't escape.

Addison fusses, ready to move on from the drama.

"We're moving," Christian assures her, offering me a smile.

We resume our path toward the playful otters, and I steal a glance at Christian. I've never seen him in doctor mode before, and I'm impressed by his calm under pressure. Usually, someone who tells you how important they are is compensating for something — and perhaps he is — but it doesn't seem to be medical skill.

A woman who was in the octopus crowd nudges my arm as we pass. "You're so lucky your husband is a doctor," she says, a note of envy in her voice. "Kids are so tough."

My lips part to correct her — Christian isn't my husband, and I'm just the nanny — but his hand comes to my other arm, halting my words before they take flight. He meets my gaze and shakes his head subtly. "It's too hard to explain," he murmurs once the woman moves on, a wry smile touching his features.

It doesn't seem particularly complicated to me. I'm the nanny, and he's my boss. But I let it go, pushing the oddity down to stir a quiet pool of questions. "Addison, look at those fish!" I point to a vibrant school darting past the glass, redirecting her attention and mine from the lingering confusion.

As we amble along, I glance up at Christian. "Can I ask again about your family? Why don't you have your dad's last name?"

He takes a moment to respond, his eyes distant. "My mother comes from wealth," he says. "She and my dad were young when they fell in love, but my grandparents… They put a lot of pressure on them."

"Pressure?" I echo, watching his jaw tighten.

He nods, looking down at Addison. "They never approved of my father, even went as far as paying him to disappear from our lives. That's when they changed my last name to my mother's maiden name."

I struggle to wrap my head around such a callous act. John, Christian and Dana's father, is such a kind man. Why would they push him away? "Sounds complicated," I murmur, unsure what else to say.

"Complicated doesn't even begin to cover it." His laugh has no humor. "Let's see what's over here," he suggests, a clear effort to step back into the present.

"Sure," I agree, but as we walk, I still feel the weight of the memories he must carry.

For now, though, Christian seems relaxed, his attention mostly on Addison. She points at a colorful fish, her finger smudging against the glass.

I try to focus on Addison as well, but my mind replays the conversation about his family. "So, your dad... You didn't know him growing up?" I ask, treading cautiously.

Christian hesitates, then nods as we turn away from the glowing tanks. "Yeah, he was more of a concept than a person for most of my life."

"That's so strange. I feel like I've known him forever. Not having him in your life must've been tough," I say.

"Didn't really have anything to compare it to," he admits, shrugging. "But, uh, things changed when I was a resident. My mom's dad — my grandfather — needed heart surgery, and suddenly, there was my dad, standing right there in the hospital. He believed in me from the very beginning."

"Did he try to reconnect with you then?"

He glances down at Addison, who's become engrossed in a display of seashells. "He tried," he says softly. "But my grandfather loved to tell me how my father had taken their money and disappeared. So when he reached out, I resisted. But he was persistent."

"That sounds like John." I find myself holding my breath for a moment. "He pushed back hard when I quit school after my grandmother died. He knew that wasn't what she'd would have wanted, but Franklin was chirping in my ear." I shake my head.

I don't even know how that happened now. "What a mistake. But John's never once said, 'I told you so.'"

Christian smiles sadly. "He's not a bad man. He just made choices, like everyone does."

I nod, understanding that forgiveness is a journey, and sometimes a long one.

Christian's gaze shifts to a nearby bench, where an elderly couple eats ice cream. "My mother, though..." He shakes his head. "She has her own ways of dealing with things."

"Like what?" I ask, sensing another piece of the puzzle about to fall into place.

"Money can solve problems, or at least, that's how she sees it. If something bothers her, she writes a check, and it goes away." A hint of resignation colors his words.

"Must be nice," I joke, but my humor falls flat.

"Sometimes," he concedes. "But not always. It can't buy everything."

His eyes meet mine, and I realize he likely knows this truth all too well.

"Right," I say, making a mental note. His mother's coping mechanism speaks volumes about her character and perhaps about the kind of love and care Christian received as a child. There's yet another layer in his complex family situation.

Addison kicks her legs in her stroller. She knows we're heading to the otters — her favorite habitat. As they move forward, I watch the way Christian interacts with his daughter — gentle, patient, and encouraging. It's a side of him that's entirely new in the past week or so, and though I don't understand it, I'm not about to complain. It softens the edges I've come to associate with him.

"Christian?" I venture. "What does your mother think of Addison?"

He watches a school of silver fish dart back and forth. "She's my daughter," he says. "For now, that's enough. But as she gets older, it's going to be harder for her."

"Harder? Why?" I ask, though I'm not sure I want to know the answer.

"Because in my mother's eyes, Addison isn't perfect. And my mother only likes perfection." He says this matter-of-factly, but there's an undertone of sadness that tugs at my heart.

Perfect is such a strange word, so final and unforgiving, so unattainable. I look down at Addison, who is now giggling at the antics of the otters who seem to be playing tag as they race around their enclosure. Could anything be more perfect than her joy, her innocence?

"Addison is perfect," I assure him. "She may have some developmental delays, but she's making great strides, and she's happy. Isn't that what everyone wants? To be happy?"

For a moment, he just looks at me, and something flickers across his face. Then he nods, a smile on his lips. "You're right, Hailey. That's exactly what we all want."

I return his smile, feeling hopeful that I'm breaking through the walls this man has built around himself. But I've had these hopes before, and they don't always pan out.

The aquarium's glow eventually wanes as Addison's energy does the same. By the time we're back at Christian's townhouse, she's ready for her nap. I feel the weight of the day's revelations pressing on my shoulders as much as the physical weight of Addison in my arms.

When we get inside, Christian takes her from me, his touch light, and heads toward her nursery. I follow, unsure what else to do. "Thanks for coming with us," he murmurs.

I nod, unable to find words that don't feel too heavy or too revealing for the moment. It's happening again. That pull between us. The way Christian's looking at me, the way the air changes when he's near. Part of me wants to give in, to let whatever this is between us take over. But what happens after that? There's no path forward. What path would I even want? So I can't. I won't.

I watch as he places Addison in her crib. She deserves better than the mess her caregivers could create. And so do I.

After all, I've been here before, standing at the edge of something that feels exciting, dangerous, and easy to lose myself in. With Franklin, I let my heart lead the way, ignoring every red flag, every warning sign, until I was drowning. But now, I've worked too hard to rebuild myself, to find solid ground again. I can't afford to let myself get involved with someone who might never be what I need.

I turn away from Christian, trying to put distance between us, physically and emotionally. But I can feel his eyes on me as I step into the hallway, and it takes every ounce of strength I have not to turn back.

"Why do you keep doing this?" he says, his voice low as he comes after me. "Why do you keep pushing me away?"

My heart clenches because he sounds hurt. I never wanted to hurt him. But why on earth does he want me? I have to protect myself. I have to put me first for once—and Addison. She's counting on me, and I can't afford to get lost in someone else's mess again.

"Because I have to," I whisper, keeping my back to him. "We need to avoid making things…complicated."

He steps closer, and I force myself to turn, not move away again. His eyes search mine for something I'm not willing to give. "It doesn't have to be complicated," he murmurs.

But I shake my head. "It already is," I tell him, my voice stronger now. "You have your life. Your work. And there's Addison. I need this job. I need to be what she needs. I can't afford to get caught up in something that could fall apart."

His jaw tightens, and frustration flickers across his face. But he doesn't argue. He just stands there.

It's killing me, this push and pull. Despite all my questions today, I still don't understand him, don't know what drives him. I look away, my chest tight. "Addison is the priority right now. We can't risk messing that up."

Christian finally steps back, giving me space. "I get it," he says, his voice low, resigned. "You're protecting yourself. I just wish you didn't feel you had to protect yourself from me."

How can he not see this the way I do? If he doesn't, it just proves we're not on the same page, don't have the same priorities. It seems obvious that Christian and I could never work the way I'd need us to.

"I've been here before," I say, finally meeting his gaze again. "I know how this goes. And I won't let myself get lost in someone else's life again."

He watches me a moment longer, and I can see the conflict in his eyes. But I hold my ground. I have to be strong—for Addison and for myself.

Finally, I escape to my room. I strip the sheets, methodically pulling each corner free and letting the fabric fall to the floor. The routine of laundry is comforting, a simple certainty I'm sure how to navigate. I shove the sheets into the washer, pour in detergent without measuring, and start the cycle.

With the laundry churning, I move to the kitchen. Dishes from breakfast still linger in the sink, and I attack them with more vigor than necessary. I scrub the dried food from the plates, lost in the monotony until a splash of water jumps across my chest, leaving an embarrassing splotch on my white T-shirt.

Christian chooses that moment to walk in. His gaze moves to the water stain, and I cross my arms over my chest, heat flooding my cheeks. He clears his throat, eyes shifting away, suddenly clouded with something unreadable. "I'm going for a run," he says, voice terse. "I'll be back before dinner."

"Okay," I reply, pulse racing.

"Let's order in tonight. Indian sound good?" He's already halfway to the door, keys jangling in our awkward silence.

"Sounds great."

"Order from Tandoori Palace in Richmond. I'll pick it up at six." His decisive tone has returned.

"Sure. What do you want?" I ask, eager to smooth over this wrinkle, to prove we can still be friendly. *Everything is fine.*

"Chicken tikka masala, lamb vindaloo, and lots of naan," he rattles off.

"Got it," I respond, scribbling a mental note.

He nods, and then he's gone, leaving me alone with the whirr of the dishwasher and the distant hum of the washing machine.

My mind won't stop racing. The truth is, I care about Christian more than I want to admit. And that's exactly why I need to be careful. I was so sure Franklin and I would build a life together, only to end up alone and blindsided when he walked out.

But Christian's not Franklin. He's steady, strong, responsible. Yet there's nothing about him that seems to be looking for a relationship. He barely has a relationship with his daughter. Work consumes his life, his identity. I sense that he's struggling with that, but forging a path forward is not something I can do for him.

I tell myself this logic is solid, but I wonder if I'm just afraid. I hate that fear has this kind of power over me, that I'm so afraid of losing myself. For now, I just need to stay on solid ground.

CHAPTER 12

Christian

The cold air bites at my skin as I pound the pavement around False Creek, trying to outrun the image of Hailey in her soaked T-shirt. It's ludicrous, really, how in sync our tastes and humor are, like two tracks running parallel on a train line destined never to meet. A 17-year age gap should mean we're worlds apart, yet here I am, struggling to keep her out of my head.

I pull in a sharp breath, the burn in my lungs matching the turmoil in my mind. Hailey has this irksome ability to remain practical, focused, entirely competent, when I seem ready to jump in on something I've never wanted before. Not that she's at all aware of that, I suppose.

Every stride is a mantra. *We can't happen.* I repeat that over and over. The notion that anything more could exist between us is a risk I can't take. For Addison's sake, just like Hailey said. A laugh bubbles up, bitter and mocking. Who knew I needed a twenty-three-year-old to be my voice of reason? But how long could it last before reality snaps back? Why is this even something I want?

My muscles protest with each step. I push harder, faster, trying to leave behind the aching desire. But even as the endorphins kick in, Hailey's image persists, something I can never have.

Panting, my feet slow on the pavement and I come to a stop in my garage, by the sleek curves of my Porsche. I could go inside and tell her I'm heading to pick up dinner, but that would only be an excuse to see her. Shaking my head, I wipe myself down with a towel, then slide into the leather seat instead. The engine purrs to life under my touch, a subtle reminder of the control I have here, at least over something.

I navigate the city toward Tandoori Palace. Its reputation is well-earned, and tonight, I need comfort food. Traffic crawls and red taillights snake ahead of me, killing my sense of control, of mastery. I'm trapped here too. My fingers tap an impatient rhythm on the steering wheel, willing the cars to part like the Red Sea.

I've always been good at keeping things separate — work, life, relationships. It's easier that way. No mess, no complications. But Hailey and my newfound interest in Addison have thrown all of that out the window.

Hailey's been nothing but good to me, to Addison, and I've responded by treating her as someone lesser, mostly refusing to acknowledge her humanity, except where my libido is concerned.

But I think for a moment and realize that's not right. That's part of my fear, my confusion. I do think of her as more. I just won't let anyone know. As usual, my fear of commitment — of losing control — runs the show.

My father disappeared from my life for years. He was never there when I needed him. Maybe that wasn't entirely his fault, but I've promised myself I wouldn't be like that. I promised I'd be better. But I haven't given myself any opportunity to try. I see the pattern now. Every time someone gets too close, I run. I push them away because I'm afraid they'll see how badly I'm broken. The only one to get past that is Addison, I suppose, and she was entirely forced on me. I've done the same thing with Hailey, and simultaneously tried to get her to offer me even more than what she already provides for me and for Addison. That's horrible. Alone in the car, my face flushes with shame.

But what if I let her in and it all falls apart? What if I'm not what she wants, or I can't be what she deserves? Maybe I'm not good enough for her, or Addison, or anyone? I know where I excel, and that's at the hospital, in the operating room, in situations I'm prepared for. But the rest of this...

The fear erodes my thinking because I know what's at stake here. If I continue to pursue her, there's a chance she could walk away. There's a chance I could lose her, taking her away from Addison. Am I even capable of the type of relationship I think I want? But if I don't take that risk, if I keep pushing her away, I'm going to lose her anyway. She'll leave on her trip with Dana and never look back. That might be even worse.

It's strange how quickly things have changed. A few months ago, I couldn't have imagined this life—sitting around at home, watching Addison play, with Hailey laughing in the background. Everything used to be so...rigid. My life was planned to the last detail. But now, they've changed everything.

Finally parking near the restaurant, I'm greeted by warm, spiced air that billows from the kitchen as they hand me my order. But as the city lights flicker past on the drive back, the scents do little to distract from the realization that distraction is exactly what I need.

"Ridiculous," I mutter, my hands tightening on the wheel. The tension in my shoulders begs for release, not through exercise or fine cuisine, but from the company of someone who doesn't stir this turmoil within me. Someone uncomplicated. That's what I know. That's how I need to manage this.

After we eat, I'll head over to the club, a club with lights that blur faces and bass that drowns out any attempt at meaningful conversation. There are rooms that are private—or public if you prefer—and it will be perfect. No reminders there of Hailey's infectious optimism or how she's fit seamlessly into a life that isn't supposed to accommodate her.

Maybe this is what I need to get Hailey out of my head, another body, another set of eager hands, and mindless sex all to quell the urges in me.

My grip loosens on the wheel, a plan taking shape. Hailey is good for Addison, indispensable even, but she's destroying my carefully structured existence. I need to take charge of that again, find a new sort of balance. This has to be the first step.

The door shuts behind me at home, the rich aroma of Indian spices clinging to my clothes. As I step into the hallway, Addison's wails cut through the silence. Hailey's soothing voice floats out from the nursery. "Shh, it's okay, sweet girl," she coaxes.

I set the food down and continue to the nursery. I watch as Hailey's every attempt to put Addison down is met with renewed cries.

I lean against the wall, catching Hailey's eye. "She's got a slight fever," she tells me, her attention fixed on Addison.

"Teething?" I hazard a guess.

"Looks like it," she responds, her fingers brushing over Addison's gums before reaching for the Children's Tylenol. She measures out a dose and gently administers it to my fussing child.

Withdrawing to the kitchen, I grab a plate, serving myself some chicken tikka masala. The spice hits my tongue, but the flavors are dulled by concern for my child. Surely, this is nothing. Hailey's got it. I was just in the way. Hailey hums softly — I can hear her through the monitor — a lullaby that works like magic. Soon enough, Addison's cries subside. She's finally calm enough to eat a little, and I have to admire Hailey's patience, her innate ability to soothe and nurture.

As Hailey rocks Addison to sleep, I finish eating and slide away silently, my resolve firming. I'll slip into the shower, wash away the sweat from my run, and once Addison is down for the night, I'll tell Hailey I'll see her in the morning. I need this— distance, detachment, a night where demands don't reach me.

The water pelts my skin, and I scrub and rinse, emerging from the steam a new man. After a few minutes more, I'm dressed sharply, hair styled just so. This is who I am, not the man beguiled by the gentle sway of Hailey's hips as she comforts a child.

When I emerge, it sounds like Addison is asleep, and the house is quiet. In the kitchen, evidence of our dinner is gone, cleaned up, hidden away. Hailey isn't there. My feet carry me to her room, propelled by a force I'm hesitant to name.

The door is ajar, and inside, the glow of the TV flickers across Hailey's face. She's sprawled on her bed, chest rising and falling evenly, lost in slumber. An action movie plays to an absent audience.

A sigh escapes me. I need to get to the club, but instead, something about her vulnerability draws me closer. I sink down next to her on the bed, careful not to wake her. Maybe it's the warmth of the room or the steady rhythm of her breathing, but I feel my eyelids growing heavy. *Just a moment,* I tell myself. *Just a moment to gather my thoughts and then I'll go.* But there are no thoughts I have in her presence that are going to be helpful. Still, somehow, the exhaustion of the day, the emotional tug-of-war, it all catches up to me and before I know it, darkness pulls me under.

The sharp cry from the baby monitor jolts me awake. My

heart thunders. The faint blush of dawn seeps through the curtains of an unfamiliar room. I glance at the clock — nearly five o'clock. Damn, this is Hailey's room. I never got to the club last night. I never sleep this well.

Hailey springs into action before I can further process the sound that woke us. She rushes out, disappearing down the hall to tend to Addison's needs. Her soothing whispers carry faintly back to me through the monitor.

Shaking off the last tendrils of sleep, I rise and dress for the hospital. I have a shift in the emergency department after I do rounds, and I'm on call for the next two full days. Responsibilities await me.

On my way out, I pause in the nursery where Hailey has just gotten Addison back to sleep. Gently, I rub the baby's back. "Be kind to Hailey while I'm gone," I murmur, though I know she understands little. It's more for me, a small plea to the universe to keep them both safe in my absence.

I turn to Hailey. "If Addison runs a fever again, please call Dr. Cordelia and go see her." It's a precaution, a safeguard against my absence, but the concern lingers. "I'll be at the hospital if you need me."

"Of course," she responds.

My hand finds the cool metal of my keys in my pocket as I clear my throat. "Hailey," I begin, and she turns to me, her expression shifting from maternal gentleness to attentive concern. "I'll call you later," I promise. "Take care of her," I add, though there's no need for me to tell her that. She gives me a small nod.

With one last glance, I push away from the door frame and head out into the crisp morning air. The hospital awaits.

CHAPTER 13

Hailey

The next night—or I suppose the next morning—the clock blinks a taunting 3:47 a.m. when I finally give up the pretense of sleep. I turn on my side, pulling the blanket up to my chin, a physical barrier against the uncertainty. But eventually, as dawn seeps through the curtains, a resolve solidifies within me.

Christian called yesterday to tell me he had to stay at the hospital, but we needed to find a time to talk. What could he want to talk to me about? Does he think I've gotten too close to Addison? Or maybe him? I know this situation is temporary, but all I've ever wanted was a family. Someone to love unconditionally who will love me back. Maybe I'm pretending a little, but I don't think that's clouding my judgment.

Franklin's name floats to the surface like a forgotten memory. I remember the way he made me feel at the beginning, like I was part of some grand, impossible dream. At first, his words promised a future that sparkled just out of reach. I fell for him hard, not because he told me he loved me, but because I needed to believe in the fairy tale he sold.

My thoughts move to Christian and the way he holds Addison. He doesn't seem to know he's falling in love with his daughter. Our day at the aquarium was fun for all of us, and I'm beginning to feel something I haven't felt in a while. *Safe.* Maybe that's the difference between Franklin and Christian.

But I know what Christian and I are. We're here fighting for Addison together. As a unit. He's not promising a happily ever after. He's likely not promising anything at all. I'm attracted to him, though, and I think I know what he wants. Why is it so bad to want the same thing? Men can be detached about sex. Dana's wrong. I can be detached too.

But I need a plan.

My mind jumps to Dana and me in a year — free. I pull the course listings from my bedside table and scroll through the real estate licensing options. It's a tangible goal, something I can focus on.

With Addison still curled in peaceful slumber next door, I do the math on a scrap of paper. Between what I have saved already and what I'll make the rest of this year, I can take some online courses before I leave. Then when we return from Europe, I can look for a place to hang my shingle.

When it's officially morning, I take a quick shower, get both Addison and myself fed and dressed, and then I'm behind the wheel of the minivan. Addison is strapped into her car seat, babbling excitedly.

An unexpected chime from my phone startles me, the screen lighting up with an incoming call. Without hesitation, I hit ignore. Driving requires all of me, especially with Addison in tow, and it's the law. "Shake It Off" comes on the radio.

"Taylor Swift is amazing," I tell Addison. "She writes all her songs, and she's super kind to her fans."

My phone rings again, cutting through my chatter. A second attempt to reach me. I turn into the parking lot of the OT's office, my curiosity piqued but patience thinning. "We're here, Addie," I say as I park and kill the engine.

I retrieve my phone, swipe open the notifications, and

freeze when I see Franklin's name—three missed calls. What could he possibly want now? An uneasy knot forms in my stomach, but I push it aside. He has no say in my life now. I switch my phone to silent and shove it into the abyss of the diaper bag.

"Okay, superstar, let's get you inside." I put Addie on my hip, and we head toward the building.

Inside the OT's clinic, the air hums with upbeat music. Addison's therapist, a woman whose patience seems boundless, reaches for her as soon as she sees us. As they get to work, I sink into one of the hard-plastic chairs that line the wall, my mind unwillingly drifting back to Franklin. What could he possibly have to say to me? My gut tells me nothing good.

I watch as the OT puts Addison in a bouncy swing, encouraging her to move to the music. Addison loves music and is happy to oblige. I think about my phone buried in the diaper bag. Should I check for a voice mail? I dig it out, and there are four messages, all from Franklin. The first is a hang up. In the second, he tells me curtly to call him, and the last two are demands to know where I am and that I stop avoiding him.

I don't have the strength to deal with this. Franklin may have once been the center of my life, but my focus is now on Addison and Christian. I don't have time for his drama. Leaving was the best thing he could have done for me.

"Addison did great today," the OT tells me a little while later as she brings her out. "But she really worked hard. Make sure she takes it easy for the next few days."

"Got it," I reply, my mind already juggling plans so I can keep Addison occupied but resting. We head out, Addison's head on my shoulder as I carry her to the minivan and feed her a bottle so she can sleep on the drive home.

The phone silently lights up with another call as I strap Addison into her car seat. I glance over, and my stomach drops— four missed calls, all from Franklin. My thumb hovers over the screen. *He's just going to keep calling…* Addison's eyes slide closed, and I finally answer the phone.

"Hailey?" Franklin's anger is evident. "My key, it's not

working. What the hell did you do?"

"Slow down, I don't understand." I close the door softly and walk around to the driver's seat. "What key? What are you talking about?"

"Are you deaf? My stuff! Where is it?" His volume rises, each word a verbal shove.

"Franklin, calm down. You took everything when you left. Including the key?" My response is steady, measured, but inside, I am a torrent of emotion, a maelstrom of anger and hurt threatening to spill over.

"Stop playing games, Hailey! You're such a fat slob, always messing things up!"

The insult stings, but I refuse to let it show. "I won't have you speak to me like this." My voice is cold, resolute. I end the call, and the line goes dead, his tirade interrupted by my refusal to be his emotional punching bag any longer.

Addison's heavy lids open as I reenter the car. "Everything's fine, baby. Let's go home." I start the minivan, fingers trembling, and navigate away from the curve of the OT's driveway and onto the open road, hopefully leaving behind whatever mess Franklin has tried to drag me into.

I drive us home and put Addison in her crib. I work on cleaning around the house while she sleeps and snack for lunch, even as I debate which frozen meal I'm going to eat for dinner.

The rain has stopped when she wakes from her nap, so Addison and I go for a late-afternoon walk along False Creek. We're both happiest in the fresh air. There are puddles along our path, and I push the stroller through the splash zone. Addison laughs. Her giggles make me so happy.

Just before we leave, I sit her in a shallow puddle, bundled tight in her rain gear, and let her spank the water. I take pictures. Addison is a pure Vancouverite with a love of the rain, and she's so happy just playing in the puddle.

Today is a great day.

After her bath and some time looking through the streaming service to find something I can watch, I read a book to Addie and rock her to sleep. The OT really did wear her out.

I'm just ready to watch my show when my phone lights up again.

It's Franklin, and my heart sinks. But maybe he's gotten the message. Things with us are not the way they used to be. "Are you calm yet?" I ask when I answer.

"You changed the locks. I need to get into the apartment now! When will you be back? I've been here waiting over an hour for you." Franklin's voice is jagged with frustration and anger.

He has lost his mind. I take a deep breath, willing my voice to be calm. "I couldn't afford the rent after you left, so I gave notice and moved out. What did you expect? That they would just let me live there for free? My guess is there are new tenants, and the landlord must have changed the locks. It's not my apartment anymore."

"Moved out?" he snaps, incredulous. "Where's all my stuff then?"

"You took everything when you left," I respond. When I packed up the apartment, I didn't see anything that belonged to him.

"No, I want to come over. Wherever you're hiding, I want to check for my things."

"Franklin, what do you think you left?" I ask. "Everything is in storage. I can look for you, but you can't just come over. I don't recall seeing anything that was yours when I packed up anyway."

"Storage? Damn it, this is ridiculous!" His voice is a low growl now, simmering with discontent.

"If you think of something specific, let me know."

Without warning, Franklin's scream explodes. The sheer intensity of it sends a chill down my spine, his anger so palpable it feels like he could leap through the phone and strike me.

My hand trembles. "Franklin, if you keep behaving like this, I'll have no choice but to block your calls."

"Block me?" he scoffs. "I'll sue you, Hailey. For everything you've got and will ever get."

A bitter laugh escapes my lips, though it's probably ill advised. "You're going to sue me? You took all the money my grandmother left me, and may I remind you, *you* left something behind, but *you* don't know what it is. This mess is on you."

There's a pause, and for a fleeting second, I hope he's reconsidering, that maybe there's a scrap of decency left in him. But then he shatters that hope with his next words.

"Remember those pictures we took?" He says this casually, as if discussing the weather. "I'd hate for them to *accidentally* appear online for everyone to see, with your name and address. And you know what they say, things live forever on the internet."

My heart stutters in my chest. "You deleted those," I counter, trying to sound more confident than I feel.

"Deleted? No." The smugness in his voice makes me want to scream. "They're safely up in the cloud. And unless you do what I ask, I'll make sure they rain down on whatever life you've created for yourself. I wonder what he would think about those naughty pictures?"

I end the call without another word, feeling like I'm going to vomit. *Why would he do this?* I need to get over to my storage unit and see what I can find. I'm sure I didn't pack anything that was outright his. We bought a bed together, and the couch, but we didn't have much. There were pictures of us, but I'm sure that's not what he's looking for. The other furniture is antiques, given to me by my grandmother. I have her will to prove it belongs to me.

My hands still are trembling, but I force a deep breath. I can do this. I am not going to let Franklin ruin anything.

I check on Addison in her crib and adjust the blanket to cover her legs. She looks so peaceful, and I envy her serenity. My world feels like it's spiraling out of control.

The moment I'm sure she's settled, I walk back to the living room and let the dam break. Tears stream down my face as I collapse onto the couch. My mind races with images of what Franklin might do, the threat dangling over me like a guillotine.

How dare he use our past, our intimacy, as a weapon against me? It's vile, a betrayal that cuts to the bone. I wrap my arms around myself, trying desperately to hold the broken pieces together.

The next time he calls, I'll either have found what he's looking for or I'll demand he tell me what it is. It's that simple. The sooner he's out of my life, the sooner I can put this firmly in my rearview mirror.

Wiping away tears with the back of my hand, I force myself to sit up straight on the couch. My phone, abandoned on the coffee table, lights up. I reach for it, squinting at the brightness of the screen.

Christian: How did the OT go today? How is she feeling?

Me: Addison's exhausted, but she's feeling a little better. She went down easy tonight.

Christian: Why was your phone off? Tried calling earlier.

I hesitate, my thumb hovering over the keyboard. The truth is a twisted web I don't want him to get caught in. He doesn't want to know about my stupid drama. Franklin only wants what is his. He's not threatening Addison. I just need to go through the storage unit and find what he could be talking about.

Me: Turned it off for the appointment and forgot to turn it back on. Busy day.

Christian: Understood. I should be home tomorrow night. Would love to do something with you and Addison. Maybe take some of the day's weight off your shoulders?

A smile tugs at my lips despite the storm inside.

Me: That sounds nice. We'd like that.

Christian: Great, I'll text you in the morning. Sleep well.

Me: Goodnight.

I power off the phone before placing it on the table.

Leaning back, I close my eyes, letting out a deep breath. Things are messy, but nothing is unmanageable. Tomorrow is another day.

CHAPTER 14

Christian

I scrub in with a haste that matches the urgency pulsing through the OR. There's a life hanging in the balance, one I'm tasked with saving. I enter the room, and it begins. There's no room for error or second thoughts as I navigate the complexities of the human heart.

The hours slip away under the bright surgical lights, but this is what I signed up for—the adrenaline, the responsibility, the unspoken promise to each patient that I will give them my all. But even as I delve into the work, part of me feels the pull of another responsibility, a personal one.

Hailey. The thought of her strikes unexpectedly, a pang of guilt amidst the triumph of a successful suture. I didn't call to tell her about the change in my plans. She'll be wondering, waiting, worrying. It's an odd phenomenon to be concerned about something like this. Previously, my life was crafted to avoid these entanglements.

Finally sealing the last incision, I step back, peeling off

gloves stained with blood. A collective sigh rises from the team. *Success.*

I shower and change, but the weight of the day presses down on me as I sit in my Porsche outside the hospital, staring blankly at the dashboard. Another emergency surgery, another life saved, but I told Hailey I'd be home hours ago. Addison will already be asleep, so I've missed yet another chance to tuck her in, to hold her for just a moment and forget the chaos.

It's like I'm living two lives now, neither of them fully mine — the one where I'm the doctor with all the answers and the one where I'm supposed to be something more. And every time I'm pulled into the OR, I feel like I'm failing at both.

The drive home is a blur. I turn the key to unlock the house, silence greeting me. Anxiety dances in my chest as I step into the living room, my eyes adjusting to the soft glow of the lamp left on.

And there she is. Hailey, asleep on the couch with Addison curled up on her chest. Addison stirs slightly as I approach. I smile as her innocence tugs at something deep within me.

"Hey, beautiful," I whisper, lifting her into my arms. She fusses, a whimper as dreams are momentarily disrupted. But she relaxes again as I carry her to her bedroom. Tucking her in, I watch over her for a few moments. Then I return to Hailey.

She hasn't stirred, and as I stand over her, a wave of affection rushes through me. With a gentleness born from six hours of holding a beating heart in my hands, I slide my arms under her, lifting her with care. Her head rests against my chest, her breath warm through the fabric of my shirt.

"Let's get you to bed," I murmur, though she hears nothing. I walk softly to her room, laying her down. I pull the covers over her, watching the way her dark lashes fan out over her cheeks.

I linger another moment, caught in the gravity of her presence. But I retreat toward my room. At the doorway, I turn and watch again. I've promised myself I will keep things professional. She's said that's what she wants, and Dana has warned me not to involve myself with her friend, who deserves better. But every time I'm around Hailey, that resolve cracks. It's not just the way she looks at me with those soft, unguarded eyes that see through all my defenses. It's how she puts Addison first, even when she's running on fumes. She makes me feel...something I've never felt, and it scares me.

I can't afford to feel that way. Not with her. Not with anyone. This life I've built — it doesn't have room for complications, for feelings that tie you down and leave you exposed. Because when you're exposed, that's when they leave you, and then you're left wondering what you did.

But with Hailey... Damn it, she's more than a complication. She feels like something I need. My heart races. I want to reach for her and hold on and never let go. I can't even begin to process what that means.

As if sensing me there, she stirs, her eyes opening to search out mine in the dim light. "Christian?" Her voice is a murmur, laced with apology. "I'm sorry. I didn't mean to fall asleep."

"Shh," I soothe, returning to perch on the edge of the bed. I brush back a stray lock of her hair. "It's okay. I had an emergency surgery. Couldn't get away." I pause. "But I'm off tomorrow. We'll do something together."

She gives a nod, faint and acquiescent, before her eyes close once more, surrendering again to sleep. I stand and retreat to my bedroom, but I lie awake, restless, until a plaintive cry pierces the silence.

Addison.

I rise, grab the bottle of formula, and head to her nursery. I find Hailey already there, cradling Addison.

"Teething," she explains softly. "I gave her some Tylenol." In her arms, Addison fusses, seeking relief from an invisible pain.

"Let me — " I begin.

But Hailey shakes her head, carrying Addison back to the rocker. "I've got this. You must be exhausted from working two days straight." They settle into the familiar motion, the soothing creak of the chair, and just like that, Addison returns to sleep.

With a nod, I slip away, my body aching with a different

kind of yearning now. Alone in my room, Hailey's image swims behind my closed eyelids, her soft smile, the gentle curve of her cheek, and I succumb to a need too primal to ignore. My hand moves of its own accord, pulling hard and fast, chasing relief, chasing her. My stomach coils as my climax builds. Release washes over me in waves, and I collapse into sleep.

It's late morning when I wake the next day, later than I've slept in years. But the emergency surgery and subsequent restless night has taken a toll. Stretching out the stiffness from yesterday's marathon in the OR, I shuffle down the hall to check on Hailey and Addison.

I find them napping on the couch—Hailey a human cushion and Addison's cheeks still flushed from fever. I'm sure it's just from teething, but I don't like it.

"Hey," I say softly, not wanting to startle them. Hailey stirs, and she looks up at me, bleary-eyed and disoriented. "You look like you could use a better nap than this."

She smiles weakly, the kind that's more about politeness than amusement. "I'm okay," she murmurs, but her eyes plead for a moment of respite.

"Go on," I insist. "I'll take over with Addison. Maybe later we can have a nice dinner. Do something different for a change." The promise of fun seems to revive her a bit, and she nods before standing, handing me the baby, and disappearing into her bedroom.

As soon as she's out of sight, I check Addison's forehead—warm but not burning with fever. I give her another dose of Tylenol, coaxing her to swallow it with a soft, encouraging voice. She does, and then, with a contented sigh, she drifts back to sleep. With her in my arms, I settle on the couch, flipping on the

Whitecaps game. I pat her gently as the players dart across the screen. But the thrill of soccer is secondary now, replaced by the simple joy of being a father.

Addison and I make our way through the day, and I manage to feed her lunch when that time arrives. After taking her for a walk in the afternoon and putting her down for a nap, I pull up the internet, determined to remove making dinner from Hailey's plate. I order food from my favorite restaurant and arrange for delivery. As I complete the transaction, an ad for Range Rover pops up. I look at the hybrid model and wonder if I should replace the minivan. The girls need a safer vehicle. With a few clicks, I can see that it seats seven, and the hybrid means it would work for longer trips. My grandfather had one, so I already know it's comfortable. I keep on clicking, comparing options and accessories, and before I know it, I've bought a pearl white Range Rover, and I'm more excited than when I bought my Porsche.

All the urgency of the hospital seems worlds away when I'm here at home now.

The doorbell chimes, and I'm up in a flash, eager to retrieve the dinner. The aroma of gourmet cuisine wafts from the boxes as I set them out on the counter.

"Hailey," I call up the stairs. "Dinner's here!"

Moments later, she comes down the staircase, her hair tousled from sleep, a faint blush of strawberries emanating from her skin—the scent of her shower gel, perhaps? My heart skips a beat, despite my resolve to maintain a professional distance.

"Smells amazing," she says, smoothing out the creases in her sweater as she approaches.

"I figured we could use something special tonight," I reply, keeping my tone light.

Addison stirs in her playpen, her big eyes blinking up at us. We exchange knowing looks. She comes first, always.

We take turns, Hailey eating while I entertain and attempt to feed Addison some finger foods, making silly faces and blowing raspberries until she giggles. Then we switch places, and Hailey cradles Addison, cooing softly to her while I savor the exquisite tastes of truffle oil and seared scallops.

"Thanks for this," Hailey says, her gratitude warm.

I just nod and smile, happy to have done this for her. The delicate gold chain around her neck catches my eye. "Tell me about your necklace. You wear it every day, right?"

"Oh, this?" She looks down at it, fingers tracing the outline of the butterfly pendant. A wistful smile lights up her face. "It symbolizes change. My grandmother gave it to me."

I've finished eating, and Addison looks like she could use her bottle. Hailey realizes this at the same time, so she mixes it, and I lift Addison from her seat to feed her.

"What happened to your parents?" I ask.

"They couldn't manage to be parents," she confesses with a shrug. "They were living on a commune in Oregon, but they got deported back to Canada. They got some money when my grandmother passed, and they said they were going to wander around Europe. I haven't heard from them since they left."

I take in her words, contemplating the resilience and lost opportunities woven into the fabric of her life. "Your grandmother raised you?" I confirm. She's spoken of that before.

"Yep." She smiles. "She didn't have much, but she was always my biggest supporter. Even when she died, she left me her life insurance policy. She wanted me to use it to follow my dreams, maybe explore Europe."

"Sounds like she was quite a woman," I say.

"The best," Hailey replies softly. "She believed in being open to change…to new beginnings."

She looks up at me, and I want to believe she's telling me she believes those things too, that the way we started won't define our relationship forever. But this is likely just a conversation I'm having with myself. It's safer that way.

We move along to lighter topics, but in the back of my mind, there's a persistent nudge, a mental note to find Cordelia at the hospital tomorrow and fill her in on how Addison's feeling. She still seems a bit warm as she takes her bottle. For now, though, I focus on the present.

Hailey toys with the edge of the butterfly again, tracing

the delicate wings. "I had this whole plan," she says, her voice wistful. "After we finished school, Dana and I were going to wander for a year. I figured maybe my parents were on to something, and I should just see the world, let each day unfold for a while."

I nod, about to confirm that this is still her plan, though I hate the thought of her leaving us, but then she sighs.

"Dana was all for it," she continues. "But then my ex — Franklin — he had this great business idea, and I wanted to be supportive since we'd talked about getting married someday."

"Sounds like you were committed to making it work," I say, trying to keep my tone neutral.

"Too committed, maybe." She looks down at her lap. "I offered to fund his idea with the money from my grandmother."

My jaw tightens at the thought — her inheritance, meant for adventures and discovery, for her own education, poured into someone else's ambition. "And he just took it?"

She looks up at me, her eyes clear, no trace of self-pity. "It was my decision to give it to him."

"Still," I mutter, anger bitter on my tongue, "it feels like this Franklin guy took advantage of your generosity."

Hailey laughs, but there's no humor in it. "Maybe. He also encouraged me to quit school, so we could focus on the food truck. But in the end, the money wasn't enough. His business flopped, and everything was wasted."

I shake my head. The helplessness I feel is unfamiliar. I want to protect her, to rewind time and redirect her path away from this Franklin ass who squandered her dreams. But all I can do now is listen, feeling the weight of her lost opportunities.

The rhythmic suckling slows, and Addison's tiny hand falls lax against my finger. She's asleep again. Hailey's gaze meets mine over the tuft of baby hair, a smile touching her lips. "See? She's always calmer when we're both here," Hailey teases.

I shake my head and walk Addison back to her crib, laying her down with Hailey by my side. "Guess we make a good team," I murmur, but suddenly, there's a tension in the air, one that's been building for too long.

I attempt to sidestep Hailey, to keep the boundaries intact, but she brushes past me first, her scent—a mix of baby powder and strawberries—fills my senses. I follow her to the kitchen, and before I know what's happening, my hands frame her face, my thumbs caressing her cheeks as I lean down and press my lips to hers.

Her mouth is soft, yielding. She makes a small sound, one of surprise or protest, I can't tell. I brace myself for the sting of rejection, for her hands to shove against my chest, for the end of whatever this fragile thing is we've been dancing around. But it doesn't come.

Instead, she leans into me with a hunger that matches my own. Her arms loop around my neck, pulling me closer, deeper. This isn't just a kiss, it's an admission, a dare, a crossing of lines we can never redraw.

She's fire and need against me, and every rational thought is drowned in the pounding of my heart. It's crazy, stupid, and I can't imagine our path forward, but God, how I want her.

"Christian…" she breathes, her chest heaving. She clutches the fabric of my shirt. "You are insufferable." Yet there's no bite to her words, just an intoxicating blend of exasperation and desire.

"Tell me to stop," I challenge, searching her eyes for any sign of regret.

When she declines to do so, I'm on her again, claiming her mouth with a fervor that leaves us both gasping. I lift her with ease, her legs wrapping around my waist as I set her on the kitchen island.

"You're so damn beautiful," I manage between kisses.

The world narrows to the taste of her, the feel of her against me, the quickening beat of our hearts. I lead her through the quiet house to my bedroom, where all thoughts of loser Franklin, wasted dreams, and consequences fade into nothing. Here, now, there's only Hailey and the undeniable truth that I've wanted this for far too long, and now I know for certain she wants it too.

CHAPTER 15

Hailey

Christian's fingers weave through mine, warm and assertive. As I follow him toward his bedroom, the air between us crackles with anticipation.

The door closes behind us with a soft click, and suddenly, we're in his world. He turns to me, his eyes smoldering. "Hailey," he murmurs, his voice low and husky. "I need to worship every inch of you."

His hands trail up my arms as he leans close, his breath hot against my neck. He whispers his sinful thoughts. Suddenly, my shirt is off, and my bra is across the room. "God, your breasts are perfect."

His fingers whisper over my nipples, which ache for so much more. Yet still… "Is this a mistake?" I voice the worry in my head.

He pulls back, and our foreheads meet. "I will stop if you want me to."

I don't think that's what I want, but in this moment, it's

really hard to know. "I have Dana on repeat in my head."

"I know she thinks I'm a cad, but I want this with you. This isn't a game to me. I can wait until you feel ready. There is no pressure."

My heart pounds in my chest. My mind races between wanting this, wanting him, and the nagging voice in the back of my head that worries this is the first domino in everything falling apart. But the way Christian looks at me, like I'm the only person in the world, drowns out the doubt, at least for now. *This is different*, I tell myself. It has to be different. I can be different.

"I do want you," I tell him, leaning in. Our tongues move in a sultry dance.

He licks the shell of my ear. "I want to trace every curve and dip with my tongue, feeling you tremble under my touch."

I close my eyes, and my pants are on the ground. He moves us to the bed and spreads my legs wide. As his fingers part my pussy, he grazes my clit. Everything he does lights me on fire. I moan.

"I want to hear the sounds you make when you come," he says. "But if you want to stop, just tell me."

He takes my hand and places it on his cock. It's hard, and it's huge. I stroke it a few times. Right now, I'd do anything he asked.

"I'm going to make you forget those boys you've been with. I'll show you what a real man can do."

I manage to nod. I want all of that and more, hanging on his every word.

"I'll stop whenever you say," he assures me, but his words are a mere formality. My body is already answering him, yearning for his touch.

His hands roam with purpose, mapping the terrain of my skin. There's a reverence to it. "Tell me," he demands, his fingers pausing at the curve of my waist. "What do you like?" His question is earnest, a genuine quest to learn what will bring me pleasure.

A nervous laugh bursts forth. "Honestly, it was always…simple before—missionary, quick, three pumps and done." The admission feels both liberating and embarrassing under his gaze, which never wavers, never judges.

"I think we can do better than that," he replies, a grin playing on his lips.

His touch becomes feathery light. It dances across my flesh, igniting trails of fire. "More," I breathe.

He obliges, and his fingers find the tender peak of my nipple, pinching slightly as I urge him, "Harder."

A deep moan vibrates from his chest as he complies, his hands moving more boldly now, claiming every inch of me. Then, his palm meets the curve of my backside in a firm spank that echoes through the room. The sting blooms into a rush of warmth that pools at the center of my desire. I can feel how wet I am, and it's as if he senses it too. "I've been waiting my whole life for you," he murmurs.

Standing before me, he watches me a moment with eyes darkened by raw need. "Suck my cock," he commands.

There's no hesitation in me as I rise, then drop to my knees and take him in my mouth, savoring the salty taste of his skin, swirling my tongue around the tip before taking him deeper.

His fingers lace through my hair, guiding me with gentle insistence until I'm taking him as far back as I can go. "Swallow," he instructs, and I feel him throb in my throat. I strum my clit and moan my own pleasure. He groans, and pride swells within my chest. I love making him come undone like this.

But just as he teeters on the edge, he pulls away, leaving me empty but eager. "Get on the bed," he says, and I scramble to comply.

"Show me how you please yourself. I've only heard it. Now, I want to see."

His confession hangs in the air, freezing me in place for a moment. My cheeks flush with embarrassment and arousal as I process his words. But then I spread my legs wide, revealing myself in all my vulnerability and arousal, glistening under his hungry gaze. I reach down to circle my wet clit, slow at first but gradually increasing in speed and pressure. My other hand travels to my breast, pinching and pulling at the nipple, just the way he did.

He groans, a guttural sound, and I open my eyes to see him stroking himself. After a moment, I lose myself in the rhythm of our mutual pleasure. My hips lift off the bed, seeking more, pushing against my own fingers as I chase my climax. Suddenly, I'm there, on the cliff's edge, and with a cry that echoes off the walls, I tumble over into blissful oblivion.

Before I can catch my breath, he's moving, the rustle of a foil packet punctuating the heavy air. He rolls the condom on, and climbing on top of me, he lifts my leg over his shoulder. As he enters, he stretches me wide, filling me completely. His movements are measured at first, allowing me to adjust to the new angle, the fullness.

"Tell me if it's too much," he says again.

"Stop talking," I pant. "Fuck me the way you like."

That's all the permission he needs. His restraint shatters, and he slams into me, hard and fast. Our bodies collide with a slapping of skin, and each thrust pushes me farther into the mattress, the forceful rhythm driving us both toward another peak. There's nothing gentle now, only raw, primal need, and it's exactly what I crave.

My fingers twist into the sheets, knuckles blanching as an intense wave of pleasure crashes over me. Holy shit—the intensity of it buckles my thoughts, scatters them like leaves in a storm. His body is an unyielding force, driving us both toward a crescendo that shudders through me, leaving me breathless and quaking.

He groans, and with a few final thrusts, I feel him tense, the unmistakable sign of his own release. The warmth spreads between us as he fills the condom, his movements slowing to a stop.

Collapsing next to me, he pants, his breath ragged and hot against my neck. After a moment suspended in the afterglow, he peels himself away and stumbles to the bathroom.

The sound of running water filters out, and when he returns, there's tenderness in his touch as he cleans me up. "That was…better than I ever imagined," he says. He pulls me in close, his arm a secure band around my waist as he spoons me from behind. In minutes, his breathing evens into the deep rhythm of sleep.

This feels good — too good — but now, in the quiet, I have to wonder what it *means*. Christian didn't make promises of forever or sell me dreams, but he did say he wanted something with me. *What?* What if I get emotionally attached? Is that what he wants? But what will that mean for me? For Addison?

The night stretches on, and I'm left to wonder if I've made a mistake. I suppose only time will tell.

I rise in the early morning, muscles sore yet strangely energized, and shuffle to Addison's room, leaving Christian asleep. It's farther down the hall than usual. Her soft coos and the rustling of blankets greet me as I enter, and as I prepare for her feeding, my thoughts churn like the formula in the bottle.

I take Addison in my arms and gaze down at her as she begins to eat, her eyes closed in trust and contentment. With each pull from the bottle, she draws more than just nourishment, she takes a piece of my heart, filling spaces hollowed by neglect.

As I burp her gently and place her back into her crib, the silence returns, my constant companion in solitude. I sit back in the glider, a sentinel in the quiet, watching over her as dawn creeps through the blinds. I chastise myself, realizing I've likely fallen into the same trap again, giving everything without expecting anything in return.

Maybe it's not about being a priority to someone else, I realize. Maybe it's time I become a priority to myself.

CHAPTER 16

Christian

I tap my foot incessantly, drumming against the tiled floor of Steaming Mugs. I'm quickly realizing I might need more than caffeine to endure this impromptu meeting with Dana, early on a Saturday morning. The time doesn't bother me. It's that I left Hailey's warm body in her bed, only to wait for my tardy stepsister.

Yesterday, Hailey and I were together with Addison almost nonstop. I don't know quite what to make of that, but I know it made for a wonderful day.

"Can I get you anything, sir?" a passing waiter asks.

I shake my head, my eyes darting once more to the entrance. Dana's request for advice was cryptic, but her lack of punctuality is entirely familiar. The minutes tick by. I have so many things to do, and sitting here is not among them. Family or not, time's still valuable.

But perhaps there's a real issue. It's not like Dana to be so vague. Usually, she's straightforward, sometimes painfully so.

What could she possibly need that I could help with? I hope it's not her love life. That's where I draw the line. I've navigated enough romantic quagmires of my own to know I'm not going to be much help. Maybe Dana could offer some advice about how to navigate things with Hailey... *No.* Scratch that. She'd put me on blast before I even had the question out of my mouth.

Come on, Dana... I check my watch for what must be the twentieth time. Her tardiness has stretched beyond acceptable limits. I take the last few sips of my espresso and prepare to leave. Something must have come up for her.

But then the door to Steaming Mugs opens and Dana rushes in. She offers a sheepish grin. "I'm so sorry," she says, but the apology is cut short by my impatience.

"Twenty minutes, Dana," I chide, folding my arms over my chest. "You could have at least texted."

She shrugs off my reproach with an ease that grates on me. "Since when are you Mr. Punctuality? Got your panties in a wad about something?"

"Never too busy to notice time wasted," I mutter as she saunters to the counter. The barista takes her order for a cappuccino, and she glances back at me with eyes that say *lighten up.* I roll mine in response.

She comes to sit across from me and sips the frothy top of her drink, peering over the brim of her cup.

"So, how's it going with Hailey?" Dana asks.

I soften, but in the same moment, my guard goes up. *What does Dana know? Has Hailey told her something?* "It's good, mostly. Just wish she'd stick to a schedule more."

"Does Addison miss her doctor or therapy appointments?"

I shake my head. "Not that I know of."

"See? She's doing great," Dana counters. "Addison loves her, and patience isn't exactly your strong suit, so you need her. You'll just have to get over yourself."

"Maybe." I concede. "But structure has its place too."

Dana smirks, lifting her cappuccino. "Spoken like a true control freak."

I can't argue with that. I've always liked having things just so. But Hailey, with her gentle resistance, challenges that every day. Maybe it's not such a bad thing after all.

Dana's eyes narrow. "So Hailey's working out. Was I right?"

I shift in my seat, suddenly uncomfortable again. "She's good with Addison. You called that from the start."

"That's why you bought her a new car?"

"I hated the minivan, and the Range Rover is significantly safer."

"That sounds dangerously close to thinking about someone other than yourself. I told you to keep your grubby mitts off her, remember? Hailey is a beautiful person, inside and out, and she's had enough troubles. If you add to them, I'll make your life miserable."

I try to brush that off, but Dana's stare doesn't waver. Finally, I sigh, running a hand through my hair, and opt for my rote answer. "You have nothing to worry about. I don't do relationships, and Hailey... She deserves more than I can give her." I wonder again, *Does she know something?* My guilty conscience sparks to life.

Dana leans back in her chair, arms crossed, her expression softening a little. "Then make sure you don't mess with her head."

I lean back in my chair, arms crossed over my chest. "All right, you've said your piece. Is this why you wanted the meeting? Just wanted to give me a refresh on your views about my life?"

She grins, a twinkle in her eye. "Nope." She pops her P. "I want to plan an anniversary party for Mom and John."

"Is that all?" I ask, skeptical yet also relieved. "How much money are you after this time?"

Her laugh is light. "Oh, come on. I don't need your money, Christian. I thought you could help plan it."

"Plan?" I snort and shake my head, dismissing the idea immediately. "No chance. I'm swamped as it is."

"Too busy for a twentieth wedding anniversary?" she

presses, her eyebrows arching in challenge.

"Fine," I relent. "Just tell me when and where, and I'll make sure the funds are available."

"Actually, I was thinking the Boathouse at Stanley Park," Dana says. "It's perfect for about forty people."

"Forty, huh?" I picture the venue in my mind. It's an excellent restaurant, and the view over the water sparkles at night. I nod despite myself. It's a fitting place for an anniversary party, and I know they'd love it. "Are you making it a surprise?"

"It would be hard to get my mom dressed the way she'd want to be for that kind of party, so I think we're better off telling them."

"Sounds good. And make sure there's enough cake to go around." I lean forward, resting my elbows on the table as I scrutinize Dana's hopeful expression. "So, do you think twenty grand will cover it?"

Dana's eyes widen, and she sputters into her coffee, coughing as she sets her cup down with a clatter. "Twenty thousand? This isn't a royal banquet we're talking about. It's just going to be family and friends, nice and low key." She wipes a drop of coffee from her chin, still looking at me like I've lost my mind. "Whatever doesn't go into the party, I was hoping we could use to send them to Hawaii. You know, a second honeymoon?"

My father married Dana's mother when Dana was three years old, and, if memory serves, they went camping on Vancouver Island for a few days after the ceremony. This would be a nice thing to do.

I nod, noting the earnestness in her gaze. "Okay," I say softly. "I'll send over a credit card in your name. Keep it reasonable, but make sure they have something special to remember."

Before I can offer my hand for a handshake, Dana lunges across the table and wraps me in an unexpected hug. I stiffen for a moment before I pat her back. Public displays of affection aren't really my thing. But Dana wears her heart on her sleeve.

"Thank you," she murmurs, pulling back with a bright

smile, her eyes misty.

"Sure," I mutter, trying to shake off the lingering embarrassment. "Just make sure they have a good time, okay?"

"Absolutely," she promises. "But you'll be there, won't you?"

"Depends on when it is and my hospital schedule." I settle back into my chair. Dana's eyes are on the clock again, and I catch a flicker of something—anticipation? Nervousness?

"I can plan around it," Dana assures me. "I know they'll want Addison there too."

I nod. "Check with Joanne in my office, and she'll know my schedule."

"Great." She takes a sip of her drink and looks at me.

"Got plans after this?" I ask, mostly to fill the silence. Dana and I have never had a lot in common.

She glances at me, a secretive smile playing on her lips. "Actually, I've got a date."

"Really?" My eyebrows rise. "First date?"

She puts her cup down. "Fourth."

"Where'd you meet him?"

"Ummm...online," she answers, shrugging as if it's the most ordinary thing in the world.

"Be careful, okay?" The protective edge in my voice surprises even me. "You can never be too sure about people you meet there."

"Always am," she assures me, but the tilt of her head suggests she appreciates the concern. With that, Dana shoves her chair back and rises, slinging her purse over her shoulder.

She steps around the table, and I stand, bracing for another hug. This time, though, it's a brief squeeze, her energy already shifting toward whatever comes next. "Remember," she says, pulling back to look me in the eye, her expression stern in a way that reminds me of my mother. "Keep your mitts off Hailey. She's my friend first, and she's way too nice for you. She's off-limits."

"Wouldn't dream of it," I lie smoothly, and she narrows her eyes. *Does she know something?*

But then she pats my arm. "Good." She turns on her heel

and heads for the door, leaving me to consider her warning.

I watch her disappear into the street crowd, always moving forward, whether it's planning parties or navigating the treacherous waters of online dating. Her resilience is something I admire, even if I don't always understand it.

Left alone, I linger over the dregs of my espresso. I should leave, but something about the empty chair across from me, still holding the impression of Dana's presence, keeps me rooted. My thoughts drift to family ties that bind and shape us.

My father, with his second chance at love, managed to find happiness with a woman who wasn't my mother. Their relationship, steadfast and unpretentious, has always seemed to me like an unattainable benchmark. Meanwhile, my own mother never settled down again, following their divorce. She danced through suitors with grace but never clung to any one of them. I can still hear her laughter when I once—half in jest, half in curiosity—asked if she'd ever consider remarrying. "*Oh,*" she had said, "*I have you. And as for the rest, I don't need a man to take care of me.*"

It's strange now, how those words echo in the quiet corners of my mind as I consider my own path. Will I ever marry? The question feels alien yet necessary, rolling around in my head. Commitment of that magnitude seems almost antithetical to who I am—a man more comfortable with fleeting connections than binding vows.

But since Hailey has been part of my life, I've felt different. It's like I don't even know myself, and I'm thinking about things that never seemed remotely appealing. Every time I see Hailey with Addison, or when she smiles like she trusts me, I feel something I can't explain. The pull of something more. *What is that?* But it's not the same as wanting marriage. I still find it strange to consider making someone more than a fleeting presence in my life. Hailey is off to Europe in less than a year.

I suspect marriage might be a societal expectation I'm not cut out for. Unlike my father, or even Dana, with her relentless optimism about love, I don't feel that pull.

I glance at the clock. I need to get going. Time slips by

when you're wrestling with the notion of your future — or lack thereof. I pocket the nagging doubts about tradition and bloodlines. After all, DNA doesn't dictate destiny, and given my parents, things could go either way.

Though I could barely drag myself away from Hailey this morning, I've avoided coming home all day, opting instead to catch up on charts at the hospital. Dana got in my head when I met her this morning. She had me second guessing every step I've taken with Hailey, so I needed time to think.

When I finally get home, I push the door open to the quiet, the scent of vanilla and something citrus lingering in the air. I toe off my shoes and hang my jacket on the rack by the door, my thoughts about how to handle Hailey still echoing in my mind.

"Hello," I say softly, careful not to disturb the peace as I enter the living room. Hailey looks up from her laptop, a tangle of notes spread out before her on the coffee table. Her brow is furrowed with concentration, but at the sound of my voice, the tension eases from her face.

"Hi." She greets me with a smile. "Addison just crashed an hour ago." Her eyes flick back to her screen. "Got this project I'm working on, but I can still keep an eye on her."

The offer is considerate, but I'm surprised to find leaving is the last thing on my mind. The idea of spending the evening alone, wrestling with my thoughts — or even trying to drown them in someone without attachments — doesn't appeal to me. Not anymore. Not when there's a better option right here, not just my daughter, but Hailey too.

"Actually, I was thinking of staying in tonight," I tell her, shuffling closer to where she sits. "Maybe we could Netflix and chill?"

Her fingers pause over the keyboard, and she raises an eyebrow. "You do know that 'Netflix and chill' means have sex, right?"

"I'm aware," I reply, a sly grin spreading across my face. The air between us crackles.

Hailey closes her laptop and turns to face me, her smirk now blossoming into a full-blown smile. "Well, in that case, I'd be up for that."

"Great," I say, eager to see where the night leads us. We settle on the couch, and I wonder if maybe life has its own path in mind for me. Maybe I need to spend less time analyzing and more just seeing what happens, doing what seems right in the moment. I let out a breath I didn't realize I'd been holding, relief flooding through me. Hailey seems up for that approach, and my pulse quickens.

"Let's do it then." I pull her gently toward me. Tonight, I'm going to deliver. Whatever she wants, whatever she needs, I'm here for it all. And as our eyes lock, I see the same hunger reflected back at me, a silent promise that yes, she can indeed keep up.

CHAPTER 17

Christian

I look over in the darkness at Hailey in my bed, her chest heaving slightly, a blissful smile curving her lips. Three times. Her pleasure is my artwork, and I've painted a masterpiece tonight.

My mind, though, is racing. Even as I enjoy this, I can't forget the stakes involved. Hailey is nothing like the women I've been with before. I've never been interested in someone like her, honestly. But she is without a doubt, someone good for me. She doesn't expect me to be perfect or have all the answers. She's strong in a way that complements my need for control, but soft enough to remind me there's more to life than chasing success. Her vulnerability challenges everything I've built around myself.

How can someone who's been hurt so much still have hope, still believe in people? She makes me question everything I thought I knew about relationships, and about myself. I just wish I knew what to do with that.

Suddenly, a faint cry slices through the intimacy. *Addison.*

"I can go," I say gently.

"No, it's okay. I've got it." Hailey is already untangling herself from the sheets, slipping on a silk robe that does little to conceal the curves I've just worshipped. She floats across the room, and I sprawl back on the bed, arms behind my head. Who would've thought? Christian Bradford, content in the afterglow, listening for the sounds of a baby. My daughter. "Bring her back with you," I call softly, hoping my voice carries. I want them both here, in this sanctuary we've created.

Time stretches, marked only by the distant sound of traffic and muffled shuffles from the monitor. Then Hailey reappears, Addison cradled in one arm, a bottle in her other hand.

"Hey, sweetness," I greet as they approach. Hailey sits on the edge, carefully positioning Addison and offering the bottle.

I prop myself up on an elbow, watching them. Addison latches on, her hand wrapping around Hailey's finger. "Look at you two," I whisper, reaching out to brush a lock of hair from Addison's brow.

"She's radiating heat," Hailey responds quietly, eyes never leaving Addison's face.

It's a picture-perfect moment, yet something twists inside me. My fingers smooth over her forehead, and sure enough, the heat there sparks anxiety in my chest.

I grab my phone from the nightstand, thumbing a message to Dr. Cordelia.

Me: Addison's had a fever on and off for days now. Not getting better. What do we do?

Cordelia's response is immediate.

Cordelia: I'm at the hospital. Bring her in now.

"Let's go. Dr. Cordelia wants to see her." The words are out before I even register them. With haste that borders on frenzy, Hailey and I dress, avoiding each other's gaze.

I race down the stairs with Addison in her car seat,

heading to the Range Rover. Hailey is hot on my heels. "Come on," I bark anyway. "Hurry up."

"I'm right behind you," she says.

I don't even remember shutting the garage door as we race to the emergency room. The world outside is a blur, every honking horn and streaking headlight merely background noise to the thudding of my heart.

The hospital looms ahead. We're ushered into one of the pediatric emergency department bays. Addison only wants to be held, but a series of nurses and PAs need to examine her. We're in a large area full of assorted equipment, and we can hear a young boy crying. Thankfully it's not long before Cordelia appears.

"Hello, Addison. I hear you're not feeling well?" Cordelia says as she takes her from my arms.

She talks to Addison like she'll understand. "I'm going to use a needle to extract some blood from your finger for a CBC. We want to measure the different kinds of blood cells in your body. It will hurt for just a few seconds, but don't worry about it."

Cordelia distracts Addison enough that she hardly notices the prick. She sends the sample off with a lab tech. Then a nurse brings in a portable echocardiogram.

"Dad? Can you hold Addison so I can take some pictures of her heart?"

"Of course," I say. We strip her down, and I hold her close.

Cordelia coats the pediatric heart wand with warm gel, keeping up a steady stream of conversation with Addison, who simply smiles and remains mostly calm. "You're doing great," Cordelia praises. As I watch my daughter's heart on the screen, my stomach twists at the realization that my little girl is ill.

The lab tech returns and hands Cordelia the results she's looking for from the blood draw. Her face falls. I shut my eyes to prepare for the bad news.

"Endocarditis," she says after what feels like an eternity. "A heart infection."

I know what endocarditis is, and it's not good for an adult, so even worse for my baby girl, especially since her Down syndrome makes her heart vulnerable. Hailey's hand finds mine, her grip a cornerstone.

"IV antibiotics," Cordelia continues. "I'm admitting her up in the peds ward. We'll start her treatment immediately. And I've put in a call to Davis. He's on his way."

"Thank you," I choke out, my throat tight with unshed tears.

"We're doing everything we can," she assures us.

As Cordelia walks away to tend to her duties, I look down at Addison, who seems sleepy and a little confused, but mostly unfazed.

We're moved upstairs to the bright walls of the pediatric ward and placed in a private room with two large chairs that extend for adults to sleep in. The nurses get Addison settled quickly and attach leads to the heart monitor and tubes to her nose for oxygen. I marvel at how fast a child's heart beats compared to my typical patient.

The rhythmic beeping of the heart monitor fills the room as a nurse enters to attach an IV line to Addison's scalp. Hailey yelps.

"This is normal for children under a year old," I assure her, though Addison's cry brings tears to my eyes as well.

Once the nurse leaves, I sit by Addison's hospital bed, my hand holding hers, focused on the fragile rhythm of her heartbeat. *Endocarditis.* The word itself is a punch to the gut. It's something I should've been prepared for, given her condition, but nothing in all my years of medicine has prepared me for this. For her.

I never thought I could love someone like this. I never expected Addison to mean so much. When she arrived unexpectedly, she was just another responsibility, a piece of the puzzle I had to figure out. But now... Now, I realize she's part of me. She's everything. Her laugh, her hands reaching out for me, the way she trusts me without question—it's more than I ever thought I could handle, but I'll do anything to keep her safe and healthy. Seeing her like this, so small and vulnerable, I feel a helplessness I've never known. I've saved so many lives, but right now, all I want is to save hers.

"I can't believe we..." Hailey's voice breaks. "We were... And she was right there suffering."

"We didn't know," I tell her. "We couldn't have known." But my reassurances sound hollow, even to my own ears. I'm wrestling with the same self-reproach. The laughter and shared pleasure now feel like a betrayal, a frivolity we had no right to indulge in.

She nods, but her gaze remains fixed on Addison.

A knock at the door pulls our attention as Davis Martin enters the room, his lab coat crisp. "Christian," he says, reaching out to shake my hand.

I introduce Hailey, reminding him she's Addison's nanny.

He nods his hello. "I'm sorry to say this, but Addison's heart is struggling. It's not uncommon for children with Down syndrome to have cardiac issues. We're going to beat this infection, but eventually she's going to need surgery for the congenital septal defect, likely before she turns two."

His words strike me, a blunt-force trauma to my already battered psyche. *Surgery.* I look down at Addison, her tiny fingers in mine, her trust absolute. She doesn't understand the trials ahead, the pain she'll have to endure.

"Okay," I reply, my voice steady despite the turmoil inside. "Whatever it takes. We'll do whatever we have to in order to make her better."

Davis nods as he explains the treatment plan in meticulous detail. I absorb every word, committing them to memory. I've said things like this to adults before. I'm well aware of the risks. But for now, my daughter needs me to be strong.

"Thank you, Davis," I say when he finishes, grateful that he's a friend as well as Addison's doctor.

"Of course," he replies. He takes another moment to assess Addison before leaving us.

I look back at Hailey, whose focus has never strayed from Addison. Even how she's stroking her finger over Addison's hand. Our roles, undefined as they may be in many ways, are clear in this instance. We are Addison's guardians, her warriors against an unseen enemy.

"We're going to get her through this," I tell Hailey. "Together."

"Together," she echoes, and in that single word, I find strength.

I rise and pace for a moment, needing to move. Eventually, I lean against the cool, sterile wall of the hospital room, focusing on Addison's small, flushed face. She doesn't seem terribly distressed, and I don't know if that makes things better or worse. I don't want her to suffer in any way, of course, but I hate that this enemy is so subtle. I feel like I may never relax again, though I'm determined to carry this burden for her as much as I can.

Davis returns with his clipboard in hand.

"How's Taylor doing?" he asks casually, glancing up from his notes. "Should we call her?"

"Taylor's pursuing her acting career in LA," I respond, the words automatic. And based on what the PI reported when he confirmed she was there, at least once, she did a little partying on the side. That was all I needed to know. "We've had no contact with her."

"Ah, and Hailey?" He looks over at her. "Would you like her listed as an authorized decision maker? I know she's usually the one bringing Addison to her appointments..." He trails off, looking at me expectantly.

Suddenly, I'm irritated. What's he getting at? "She's the nanny," I answer too quickly, too curtly. "She'll continue to be part of Addison's care."

A flicker of pain crosses Hailey's eyes so quickly I almost miss it. But before I can react, she murmurs an excuse and slips into the restroom.

Davis watches her leave, then turns back to me, a knowing look in his eyes. He sees through the facade I've tried to put up.

"Let's go over the treatment plan one more time," Davis says, returning to the reason we're here. "Endocarditis is tricky, but we've caught it early enough."

He details the regimen of IV antibiotics, explaining that if they work well, Addison could continue receiving them orally at home after the initial assessment. Antibiotic treatment will be roughly four to six weeks, he estimates, depending on her response.

I hate that immediately. The hospital is a warren of bacteria, viruses, and fungi brought in by patients, visitors, and staff. My little girl has a weakened immune system. This seems the last place she should be. "We need to get her out of here," I blurt. Addison should be somewhere other than this cold room filled with beeping machines and antiseptic smells, somewhere familiar and warm.

"Exactly," Davis responds, closing his folder with a snap. "It's always better for recovery if the patient is in a comfortable environment. If we can get the infection under control, I'm sure we can shift her to home care and oral antibiotics sooner rather than later. We'll get her managed as quickly as we can and be vigilant in the meantime."

"Thank you, Davis," I say.

"Anytime," he replies and heads out again.

I sit there a moment, my gaze moving to the closed bathroom door. It's been several minutes since Hailey slipped inside, and I know she's upset. The silence is killing me.

I take a step forward, my hand raised to knock, hesitating as if it's not just the door I'm about to breach, but something far more intimate and fragile. "Hailey?"

There's no response. With a steadying breath, I tap lightly, and then, without waiting for an answer, I push the door open.

Hailey sits on the edge of the toilet, her face buried in her hands. When she looks up, her eyes are red-rimmed, the remnants of tears glistening on her cheeks.

"Hey," I begin, my throat tight with emotion. "I'm sorry, Hailey. I didn't mean to—"

She shakes her head, dismissing my words before they're fully formed. "It's fine. You told the truth. You don't have to explain. This is on me. Dana's always been clear who you are. I'm the nanny. I would do well to remember that."

Her admission stuns me. *That's not true.* "No, I want us to be something more. You are something more. But I don't talk about my personal life with anyone. It's not their place to know." I pause, searching for the right words. "But that doesn't mean you're not important, and not just because of Addison."

There's a spark in her eyes, and it strengthens my resolve. "What we have, our relationship? It's ours," I tell her. "No one else's business."

Her gaze holds mine. Then she nods, just once, and the simple gesture feels like a truce. But the wall she's built is high, and it's my fault.

What does she want from me? I'm not the settling-down type. Clearly, Dana told her. Do I need to tell her? Do I want to tell her? I don't really know what's true for me anymore, and right now, with Addison in crisis, there's no way I can find clarity.

Her phone pings, then twice more in rapid succession. Her hand clenches into a fist, and she takes a deep, shaky breath.

"Are you all right? Who's trying to reach you?" I ask.

She hesitates for just a heartbeat before answering. "It's Franklin. He says he left something in the apartment, and he wants it back." Her brow furrows. "He won't say what it was. And I'm certain I didn't pack up anything that was his when I moved everything into storage."

"Are you okay handling it?" I ask. "How can I help?" Her stress levels seem to rise with every vibration of the device.

Hailey nods, though it's clear she's far from okay. I fight the impulse to take matters into my own hands. "Let me know if you need help," I offer instead, making sure she knows I'm here.

"I can handle it," she asserts softly.

"Okay." I nod. There's just so much on our plates already. "Thank you for being here with me, and with Addison. She needs you. I appreciate all you do for us."

She offers a small smile, one that doesn't quite reach her eyes. With a final nod, I step back into the hospital room and return to Addison's bedside, where I pull out my phone. It's after eight now, and we've been awake all night. My thumb hovers over the screen for a moment before I dial my mother.

"Mom, it's Addison…" I say when she answers. "She's in the hospital."

"Christian! What happened?" There's panic in her tone, and I take a deep breath, trying to steady myself enough to explain.

"Endocarditis. We're at the hospital now. She's getting treatment," I tell her, the words tasting like ash in my mouth.

"I'm coming," she says, and we hang up without further pleasantries.

I turn to Hailey. "My mom is on her way. I need to run home and get a few things, but if I go now, I should be back before she arrives. It seems we'll be here for a while."

"That sounds fine. I'll be here when you return."

The drive home feels longer than usual, my mind racing with concerns. Once I arrive, I hastily grab fresh clothes. I have a shaving kit and toiletries already in my locker at the hospital. I debate packing things for Hailey, but it feels too personal. She will need a break and can come home herself after I return. Maybe even get some sleep.

I retrace my steps to the hospital and upstairs to Addison's room without pausing. But when I reach the doorway, the sight that greets me stills my frantic pace. Mom is here, her elegant frame bent slightly as she leans over to gaze at Addison. Hailey stands beside her, a steady sentinel whose conversation with my mother halts abruptly upon my arrival. There's tension in Hailey's shoulders, an unspoken upset in the air, but she avoids my gaze.

"Hi," I greet them.

Mom looks relieved to see me, but it's Addison's reaction that tightens my chest with emotion. She squirms in her bed, her little hands reaching for me, her face scrunched in discomfort. As soon as our gazes meet, she releases a tiny, plaintive whimper.

"I'm here, sweetheart," I say softly. Addison clings to me instantly, her small body curling toward me as if she could burrow away from all her ailments. My heart aches with a father's love, fierce and protective.

"Mom, thanks for coming," I murmur, stealing a look over

at Hailey. I vow to find a moment to mend whatever has upset her.

My mother strokes Addison's wispy hair, a tender gesture that feels foreign coming from her. "I don't like grandma or grandmother. I think I'll have her call me Mimi," she declares.

"Okay, Mimi it is," I reply.

"Christian, dear, should we...?" My mother hesitates, her polished facade cracking with concern. "Should we consider flying in a specialist? Someone with expertise in pediatric cardiology?"

I shake my head. "No, Mom. Davis Martin is overseeing her treatment. He's top notch, the best out there."

Her shoulders relax, relief washing over her. "Good, good." She pats my hand, needing the assurance that only the word *best* can bring.

As Addison's eyelids flutter closed, my mom leans in closer, her tone shifting to something lighter. "We should discuss her first birthday party, Christian. You never sent out birth announcements, and I want to make it unforgettable when we introduce her."

"That's more than five months from now. What do you have in mind?" I ask, though my thoughts linger on Hailey's unreadable expression.

"I'm thinking a grand garden celebration, pastel balloons, a petting zoo..." She launches into a list of ideas, each more elaborate than the last. I listen, nodding along, but I can't entirely focus. What's happening now seems way more important. Five months is an impossibly long time away.

Hailey rises from the chair she's perched on, a shadow of discomfort in her eyes. "I'll be right back," she murmurs.

"Mom, I should—"

"Christian, stay. We need to finalize these plans," she insists, her voice a gentle command that no one, least of all me, can refuse.

So I nod, fidgeting with the hem of Addison's blanket, my gaze flickering to the door Hailey vanished through. "Can't it wait? Addison may still be here in the hospital on her birthday."

I'm pretty sure this is a lie, based on my conversation with Davis, but I need to buy some time.

"What are you talking about? Hailey told me she'd be home with you for most of her treatment. This is important. Addison will only have one first birthday." She doesn't even glance up from her tablet, where I suspect she's already recruiting a party planner.

"Fine," I relent. "But it needs to be at our house, and it needs to be small. She will have just recovered, and infection is a risk." As we delve further into the details of a party that seems too grand for a one-year-old, I feel like I'm betraying Hailey with every nod, every forced smile.

Suddenly, a soft whimper disrupts the conversation. Addison stirs, her fussiness cutting through the talk of ice sculptures and mini carousels.

Without thinking, I rise and carefully find a way to lift her, patting her gently, my movements surprisingly instinctive. "Shh, it's okay, princess," I whisper.

"Look at you," my mother says, her eyes wide as if truly seeing me for the first time. "You've really taken to fatherhood."

I look down at Addison, her hand gripping my finger, and feel a swell of protectiveness. "I'm growing to love her very much," I admit softly.

"Who would have thought?" Mom muses, her astonishment a rare crack in her polished demeanor.

"Certainly not me." I glance once more toward the door, wishing Hailey were here to see this — to see us.

I'm smoothing the creases from Addison's blanket when the question comes, unexpected and sharp as a pinprick.

"And Hailey?" Mom asks. "How does she fit into all this?"

"Addison adores her," I say. "She's been a godsend."

Mom tilts her head. "Christian," she begins, her voice taking on the tone I recognize from many a childhood lecture, "she's young and rather naïve. It's not…appropriate for her to be overly involved. Stay away from complexities you don't need."

"Thanks for the advice, Mom," I reply, though the words are more dismissal than gratitude. "Right now, I'd just like to focus on Addison."

"Of course," she concedes, but there's an edge to her acquiescence as she gathers her purse. "Please keep me posted on how things are going. And just remember what I said." With a final look that tries to pierce through me, she leaves, the door closing behind her.

The silence left in her wake is brief. The door reopens, and Hailey returns, looking slightly disheveled.

"Everything okay?" I ask as she settles into the chair beside the small hospital bed.

"Your mother arrived just before you did," she says. "But she had time to ask a few questions."

"Nothing too invasive, I hope?" I'm well aware that my mother's few questions could be akin to an interrogation.

"Nothing I couldn't handle," Hailey assures me.

"Good." I nod, letting the subject drop for now.

I return Addison to her bed now that she's settled and step back to lean against the doorframe. Hailey's fingers trace circles on Addison's back. The tension from earlier has ebbed away.

"I'm sorry about last night," I tell her. "How everything turned out... It's not what any of us expected."

She offers a tired nod.

"It's tough, juggling all this," I continue, gesturing vaguely to encompass the hospital room, the unspoken worries, the weight of responsibilities that neither of us asked for. "But I need you to know, I need your patience. With Addison, with me. We're navigating untraveled waters here."

Hailey's gaze holds mine, searching. I feel a twist of unease at the vulnerability exposed between us. "This is new to me as well," she reminds.

I nod, wondering exactly how much of our current situation she's referring to. "When all this is over," I tell her, stepping closer, "I have other plans for us, plans that involve just you and me, no interruptions, no hospitals... I want to show you how much you mean to us, how much you mean to me."

Her lips part, but she doesn't speak, and the silence stretches out. I watch the emotions play across her face, hoping she reads the truth in my eyes, the truth of my intentions, both spoken and unspoken.

CHAPTER 18

Hailey

The heart monitor's incessant beeps are a constant reminder of the three weeks in the hospital that have stretched out since Addison's diagnosis. But the fact that the sounds are steady and strong reminds me that we're making progress. When Christian is not with his own patients, he's joined me at Addison's side, holding her whenever he can as she fights the infection in her heart. We've both been sleeping in the parents' chairs here in her room, which is not the easiest with all the noise and constant interruptions. I try to get away for a few hours every day, just to breathe some fresh air and take a break.

Currently, we're seated at Addison's bedside, listening as Dr. Martin reports on her progress after three weeks of IV treatment. She's able to take the oral antibiotics well, so we will continue that for a while at home. She's dozing calmly, blissfully unaware of the monumental step she's about to take.

"Rest is paramount," Davis says, "even if she's not in-patient anymore." His eyes move between Christian and me.

"Therapy appointments only for now. Walks in the park are good, but any socialization can wait—no play groups, classes, going where there are lots of people you don't know. Her body is working hard to recover, and getting sick will slow that down."

"Please limit yourselves to a few visitors—family only," Dr. Cordelia adds. "Keep her environment calm, familiar."

Christian's brow furrows slightly, but he nods, absorbing every word. He's become a sponge for their advice, and I know he'll do everything in his power to make sure Addison thrives.

"We've got this," I assure him. Being at home again has to be better than this, for all of us.

With the discharge paperwork complete and antibiotics in hand, we pack up and leave the hospital. Addison looks so fragile as Christian places her in the back of the Range Rover and drives cautiously out of the parking lot.

The moment the front door clicks shut behind us, a sigh escapes my lips, one that feels like it carries the weight of all of our sleepless nights. Addison snuggles against my chest. "Finally," I breathe as Christian sheds his coat and shoes.

He looks over at me, a silent conversation passing between us as he crosses the room to wrap an arm around us. "Let's get you two settled," he murmurs.

I nod. We shuffle toward my room, where I place Addison in the bassinet we've set up next to my bed. Without bothering to change out of my day-old clothes, I lie down. Sleep overtakes me before I can even pull the covers up.

Sometime later, the bed bobbles and wakes me enough to know Christian has lain down beside me, his presence a reassuring warmth at my back.

Time blurs, soft and indistinct as we sleep the day away, until Addison's stirring pulls me back to consciousness. In the dim light filtering through the curtains, I hold a bottle to her eager mouth, watching her eyes flutter shut as she drinks. My heart swells with every gulp she takes. She's so much stronger than she was before she went into the hospital. When she's sated, I rock her gently back to sleep.

Her eyes close, her breaths even out, and I lay her in the

bassinet. I turn to find Christian watching me.

"She's doing so well," I whisper, my voice low. "I can tell she's glad to be home."

"Thankfully," he agrees, his voice thick with the kind of exhaustion that comes from more than just sleepless nights. "We've come so far."

There's a pause, a shared moment where the weight of everything we've been through—the hospital stay, the endless stress—settles between us. I can see it in his eyes. He's just as overwhelmed as I am. But beneath the weariness is something more, a need for reassurance, for connection. A need for me.

Christian's hand finds my waist, gentle at first, but then his fingers tighten. In his eyes, I see the same mix of exhaustion and longing I feel. It's not just about passion. It's about finding solace after days of feeling powerless.

He doesn't say a word, but when he pulls me closer, I understand. This is about reclaiming a part of ourselves, something that's been lost in the chaos of hospitals and worry. His lips brush my forehead, a tender gesture that quickly turns into something more.

"I need you," he murmurs. His kiss is soft at first, but it deepens with every heartbeat, the warmth of his body pulling me in, anchoring me to this moment.

His kiss transports me right to where I need him. "Hard and fast," I urge. I need to reclaim control of a world that's been turned upside down.

"Let's go to my room," he suggests. "We'll have the monitor, and I want to hear you call my name."

Moments later, he shuts the door behind us and backs me over to his bed. "God, I've missed this with you." He pulls my sweater over my head and pushes my jeans to the ground. I lie back on the bed and watch him rip his clothes off in mere seconds.

Then Christian's mouth is on me, tender yet demanding, his tongue tracing circles around my nipple before he draws it between his teeth. A shiver races through me, a delicious tension building as he bites down gently, sending shockwaves of pleasure straight to my core.

"Christian," I moan, arching into his touch. His fingers part me, deliberate and slow, before one slides in, a single finger that knows exactly where to go.

He groans. "You're so wet for me. What a fucking turn on."

The praise, the sensation of being filled, sends a surge of warmth flooding through me. He adds another finger, and then another, stretching me, pushing deeper. I gasp at the sense of fullness, the intensity growing with each movement.

"More," I plead, my hips rising to meet his hand, desperate for the relentless pleasure only he can give. He obliges, a fourth finger joining the others, moving inside me in a rhythm that has my head spinning.

He's good at this—too good—and I'm teetering on the edge, the coil in my stomach winding tighter. I reach for him, my fingers tangling in his hair, pulling him closer as I seek something to ground me in the whirlwind. "Please," I whisper, and he understands, his mouth returning to my nipple. This time when he bites, it's sharper, a jolt of sweet pain that tips me over the edge. My climax crashes over me, ripples of ecstasy that leave me breathless and trembling.

"Christian," I gasp out his name as the world narrows to just the two of us, the connection we share outstripping everything else. There's no room for doubt or fear. There's only this moment, this perfect release.

Before the tremors have fully subsided, Christian is rolling a condom over himself. The sight of his readiness ignites a fresh fire within me. He aligns himself with my body, and with one fluid motion, pushes inside. A shared groan fills the air. "Perfect," he breathes. His fingers grip my hips. I'll wear the memory of this moment on my skin. "Open for me," Christian commands softly, pressing his fingers, slick with my arousal, to my lips. I taste myself on him as I suckle gently.

The room echoes with the slap of flesh against flesh, a testament to our urgency, our need. I'm climbing again, chasing the high he offers so skillfully. With a shift of his hips, he changes the angle, and suddenly, he's there, stroking the bundle of nerves that sends sparks shooting through my veins. My climax looms large, and when he adds a rhythmic tap against my clit, it detonates. I scream, a raw sound of pure ecstasy, as my body shakes uncontrollably beneath him.

"Hailey," he groans as he reaches his own peak, his voice laced with satisfaction.

In this moment, spent and satisfied, I'm candidly vulnerable. "You've probably ruined me for all other men," I murmur.

"Good," he replies, his voice husky.

Exhaustion melts into my limbs, with the warmth of Christian's body curving around mine. He spoons in behind me, his breath ghosting over the nape of my neck, pulling me into an intimate cocoon.

"Thank you for that," I whisper.

He chuckles, his chest vibrating against my back. "I wanted to take you into the bathroom at the hospital and fuck you there… But I couldn't do it."

Curiosity piqued, I roll over to face him, our noses nearly touching. His eyes are a stormy sea of blues and greens, emotions churning just beneath the surface. "What stopped you?"

"I worried it would make me a bad father," he confesses.

I press my lips to his. "You're a good father. You were there with Addison every day, even on days you worked. And yes, you'll make mistakes — we all do — but it's okay. No parent is perfect. That's how we learn, how we grow."

For a long moment, he simply looks at me. Then, slowly, he smiles. His lips brush the tip of my nose, a tender gesture that sends a ripple of warmth through me. "How did you get so wise?"

I can't help but laugh. "Must be the injections you're giving me."

For a moment, confusion knits his brow, and I seize the chance to shift the mood. My hand finds him, still warm from our previous union, and with deliberate strokes, I coax him back to life. His confusion fades, replaced by dawning realization as his body responds to my touch.

"Ah…" He breathes out a soft laugh.

When he's ready again, I roll the latex down his length, ensuring we're safe before I position myself above him. I lower onto him, guiding him inside, and the connection is immediate and electrifying. The room fades away until there's nothing but Christian and me, moving together in a rhythm as old as time.

CHAPTER 19

Hailey

I'm barely awake when the front door chimes. Addison is not back on her previous schedule yet, and she was up throughout the night, though now, of course, she's sleeping. The clock glares 7:17 a.m. at me, and I know it can only be Dana. She's the only one who'd come by at this ungodly hour without a call first. We've been home for a few days, and Dana has restrained herself from coming by so far. Wrapping my robe tighter, I shuffle to the door and open it.

"Hey," Dana says, stepping into the living room with a cardboard tray of coffee cups and a bag from our favorite bagel shop. "I heard Christian got called to the hospital in the middle of the night. I thought you might need some company."

"Thanks, Dana." I smile, taking the warm tray from her hands and setting it on the kitchen counter. We settle on the couch and arrange the feast before us.

"Everything okay?" she asks, biting into a cinnamon-raisin bagel.

"I'm fine," I assure her. "Christian woke me when he left," I explain, cradling the coffee cup in both hands. "I couldn't sleep after that, just kept tossing and turning. I feel so bad for him. He can't catch a break."

Dana nods. "That's rough. But I'm more worried about you right now."

I force a smile, though it feels brittle on my lips. "Why? It's not like it's the first time he's been called away in the middle of the night. He used to not come home at all. And Addison's infection is no fun, but it's so much nicer to be home now."

She opens her mouth but doesn't respond to that. I busy myself with my bagel, and we sit in silence for a few minutes. Then, biting the inside of my cheek, I decide to broach the subject that's been haunting me all week. Franklin was mostly quiet while we were in the hospital after I told him in no uncertain terms to buzz off, but now that he knows we're home, he's back to full throttle.

"I'll tell you what has been a little stressful, though," I begin, watching as Dana raises an eyebrow. "Franklin has reappeared and is acting weird. Like, more than his usual oddball self." I take a deep breath. "Something's not right."

"Weird how?" Dana sets down her bagel.

"Edgy, paranoid," I explain. "He didn't seem to realize I'd moved out of the apartment. Then he said he left something there and insists that I have it. But I have no clue what he could be talking about because he took everything before I moved out."

"Does he think something you bought together is his?"

"I keep asking him what he's missing, but he's being very vague."

"Sounds like we've got a mystery on our hands." Dana's eyes gleam. "We should go through those boxes, see what's got Franklin all wound up. There's got to be something fishy there."

"Could be nothing…" But even as I say it, I feel the certainty in Dana's intuition. She has a way of sniffing out trouble before it fully emerges, a trait that has saved us more times than I care to count. Besides, there's no *good* reason Franklin would be trying to get in touch with me again.

"Or it could be something big," Dana counters, finishing her coffee with a decisive slurp. "Either way, we won't know until we look. What do you say? Ready to play detective?"

I just dumped everything in the storage unit initially since I was short on time that day. A reluctant smile tugs at the corners of my mouth. Despite my reservations, I find myself nodding in agreement. "Let's do it," I say, stretching out the stiffness in my limbs. "But first, another bagel. I'm going to need all the energy I can get if we're going to sort through that mess in storage."

"This is the perfect chance to straighten it all up," Dana says.

Dana follows me upstairs so I can change and she can see Addison. Sunlight filters through the blinds in my room, where Addison's just starting to stir, casting a lattice of shadows over Dana's concerned face.

"Okay, little munchkin," Dana coos. "Let's get you ready for your big day out."

I hand her a fresh diaper and a change of warm clothes for Addie.

I pull out my own clothes, quickly putting on a bra as I realize I need to hide small but damning evidence of last night's indiscretion.

Dana's hand pauses mid-air, her eyes zeroing in on the purplish blemish staining my skin. "Hailey," she says slowly, "what's that?"

"Uh, nothing," I stammer, pulling my shirt down hastily. "It's just a birthmark, you know?"

"Birthmark?" Dana raises an eyebrow, her expression skeptical. "We lived together for nearly two years. I think I'd remember if you had a birthmark that looks like a hickey on the side of your boob."

I bite my lip. If I tell her the truth, that Christian left this mark on me, she'll be so upset.

"Actually, it's not a birthmark," I confess, feigning nonchalance as I lie my butt off. "Ray and I... We're seeing each other."

For a moment, I almost believe it myself. Dana's eyes

widen, her usual enthusiasm bubbling up, and I know I've dodged a bullet—for now.

"Ray? Since when? Why didn't you tell me? I want details!"

I force a smile, pretending to be casual, but my chest tightens. Part of me wants to tell her everything, that it's not Ray I'm seeing, that it's Christian. That I've never felt this way about anyone before. But I can't stand the thought of disappointment in her eyes, the 'I told you so' on her lips.

I'm not ready for that conversation. Not yet. So, I lie. Again.

"Oh, you know me," I say with a forced chuckle, avoiding her probing gaze. "I don't kiss and tell."

"Come on," she presses, leaning against the doorjamb with folded arms. "Since when?"

"Trust me, there's not much to share," I deflect, hoping my smile looks more genuine than it feels.

"Fine, keep your secrets." Dana sighs, though her eyes glint with mischief. "But promise me one thing. You won't let any guy distract you from what's important. We're going to go to Europe."

"Promise," I assure her, grateful for the change in topic. I can't afford to lose Dana's trust.

I zip up my jacket as Dana lifts Addison into her arms.

"Are you sure this is okay?" Dana asks.

"The doctor told us not to expose her to people who are sick, but I think we're fine at the storage unit. I've never seen anyone else there when I've been there before."

"Good. Let's do it," Dana says.

"Ready for our treasure hunt?" I ask.

"More than ready," Dana says with a grin.

Downstairs, we pile into the Range Rover and make our way across town to the storage unit. My thoughts keep drifting back to Christian. I try to focus on Dana, on Addie, on the task at hand, but it's impossible not to feel his presence lingering.

His words from last night still echo in my head. *"We'll figure it out together."* The way he held me after putting Addison to bed, the steady reassurance in his touch — it felt like more than just comfort. It was a promise. And that scared me, in the best way. Because as much as I try to keep this casual, to tell myself it's just physical, there's a part of me that wants more.

"So, what's it like dating while you're someone's nanny?" Dana asks, her voice cutting through my thoughts.

I hesitate, my mind flashing to Christian. Last night, the way he kissed me, the way his hands found their way under my sweater — it felt like he was erasing everything that had come before him. But I can't say that. Not to Dana. Not yet.

"It's fine," I manage, forcing a smile as I park. "You know, nothing serious. I didn't see him much while Addie was sick, but I do get some time off, especially now that she's back at home."

Dana nods, seemingly satisfied, and we head inside and up to my storage unit, rolling Addison in the stroller. I open the lock and roll the metal door up with a clatter, revealing the clutter inside — stacked boxes and furniture draped in my old bed sheets like ghosts of the past. We start with the boxes, methodically opening each one to sort through its contents. It feels good to be doing something tangible, even if it's just organizing old things. We dig and organize, looking for anything that could be Franklin's. There's an old bottle opener that might be his. His tax file. But nothing that should make him so upset.

A little while later, I pause to check on Addie, who's playing with her doll in her playpen. But then I'm right back to being knee-deep in trinkets, papers, and memories. Dana is rummaging through a drawer, her brow furrowed as she sifts through antique silverware. She pauses, gasping as she unearths the tarnished locket my grandmother always wore.

I take it from her and put the necklace on.

We talk about mundane things — the rain that's pouring from the sky, how we're adjusting to Addison's post-infection life at home, Dana's job, and eventually her boss.

Dana's expression hardens. "Can you believe Tate's ex? Just drops the kids off and scampers away whenever we have plans." She huffs. "This last time the boys were so excited to see their dad, and we thought they were just stopping by to get something. Then we realized she'd left them with us, without saying a word. Tate didn't discover she was gone until nearly an hour later."

I stack a pile of old books, carefully aligning their spines. "Sounds like she knew exactly what she was doing," I reply. "It's terrible to manipulate people like that."

"Exactly!" Dana slams the drawer shut in a side table. "I swear, it's like she has a sixth sense for ruining our nights together. And she's using her kids as pawns."

My heart goes out to her. "You know dating a man with kids means dealing with his past, and that includes his ex." I hesitate, choosing my words with care. "Maybe it's time for a real talk with Tate. Then you two could sit down with her, no kids around, and lay some ground rules that work for everyone."

She bites her lip, considering. The thought seems to weigh on her.

"Is that what you want, though?" I prod gently. "To be in the middle of all that? Does that work for you?"

She leans against a stack of boxes, crossing her arms. "I don't know. I really don't. But if he's worth it..."

"Then you'll figure it out together," I assure her. "But only if you're both serious about making it work. Otherwise, you might need to reconsider where this relationship is going."

Dana nods slowly. "Thanks, I needed to hear that."

We turn back to our sorting, and I sift through yet another box.

"Nothing here but old records and a few books," Dana announces. "And a bag of clothes you should give to the thrift store."

"Same," I reply, holding up an antique lamp that doesn't likely belong to Franklin either. We've been at this for hours, and the only item that's raised an eyebrow is a small baggie with a single joint inside.

"Franklin losing his mind over this?" Dana asks, pinching the baggie between her fingers. "Doubtful."

"Right?" I chuckle, shaking my head. "There's got to be something else."

But there isn't. Not that we can find, anyway.

We finally give up, the mystery of Franklin's possessions still unsolved. But the storage unit is better organized. The furniture is neatly arranged on one side, and the boxes are labeled and stacked on the other. If nothing else, I feel like I accomplished something.

Locking the storage unit behind us, I push the stroller to the parking lot. The crisp air outside bites my cheeks, and Dana slips her arm through mine. "Europe is going to be so much fun, you know?" Her eyes twinkle with excitement. "Just you, me, and endless adventures. No Ray and no Tate!"

I smile at the thought. No Ray is no problem. It's no Christian—and even no Addison—that will be an adjustment. "I can't wait."

We return to Christian's townhouse, and as we reach the door, Dana leans down to kiss Addie on the head and pulls me into a hug, a fierce one that seems to convey all her worries and affections without a single word.

"Listen," she says. "I'm sorry we didn't figure this out today, but no matter what happens, I'm here for you."

I nod, grateful for her presence in my life.

Dana gives my hand a final squeeze before stepping away. As I watch her leave, I unlock Christian's door and step inside with Addison, who is babbling away.

"Europe," I whisper to myself. "Adventures await." And for a moment, I let the possibility of all the places I want to go wash away the complicated mess of feelings in my current life. But then it all comes crashing down.

"What the hell am I doing?" I murmur to the empty room. I can't imagine just picking up and leaving at the end of this year. But I have to. Everything I've done has been so I have the means to explore and have fun and get on with my life.

But even as I remind myself, I wonder if I'm already too far gone—too entangled in the thrill of whatever this is with Christian, too invested in Addison—to find my way back to solid ground.

CHAPTER 20

Christian

I open the door at home, a box of tacos like an offering in my hands, casual comfort food for what I hope will be an easy evening. "I come bearing gifts," I announce, setting the box on the kitchen island.

Hailey looks up from the couch, her face lighting up with a smile that makes my chest tighten pleasantly. "You didn't have to do that," she says, but her eyes are already on the box, hungry.

I shrug off my jacket and drape it over a chair, feeling the day's weight lifting. "Where's Addie?"

"She's in bed, sleeping. I almost have her back on her old schedule."

"So, what did you and she get up to today?" I ask. I find I'm eager to hear about the mundane details, to picture them moving through the day.

She walks toward the tacos and tucks a loose strand of hair behind her ear, which I've learned she does when she's uncertain. "Actually, I spent the day with Dana," she says.

"Oh?" I lean against the counter, crossing my arms.

Hailey nods, drawing in a deep breath. "We went to my storage unit. Like I told you, my ex, Franklin, he thinks he left something when he moved out of our apartment."

She rolls her eyes, but I keep my expression neutral. "And did you find whatever he left?"

She shakes her head. "No. But I needed to get it straightened up anyway. When I dropped my stuff there, I was in a hurry because someone was sailing to Victoria with friends."

"Hmmm…yes. I do recall something about that. Not my finest moment. But I'm sure I can find a way to make it up to you." I pull her in close and kiss from her collarbone to her ear.

"We need to eat, and you need to spend some time with Addison." Hailey grabs a plate and crosses to the couch.

"Anyway, that sounds like a day." I move to join her.

"Whatever he thinks he left, I can't find it," she says, meeting my gaze squarely. "Tacos?"

Her attempt to change the subject doesn't go unnoticed, but I decide to let it slide — for now. "Definitely tacos," I agree.

I adjust my position on the couch. "How did Addison do at the storage unit? Weren't things a bit grimy for her? That can't have been easy."

Hailey chuckles. "It's all inside, climate-controlled," she explains. "Not as dusty or dirty as you'd think. Addison mostly slept and just kept us company. There wasn't anyone else around."

I'm relieved to hear that, but then Hailey drops a bombshell that shifts my concerns.

"By the way, Dana saw your artwork," she says, lifting her shirt to show me the love bite on the side of her breast.

I can feel my pulse quicken. "What did you tell her?"

Hailey's gaze flits away before returning to mine. "I told her it was someone else," she admits.

I feel a bit stung by the lie, but I understand her protective instincts. "Dana's not always my biggest fan," I agree, trying to make light of it. "But I'm working on it."

The conversation lulls for a moment as we both reach for

a taco. I take another bite as Hailey's next words catch me off guard.

"Dana… she's actually warned me about getting involved with you," she confesses.

"She warned me away from you too," I say. "She thinks I'm too careless with my love life."

Hailey nods.

Before we can wade in any deeper, Hailey's phone rings. The sudden sound startles us both, and she fumbles for the device, eyes apologetic as she answers with a brisk, "Hello?"

She rises and goes to the kitchen to speak in hushed tones I can't quite make out, so I'm left to stew in my thoughts. It's unsettling, her not telling Dana about us. Why does it matter so much? Why does the secrecy leave me cold? I've always been a proponent of discretion. Isn't that all she's really doing?

"Sorry about that," Hailey says, ending the call with a sigh.

I shake my head, trying to dislodge the unease. "No worries."

"It was the storage unit place," she says as she returns to the couch. "They wanted to know why I didn't lock up my unit when I left. I could've sworn we did." She bites her lip, a hint of frustration in her voice. "Anyway, they've put a lock on it now. They said I need to swing by for the key."

"Sounds like a hassle," I say. "But good that they didn't just leave it open. What are you going to do about Franklin?"

"I don't know," she exhales, a tired smile touching her lips. "What's in there is mostly just my grandmother's antiques, some keepsakes, and my important papers." She shakes her head. "It's everything I have that isn't with me here."

"That's important stuff," I acknowledge. "And Franklin won't say what he's missing?"

"He's always vague. I mean, we did find an old joint, a bottle opener, and some tax files, but he shouldn't be this upset over any of those things."

My chest tightens. "What do you mean he's upset?"

"He keeps demanding that I return whatever he left

behind."

She doesn't look at me, and I have a feeling there's more to this. "You know," I tell her, "I have this whole empty basement downstairs. You could move your stuff there."

She blinks, and for a moment, the stillness between us is palpable. "Thank you."

"Yeah." I nod, surprising myself with how much I mean it. "And if you want to put some of your things around the house, make it more of a home for you, I'd like that."

Her stunned silence fills the space, and I'm not sure why I've made the offer, why the thought of her things mingling with mine feels so right.

"I..." she trails off, her fingers tracing the edge of the cushion.

"Think about it," I say quickly, feeling the need to escape, to breathe, to understand the rush of emotions inside me. Without another word, I retreat to my room, trading my clothes for running gear and shoes.

"I'm going out for a run," I tell her when I return to the living room, and I don't even wait for her response.

The door closes behind me, and I'm alone with the cool evening air of Vancouver. False Creek awaits, its winding paths a welcome distraction. My feet find their rhythm, pounding against the pavement, each step propelling me forward, away from the townhouse, away from the confusion.

Hailey's face flashes in my mind, her expression when I mentioned the basement to store her things. I think of her laughter, the warmth of her skin, her nurturing care. Why does she stir these feelings within me? Why does her happiness suddenly feel like my own? And at the same time, why does that send me running away? Literally.

I'm running harder now, trying to shake off the weight of my thoughts. But then a tap on my shoulder pulls me out of the storm in my head. I stumble, irritated at the interruption, only to find Cinnamon standing there, her ponytail bouncing like she doesn't have a care in the world. It's the same old vibe with her — flirty, easy, no strings attached. Once this was exactly what I wanted, someone uncomplicated. But now, it feels…off.

"We missed you," she says with that playful smirk she always wears. "Savannah and I had a blast without you."

I draw a blank for a moment, and then I remember. We had plans to meet the day Addison arrived, months ago. I totally forgot. My life would be entirely unrecognizable to her now. Honestly, I'm not sure how I ever thought being with Cinnamon was enough.

She takes a step closer, her eyes locking on mine. "I've missed you," she adds, her fingers grazing my skin. It's a deliberate move, one that should set off a familiar thrill, but all I feel is a hollow echo of what I once enjoyed.

It would be so much simpler if I could fall back into this. No strings, no mess. But what kind of man would that make me? Someone who runs when things get complicated? Someone who can't handle feeling something real? What kind of father would I be?

"I'm not single right now, Cinnamon," I say, surprising even myself.

Her eyes widen, taken aback, and for a second, I almost regret it. Almost.

She laughs. "Really? Well, when you tire of your vanilla friend, you know where to find me."

As she jogs away, I'm left standing there, my old life still tugging at the corners of my mind. But it's not strong enough. Addison and Hailey have changed something in me, something I didn't know I wanted to change. And for the first time, I realize I'm not just scared of falling for Hailey, I'm scared of who I might become if I don't.

Turning back to the path, I push forward. I feel pretty sure now that Hailey is not just a passing fancy. She's an integral part of my world, and not just because of Addison. That realization propels me faster.

Soon, I'm pounding the pavement again. I can't shake off the ease with which I turned Cinnamon down. Hailey and I haven't drawn any lines for ourselves, haven't shared promises of fidelity. Yet here I am, barreling toward a commitment as if it were magnetic north.

The townhouse appears ahead, its windows dark except for one soft glow on the lower level. My pace slows as I approach, my thoughts racing ahead. Inside, the silence greets me, clean kitchen counters reflecting the dim light.

Climbing the steps, I find Hailey cocooned in bed, her eyes dancing over her tablet screen. She doesn't notice me at first, lost in whatever digital world she's immersed in, but then she looks up, her smile tentative, questioning.

"Hailey," I tell her, "things have changed between us." I wait for her reaction, for a sign that she feels it too. "I want us to be exclusive."

As soon as the words are out of my mouth, I wish I could reach out and take them back. I should have said that so differently. "What I mean is, I don't want to share you with anyone else. And I don't want to be with anyone else either. I want us to only see each other."

Surprise flashes across her face before it softens into something more profound. "I would like that very much."

I take her hand, feeling its warmth, and guide her to my room, a place that suddenly feels more intimate than ever. "Is Addison down?"

She nods. "For the night."

The air is charged with something new and fragile, like the first breath of dawn. I lead her into the en suite, turning on the shower until steam curls around us. With gentle hands, I undress her, and together, we step into the warm embrace of water.

I take my time, letting the droplets cascade over her, watching them trail down her skin. There's a reverence in the way I shampoo her hair, in the way I rinse the suds away, my fingers massaging her scalp. The mundane act becomes an exploration.

As she faces the wall, the curve of her back speaks volumes, and I'm drawn to her with a magnetism I can't deny. I reach to where desire pools, where heat gathers, and I massage her, slow circles coaxing out soft sighs and shivers. She leans into my touch, seeking more, and I find myself lost in the rhythm of her pleasure.

"I need you," she whispers, the urgency in her voice sending a jolt straight through me. She turns and her hands, slick with water and soap, find their way to my hard cock. She strokes me until my breath hitches in my throat.

She lowers herself onto the shower seat, pulling me closer. She looks up at me with those mesmerizing eyes before taking me into her mouth. The warmth, the wetness—it's almost too much. She licks away the precum beading at the tip, sending waves of pleasure radiating through my body.

Then, she massages my balls as my cock hits the back of her throat, and I'm forced to look up at the ceiling, fighting the urge to let go right then and there. But I want this moment to last.

She releases me with a pop, looking up at me with a devilish grin. "Where do you want to come? On me or down my throat?" she asks.

"Down your throat," I groan, my voice ragged with need.

"Show me how you like it," she challenges.

I place my hands gently but firmly on the sides of her head, guiding myself into her inviting mouth once more. "Just like this," I whisper. "I love the way you take me."

"Then fuck my face," she breathes against my cock, and the raw words send a shiver through me. "Harder," she urges, squeezing my balls just the way I like it. It's perfect. Everything about this—about us—in this moment is exactly right.

I thrust deeper, the edge of control slipping as I succumb to the intensity of the sensation. "It's so sexy watching you take my cock," I praise between labored breaths. And when I can't hold back any longer, I give in to the abyss, letting go completely as I come, waves of release crashing over me.

She swallows deeply, and in the aftermath, I'm left panting, adrift in the blissful haze of fulfillment, marveling at the connection we've found and the surprising depth of our desires. I glance down, and there she is, caught in her own world of pleasure, fingers dancing between her legs. A surge of pride and fascination washes over me. Could she be the one who matches my hunger, my intensity?

"God, you're amazing," I breathe.

We linger under the cascading water a moment longer, but it's clear the day has taken its toll on her energy. With care, I turn off the water and open the shower door, reaching for the plush towels. Wrapping one around her, I pat her skin dry.

"You must be exhausted," I say.

"Maybe a little," she admits.

Arm around her shoulders, I guide her to the bedroom, where we sink into the cool sheets. The need within me still smolders, but seeing her nestled against the pillows, I can't bring myself to ask for more tonight. Instead, I pull her close, feeling the steady rhythm of her heartbeat against mine.

"Do you still think you're a bad father?" she murmurs.

The inquiry stings, reopening old uncertainties, but I owe her honesty. "It's hard not to sometimes. I never had anyone to show me how it's done." I stare up at the ceiling as if it holds answers. "My dad left with a check… That's all he thought parenting was. And Mom, well, money was her way to make problems disappear."

"Despite what you may think, you're doing a great job. Honest," she says, her lips pressing against my shoulder.

Her words are simple, genuine, and they settle somewhere deep inside me. Maybe I can be different. For Addison, for Hailey, for us.

CHAPTER 21

Hailey

The buzz of my phone jolts me from sleep before my alarm has the chance this morning. My muscles protest after last night's acrobatics as I grope for the device on the nightstand, squinting against the light of the screen. As my eyes adjust, Franklin's words come into focus, each one a targeted missile designed to wound.

Franklin: Thought you could ignore me? Think again.

Franklin: I'll show everyone who you really are. And your future earnings? They're mine.

My heart stammers in my chest as I scroll through his messages, each more vindictive than the last. Then comes an image—a photo of me, barely clothed in a whisper of lingerie. Another follows, and this time, there's no barrier between my skin and the lens. I can't bring myself to look at any others. Shame is a hot flush that spreads across my cheeks. Why did that ever seem like a good idea?

"Hailey?" Christian asks. "What's going on?"

"Nothing," I lie, but tears betray me, spilling over despite my efforts to dam them.

Christian reaches for the phone, and I relinquish it, watching as his eyes darken as he reads. When he sees the photos, something in his expression shifts. "Tell me about these," he says, voice tight with anger.

I draw in a shaky breath, trying to stitch my fraying nerves together. "Franklin and I...we were serious. I thought...I believed we'd get married one day."

The words feel hollow now, a bitter reminder of how easily I fell for his act. Looking back, it's clear that Franklin never loved me, not the way I wanted to be loved. I shake my head. The moment I couldn't support him anymore, the moment I became more of a burden than a benefit, he turned cold. Distant. It had never been about me or about a partnership. It was about what I could give him.

Now, I see his manipulation for what it was—survival. Franklin was always scrambling to keep his head above water— probably still is—and I was just another lifeboat he latched onto.

But I'm not that girl anymore. I won't let him drag me down with him again.

Christian's hand tightens over mine, pulling me out of the memory. "He can't bully you into something if he won't even disclose what's missing," he says. "I'm sorry this is happening to you, but I'm here to help. We'll deal with this together."

I nod, feeling a weight slowly lift. I'm ready to fight back. I don't need to be afraid of Franklin and his threats.

"Did you want to take these photos?" Christian asks.

"Not particularly," I whisper. "But I wanted him to be happy. To love me."

"Hey," Christian says with a nod, thumb brushing a tear from my cheek. "It's going to be okay. We'll figure this out."

His assurance calms me, but my stomach doesn't entirely uncoil.

Christian's jaw clenches as he captures the screen with quick, precise movements. Then he taps out a message with a ferocity that matches the thundering rhythm of my heart.

"Who are you sending those to?" I ask, trying to keep my voice steady. Though I don't know why it matters. Once Franklin decides to do it, they'll be everywhere.

"Someone who can help," Christian answers. "I promise, Franklin won't be able to touch you."

"But what if he posts the pictures? With my name and I don't want my mistake to cause you problems?" The words tumble out in a rush, echoing the panic inside me.

Christian looks at me, his eyes fierce. "He won't get that chance. I've sent everything to my family lawyer, Miller Crawford. He's good, very good. Franklin's about to learn he can't mess with people's lives without consequences."

More people viewing these pictures and more people I never want to meet. "If I have anything of Franklin's, it needs to go back. I don't want any part of him near me."

Christian nods. "That's fine, Hailey. But he hasn't told you what's missing."

I can't look at him.

"He has to disclose what he's looking for. I'm here to help you." His hand finds mine, strong and warm, a promise of protection.

Addison fusses, and with a nod, I go to her. She's hungry, and as I prepare her bottle, I notice the sun is shining for once. We should use that to our advantage today.

I scramble eggs for all of us, and Addison eats on Christian's lap, happy and full of giggles.

"I was thinking I'd take Addison down to the seawall at Stanley Park for a stroll this morning."

"Can I come with you?" Christian asks.

"You're not working? We'd love that."

Christian kisses Addison on the forehead.

When we've finished breakfast, we all get dressed, and then Christian drives us in the Range Rover. "I feel so much better with you in this vehicle," he remarks. "I had no idea the minivan was so bad."

"It wasn't that bad." I laugh. "You're just used to those little dick compensators."

"What?"

"You know, most women figure a guy needs a sporty car to make up for having a small dick."

His brow furrows. "I don't have a small dick, and women gag for my Porsche."

I've found a nerve. This is fun. "I'm not super knowledgeable on dick sizes, but yours fits tightly. But really, the minivan is a mom car."

"That's right. My dick size is extra large." He pulls into the parking lot at the Totems, and we get out.

I find it funny that he's so sensitive. I wince slightly as we walk, the dull ache a reminder of how truly large his dick is. Christian doesn't seem to notice. He's lost in thought until we reach the seawall. The ocean breeze tousles my hair as we start off, Addison in the stroller.

"Tell me about your grandmother," Christian says, his voice soft against the rush of the waves.

The question catches me off guard, but he smiles encouragingly. "My parents were always just the two of them," I begin, my gaze fixed on the horizon where the sea meets the sky. "They had their world, filled with causes and ideals that felt like something out of the sixties—a love for communes and free spirits." I pause, the memory bitter. "They left me with Grandma when I was eleven, and it was the two of us against the world. She was there for skinned knees, mean girls, and boys who broke my heart. I loved her more than anything. But…" My voice trails off.

"But what?" Christian prompts.

"Once she passed away, I was pretty much alone."

Christian reaches for my hand, and I savor the comfort.

Then, an odd chirp sounds from his pocket. Christian pulls out his phone. "It's a notification from the Ring doorbell at home," he says. His eyes widen as he views the video feed, the blood draining from his face.

"Who is it?" I ask, my throat tightening.

He doesn't answer, just grabs my hand tighter. "I need to take care of something. My dad has been asking to see Addison. Can I drop you there for the afternoon?"

Something about his tone sends a shiver down my spine. But I nod, trusting him despite the fear. *Did Franklin do something?* We make our way back to the Range Rover, and soon enough, we're over the Lions Gate Bridge and winding through West Vancouver's plush neighborhoods.

He pulls up to his father's house, high in the hills on the north shore. His father's warm welcome washes over us, especially Addison, who clings to me for only a moment before her giggles fill the air, mingling with the sound of the ocean below.

"Everything's going to be okay," Christian whispers as he slips away. I want to believe him.

His stepmother, Tasha, smells of jasmine and something citrusy, her arms enveloping me in a maternal hug I haven't felt since my grandmother passed.

"It's been too long," she says, looking at me with genuine affection in her eyes.

"Too long indeed," echoes John, Christian's father.

As we settle into the living room, Addison sits comfortably on Tasha's lap.

"How are things going with Addison?" John asks.

"She's doing great and feeling a lot better. Giving her medicine at home is so much better than being in the hospital. I'm loving this work," I tell them. "I'm not even sure it's fair to call it that." Addison smiles and giggles. "Who doesn't love that face?" I say with a smile.

"The infection gave us quite the scare." Tasha holds Addison tighter.

"Indeed," I agree. "But she's getting so much stronger."

We move on to talk about how great Dana's doing, though I don't mention she's seeing Tate. I'm not sure what they know, and it's not my story to tell anyway.

After a little while, John claps his hands together. "We

were thinking burgers on the grill for lunch. Would you like one?"

"I don't want to impose…"

"Nonsense." Tasha waves my concern away. "We're just glad to get more time with Addison."

"That sounds good, but let me just check in with Christian," I tell them. *Did he go home or to the hospital?* I wonder as I text him.

Me: How's it going? Everything okay? Would you like me to get a rideshare home?

It takes a few minutes, but I get a reply.

Christian: No. Please stay where you are for now.

CHAPTER 22

Christian

I grip the steering wheel tighter. Can't this red light hurry up? My knuckles whiten as I stare at the notification on my phone. *Motion detected at front door.* In the accompanying photo, Taylor Hearst sits hunched on my front step, waiting. A woman I barely know yet can't shake.

My finger hovers over the live feed from the Ring camera. I tap the screen, and the image loads, grainy at first, then clearer. Taylor, the mother of my child, is a stranger to me in all the ways that matter. She still sits on the top step, arms folded across her chest, clearly impatient.

What the hell is she doing here?

She's a walking reminder of the worst parts of myself—the reckless nights, the meaningless encounters, the carelessness I wore like armor.

I stare at Taylor as though the act of watching her will somehow jog my memory. But there's nothing, just emptiness where those memories should be. Addison wasn't planned. She was a consequence — a beautiful, unexpected consequence — but a consequence of my own failure to be responsible, to take my life seriously.

How could I have let it happen? How could I not have known?

A honk behind me jars me back to the present, and I continue driving as rain streaks down the windshield. Addison could've grown up without me ever being in her life. And now her mother reappears? As if she can undo the damage she's done.

Could this be a scam for money?

Taylor doesn't belong here.

But then again, neither do I, not in this version of my life, not in this role of father. I'm still learning how to be steady, how to be someone Addison can depend on. Some days, I still feel like the man who doesn't care who he hurts as long as he doesn't have to feel anything himself. But I can't be that person anymore. I don't want to. Addison deserves more, and so do I.

When I get to my alley, I look back at the screen. Taylor shifts slightly, glancing at her phone, unaware of my silent surveillance. Does she ever think about that night? Does she remember what I can't?

I can't quite bring myself to ask, as facing those answers means facing my own failures. But for Addison, I have to try.

I pull into the garage behind my townhouse and park in my dimly lit space. Before I can even gather my thoughts, I'm pulling up the app on my phone to check the front door. Taylor is still waiting. Scrolling through contacts, I find my family attorney, Miller Crawford, and dial.

"Miller," I say the moment he picks up, "it's Christian."

"I have good news," he replies.

"Tell me."

"I've spoken with a judge. A restraining order against Franklin Richards has been issued and will be delivered this afternoon." There's a pause, a shuffling of papers on his end. "The order is crystal clear. If he posts any of the photos, he'll be prosecuted for harassment."

I sigh, one layer of tension peeling away. Legal protection for Hailey is now in place. "Thanks. That's one less thing to worry about."

"Always here to help. Anything else you need?"

I look up at the ceiling of the garage and clench my jaw. "Taylor Hearst is sitting on my front doorstep."

"I'll be right there," he says. "Please don't engage with her until I arrive. I can be at your place in fifteen minutes. I'll let you know when I drive up."

"Understood. I'll wait for you."

As I disconnect the call, I lean back against the seat and my fingers tap against the leather, a staccato beat to accompany the racing of my thoughts. Taylor's return, the restraining order, the ever-present weight of responsibility—how did I get here? I stew on that for a few minutes and then with a deep breath, I gather my resolve and step out of the car, ready to face whatever the day may yet hold.

I walk into the house and wait some more, glancing at the Ring feed. Taylor's still there. Waiting. *Like she has any right to.*

The doorbell chimes again, echoing through the townhouse. I take a deep breath, but fortunately, my phone also vibrates. Miller is three minutes out. I wait impatiently until I see him pull up outside, and then I open the front door just as Taylor's hand rises, about to knock again.

Relief flickers across her face, quickly replaced by annoyance. Her arms fold across her chest, a protective gesture that tells me this won't be easy.

"Christian. Why didn't you answer the door?" Her voice is sharp, accusatory.

Like she has any right to question me. I gesture to the camera above the door, keeping my voice calm. "I was out when you rang. I saw you on the camera. Figured this was important enough to involve legal counsel."

Her eyes flick toward the camera, then to the man now standing behind her—Miller, briefcase in hand, suit immaculate.

Her posture stiffens. "Legal counsel?" Her voice is tight. "I only came to see my daughter. Why do you need a lawyer for that?"

I don't respond immediately. Instead, I take a step

forward, folding my arms across my chest, mimicking her stance. She wants to play this game like we're equals, like we have the same rights. But we don't. "You came all the way from Los Angeles just to see Addison?" I ask. The silence between us stretches, thick with tension. I don't fill it. I want her to squirm.

"I..." she starts, then stops, her eyes flitting to Miller. "I needed to see her. It's been too long."

I raise an eyebrow, keeping my expression neutral. "Too long? You didn't seem to think it was too long when you dropped her off with Erica and disappeared for months. You forfeited the right to see her the moment you decided chasing your dreams in LA was more important than your child."

Her lips press into a thin line. "It wasn't like that. It was only supposed to be for a few days. I landed a paying part. I didn't know it would take this long. But now, I'm back, and I intend to stay."

I laugh at that. "You're back? You were gone longer than you expected? And what was the plan before that, Taylor? Were you hoping I'd never find out I was a father?"

She flinches. "I didn't tell you because..." She pauses. "I didn't want you to feel trapped."

"Trapped? You didn't want *me* to feel trapped? Or *you* didn't want to be trapped? There's a difference."

Her gaze falters, dropping to the ground for a moment before she looks back up, defiance creeping into her voice. "I did what I thought was best at the time."

"And now what? You expect to just waltz back into Addison's life like nothing happened?"

She takes a step forward, her voice rising. "I'm her mother, Christian. I have the right to see her."

The words hang between us, but it's what she's not saying that sticks in my throat. She is Addison's mother, and that gives her a claim. But where was she when Addison was hospitalized with endocarditis? Where was she when our daughter cried in the middle of the night? There's a whole lot Taylor hasn't been a part of, and now, she wants to pick up the pieces when it suits her.

"You lost that right when you left her behind," I say. "You made your choice."

Taylor's eyes harden. "I didn't choose to leave her. I needed to earn a living to keep a roof over our head and food in our mouths."

I snort. "Partying in LA puts a roof over your head and food in your mouths? I saw the drugs. I hired a PI, and I've got pictures."

Her face pales. "You don't know anything about my life in LA," she whispers, but her voice lacks conviction.

"I know enough," I say. "And I know Addison deserves better."

She takes a deep breath, her eyes growing glossy. "I didn't plan for it to go this way," she says softly, almost pleading. "I didn't want this."

"And yet here we are." I cross my arms, my stance firm. "What do you want, Taylor? What do you really want?"

Her eyes snap to mine, blazing. "I want to see my daughter. I want to be in her life."

I meet her gaze, unflinching. "And I want to protect her."

I turn to Miller, who hands me an envelope, which I extend toward her. "Sign the papers. You can walk away with a clean slate. A hundred thousand dollars, and you don't ever have to worry about Addison again."

Taylor's eyes drop to the envelope in my hand. She looks hurt, betrayed. But there's something else too. She shakes her head, her voice trembling. "You think you can just buy me off? Erase me from her life with a check? I'm a good mother."

Her words sting, but I let them roll over me, cold, detached. "It's your way out, Taylor. Take it. She's happy with Hailey. She's thriving."

Her hands hang at her sides, fists clenched as she stares at the envelope. The silence stretches, and then, with a bitter smile, she shakes her head. "No," she whispers, her voice cracking. "I'm not giving up my daughter."

Without another word, she turns and walks away, her figure disappearing as she turns the corner.

Miller steps forward with me as I return to the house, and the door swings closed. "You did the right thing," he assures me.

"Like you did with my father?" The question leaps from my lips before I can catch it.

"Yes," Miller replies with a sigh. "These situations are never easy. But you have to protect Addison, just like your grandfather wanted to protect you."

His words are meant to comfort me, but I'm not so sure I was protected, which makes me question my choice here too.

"Let me know when she returns," Miller says. "Because we know she will."

I nod as he gathers his things and returns to his car. Once alone, I collapse onto the nearest chair, the fight draining from my body. I should feel relieved. I handled it. Miller handled it. But did he?

Taylor's face — the hurt, the desperation — floats before me. I wanted to feel justified, vindicated, but all I feel is...uncertain. Taylor is clearly struggling, yet once upon a time, she cared for Addison.

My mind drifts, unbidden, back to my grandfather. He thought he was protecting me too. That's what he told me, years later, when I demanded answers, and that's what Miller said too. He thought he was doing the right thing, just like I did today.

But my father leaving didn't protect me. It broke something in me. I spent years trying to make sense of it, trying to prove I didn't need him. But the truth is, I did. And now, facing my own choices, I'm terrified that Addison will feel the same way about me, that no matter what I do, I'll end up failing her the same way my father and grandfather failed me.

I rub my hands over my face, groaning into my palms. The weight of it all feels crushing. I don't want to be like them. I don't want to repeat the same mistakes. But the more I try to control things, to protect Addison, the more I see myself in my grandfather's shoes. And that terrifies me more than anything Taylor could throw at me.

I need to go get Addison and Hailey. Suddenly, the desire to have them here with me is nearly overwhelming.

Twenty minutes later, I pull into the driveway of my father's house. When I enter, the familiar scent of home-cooked food wafts through the air as they clear the last of the dinner dishes. My stomach knots, not from hunger, but from the anticipation of the impending conversation.

But first, I check on Hailey and Addison. "I need to talk to my dad. Can you hang a while longer?"

Hailey nods. "Sure."

I find my father, and his eyes light up. "Can we talk?" I ask.

"Of course." He nods and leads me past the familial chatter into the refuge of his home office. The room is lined with bookshelves and has a spectacular view of the sound.

"Hailey's been wonderful, you know," he begins, settling behind his mahogany desk. "She's good for you...for Addison."

"I agree," I say, but I hesitate before diving into the depths of our past. "I need to understand something. Why did you leave me?"

He leans forward, elbows resting on the polished wood, fingers interlaced as if in prayer. "It was complicated, Christian. Your grandparents never approved of your mother and me. It was very hard for her, and we struggled to get by. When things got tough, she reached out to her father for help."

"Help?" I echo.

He nods. "They wanted her to come home with you, but not me. She had to make a choice, and she chose them. I was angry about that for a while, but I've forgiven her. Anyway, to convince me to walk away, they offered me money. A lot of money." His voice is steady, but I catch the flicker of old pain in his eyes. "I refused at first, tried to fight for joint custody. But then..."

"Then what?" My heart races, fearing the answer.

"Accusations started flying. My co-workers were told I was abusive." He shakes his head. "I didn't want their money, but then I realized I could put it in your name. Assuring your well-being? That was more important than any courtroom battle. And I thought it might spare you the pain of our arguments. It nearly killed me, but I took the deal."

He reaches into a drawer and pulls out a stack of papers, decades' worth of monthly statements, neatly filed. "This is it," he says, sliding them across the desk. "The money they gave me. It has your name on it, nearly three-million dollars now."

My hands tremble as I touch the proof of a lifetime's struggle and sacrifice. The silence between us stretches, filled with the unsaid and the unforgettable. Here, in the quiet sanctity of my father's office, the truth lays bare, and with it, the question of what comes next.

I'm still reeling from my father's revelations as he leans back in his chair, studying me with a concern that has aged him. "Christian," he says, "You've never been interested in this before. Why now?"

"Taylor Hearst, Addison's mother, showed up today. She says she wants to be in Addison's life, which feels like the first step in taking her away from me. I can't let that happen."

"Of course you don't want her taken away, but why do you think that's her plan?"

"She just dumped her. She followed her dream and left her behind because Addison was hard. Now, she's changed her mind? She's not a trustworthy person. I don't trust her motives."

"Is that what she said about why she left?"

"No. But it's clear enough. I've finally got things figured out now, and she wants to come back and make it all chaos again."

"That may not be what she wants. Maybe you should talk to her. Maybe there's a middle ground you haven't seen yet."

I nod. It's difficult to picture any compromise with Taylor, but the sincerity in Dad's eyes reminds me of the stark contrast between what is easy and what is right.

"Life isn't always black and white. As a doctor, you know that," he continues. "People change, circumstances change."

When I don't respond, he shifts the conversation, likely to give me space to process. "By the way, have you been keeping up with the Mariners?"

A smile tugs at my lips despite the storm inside me.

"Honestly, no. Baseball took a backseat to…well, everything else."

"Understandable." Dad chuckles. "But they're not doing too bad this season. Might be worth catching a game or two when things settle down. Tasha and I were thinking of going down to Seattle for a weekend. We'd love it if you wanted to join us."

"I'll think about it. Depends on my work schedule." The suggestion feels like an olive branch, an attempt to create something more substantial between us. "I'd like to do it," I assure him.

"Sounds good," he agrees. "Just let me know."

We stand then, and as we walk out of the office, I put a hand on his shoulder. "Thank you for everything you've done for me, for all the sacrifices." My voice feels thick with emotion.

He looks at me, and there's a depth of understanding that transcends words. "I was just trying to be a good parent. Now, you take care of yourself and that little girl of yours."

I nod. He's given me a lot to think about.

I find Hailey and Addison in the living room and help them gather their things. After saying our goodbyes, we get into the Range Rover, and I drive us home.

It's Addison's bedtime when we arrive, and I watch Hailey's silhouette glide through the dimmed hallway, Addison cradled against her chest, until they disappear, climbing the stairs to the nursery. Alone in the living room, I settle onto the couch, looking out the wide windows to False Creek. The city lights dance on the water's surface.

I'm not sure how long I sit there before I sense Hailey's presence. She moves silently, but her energy shifts the air around us. "Who was at the house earlier?" she asks as she takes a seat beside me.

"Taylor," I say. I feel her body tense next to mine. "She wants back into Addison's life."

She's quiet a moment. "How do you feel about that?"

I draw in a breath, exhaling slowly. "Miller Crawford, my attorney, brought up something today…about my father." My voice is hesitant as I navigate the memories. "He said he did the same thing for my grandfather, and it was meant to look out for me." I pause. "That stopped me cold."

Her hand finds mine, fingers lacing. "What happened?"

"That's what I pulled Dad aside to talk about at the house earlier. I wanted to understand." I recount the conversation in brief strokes. "I remember missing him so much, blaming myself because he wasn't there, thinking it was my fault he left."

Hailey squeezes my hand, a silent comfort. "Christian..."

"I don't want Addison to go through what I did."

Hailey's eyes search mine. "Maybe Addison would do better with her mother *and* father in her life," she suggests.

I look at her, and my heart tightens. A child deserves both parents, regardless of whether they're together. But that thought clashes with everything I've planned, every safeguard I've put up to protect Addison, to protect myself. The plan was never to share custody, to let Taylor back in after all this time. She did the unthinkable when she didn't tell me I was a father and then dumped her baby at her sister's to pursue her dream. "You might be right," I admit. "But that wasn't part of my plan."

Her hand remains steady in mine. "What happens to your plan when you're in surgery and something goes sideways?"

I sigh. "I change the plan."

"So maybe it's time to change your plan," she says simply.

"I need to think about it," I say finally, a concession to her wisdom, and to the possibility of a different future than the one I'd so carefully mapped out.

CHAPTER 23

Hailey

For the last week and a half, everywhere I've gone, I've been worried I'll run into Taylor. It's curtailed my walks and activities with Addison, but I saw how her appearance affected Christian, and I don't want to encounter more trouble.

Today, though, we have Addison's checkup, so we're headed to the doctor's office. I can't hide forever. I push Addison in her stroller as we navigate the maze of hallways to the medical offices at the hospital and then to Dr. Cordelia's clinic.

We wait in the front area only a few minutes before a nurse whisks us back to a brightly colored room, adorned with cartoon animals and alphabet posters. It's designed to be cheerful, but my anxiety renders it all a bit garish. I lower Addison onto the padded exam table, and the nurse takes her vitals before assuring us Dr. Cordelia will be right along.

When the doctor appears, she gets down to business and begins her assessment right away, her hands gently probing as Addison smiles.

Most things seem normal and as expected, though Addison once again has a bit of the sniffles, but at the end of the exam, Dr. Cordelia turns to me. "Addison isn't showing the level of vitality I'd expect at this stage," she explains. "She's not trying to crawl yet, though that's not entirely unusual for a baby with Down syndrome." She pulls out a bright green stuffed worm, and Addison tracks it with her eyes. "She's following objects."

I nod, watching Addison's gaze move to the dangling mobile above her. "Yes, and she can sit up without support."

"That's definitely a positive sign," Dr. Cordelia confirms. "We'll keep monitoring her progress. Hopefully, by her second birthday, she'll be walking."

"Hopefully," I echo, feeling a tightness in my chest. Addison is nine months this week, and her first birthday looms closer each day and, with it, the weight of expectations.

"How was Taylor as a mother?" I ask. "Before..." My voice trails off, not wanting to dredge up the details of Taylor's departure.

Dr. Cordelia pauses, considering her words. "Taylor was...very involved. She seemed competent and connected to her child," she says. "But right now, we need to think about the present. I'm worried about Addison's heart. Children with Down syndrome are slower to meet milestones, but Addison should still be farther along, and I think it's because of her heart. We need to keep her environment controlled and low-key so she can stay healthy and gain some strength. Stress is not good for her, and neither is additional illness, so continue to avoid large crowds and germs as much as possible. When we think she's strong enough to schedule surgery, we will."

"Understood," I reply, gathering Addison's clothes to put her back in them. "Thanks, Dr. Cordelia," I add as the doctor departs.

Once we have ourselves back together, we leave the sanctuary of the clinic, stepping out into the uncertainty of the real world. I push Addison along, looking for a ray of sunshine before it becomes too hot for her to be outside.

The sun filters through the branches above us, casting

dappled shadows on the walkway as I push the stroller, my mind a whirlwind of concerns for Addison's health. I hardly register the approach of a woman until she steps directly into my path, forcing me to halt.

Taylor. I glance down at Addison, brushing a stray curl from her forehead. My pulse quickens. Taylor looks different than I expected—anxious and…desperate. There's an intensity in her gaze that makes me tighten my grip on Addison's stroller.

This is the moment I've been dreading, the moment Taylor forces her way back into Addison's life.

"Hailey, right?" Taylor's voice is thin, stretched. Her eyes flicker to Addison, and I shift, putting my body between them.

I know she noticed.

"How do you know my name?" I ask. She's already in my space, closer than I'd like.

"Christian mentioned it," she says, her gaze locked on Addison. There's an edge in her voice, like she's barely holding it together.

Her hand twitches toward Addison, and I step back and pick her up.

"I'm Taylor, Addison's mother."

"Don't," I say firmly. "I know who you are. Please don't touch her."

Taylor's eyes narrow. "I miss her so much."

"Why did you leave?"

Her shoulders sag. "Having her wasn't easy from the beginning. I found out at twenty weeks that she had Down syndrome, and my family thought I should give her up. But I couldn't. I was on birth control, and we'd used a condom, so I figured someone was sending me a message to have this baby."

She reaches for Addison again, and I relent. I can see the pain in her eyes. This must be so hard for her. "Be really careful. Her health is fragile."

Addison is rigid in her arms, fusses, and reaches for me.

"She doesn't remember me," Taylor whispers.

"Let's sit down." I motion to the park bench, praying she doesn't just run off with her.

"I thought I could take care of her on my own, but it was so much work," Taylor says, shaking her head. "I got her the best doctors, and I made sure she had everything she needed."

I nod, and she finally gives Addison back. Addison puts her head on my chest, and I rub her back the way she likes while she watches Taylor. Relief washes over me in waves.

"I have postpartum depression," Taylor says. "I'm doing a lot better now, but I knew if I didn't take the job in California, being a mother would crush me. I love her, though."

"I'm sorry to hear that. It sounds very difficult. But you should know Addison is doing great. I'm only the nanny, though. I'm not a decision maker in this situation."

She nods. "You take her to all her checkups?"

"I do." Addison gives me a toothless smile. "And to all of her therapy appointments. She's doing great. She's right on track for a baby with Downs." Until I speak with Christian, I'm not telling her anything Cordelia has shared.

"I miss her."

"I'm sure she'd love it if you were in her life—at least sometimes. I know leaving couldn't have been easy for you, but I also know what's been hard for Addison." I meet her gaze head on. "She's been sick. Her Downs makes her heart fragile. She needs calm, consistency, things you haven't been able to provide. I understand that you want to be a part of her life now, but you have to work it out with Christian, and I know he's going to put Addison's needs before any others."

"I'm not here to cause problems," Taylor says. "I'm here because I love her. Because I'm her mother."

I swallow hard, my heart thudding in my chest. "Then be her mother," I say. "But you need to do it the right way. Addison deserves better than this back and forth, and her health conditions demand it. You can't just come and go when it suits you."

Taylor's face tightens, her lips parting as if to argue, but then she takes a deep breath, her shoulders slumping slightly. "I just want to see her," she says. "I just… I want to hold her."

My heart aches, but I don't let myself soften. Not now.

Addison squirms against me, fussing, and I know it's time to go. "We have to figure out what's best for Addison," I tell her. "You'll have to talk to Christian about what you want. Right now, we need to go."

Taylor's gaze lingers on Addison, but she doesn't argue. Then her face crumples with emotion as she turns and walks away, disappearing into the crowd at the hospital.

I watch her go, adrenaline coursing through my veins. My legs feel weak, like they might give out, and I can't let that happen. I kiss the top of Addison's head, her soft curls tickling my cheek as I return her to the stroller.

"You're okay," I whisper. "We're okay."

But as I look down at Addison, the weight of what just happened settles over me. I need to tell Christian.

The drive home is a blur, Addison's soft breathing the only sound that grounds me. But as I pull into Christian's garage, my heart hammers anew. Franklin suddenly appears next to the car, his body tight with anger, veins bulging at his temples. He must have been hiding in the alley somewhere.

"Where is it, Hailey? Where did you put my stuff?" he shouts, pounding on the driver's side window with a force that sends shivers down my spine.

"Franklin, just calm down, please," I plead, fumbling with my phone and making sure the doors are locked. My fingers tremble as I dial 911, reporting the situation in hurried, hushed tones. I climb into the backseat and sit next to Addison's car seat, ready to protect her from broken glass or whatever he's ready to throw our way.

"Hailey!" Franklin's voice is a jagged edge, slicing through the refuge of the Range Rover. "Give me my damn things now!"

Addison stirs and whimpers. Franklin steps away and looks around Christian's garage. There isn't much. He hurls a plastic recycling container against the window, and it boomerangs right back at him. The police can't come soon enough. Time stretches, each second a weight upon my chest until I see the flashing lights.

Officers step out, their authoritative presence a relief as they approach Franklin. They speak with him, their voices firm but controlled. Soon, one of them comes over to me and knocks on the window.

I open the door, just in time to hear Franklin yelling expletives at me.

"Ma'am, with the restraining order against Mr. Richards, he's been arrested. He's not supposed to be here," the officer explains. "He's violating the order."

My breath catches, a mixture of fear and solace wrestling within me. Addison reaches out for my shirt, sensing the disquiet. As the police take Franklin away, his rage-filled eyes find mine one last time. "You're going to pay for this!"

After I answer the police's questions, Addison and I finally get inside. The quiet hum of the air purifier is the white noise that calms us for the rest of the day. After her dinner, Addison's sprawled across my lap, her tiny chest rising and falling in the jerky rhythm of an overstimulated infant on the brink of sleep. Dr. Cordelia's words haunt me. Too much excitement is not what Addison needs. Today has been a tempest, one I certainly didn't plan for.

I gently pat Addison, tracing circles until her breath evens out and she succumbs to exhaustion for the night. But I can't shake the anxiety that sparks within me. I should have protected her better, shielded her from the drama.

I glance at the clock. Christian will be home soon, and I need to create some semblance of normalcy out of the day's wreckage. With utmost care, I transfer Addison to her crib, ensuring her comfort before tiptoeing to the kitchen.

Dinner is a simple affair, a pot roast I prepared earlier. But the tension in my shoulders doesn't ease, not when the memory of Franklin's furious eyes still burns behind my eyelids. I set the table mechanically, arranging utensils and plates while my mind races with the potential fallout from his rage.

The beep of the back door opening signals Christian's arrival. His footsteps are heavy, the sound of a man bearing the weight of long hours and life-and-death decisions. "Hi," he murmurs, his voice gravelly with fatigue. He drops his bag and wraps me in a weary embrace.

I melt into him for a moment, allowing myself the illusion of safety. "Hi," I reply. "Dinner's ready."

We sit, and he eats with an absentminded appreciation, his thoughts clearly elsewhere. I hate to add to his load right now, and it takes me until we've cleared our plates and started dessert to summon the courage to broach the subject of Franklin.

"Something happened today," I start, my fingers entwined tightly in my lap. "Franklin showed up. He was… It was intense. I called the police."

He pauses, a forkful of pie halfway to his mouth. "Are you and Addison okay?" He sets down his utensil, giving me his full attention.

"Yes. But he frightened me and was trying to get into the Range Rover, so I called the police. He was arrested for violating the restraining order. When he left he said he was going to make me pay, so that means he'll release the photos."

Christian reaches across the table, covering my hand with his. "Did anyone else hear this?"

I roll my eyes. "Just everyone in the neighborhood and the officers who arrested him."

His thumb strokes my skin. "Don't worry about Franklin."

I stare at him. How can he be so calm?

"We've got this," he assures me, reaching for his phone.

He finds who he wants to call and dials. "Miller? Sorry to bother you again. Franklin Richards showed up at the house this afternoon and was arrested, but he also insinuated that he was going to release the pictures." He's quiet a moment, then looks at me and smiles. "Great," he says into the phone. "Hailey will be glad to know that."

He disconnects his call. "Miller will be at Franklin's arraignment, so we can keep track of what happens after this, and he has one of his teammates working on getting into the cloud and deleting the photos."

"You can tell them Franklin's password is usually pound sign, the number one and the word gamer with the G capitalized and an exclamation point."

Christian types it out, and when he shows it to me I nod. "That's really easy to break."

I shrug. "Well, he did fall out of the stupid tree and hit every limb on the way down."

Christian cracks a smile. "He won't get far with this nonsense. I promise."

I nod, trying to believe him. But the reassurance feels thin against the reality of Franklin's venomous threats. I've seen how he exacts revenge. An older man took what Franklin believed to be his seat on the SkyTrain, and he harassed the guy relentlessly, despite my urgings to stop. He can be cruel, and he doesn't like it when things don't go his way. I just never thought he'd turn on me.

"I'm beat, but I've missed you," Christian says, attempting to move us to lighter topics. His gaze holds a familiar heat, one that momentarily pushes aside the concerns clotting my thoughts.

"Me too," I respond, a smile touching my lips.

He reaches for me, and the turmoil of the day recedes, replaced by the promise of intimacy and connection. Tonight, at least, there is solace in each other's arms.

Lying beside Christian in the dark, I trace idle patterns

across his chest, watching as his eyes close with the contentment that follows our lovemaking. But as the pleasure and release ebb away, my heart returns to being a clenched fist inside my ribcage. There's more I have to share about today, and it really shouldn't wait.

"Thank you for that," I tell him. "Today was such a shitty day. I also need to tell you that Taylor showed up outside Dr. Cordelia's office after our appointment."

Christian bolts upright, his face hardening into sharp lines of anger. "What? Taylor?"

I nod. "She approached us on the sidewalk outside the hospital, wanting to see Addison."

Christian is on his feet now, pacing like a caged animal. "What was she thinking? Was she high? Did she try to take Addison away from you?"

"No. Nothing like that. We were in a very public place. She wanted to hold her and explained why she left. She has postpartum depression."

His hands clench and unclench. "She told you that?"

I nod.

"Damn it." He stops pacing, his gaze searing into mine. "I'm home tomorrow but I'm on call. We'll figure this out."

"Okay," I whisper.

After a moment, he returns to the bed and pulls me to him. "Are you on birth control?" he asks, even as his hands begin to move over my body again.

"Yes. I've had the shot." I gasp as he grips the back of my neck.

"Would you be okay if we didn't use condoms? I'm clean and haven't been with anyone."

I nod, my breath coming in pants. "I'm clean too."

He pulls away and looks at me. "I've never had sex without a condom. But I trust you, Hailey."

I nod, unable to form words. He's telling me something here, drawing a contrast between the life he had before and the life we have now. I feel like I should figure out how to respond, but then the world tilts on its axis when Christian's lips crash against mine, stealing my breath and the chaotic thoughts swirling in my head. Taylor's back. Franklin's threats are closing in. But none of it matters when his kiss devours the fear, leaving only a hunger that claws at my insides.

"I need this," he breathes against my mouth, his voice gravelly with emotion. "We both do."

I can't argue. I'm desperate to cling to anything that feels real, feels like us. His hands — those strong, capable hands — slide into my shorts, past the flimsy barrier of my panties, and find evidence of my own need all over again. I shudder under his touch, heat pooling low in my belly as I shove the fabric down my legs and kick them off in a rush of urgency.

My heart races in tandem with his ragged breaths as he parts me wide, exposing the raw desire glittering between us. A thrill shoots through me at the sight of his approval, the hungry gaze drinking in my vulnerability.

"Look at you," he murmurs, stepping back just enough to showcase the prominent bulge once again straining against his boxer briefs. "Open wide and show me what I do to you."

It's an intoxicating power, knowing I inspire such lust in him. "What are you going to do about it?" The words roll off my tongue, thick with suggestion, my body coiling in anticipation of his next move.

His eyes darken, a storm brewing in their depths. Without a whisper of hesitation, Christian's fingers thrust inside me. I gasp, the sudden fullness making me feel stretched, almost to the brink of being overwhelmed, but it's a sensation that borders on exquisite.

"Better hang on," he growls with an edge that promises this ride will be anything but gentle. His fingers pivot, drawing out only to push back in with a rhythm that leaves no room for thought, only the mounting pressure of need building inside me. I grip the edge of the mattress, knuckles white, as my body tries to keep pace with the fervor of his movements.

I lean back, a silent plea for balance, and Christian — ever attuned to my desires — seizes the opportunity. His mouth finds me, hot and insistent against my clit. The sensation rockets through me, amplified by the relentless dance of his fingers within. I'm spiraling, hurtling toward a precipice I can't see but am desperate to tumble over.

"Christian...!" His name escapes as a moan, ripped from the depths of me as pleasure blurs my vision. The climax hits hard and fast, a wave crashing over me without mercy. But he doesn't stop. He continues, his mouth and fingers a symphony of relentless pleasure that refuses to let the echoes of my release fade away.

The tremors of my first release still linger, a low hum in my veins, as the second wave swells within me. It's building, intense and unstoppable, when suddenly Christian withdraws his fingers. Air rushes into the void he leaves, and I gasp, eyes snapping open to find his gaze locked on mine, his face glistening with my arousal.

"I want to come inside you," he breathes. The intensity in his eyes anchors me, but his words seem distant, like they're coming from far away. My brain can't latch onto them. All I feel is the sudden absence of him and the desperate hunger for more.

"Lean over the bed," he commands, and I obey without hesitation. I bend forward, offering myself to him. Then comes the sharp smack against my ass, a sting that blooms into heat and sends my arousal spiking even higher. "Please, make me come," I beg, my voice laden with all the desire he has stoked within me.

His fingers trace up my spine, then curl around to my front, finding my nipples and twisting them gently, skillfully. A moan escapes, riding the edge of pleasure and pain.

"Tell me if it's too much," he says.

I nod but it never is. Not with him.

He steps away, leaving me exposed, craving his touch again. Then he's in front of me on the bed, his eyes dark with desire. "Get me wet," he orders. "Wet enough so I can fuck you just how I like."

Eagerly, I take him into my mouth, the saltiness of his skin mingling with the remnants of my own taste on his flesh.

Christian groans, his hands finding my hair, not pushing or guiding, just holding. "That's it, Hailey...just like that." He fondles my breast, thumb brushing over my nipple in tandem with his deep thrusts.

His cock hits the back of my throat, and I take him deeper with each movement. My eyes water, but the burn is exhilarating. It's a challenge, one I accept willingly, wantonly.

Just as I think he might push me farther, he pulls back, cradling my jaw as he looks down at me. "You okay?" he asks.

With heavy-lidded eyes, I nod and whisper between breaths, "Don't stop, Christian. Please, don't stop."

Satisfaction flickers across his features, and his eyes hold mine as he helps me to my feet. The silent exchange is electric, our connection palpable. We're in this together—every gasp, every touch, every moment of surrender.

Christian moves behind me, bending me over the bed again. His presence is a force, and when he pushes inside, my breath catches. His thickness demands an adjustment, a moment of acclimation, but there's no pain—only a fullness that sends my senses reeling.

"Hailey," he breathes. "You're heaven." He speaks against my neck, his hot breath sending shivers down my spine. "I could live here forever." Each word is punctuated with a push deeper into my tight embrace.

I gasp, my fingers clawing at the surface beneath me. The stretch, the pull—it's all-consuming, and I'm lost in the sensation of him filling me again and again.

Once he's settled into a rhythm, his hands roam over my body. Eventually, one finds its way to my hair. He tugs gently at first, then more firmly, tilting my head back to meet his gaze. There's a wildness there, a fervor that mirrors my own. And when he draws out slowly only to pound back into me, it ignites every nerve ending I possess.

"Christian!" My voice climbs as the crescendo of pleasure builds within me. The sound of our bodies meeting in relentless strokes echoes through the room. Heat coils tighter in my core, and when he pulls my hair just so, tipping my world off-kilter, I shatter.

The climax washes over me in a roaring wave, and I

scream his name, a vocal surrender to the overwhelming bliss that wracks my body. Christian doesn't relent. He drives into me, chasing his own release with a fervor that pushes me to new heights. Every motion is a promise, every touch a claim — his on mine, and mine on his — in this dance of desire that refuses to end.

As we gasp for air, Addison fusses over the baby monitor, piercing through the fog of our passion. Christian's rhythm falters, and for a heartbeat, we're both suspended in the sudden silence that follows.

"Christian... Are you ever going to finish?" I tease, breathless, my voice laced with frustration and longing. It's bratty, sure, but I can't help it. He's brought me to the edge and back, and I'm greedy for his cock.

He responds with a sharp spank, a crack of flesh that resonates in the charged air. "You're going to pay for that," he growls. His hands grip my hips with an intensity that speaks volumes. He's staking his claim, leaving marks that will remind me of this moment for days to come.

The room fills with the sound of our skin slapping together as he finds his pace again. My body is alight with sensation, each thrust pushing me farther into the abyss of pleasure. And when he comes, it's with a primal force that leaves me gasping, his warmth flooding inside me in a rush that's almost too much to bear.

"I love that my cum is deep inside you," he breathes, his voice thick with satisfaction. "I've marked you as my own."

We're sticky and spent, but the hunger between us hasn't abated. It's merely transformed, simmering beneath the surface. Christian pulls me close, his eyes dark with renewed desire. "We're not done yet," he murmurs against my lips, and the promise of more ignites a fresh wave of anticipation. The night is ours, and I'm ready to lose myself in him all over again.

CHAPTER 24

Christian

With tray in hand, I navigate through the bustling cafeteria, grabbing a quick lunch before the emergency room needs me for a consult or surgery. It's been a busy morning, but it's quiet now, so I'm going to take advantage of it.

"Christian," Davis calls, intercepting me near the condiment station.

"Hey, Davis." I greet him as I set my tray down. "What's up?"

"Addison," he starts, leaning in closer. "Cordelia tells me she's been under the weather."

I exhale slowly. "Yeah, she has been a little sick this last week. Nothing like before the infection, though."

Davis nods and picks up his phone. "I'm in the cafeteria with Christian. Are you coming down?" He looks at me and smiles. "Great, come find us."

I briefly wonder if I'm being ambushed.

"Cordelia's on her way. She and I thought we should get

together and talk about Addison when we were all free."

Cordelia walks in, and Davis waves her over. She holds up a finger and gets into the food line first. Looking at her profile, I realize she's pregnant. I'm thrilled for her and her husband, William. She told me once that she wants a dozen kids. I used to think she was trying to be funny, but I've seen her with her daughter, and I really think she's serious.

Cordelia joins us a few minutes later with a tray of steamed vegetables, a sad-looking piece of meat that I think is chicken, and sliced apples.

"That looks way too healthy, even for you."

She looks at her plate and laughs. "I find when I'm pregnant I can't digest salad, so they make this for me, but I was twenty minutes later than I'd planned. It's no longer at its best."

"Congratulations!" I tell her. I would never have been truly excited for anyone becoming a parent before Addison, but now, I think I get it.

"Thank you," she says. "Anyway, I'm sure Hailey filled you in after my appointment with Addison last week, but her condition..." Cordelia pauses as she cuts into her chicken. "I believe the endocarditis has damaged her already weak heart."

Davis crosses his arms. "Is she strong enough for surgery?"

"Eventually, yes," Cordelia confirms without hesitation.

"I need to get her on my calendar then," Davis says. "We've been monitoring her closely, and I want to see her do a few things before we go in that will help with her recovery."

"A few things?" My voice is barely audible over the lump forming in my throat.

As Davis speaks about the surgery, I force myself to nod, but all I can see is Addison in a hospital bed. The thought of her enduring open-heart surgery before her first birthday is almost too much.

"She's not ready yet physically," Davis admits. "But we have time to strengthen her, get her as healthy as possible before we move toward operating."

Cordelia reaches for my arm. "We're keeping an eye on

her."

Nodding, I mumble my gratitude and make my excuses. I need to get back to the emergency department, so I thank them both for their time and extra care.

"I'll have my office call Hailey and get her on my schedule," Davis says.

"Thank you both. Truly. I'm glad Addison has the best."

CHAPTER 25

Hailey

I can hear the soft rhythm of Christian's breathing as the morning light filters through the curtains. I lie still a moment, watching the rise and fall of his chest. Ever since Christian and I stopped using condoms a few weeks ago, he's been absolutely insatiable, and I've loved every moment of it. Our time has been more than just fun. It's peeled back another layer of Christian, and with it, my own defenses. The laughter, our night out at his club, the way he looks out for me without smothering. It's all creating something tender inside me.

And we really are more of a team these days, he told me about his meeting with Cordelia and Davis not too long ago. Surgery for Addison is coming sooner rather than later, and that is a huge source of stress. I'm grateful he's keeping me in the loop, though. I'm doing everything I can to make sure she'll be ready.

Yet even with so many connections, so many shared goals, part of me waits for it all to fall apart, reminds me that it's temporary, something I've scheduled myself out of at the end. As Christian sleeps, the silence wraps around me, pressing in on all sides, reminding me of the emptiness I've known for far too long. The emptiness that started when my parents left me behind.

I was eleven when they took off, too young to fully understand why but old enough to feel the sting of it. One day, they were there, promising to come back after their "trip," and the next... They just didn't. I waited. I waited for weeks, then months, thinking every car that passed by could be them, thinking every ring of the phone might bring news that they were on their way back. But no one ever came.

My grandmother tried her best, but I could see it in her eyes. She wasn't meant to raise a child at her age. And then, when I was nineteen, she got sick.

I watched her fade, just like my parents had, but in a different way. Then one day I received a phone call at school. She had gone peacefully in her sleep.

Abandoned. That's what I was. First by my parents, then by my grandmother — though it wasn't her fault. I know that now. But the scars it left haven't fully healed. I guess that's why I got tangled up in Franklin's nonsense, and why I've held on so tightly to Addison, to Christian, to this life we've built, even if I'm just waiting for it to be taken away.

I slide out of bed, careful not to disturb him, and tiptoe to Addison's room to check on her. She gurgles softly in her crib, and I reach for her to get the day going. After her morning feed — she took to the bottle eagerly today, thank goodness — I feel the itch to stretch my legs outside, to show her the world beyond these walls. Her visits to the physical and occupational therapists continue to show that she's weaker than she should be, and she's also fighting yet another cold, but a walk around False Creek would do us both good.

"Let's check the weather, sweet girl." I hoist her onto my hip as we pad over to the window. The sky is a clear blue, promising warmth and the kiss of the sun. Perfect for a walk. But then I see her — Taylor — standing by a tree along the path that skirts the inlet. The path we would walk on. Her presence is enough to stir the pot of unease, knowing how much she unsettles not only me but Christian.

I sigh, turning away from the window. No, I won't wake Christian. He needs the rest, and I don't want to add to his burdens.

"Looks like it's indoors for us this morning," I whisper, kissing Addison's forehead. We'll just avoid any confrontation with Taylor for now. Her big eyes blink up at me, unaware of the drama unfolding around her. She's content, snuggled close to my heartbeat, and that's all that matters.

We retreat to the living room, building a fortress of pillows and soft toys, while Christian sleeps.

After a bit, I notice Addison's breaths are shallow, a sign she's not feeling her best today. I cradle her against me, and she feels warm, too warm. Her little nose is a battlefield of sniffles.

"Shh, it's okay," I murmur, brushing away the wisps of hair glued to her damp forehead.

Just then Christian stumbles out from the bedroom, his eyes squinting against the light. His sleep-tousled hair and bare chest paint the picture of a man at ease in his domain. But as he stretches, revealing the line of his boxers and the evident outline beneath, my cheeks flush.

"Morning," I tease, unable to resist. "Looks like someone else is up early too."

His groggy smile falters, and our playful bubble bursts with the sound of Madeline, his mother, clearing her throat.

Where did she come from? I didn't hear the door chime when it opened.

Christian hastily sidesteps out of view, his tanned skin disappearing behind the doorway.

I turn to the matriarch now occupying the room. Her arched eyebrow tells me she has seen far too much already.

"Would you like some coffee, Madeline?"

"Mrs. Bradford," she corrects sharply. "And no, thank you. I'm concerned about Addison." Her gaze moves over her granddaughter with the scrutiny of a general inspecting troops.

"Of course, Mrs. Bradford," I reply, the title cumbersome

on my tongue. I shift Addison's weight, trying to soothe her without making it seem like an excuse to avoid further confrontation.

Christian re-emerges, joggers and T-shirt in place. "What's got you here so bright and early?" he asks.

"Nearly eleven isn't early, and I've been trying to reach you," she says, her tone implying negligence on his part. "We need to discuss plans for Addison's first birthday."

"Right," he nods, folding his arms across his chest. "Sorry I missed your calls."

"Why isn't she crawling yet?" Madeline's question feels more like an accusation.

I glance down at Addison. "She just needs a little more time," I murmur. But my soft reassurance is not meant for Madeline's ears.

"You coddle her too much." Her sharp tone cuts through the room. "She'll miss her milestones if you keep this up."

Christian steps in. "Mom, milestones for kids with Down syndrome can be different. She will reach them, but on her own schedule."

"Addison can do anything," Madeline insists.

"Absolutely. She's fine," Christian assures her, patting Addison's back. "On her own time."

Madeline's lips press into a thin line, and then she abruptly turns her focus to me. "You can leave us now, Hailey." It's a dismissal, clear and cold.

I hesitate, but I know better than to argue. With a final, soothing stroke on Addison's back, I hand her over to Christian and retreat to my room, closing the door behind me.

I don't understand this rush to plan a small family party. Addison isn't quite ten months now. I know Christian appeases his mother to keep the peace, but sometimes, she doesn't understand Addison at all. I'm so grateful Christian does.

After I fold and put away the clean laundry, I get into the shower. I have the time if Madeline is going to monopolize Christian and Addison.

But I find myself fuming under the hot water. Madeline

has a way of making me feel small and insignificant. I am the hired help, yes, but it stings to be reminded of my place so bluntly.

When I finally emerge, wrapped in a towel, the house is quiet.

"She's gone. You can come out now." Christian's voice carries from the living room.

I dress quickly and find him downstairs, standing with Addison perched on his hip, her head resting against his shoulder. He holds out a mug, steam curling from the top in lazy wisps. "I made you some hot chocolate," he says.

"Thank you." I take the mug, feeling the heat seep into my palms. I can smell just a hint of cinnamon, exactly how I like it.

"I'm sorry about my mother," he adds. "She can be…a lot."

"Understatement of the year," I mutter.

"Anyway, we've planned Addison's party. My mom's party planner is coming by tomorrow morning to assess the space for setup." He shifts Addison to his other hip, and she snuffles against him.

"Isn't it a bit early?" I ask.

"Yep, and she knows it needs to be only family and friends, but this is what she wants." His gaze drifts off for a moment, pensive. "We'll have to keep my parents separated, though. They're like oil and water."

"Does she know you're seeing your dad?"

Christian's jaw tightens, and he shakes his head. "I haven't directly told her, no. I know it won't make her happy."

"Are you going to invite Taylor?" I ask, trying to get a gauge on things.

"I don't know how I'd get ahold of her," he says with a shrug, but there's a flash of something in his eyes.

He knows, but he's not ready. I'm not going to push it.

So maybe I'll go for the other elephant in the room. "Your mother…"

He looks up, his brow furrowing. "She didn't mean anything. She's just…old-fashioned."

"Old-fashioned?" I repeat. "She treats me like I'm nothing! Like I don't belong here, and I don't matter to Addison—or to you."

He sighs, clearly uncomfortable with the confrontation. "You know that's not true. You matter to Addison. And you matter to me."

I shake my head, feeling frustration build into something hotter, something I'm struggling to contain.

His expression tightens, his patience wearing thin. "I'm trying to keep the peace. My mother's difficult, and she has her opinions, but she'll come around. She always does. You just need to give her time."

I stare at him. How can he possibly believe that? His actions indicate the exact opposite. He placates her because she'll never change.

"It's complicated, Hailey. My mom... She's just protective of Addison, and she's old-fashioned about family. She doesn't understand our situation."

"'Our situation?'" I repeat, stunned. "I'm a situation?" Anger and hurt rise in my chest. "I'm not just the nanny. I love Addison like she's my own, and I've been here for you every step of the way. But your mother looks at me like I'm disposable, and you never say a thing. Sometimes, I feel like you see me that way too."

His eyes widen in shock. "That's not fair, Hailey. I've never treated you like you're disposable. You know I care about you." His face softens for a moment, but then he shakes his head. "I've got a lot going on right now. Addison's eventual surgery, work, Taylor coming back around, my mom... I'm trying to keep everything together."

"And what about me?" I ask.

Christian's shoulders sag, and for the first time, I see the cracks in his armor. He looks exhausted, worn down. "I'm not trying to push you aside. I'm just... I don't know how to deal with all of this. I'm scared, Hailey. I'm scared I'll lose Addison. I'm scared I'll lose you. And when my mom's here, I don't know how to navigate it. It's all too much."

I look up at him, tears stinging my eyes. "I don't want to be on the outside anymore, just because that's convenient for you."

He holds out the arm that doesn't have Addison, pulling me tightly against him. "You won't be," he murmurs. "I promise, I'll do better. I don't want to lose you, Hailey."

Before I can speak further, his phone rings. He fishes it out of his pocket and reads the screen. "It's the guys. They want to go golfing. Is that okay?"

I nod, because what else can I do? "Go have fun. We'll be fine here."

"Call if you need anything." He presses a kiss to Addison's forehead before setting her in her playpen, her little hands reaching up as if to keep him close.

"Will do," I promise, but as soon as he's gone, I begin to worry. Addison's been too quiet today, too lethargic. "Hey, sweetie," I coo, reaching for the thermometer. Her skin remains warm to my touch, and her nose is a red, snotty mess.

"Let's see how you're doing, huh?" I take a video of her with the thermometer reading and send it to Cordelia, hoping I'm just overly cautious. She texts back almost immediately.

Cordelia: Monster cold. Hang tight. Worst is over.

I let out a breath and pull Addison into my arms, whispering reassurances I hope are true. We spend the day curled up together, her tiny frame fitting perfectly against me, despite Madeline's earlier admonitions.

"Nobody knows you like I do," I tell her, brushing a kiss to her forehead. "You'll hit those milestones when you're ready, and not a second before."

The day is done, the night is still, and the clock on the nightstand reads 11:22 p.m.

"Stop it," I whisper to myself, a stern admonition.

Christian has never promised me anything—not a future, not even an actual relationship other people know about—yet I got myself into this. We did agree to be exclusive, and I have no reason to doubt that, so why does jealousy rear its head now? I flop over to my other side.

The sound of the back door closing rouses me from a restless slumber. My heart thumps as I feign deep breaths, eyes closed but mind acutely awake. The familiar creak of floorboards signals his approach, and then he's here, slipping into bed beside me. A cloud of cheap perfume invades my nostrils, a scent that's all wrong for him.

"God," he mutters under his breath, likely assuming I'm asleep. "Why can't you just move into my room already?" There's a longing in his voice that tugs at something within me, but I fight the urge to respond.

His breathing eventually evens into the telltale rhythm of sleep. I lie motionless, tears tracing warm paths down my temples. What did he do all night that he couldn't check in? Why didn't he think of Addison or me even once?

A small sob catches in my throat, and I stifle it with a pillow pressed against my face. A harsh truth settles in my bones. I'm falling for him, and that has to be a mistake. Once again, I've chosen a man who doesn't have what I need to give. Things have to change. Otherwise it relegates me to the role of convenience, always there, never chosen.

CHAPTER 26

Hailey

I jolt awake to the sound of Dana's voice, her words tumbling through the half-open door. "Hailey, are you up? I have Timmy's," she calls.

"Give me a sec," I call back. Beside me, Christian stirs, his eyes meeting mine for a brief moment before he slips out of bed and pads silently to my bathroom, disappearing just as Dana bursts into the room holding a box of donuts.

Her face is a storm cloud of emotion, her eyes red-rimmed, her lips quivering. She collapses on the edge of my bed, hands wringing. "It's Tate." She exhales. "He's still so tangled up with his ex. I can't do it anymore, Hailey. I want to be someone's first choice, not an afterthought."

I shift closer, reaching for her hand. "You deserve to be a priority, Dana."

"I thought things would be different with him, but every time I feel like we're finally making progress, she pulls him back. And he lets her." She pauses, wiping a tear from her cheek.

"Sometimes, I think I'm crazy for getting involved with my boss, like I'm not enough for him, and I'll never be enough."

I squeeze her hand. "You are enough. It's Tate who's trying to navigate this."

"But what if this is all I get? What if no one ever chooses me first? I've spent so much time waiting for him to let go of her, but maybe I'm the one holding on to something that will never be mine. What does that say about me?" Dana's voice falters, vulnerability replacing her usual confidence. "I'm scared I'll always be chasing someone who isn't fully there."

My heart clenches. "You deserve more than this, Dana. You deserve someone who knows they want you, without hesitation."

She nods, a tear slipping down her cheek. "I just don't know if I have the strength to walk away. What if he does choose me someday, and I've already given up?"

"I know."

"Anyway, I should get going," Dana says, glancing at the clock with a resigned sigh. "I have an actual in-person meeting this morning. If it weren't for this Europe trip, I swear I'd start job hunting."

"Let's grab drinks soon," I suggest.

I hear the back door chime, and I know Christian has escaped without being seen. I feel relief and like crap all at the same time. I pull Dana into a hug.

"I need an update about Ray," she mumbles into my shoulder.

"Ray?" I pull back.

"The hickey guy," she reminds me.

Crap! I'm such a terrible liar. "Haven't seen him much. But let's get dinner and drinks at our favorite place tonight. We don't need men. We'll make a date."

"Sounds perfect," she smiles, the ghost of her usual spark flickering behind her eyes.

"Take care, Dana," I say as she waves and heads out the door. "I'll see you later."

Left alone, I exhale slowly. I'm not even sure how to

process that. I pick up my phone and scan my email. Audrey Henry, Madeline's party planner, is coming over this morning. I have twenty minutes to get ready.

I grab Addison and put her in a bouncy seat in the bathroom, so I can keep an eye on her while I shower. I dry my hair but pull it into a ponytail.

I run my hands down the front of my sundress, nerves fluttering as I glance at the clock. This will have to do. I know Christian trusts his mother, and he wants what's best for Addison, but I still worry, like I'm being kept at arm's length from decisions that matter, decisions that affect what the doctor wants for Addison.

Right on time, I hear the front gate, and my stomach tightens. This isn't just a birthday party. This is her grand gesture. For a moment, I wonder how much I'll really be involved — if at all — probably just to help with the decorations or smile politely when it's all set up.

As I lift Addison into her carrier, her eyes blink up at me. "Don't worry, sweetheart. I've got you."

But deep down, I don't know if that's true. Madeline always seems to have the final say.

Audrey Henry, party planner extraordinaire, arrives, introduces herself, and walks in like she owns the place. She strides through the house and into the backyard, clipboard in hand. She immediately launches into plans for the party — white and gold, ethereal elegance, balloons, and lush floral arrangements.

It sounds beautiful, yes. But extravagant. And not what I'd imagined for Addison. I was hoping for simpler, but I know that is not Madeline.

I nod along, though my thoughts are elsewhere. Christian said we'd keep this simple, didn't he? Dr. Cordelia specifically recommended something small, for Addison's sake. So why does this feel like an event designed to impress everyone but our daughter?

"It's Madeline's vision," Audrey says with a bright smile. "She really knows how to pull off a party." She waves a piece of paper packed with names. I force a smile, but the unease festers. "Could I get a copy of the guest list? For Christian?"

Audrey's professional smile never falters. "Sorry, Madeline instructed me to keep it under wraps until the day of the event."

Her response makes my pulse quicken. I'll have to make sure Christian knows that. My jaw clenches as Audrey's pen moves swiftly across the paper, jotting down notes. She talks about tables, and I don't get the impression it's two, but closer to twenty. My radar is on high alert.

When she puts her files down and steps away to run a tape measure, I jump into action. This isn't just about a birthday anymore. It's about control. As Audrey turns her back, I make a decision. Before I can second-guess myself, I lean over her open file and snap a picture of the guest list with my phone. There are at least a hundred people on it!

My heart pounds in my chest. But this is about Addison, and Christian has every right to know who's attending.

Retreating to the solitude of the living room with Addie, I send the image to Christian, along with a text.

Me: Over 100 guests — and I only have it because I stole this photo. Seems excessive for a toddler's birthday. Didn't you tell her what Cordelia said?

As I hit send, the weight of all those names — all those strangers — presses down on me. This isn't just a party. It's a production, one where Addison will be exposed to so many.

I close my eyes, just for a moment, trying to decide whether we need to return to the backyard. My heart skips when my phone rings, and I fumble for the device, careful not to upset the baby.

"Hey," Christian's voice comes through. "Are you sure this is the guest list?"

"Yes. She wouldn't let me see it, so I took a picture when I had a chance, and I'm not even sure there isn't a second page. It's more gala than toddler birthday party."

Addison stirs in my arms, her tiny face scrunching in discomfort. I begin to rock gently. "Dr. Cordelia said we should keep things low key, remember? For Addison's sake."

"Right." There's a pause on the other end, and I imagine Christian running a hand through his hair. "I'll talk to my mother. This isn't what she promised me."

"Thank you," I whisper. "Just thought you should know." The line goes dead, and I focus on Addison, who's now gazing up at me with watery eyes.

"Shh, sweetheart," I murmur. We start the rhythmic creak of the rocker as I read from the worn pages of her favorite book, *Where the Wild Things Are.* Her little hand clutches my finger, her need wrapping around my heart, grounding me in this moment.

I hear the door open and close, and I think that means Audrey is leaving without saying goodbye. This is going to be a fun party. I lean my head back and think about Europe, and I wonder how I'm going to manage not seeing Addison every day. Who is going to take care of her?

The doorbell sounds, and Addison's eyes pop open, round and startled, but thankfully, she settles back against my chest with nothing more than a soft murmur. I rise from the rocker with careful, silent steps, set her in her crib, and make my way to the front door.

Peering through the peephole, I spot a delivery driver holding a large, insulated bag. My stomach growls in response, a Pavlovian reaction. But I ordered nothing. With a gentle push, I open the door just wide enough to communicate.

"Can I help you?" I ask.

"Delivery for Hailey," he says. "Got an order of chicken poutine from La Belle Patate here."

"Chicken poutine?" My eyes widen in surprise. French fries with chicken, peas, and cheese curds all smothered in brown gravy, a culinary hug of my favorite comfort food from the best spot.

"Yep, already paid for and everything." The driver hands over the meal.

"Thank you," I say, still grappling with the mystery of this kindness as I close the door.

No sooner do I set the package on the kitchen counter than the phone rings. I quickly answer, tucking the phone between my ear and shoulder.

"Hey," Christian's voice is warm. "I hope I'm not interrupting."

"Actually, you're right on time," I reply. "Just received a surprise delivery of chicken poutine."

"Good." I can hear him smiling. "Sorry about sneaking out this morning. Dana needed you, and I had to rush to the hospital."

"No one has ever done anything quite like sending me lunch from La Belle Patate. It means a lot. Really."

"Anything for you, Hailey." There's a pause. "You've been juggling so much lately. I wanted to take care of you too."

"Promise me you'll let me thank you properly when you get home," I say.

"Counting on it," he assures me before we say our goodbyes.

As the call ends, I hear Addison upstairs. "Looks like lunch is served," I whisper, starting up the stairs to get her. For a fleeting second, I feel like everything might just be okay.

We spend the afternoon quietly, and when the weather gives us a small reprieve, we go for a walk along False Creek. Addison just watches as I talk away, pointing out what I see — Science World's geodesic dome, the Vancouver Tigers stadium, sailboats, yachts, and greedy seagulls.

When we complete our walk, we return home, pulling in just as Dana arrives.

"Perfect timing," I say.

Dana's tear-streaked face greets me before I can even get Addison out of the car, and she practically falls into my arms, her body shaking with sobs.

"He wants me back," she chokes out between gasps for air. "Tate," she clarifies.

I nod and just hold her for a moment. Eventually, she's calm enough to greet Addison, and we head inside. I open the door and lead her to the couch, putting Addison in her highchair with some Cheerios for a snack.

I sit beside her, my heart heavy. She's caught in a love she can't seem to navigate, and I see myself reflected in her turmoil.

"Does he only want me because we're together all the time?" Dana's eyes search mine for answers I'm not sure I have.

"Hey," I say gently, reaching for her hand. "Do you love him, despite all the mess?"

She hesitates, then nods, wiping away tears. "I do."

"You know, Tate has a lot on his plate. Divorce, kids… Maybe be patient with him."

Dana leans into my embrace, still trembling. "I love you," she murmurs into my shoulder. "I don't know what I'd do without you."

"Always here for you," I whisper back, holding her tight and pushing my own uncertainty aside. I need to be strong for my friend.

CHAPTER 27

Hailey

Christian has been busy at the hospital, and Addison and I have stuck close to home these past few days. Today has had a bit of excitement, but not the kind I wish for. Right on cue, my phone buzzes again, sending a shiver down my spine. *Franklin.* Another missed call, the fifth one today. He was arrested weeks ago, but now, it seems he's out, released as a first-time offender. I'm supposed to call if he contacts me, but why? They can't do anything unless he does something. I just want this to be over. Each voicemail is a verbal stone thrown harder than the last. He says he doesn't care about the restraining order. He's going to release the pictures.

I take a shuddering breath, my fingers trembling as they hover over my phone. I was so naive back then, so trusting. Too trusting. "Christian," I say, turning toward where he's buried in some medical journal, "What nights are you home this week?"

He glances up. "Tonight and tomorrow," he replies. There's concern in his voice, a silent question he doesn't ask.

I turn away before he can probe further. I'm just going to get this over with myself. My fingers move across the keyboard, typing out a message to Franklin.

Me: I can meet you tonight. Let's go to the bar where we first met.

The place where it all began, where I thought we were just two people who randomly met and fell in love. I believed he wanted the same things I did—security, commitment, a future. But it was all a lie.

Anyway, this will be a meeting in a public place. He can't do anything too terrible with others around, and I need to find out what he wants, once and for all.

Almost instantly, his response buzzes back.

Franklin: I'll be there in an hour.

I swallow hard, my heart pounding as I stare at the screen. *Am I really doing this?* My mind races through every possible outcome. If I confront him, will he give me what I need? Or will he just toy with me, like he always does? *Could I provoke him into something big enough to land himself back in jail?*

I get up and excuse myself, heading for my bedroom. After some rummaging in my closet, I stand before the mirror, tugging at the hem of a deep blue blouse that clings just enough to suggest a confidence I don't feel. The jeans I slip into are comfortable, familiar, but my skin prickles with anxiety. I was so honest with Franklin once, so vulnerable. Told him what I wanted, what I needed. And he used it all against me. Every moment of weakness, every confession I thought was safe. I can't stop thinking about how he'd smile, how he'd make me feel like I was finally being heard, only to twist my words later, make me doubt myself.

I was a fool to trust him. Never again.

With one final glance at my reflection, I grab my phone and send a quick message to Dana. My safety net. My backup plan.

Me: I'm meeting Franklin at the bar we used to go to. If you don't hear from me in an hour, call me, okay?

Dana: Are you sure you don't want me there?

Me: No need to worry. It's a public place. I'll be fine.

I hope. I bite my lip, staring at her response. I should have told her more, explained why I'm going. But what would I even say? That I'm scared he'll release the pictures? That I'm ashamed I let someone like Franklin have power over me for so long?

"I'll be back shortly," I tell Christian, already moving to the door.

"Are you meeting with Dana?" he asks, looking up from his medical journal.

I shake my head. "No, but I shouldn't be long. And Addison should stay asleep." I force a smile, hoping it hides the storm brewing inside me. Christian's phone rings, and I wave goodbye quickly, not giving him a chance to ask more.

The summer evening still has sun in the air, and it's warm outside as I walk to the bar. This is my favorite time of year. But I can't distract myself. I need to get this thing with Franklin done and over with.

Inside, the bar is dim, the kind of place where bad decisions are made in the shadows. Franklin's not here yet, thank God. I slide on to a stool at the bar in the middle of everything. This is hopefully a spot where he won't become too evil. After ordering a drink, I try to calm my racing thoughts, but my mind won't stop replaying every argument, every moment I let my guard down with him. How could I have been so naive? How did I let him manipulate me into thinking we were partners and give him all my money?

And now, here I am, waiting for him again, scared of what he might say, what he might show me. *What if I'm still that weak girl who trusted the wrong man?*

The bartender sets down my mojito, and Franklin walks in, his eyes scanning the room until they lock onto mine. My heart sinks. He thinks he has the upper hand. And the worst part? I'm terrified he might be right.

Franklin moves with a swagger, but there's something off about it—too sharp, too deliberate. There's a frantic energy radiating off him, like he's barely keeping himself together. He slides in next to me at the bar, not bothering with any pleasantries, his fingers tapping erratically on the wood as his eyes dart around the room. "Where is it?"

I blink, trying to stay calm. "This is all I could find." I push his tax file and the broken bottle opener at him. "There was a joint too, but I threw it away. I can't have drugs in the house."

"This isn't what I want." He leans in, his breath hot and sour. "Don't play dumb," he snaps. "You know exactly what I'm talking about."

"I don't," I say carefully, trying to gauge his mood. There's a manic gleam in his eyes, something wild and unpredictable. His leg is bouncing, the constant motion making me nervous.

"You took it. I know you did!" His hand slams onto the bar top, causing me to jump. His voice rises again, drawing the attention of a few people nearby. "You think you're so clever, don't you?"

"What are you talking about?" I ask, my heart racing. "I haven't taken anything from you."

Franklin laughs, a sharp, humorless sound. "Oh, come on. You always thought you were smarter than me, but guess what? You're not. You've never been." His hands are trembling now, the erratic tapping getting faster. "You think I don't know what you're doing? You think I don't see you, plotting against me?"

I stare at him, unsure how to respond. The man sitting next to me is a far cry from the controlled, manipulative Franklin I once knew. He's unraveling, his paranoia spilling out of his pores.

He suddenly grabs his phone, shoving it in my face. "You see this?" he snarls, scrolling through the images at a dizzying pace. "I've got everything I need to ruin you. Everything." His finger jabs at the screen with such force, I'm surprised it doesn't crack. "You thought you could hide from me? Think again."

I realize I'm looking at a picture of someone I don't recognize. It's not me. "Franklin, you're not making any sense," I say. But inside, I'm panicking. He's not just angry. He's spiraling out of control, and I have no idea what he's going to do next.

His eyes flicker with a dark light, and suddenly, he's laughing again. "Oh, I'm making sense, all right. Perfect sense. You think you can steal from me? You don't know what's coming." He leans in closer, his voice dropping to a sinister whisper. "I'll destroy everything you've built, Hailey. Everything. I'll make sure everyone knows just what kind of person you really are."

He slams his hand on the bar top again, the noise echoing through the tavern. People are staring now, but Franklin doesn't seem to care. His movements are jerky and uncoordinated. "You're nothing."

For a moment, I'm frozen. He's unraveling so fast, I can barely keep up. I've seen Franklin angry before, but this? This is something else. This is desperation. Chaos. And I know, without a doubt, that he's on the edge of something dangerous.

"Find it," he seethes, his breath hot on my skin. "You have forty-eight hours, or everyone will see just how much of a —" He doesn't finish the sentence. Instead, he grabs the front of my blouse, fabric tearing beneath his fingers.

I gasp, the sound lost in the sudden commotion. The bartender steps in, her bar gun aimed.

"Enough!" She sprays Franklin squarely, the stream of water a clear command. "Get out of my bar, now!"

He reels back, the shock of the cold water breaking through his fury. With a final glare, he stumbles back, leaving the remnants of my dignity soaked and scattered on the floor.

The bartender's voice slices through the tension. "I'm calling the cops."

Franklin's eyes narrow, fixed on me with a sinister glint. "Tick-tock," he hisses, pointing a finger. Then he wheels around and marches out the door.

My heart is racing. *What does he mean?* This meeting was pointless. I still have no idea what he's searching for.

The bartender shakes her head and turns to me. "I've already called the cops," she says quietly, wiping her hands on a towel. "They're on their way. You should sit tight."

I nod, but my mind is racing, heart still pounding from the confrontation. My hands tremble. I've never seen him acting like that. What could be going on?

The door swings open a few minutes later, and two police officers walk in, their presence commanding attention. My stomach churns as they approach, the relief I thought I'd feel elusive. What do I even tell them? That I'm scared of a man I used to trust with everything? That I don't know how far Franklin will go to hurt me?

The officers approach the bartender, and they talk for a few minutes before she points them to me.

"We understand you had a confrontation with a guy who got a little aggressive."

I nod.

"Do you have any identification on you?"

I pull my driver's license from my purse. One of them jots the information down.

"Why don't you tell us what happened?"

My hands tighten around the edge of the stool, my knuckles white. I try to speak, but the words get stuck in my throat. The whole scene replays in my mind—Franklin's rage, his wild threats, the way he grabbed me, the way he... I shudder, and it's like I can still feel his hands on me.

"I have a restraining order against him, but he kept calling. So, I—I said I'd meet him here," I finally manage, my voice trembling. "I thought I could...reason with him. But he's not... He's not the same anymore. He's dangerous. He grabbed me. He threatened me."

"Take your time," the first officer says gently. "You're doing fine."

I look down at my hands. "He has pictures of me—private

ones. He's threatening to release them if I don't give him what he wants. But I don't know what he wants." My voice cracks, and I feel a wave of panic rising in my chest.

The officer's brow furrows, and he exchanges a glance with his partner. "Did he say anything specific that makes you think he's a threat to your safety?"

I swallowing hard. "He said he would destroy everything. I've never seen him like that before. He was completely out of control."

"Has he hurt you before?" the second officer asks.

I shake my head. "Not physically, no. But he's manipulative. He knows how to...get under my skin. He used to promise me we'd be together forever. He got me to give him the money from my grandmother's insurance policy, and then he just stopped working."

"Why the restraining order?"

"We don't live together anymore, and he keeps saying I have something of his. But he won't tell me what it is. He's harassing me. I've looked, and I can't find anything. I gave him back everything I've found that belonged to him. But he keeps threatening to release those pictures of me..." I look around the bar, and everyone is listening. Of course, they are.

The officer picks up the folder and looks through the old tax forms. "Where is the restraining order?"

"It was filed with this officer." I pull out the business card Christian gave me.

"You should have called us once he made contact." The second officer lowers his voice, stepping closer.

"We'll need to know if he tries to contact you again. And we recommend filing for an emergency protective order. It'll reinforce your current restraining order."

My mind swirls. Another protective order? More paperwork. But will it really stop him? Will anything stop him?

"I don't know what to do," I admit quietly.

The officer nods. "You did the right thing by talking to us. We'll do everything we can to make sure he doesn't hurt you."

For a second, I sit there, trying to let their words comfort me. But the fear still lingers. Franklin's face flashes in front of me again—the anger, the chaos. The way he looked at me, like he was ready to destroy everything.

I take a deep breath. The officers are still talking, but their voices blur together as the weight of the situation bears down on me. This is real. This is happening. And I have no idea what comes next. "Thank you," I manage to say, my voice almost lost in the noise of the bar around us. "Thank you for coming so quickly."

"We're here to help," the officer says, giving me a reassuring nod. "If you need anything, don't hesitate to call. We'll keep an eye on things."

I nod again, my head spinning. "Okay. I will."

"Can we give you a lift home?"

I stand up straight. "No, I, uh… I can walk."

"Given he might be waiting for you, I think we should give you a ride home."

Of course. If Franklin is out there, I should let them take me home. I thank the bartender and leave her cash for my drink. It's not nearly enough for the trouble I caused.

The drive home in the back of the police car is embarrassing. At least the lights and sirens aren't going, but I'm still locked in behind the protective glass. I can't believe this. They pull to a stop in front of Christian's townhouse, and it seems like everyone is stopping to watch.

Before I even get out of the backseat, Christian's figure emerges from the front door. He rushes over, his eyes searching mine for answers.

"Let's go inside," I murmur.

With a nod, Christian ushers me back toward the safety of our walls. Once the door closes behind us, shutting out the curious eyes, Christian rounds on me, his frustration palpable. "What happened?"

I tell him everything—the calls, meeting Franklin, and the bartender stepping in.

"Why didn't you tell me you were going to see him? You could have been hurt!"

I flinch, not from his tone, but from the truth in his words. "I thought… I thought I could handle it. I didn't want you caught up in my mess," I confess, feeling tears threatening to spill over. "This is all my fault."

Christian steps closer, the anger melting from his face. He wraps his arms around me, pulling me into the solid warmth of his chest. "Your mess is my mess," he says, his voice a gentle rumble against the top of my head. "We're in this together, remember?"

CHAPTER 28

Christian

I set my coffee down with a heavy clink, the dark liquid inside barely touched. I stare at it, the weight of everything pressing down on me — the cops driving Hailey home yesterday evening, my mother doing the opposite of what we'd agreed to. My head throbs, hence my drinking coffee in the middle of the day.

Franklin could have hurt Hailey, and it kills me that she thought that was something she needed to handle herself. Honestly, it also kind of kills me that I feel that way.

I watch Addison play on a blanket on the floor, and my phone rings. It's my mother. At least she didn't just walk in this time.

I answer and can barely get a word in edgewise for the first couple minutes. Mom has so much to say about this magical event her planner is putting together. Finally, she pauses to take a breath, and I bring up the extensive guest list she's concocted for the party.

"Christian, darling, you worry too much," she says, brushing off my concerns. "Everything is under control."

"Mom, Addison just got out of the hospital," I remind her. "She's still recovering from a terrible cold, and she's probably going to have heart surgery before we get to the party. We can't have her surrounded by strangers."

"Strangers?" Mom scoffs, unfazed. "They're our family and friends."

"Friends who could make her sick again," I press, hoping to get through to her. But it's like talking to a wall, a well-dressed, immovable wall.

"Your daughter needs to build her immunity," she counters. "And besides, I've arranged everything. I've got everything covered."

Her tone says she's dug her heels in, and no amount of reasoning will budge her. I clench my jaw, trying to keep my cool as she goes on to lay the blame for Addison's health issues squarely on Hailey. "She's coddling Addison," she insists. "Carrying her everywhere. The girl will never learn to walk at this rate."

"Mom," I interject, but she barrels on, steamrolling my objections.

"These are people who've watched you grow up, Christian. They're eager to meet your daughter and celebrate her first year."

And suddenly, it's all clear. There's no way to work this out, to come to compromise, to provide the information that will help everyone understand. One party here doesn't want to compromise, so that makes it impossible. But this is too important to just let my mother have her way.

"Listen," I begin, steeling myself for the confrontation. "The party will be small. Just Dad and Tasha and their family and—if you want—you."

Her silence tells me she's poised to argue, to insist on having things her way as she always does.

"This is *Addison's* first birthday," I continue. "It isn't about you. It's about her. She shouldn't be overwhelmed, especially not after being in the hospital."

The silence continues, heavy and electric. My heart races, thumping a fierce rhythm against my ribs. Standing up to my mother, possibly inviting her wrath… It's a gamble.

"That will not happen," she declares.

"Mom, it's not up for discussion. Addison needs something small, something intimate. I am her parent, and I am making the call."

She scoffs. "Why are you so determined to ruin your life?" Her words cut deep, suggesting my choices are the blueprint for disaster.

I draw in a breath. "I'm doing what's best for Addison. Your party is canceled." My voice is firmer now, more certain than it's ever been when speaking to her. "We'll have a family gathering, as we originally agreed. You're invited, if you want to come."

A big blowup ensues, but instead of feeling awful, I realize she sounds a lot like a toddler—worse than a toddler. I can't imagine Addison ever behaving like this. I don't back down, so she moves back to attacking Hailey, and at that point, I've had it.

"Mom, you should know that Hailey treats Addison like her own. She loves my daughter, and she's spent enough time caring for her to know what's best for her."

"Fine!" she hisses. "Ruin your life. But remember who tried to stop you." She hangs up.

I still can't fathom how not having a big, splashy birthday party is equivalent to ruining my life. But nonetheless, it's a hollow victory.

I glance over to where Addison is still lying on the floor, her little hands gripping a teething toy, manipulating it with intense purpose. She looks up at me, so proud of her hard work, and for a moment, the noise in my head fades, and it's just me and her. My daughter. My reason for all of this. I know I'm making the right choices.

As I watch, Addison discards the toy, rolls from her back to her stomach then keeps going. With a grunt of effort, she suddenly sits up, all on her own! She's grinning. She knows she's just accomplished something great.

I scoot myself down next to her and reach out, gently placing a hand on her back to steady her, but she doesn't need me. Not right now. She's sitting tall, smiling with pride.

"You did it, sweetheart," I whisper, my voice thick with emotion.

This is it. This is what being a father means. It's not just about protecting her or providing for her. It's about being here, witnessing these moments that shape her, that shape us. It's about being part of her journey, one milestone at a time.

I swallow hard, blinking back the tears that blur my vision. She's so small, so vulnerable, and yet she's showing me just how strong she can be. And in that strength, I see all the possibilities for her future. All the things she can become. We just have to keep her safe and give her the chance she needs.

I brush a hand through her soft hair, trying to focus on my pride rather than fear. "I'm so proud of you," I tell her. "You're growing up so fast."

Addison babbles in response, a soft sound that makes me smile.

"Hailey!" I call. "Come quick!"

I lean down and kiss the top of Addison's head. "I'll always be here for you," I whisper. "No matter what."

Hailey rushes in. "Everything okay?"

Addison sees Hailey, lifts her arms, and says, "He he he he he."

My eyes widen, and Hailey's do too. What did she just say? "Yes, that's Hailey," I tell her.

Hailey covers her mouth with her hands.

"That's not even why I called you in here," I tell her through a huge smile. "Addison did this all on her own," I say, presenting her like a prize.

A grin as wide as the Grand Canyon erupts on Hailey's face, and she pulls out her phone to snap a few pictures. "You did it!" she says. "You sat up! What a big girl!"

Then Hailey's arms encircle me. Her touch is gentle, a stark contrast to the harshness that transpired earlier with my mother. "What's wrong?" she murmurs against my shoulder, her concern piercing through my defenses. "You're not jealous she didn't say dada first, are you?"

I narrow my eyes and give her a playful swat. "Of course not," I tell her. "I stood up to her today," I say. "My mom. For the first time, I wasn't afraid to make the right choice, even if she didn't agree."

Hailey shifts so I can see the pride shining in her eyes. "Your mother is a lot of things, but she loves you, no matter what. You've always been enough."

I nod. In her embrace, something shifts inside me, settles into place. I feel whole, not fragmented by fears and insecurities. It's a completeness I've never known, one that only Hailey seems able to bring.

"We're going to keep the party small," I tell her, the words flowing more easily now. "Just my dad and his family, us, and maybe my mother if she comes."

"Sounds perfect," Hailey agrees.

We talk quietly, discussing perhaps inviting Davis and his wife, and Cordelia and her family. These are simple plans for a celebration that feels true to who we are, and what Addison needs, not what my mother demands.

I'm jolted awake the next morning by a persistent pounding on my front door. The clock says it's just after six thirty as I untangle myself from the warmth of the bed and Hailey's soft limbs.

I open the Ring app on my phone, and a delivery driver is there. "Can I help you?" I ask over the intercom.

"I have a delivery." He shows the envelope to the camera.

"Can you leave it on the step?"

"Unfortunately, I can't. You need to sign for it."

"I'll be down in a minute."

"Stay," I murmur to Hailey as she stirs, her eyes concerned. "It's probably nothing."

But the knot in my stomach tells me otherwise as I pad to the door after throwing on a pair of joggers and T-shirt. When I swing the door open, a man with disheveled hair and indifferent eyes greets me, envelope in hand.

"Christian Bradford?" He doesn't wait for confirmation before thrusting the envelope at me. "You've been served."

My hands shake as I take the envelope. The process server turns on his heel and leaves without another word, leaving me staring down at an envelope from a lawyer's office.

"Christian? What is it?" Hailey's voice floats down from the bedroom, laced with sleep and worry as I step back inside.

"Give me a minute," I call, trying to keep my voice steady as I break the seal.

The legal jargon swims before my eyes, but the accusations pierce through, sharp and clear. *Full custody. Lack of presence. Raising Addison with a nanny instead of family.* My heart clenches at the mention of Hailey, whose words have been twisted into weapons against me. Taylor's demands scream from the page—money, a home, a life equal to what I've provided here for Addison.

"Damn it," I curse, crumpling the papers in my fist. *I knew this would happen.* How did everything spiral out of control so quickly?

Hailey appears beside me, her hand light on my arm. "What's wrong?"

"Taylor," I say, the word tasting like bile. "She's suing for full custody."

Her face pales, her eyes scanning the document as I hold it out. Her reaction is a mirror of my own—shock, pain, betrayal. But beneath it all, I can see her gathering herself, preparing to be the support I need. "We'll figure this out," she says.

I want to believe her, to lean on her like I have these past months. But a poisonous thought slithers into my mind, dark and consuming. Maybe she's what's left me in this position. Hailey, with her plans to leave for Europe, her temporary presence in my life… How could I have trusted her with my daughter's care? In my quest to fill the void, to find solace, have I jeopardized Addison's future?

"She's taken me out of context," Hailey protests, still reading the document. "She makes it sound like I was complaining. I was never." Emotion laces her words.

"I understand," I lie, squeezing her hand before letting go. No reason to start an argument before I've thought this through. "I just… I need to think."

She nods, giving me space, and the distance between us grows tangible. Have I been a fool to let them grow so close, knowing the inevitability of her departure? Trust, once unshakable, now trembles on a precipice. Hailey is the wrong person to care for Addison, not because she isn't capable or loving, but because she's not permanent. And in that clarity, I realize the hard truth. I can't do this anymore. Not with everyone judging me from the outside, finding fault and using it to take my daughter away.

With every second that ticks by, the pressure mounts, and the fear of losing my daughter eclipses everything else.

I stride into Hailey's room, her eyes already red-rimmed from crying. The words feel like boulders in my throat, but they tumble out with a force I can't control. "You have three hours to get your things and leave. You're fired."

Hailey gasps, her hand flying to her mouth, eyes brimming with fresh tears. "Please," she pleads, her voice cracking. "Why? What do you think I…?" Her eyes widen. "Taylor cornered me. I thought we were just having a conversation. I didn't tell her anything about how you care for Addison. I didn't mean to give her ammunition."

I shake my head, a cold numbness seeping through me. "It doesn't matter. You talked to her. You gave her a chance to make this claim. You were the wrong choice from the start, and I knew it."

"Please, I—" Her words break off as a sob overtakes her.

"Go," I say, turning away to shield my face from her anguish. I can't watch her crumble; it's too much. But even as she sobs, my resolve firms. This pain is necessary. For Addison. For the broken trust that can't be mended.

The sound of shuffling and soft weeping fills the house as Hailey moves through the rooms, collecting the pieces of her life she'd woven into ours. It's a tangible dismantling of what could've been a future together, now packed away into bags and boxes.

She walks past me to the door, a duffel bag slung over her shoulder, her face streaked with tears. Our eyes meet for a fleeting moment, and the hurt in hers is almost enough to make me falter. Almost.

"Goodbye," she whispers, her voice barely audible.

"Goodbye," I manage, though my voice feels detached, foreign.

The door closes behind her, and I'm left in the echoing silence of the house with the weight of decisions made and paths irreversibly taken.

Outside, I watch through the window as Hailey hesitates on the front steps before requesting a rideshare on her phone. A few minutes later, a car pulls up, and she gets in without looking back. As it drives away—away from me, from us—I tell myself this is for the best, that the sharp sting in my chest will dull in time.

I did this for Addison.

CHAPTER 29

Hailey

The rain pelts down like icy needles as I wait on Dana's doorstep, soaking through my jacket and into my bones, but I barely feel it. Christian's words echo in my head, over and over again. *"You have three hours to get your things and leave. You're fired."* It plays on repeat, each time cutting deeper.

I hug my jacket tighter, but it's no use. The cold isn't just outside. It's inside too. Everyone I've ever loved has found a way to push me aside.

The buzzer sounds, and I pull the door open, stepping into the dim hallway. I haul my suitcase down the narrow corridor, and Dana meets me at the door. "Hailey…" she says. She offers me a hug, but in her eyes is that same look of pity I've seen a thousand times before.

I want to tell her everything—how I didn't mean for any of this to happen, how I never wanted to hurt Christian or Addison, how terrified I am of losing them. But the words don't come.

"Christian called," she says after a moment. "Are you okay? What happened?"

Tears stream down my face, and I shake my head. I can't even talk about it right now. What if Dana doesn't understand? "I just need a place to stay for tonight," I whisper. "I won't be here long."

She steps aside, letting me in without a word.

I drop my suitcase by the couch and collapse on the cushions, sinking into the familiar softness. All I feel is emptiness. *How did I get here?* How did I let myself believe Christian cared about me, not just what I could do for him? That he wanted me to be part of his life?

But I know how. It's the same way it always happens. I fall for someone. I give them everything I have, and in the end, they leave. Or worse, they kick me out, like I never mattered in the first place.

Christian wasn't supposed to be like that. *He wasn't supposed to hurt me like this.*

I bury my face in my hands, fighting back tears that burn behind my eyes. But it's no use. They spill over, hot and bitter, sliding down my cheeks like the rain outside. I thought I'd stopped crying over people who don't love me back, but here I am. Again.

Dana comes and sits next to me, rubbing my back. After a few minutes, I wipe my face with my sleeve, trying to hold myself together, but the cracks are starting to show. I've always been good at pretending to be strong, at pretending I can handle anything. But not this. Not again.

I gave everything to Christian, to Addison, to this life we were building, and still, he pushed me away. He didn't even think twice. One mistake, and I was gone. No second chances, no forgiveness. Just gone. And now, I'm here, sitting in a life that's crumbling, wondering why I ever thought things would be different.

It's always the same. I love them, and they leave. Every single time.

"Why don't you get in the shower?" Dana suggests. Her

concern stifles my guilt for a moment. She thrusts a pair of black joggers at me, the word *Juicy* emblazoned across the back in bold, shimmering letters. I have to smile at that, a classic Dana fashion statement.

The steam from the shower envelops me, a fog that washes away the chill and turmoil if only temporarily. As water cascades over me, I hear muffled voices. My heart sinks as I recognize the sharp cadence of Dana's speech. She's on the phone with Christian again. His name, spat out with venom, confirms it. If she didn't have the whole story before, I bet she does now.

I shut off the water, wrapping myself in a towel that smells faintly of lavender. Dressing in the borrowed joggers and a soft, oversized shirt Dana must have left for me, I brace myself for the impending storm outside the bathroom.

Dana is silent when I emerge. She's holding two steaming cups, the scent of chamomile tea drifting between us. She hands one to me, her fingers brushing mine.

"How long was it going on?"

I hesitate, my throat tightening around the confession. "It…it just happened," I admit. "We were both lonely, and it was—"

"Stop." Dana cuts me off, a hand raised. "I don't need the details. It's just…" Her eyes meet mine, filled with hurt and exasperation. "You know how fragile Addison is right now. And why would you do this to yourself? How could you risk everything for someone who isn't capable of a healthy relationship?" She looks down at her mug. "You promised me."

I can't think of a response to that, but then her disappointment continues.

"And you told Taylor things. How could you?"

I sit at the edge of Dana's plush couch, my fingers digging into the fabric as if I could anchor myself against the storm brewing in her eyes. "My words were taken out of context. She cornered me after a doctor's appointment. I thought it was better to talk with her than cause a scene." My voice breaks. "I told Christian about it when he got home. It didn't seem like a big deal at the time."

Tears carve hot trails down my cheeks, and I let them fall, unrestrained. "Poor Addison," I sob. "Her little heart doesn't deserve this mess. She won't understand."

"You weren't thinking about Addison when you fucked him," Dana scoffs.

I recoil. "It wasn't like that."

Dana's silence is a living thing, heavy and suffocating. She stands there, her arms wrapped around herself as if she's the one who needs protection. When she finally speaks, her words are measured but laced with hurt. "Christian isn't innocent in any of this," she says slowly. "But God, I didn't think you'd be so reckless."

The air between us chills, and I watch helplessly as Dana grabs her keys and leaves, shutting the door behind her. Alone, I curl up on the couch, wrapping my arms around my midsection as if I could hold together the pieces of me threatening to scatter.

I turn on the TV and stare at the screen for a while before picking up my phone. I've never been this scared to text Dana before, but everything feels different now, fragile, like one wrong move will shatter everything between us. I know I messed up. I know I hurt her. But if I don't reach out now, I might lose her forever.

Me: I'll leave as soon as I find a place. I'm so sorry.

My thumb hovers over the send button for what feels like an eternity. What if this is the last text I ever send her? What if she doesn't respond? Or worse, what if she does, and it's not the answer I'm hoping for?

What if she hates me?

I press send, my stomach twisting into knots as I watch the message disappear. *Delivered*, it says after a moment. But that's it. No reply. No typing bubble. Nothing.

The silence is suffocating. I hold my phone in both hands. *Please, Dana. Just answer me. Just let me know I haven't lost you too.*

Minutes pass. I pace the room, still clutching the phone, my mind racing. What if she doesn't answer? What if she's done with me? I can't lose her too. She's the one person who's always been there for me, the one person I thought I could always count on.

But maybe I've pushed her too far this time. Maybe she's sick of cleaning up my messes. Maybe she's finally realized I'm not worth it.

I glance at my phone again—still nothing. *God, why isn't she answering?* My throat tightens, and I swallow hard, fighting the panic rising in my chest. My heart hammers so loudly I can barely think straight. I know I hurt her. I know I let her down. But she's my best friend. Doesn't that count for something?

What if it doesn't?

I sit down on the edge of the couch, my leg bouncing nervously as I stare at the phone, willing it to light up. *Please, Dana. Please. Don't let this be the end.*

I think back to the nights she stayed up late, listening to me cry over my mistakes. She was by my side at my grandmother's funeral and helped me get through that loss. She's picked me up countless times when I fell.

Another minute passes. Then another. My hands are shaking now, and I can feel the tears welling up. *She's not going to answer. She's done with me. She's finally done with me.*

I open my messages again, reading over what I sent, wondering if it was the wrong thing to say. Should I have said more? Should I have begged for forgiveness? I run my hand through my hair, gripping the strands tightly as my mind spirals. What can I do to fix this? How do I even begin to make things right?

My phone buzzes, and I nearly drop it in my haste to check the screen. The relief is immediate, but short-lived.

Dana: Thank you.

Two words. That's it. Her message flat and cold, no hint of the friend I used to know. My heart sinks. *Thank you.* What does that even mean? Is she just being polite? Is this her way of telling me she's done?

I read the message again, hoping for some hidden meaning, something that will give me hope. But there's nothing. No follow up. No offer of support. Just a quiet dismissal. The kind of response you give to someone you don't want to deal with anymore.

I set the phone down on the couch beside me, feeling hollow, like the last piece of me has been ripped away. I lean forward, burying my face in my hands. *I've lost her.* My agony is complete. Everything I once had is gone.

My phone sounds, and I fumble to unlock the screen. But instead of a text, it's a notification from the bank. The numbers in my balance blink back at me, staggeringly higher than they should be. Christian has made a deposit, an enormous sum that drowns the amount he owed me. My chest tightens as I realize he's paying me to disappear. Each digit is another crack in the already shattered vessel of my heart, not just for him but for Addison too. Losing her sweet, innocent admiration is a separate anguish, one I can scarcely bear to acknowledge.

But then a calm comes over me. Shaking off the weight of betrayal, I focus on what needs to be done. The storage unit, a tangible problem to tackle. I never did go pick up my new key, and I can look again for what Franklin seems to be missing. I grab my purse and head out, the city still rubbing sleep from its eyes.

As hours bleed into the afternoon, I sort out what I want in my new apartment and what should stay here in storage. And I try to organize what's left better than the last time I was here. My legs grow numb, but I press on, with Christian and Addison in the front of my mind, wondering what they're doing, what our day would be like if I was there.

When I've gone through everything, the storage unit slowly returns to a semblance of order, yet I can't shake the feeling that something vital is gone, hidden in the jumble or spirited away by Franklin's greedy hands.

With a sigh, I lift the final box onto the stack and rub the small of my back. The unit looks almost as it did before, the chaos tamed. I pull down the door with a resounding clang, locking away my past once more.

The sky is dusky as I return to Dana's apartment, my feet dragging. I pause at the door, hand trembling over the knob, bracing for what awaits. When I enter, the note, crisp and white against the dark wood, is like a dagger.

Hailey,
  I'll be at my father's. Let me know when you're gone.
-Dana

Each word cuts deeper than the last. "Where did I go wrong?" I whisper to the empty hallway as I slide to the floor. What cosmic debt have I incurred to warrant such relentless loss? The silence offers no answers.

Thanks to Christian, I can move into my own place, but the rental market is very tight. A short-term rental might be my answer. I used to walk by one all the time down on Hastings Street. I look it up on my phone and call about vacancy. They can take me for a month starting tomorrow.

So, I gather myself, rising from the floor. Inside, the apartment is still, haunted by the ghost of friendship. I curl up on the couch, surrounded by shadows and the scent of chamomile tea, and let the darkness swallow my sobs.

I wake two mornings later, having forgotten where I am. It comes back in a rush. I'm in my rental for the month. The walls are like paper, and I could hear my neighbors all night. Pushing myself off the bed, I make my way to the tiny bathroom and shower, determined to figure out my life. Once dressed, I pull up the online wanted ads and see nothing. I applied yesterday at a nanny service, and they said they thought they had work for me. But I left Christian as a reference. He's the only one I had. Now, I haven't heard from them, so I'm guessing he didn't have anything helpful to say.

A little while later, I sit at the dining table, scraps of colored paper, stickers, and photographs scattered around me, but my hands feel heavy. I stare at the pictures. The plan was to only stay a year and move on, but it was becoming harder and harder to imagine doing that. I'd thought about talking with Dana and with Christian about other options, but now, none of it matters.

The scrapbook lies open in front of me, half-finished, its empty pages staring back like a reminder of all the things I'll never get to be part of. I trace a finger over the photo of Addison's tiny hand wrapped around my finger — the first day I met her. She was so small, so fragile, and I remember the way she looked at me with those big, innocent eyes. Like she trusted me. Like I belonged in her life.

But I don't anymore. I don't belong anywhere near her now.

The thought pierces through me, sharp and cold, and I have to blink back tears. I pick up a picture of Addison at the park, her face lit up with laughter as she swings in the baby seat, her little legs kicking in the air. It had been a perfect day. And now, it feels like a memory from someone else's life.

How am I supposed to do this? How am I supposed to create this gift for her, knowing I'll never get to see her grow up? Never get to be part of her milestones, her birthdays, her ordinary, beautiful days? I won't get to hear her call me He-he-he. Every picture I paste onto the page is another piece of my heart breaking.

I cut a strip of decorative paper, my hands shaking as I glue it next to a photo of Addison sleeping in my arms. That was a night she had a fever, and I stayed up all night, watching over her, terrified something might happen. I remember the way Christian looked at me in the dark, like I was the one person he could count on to keep her safe.

But not anymore.

I swallow hard, pain rising in my throat. I thought I was

building something with them. A family. But now, that's all gone, and here I am, stuck in the past, creating a scrapbook she'll probably never even know is from me.

I place a sticker next to the photo, a tiny cartoon sun shining bright against the pale blue background. I have to force myself to keep going, to finish this. I owe it to her. Even if she never knows I was part of her life, I want her to have this.

I reach for the next picture, a candid shot of Addison looking up at Christian, her eyes full of love. He's cradling her in his arms like she's the most precious thing in the world. I stare at the image for a long time, my heart aching. How do I say goodbye to her? How do I let go of this little girl who became everything to me?

I press the photo onto the page, smoothing it with trembling fingers. When I sit back and look at the page, the tears finally spill over, silent and steady. I pick up a marker and write in careful, deliberate letters under the photo: *Always in my heart.*

Because that's where she'll stay, even if I can't be with her. Even if she forgets me. She'll always be in my heart.

I never wanted to love her like this, to need her like this. But now that I do, the thought of losing her is unbearable.

I close the scrapbook and press it to my chest, as if holding it close will somehow keep her close too. But deep down, I know the truth. She's already slipping away, and there's nothing I can do to stop it. There's also little I can do to distract myself, as the plans Dana and I had drawn for our European adventure are likely now just another discarded dream.

"Time to make new plans," I murmur, pulling back the curtains to gaze out at the city sprawled below. The world moves on, indifferent to the chaos of my life. Somewhere out there is a place for me, a niche where I fit without having to force the pieces together. It's time to stop looking backward, to stop picking at old wounds and start fresh.

CHAPTER 30

Christian

I shuffle through another stack of résumés, the edges of the paper fraying under the stress of my thumb. Addison sits on the floor, her small fingers fumbling with the buttons of a doll's dress, uninterested in the parade of potential caregivers that has come and gone. Each one leaves with the same polite smile, a facade barely concealing their relief at escaping the scrutiny of a toddler who refuses to be won over.

Miller Crawford leans against the doorframe, his arms folded across his chest, watching the latest applicant make an awkward exit. "You know," he begins, the lawyer's tone casual but eyes sharp, "it wasn't Taylor who left Addison on your doorstep. It was her sister."

I feel a tightening in my chest, the involuntary acknowledgment of a truth I've been reluctant to face. Taylor, despite her failings, did care for Addison well before it all fell apart. The silence that follows Miller's statement is heavy with implication.

"Look," he continues, shifting into his professional persona. "I've been working on the counter proposal to Taylor's petition, and I think we should consider joint custody."

"No." The word echoes through the high-ceilinged room. "Taylor isn't responsible. She promised her sister a few days, and that turned into weeks. She was using drugs. Her sister couldn't handle it anymore, and Taylor didn't even call to check on her own daughter. Not once in four months." The frustration boils within me. How could anyone claim to love their child and yet walk away so easily?

"I understand," Miller soothes. "But we have to think about what's best for Addison in the long term. You need help with her care, and perhaps her mother is the obvious solution."

I look down at my daughter, whose innocent blue eyes flick up to meet mine. She's all that matters. And as her father, it's up to me to protect her, even if it means standing alone against everyone else's advice.

I carefully balance Addison on my hip as I knock on my father's door. It's been two weeks, and I still haven't found anyone who meets my expectations to care for her. I haven't worked, and she's not been her best. She doesn't like the change in her routine and calls for Hailey regularly.

"Damn it," Dana's voice slices through the thick air as soon as we step inside. This is supposed to be family dinner. "You're such a self-centered asshole! All I asked was for you not to sleep with my best friend. Was that so hard?"

Her words are like whips, lashing out with disappointment and anger. I wince. "Dana, I—"

But she's relentless, her face flushed with fury. "You took advantage of Hailey when she was vulnerable! And you're too old for her, you sack of shit. You should know better."

The rebuke is a gut punch, leaving me momentarily breathless. Addison tugs at my shirt, her small voice chiming in amidst our heated exchange. "He he he he he." Each syllable is a plea, a call for the one person who isn't here.

"Your daughter needs you to be better than this," Dana spits before storming off.

"What the hell happened?" My father's voice booms from the hallway.

"Dana's mad about Hailey... But she betrayed us," I manage, struggling to keep my voice steady.

"Betrayed how?" He steps closer, his gaze searching mine for answers.

"By talking to Taylor, by..." I explain the whole thing — the lawsuit, my reaction, Hailey's dismissal, and the subsequent chaos. The details feel sordid now, irrelevant in the face of Addison's incessant calls for *he he he he he* — a mantra that grows more desperate with each repetition.

"He he he he he," Addison chants again. The sound is a dagger, a reminder of the gaping hole left behind by Hailey's absence.

"Addison wants Hailey," I admit, feeling a twinge of guilt as I speak the truth aloud. "She keeps asking for her."

"Then maybe you need to think about what that means," my father says, his voice softening. "You should be sure you've assessed the situation the right way. For Addison."

I nod, swallowing past the lump of uncertainty lodged in my throat. Addison's persistent calls for the woman who's no longer here is a clear message. My actions have consequences. *But she was going to leave eventually anyway*, I reason with myself.

"Hailey betrayed us," I snap, my grip on Addison tightening ever so slightly. "She told Taylor things she shouldn't have. Now, I have this giant custody battle, and it's all her fault." The words are a shield raised against the doubts creeping into my mind.

"Did Hailey tell you she'd spoken to Taylor?" my father asks.

"Yes, she told me."

"And was what Taylor quoted her as saying true?" he presses, undeterred by my defensiveness.

"No," I start, faltering, then admit with a reluctant sigh, "Yes, some of it. Hailey… She took Addison to all her appointments because I have a full-time job." I look away, unable to hold my father's gaze.

My father lets out a long breath. "Son, I can't imagine Hailey would do anything to hurt you or Addison deliberately. Tasha and I could tell she loved Addison."

I shift uncomfortably, not ready to face that.

"Your mother cut me out of your life, and I left because I thought it was better for you. We can look back at that and decide it was a mistake, but I thought I was helping you at the time. All I wanted was to be a part of your life." His words are gentle, coaxing me to understand. "Whatever your choice about Hailey, maybe it's time to reconsider your stance on Taylor. She was a good mother. You've said that. And before things got to be too much, she handed Addison over to her sister to protect her."

I shake my head, even as my resolve begins to crack, my decisions now murky and uncertain. "Hailey was supposed to be on my side, not theirs. Not Taylor's." The thought makes my blood boil, but deep down, something else is simmering — fear. Fear that maybe they're right, that I've messed this up, that I'm the one who's wrong.

Addison nestles against my chest, finally seeming to settle, but then I hear it, a wheeze with each breath she takes, subtle but undeniable.

"Hey, what's this?" I ask, though I know she can't answer. I look her over carefully and decide not to take a chance.

I dial Cordelia's number. The phone rings, and she picks up.

"Christian? What's wrong?" she asks.

"Addison, she's…she's wheezing." The words tumble out. "I'm at my dad's house. It just started. I don't know what to do."

"Okay, bring her in," she says calmly. "I'll meet you at the ED. We'll take a look at her as soon as you arrive."

"Thank you. We're on our way." I end the call and look at Dad. "I need to go."

He nods. "We'll be right behind you."

I grab the diaper bag, check for her favorite blanket, and hustle to the car. Every breath she takes sounds like a ticking clock in my ears. As I secure her in her car seat, I whisper promises I can only hope to keep. "You're going to be okay, baby girl. Daddy's got you."

When we reach the hospital, I dump my car in my reserved parking spot and nearly sprint to the ED. I can't tell if I'm imagining that her lips are slightly blue. As Cordelia promised, we're ushered into an examination room as soon as we arrive. I place Addison on the bed, and Cordelia snaps her gloves on and starts listening to Addison's chest.

"Christian." Davis greets me as he walks in and then turns his attention to Addison. He works with methodical precision, conducting the echocardiogram. He clicks through images, measurements, and waveforms, each a silent testament to the battle raging within my daughter's chest.

"Her heart is weakened," Davis finally says. "The endocarditis from her previous infection… It's taken a toll. We need to operate to repair the damage."

My vision tunnels, the words echoing in a void where time slows. *Surgery.* My mind recoils. I knew this was inevitable, but we were working to get her strong enough. She's vulnerable on an operating table. I'm supposed to protect her, not throw her into danger. "But is she ready? Will she be strong enough?" I ask.

"I don't think we have a choice," Davis says, putting his hand on my shoulder. "I'm going to do the best I can. She's a fighter. Don't give up on her."

"Okay," I agree. "Do whatever you need to do."

I step out into the hallway as nurses come in to work with Addison. I lean against the cold wall and slide down to the floor, hands clasped tight. I look up to see concern on my father's face and soft empathy in my stepmother's eyes.

"Christian," my father breathes, offering a hand to help me to my feet.

Dana arrives as I stand to face them.

"They need to do the surgery on Addison's heart now," I choke out, my eyes flooding with tears.

Dad's arms circle me, and I can't hold back. Tears stream down my face. "It's going to be okay," he says. "Addison may be an infant, but we know she's strong."

Davis appears with some paperwork for me to sign. "We're going to take her up to the OR," he says when I've finished. "She's been sedated, and her numbers are in a good range to do the surgery." He goes on to tell me what he's going to do. It's a little different than working with an adult heart, but I know he's done this a dozen times this year alone. "The surgery will be a few hours," he concludes. "Do what you need to do. I can page you when we're done."

I nod. "We'll be in the surgical waiting area."

I pace the sterile hospital corridor, each step a silent prayer. Then a shadow appears at the periphery of my vision, halting me. There, distancing herself from the cluster of family, stands Hailey.

"Hailey?" I approach, though caution tightens every muscle. "Why are you here?"

She swallows hard. "Dana called me… I had to come. I love Addison." A pause, heavy with resignation. "Even if…even if I'm not part of her life anymore."

The words sting, a reminder of the chasm my actions have created. Before I can navigate this fresh wave of guilt, she extends a hand, offering a book bound in soft leather.

"Please, take this," she urges.

I scan the room, finding my family's eyes on us, and look back at Hailey. "It's going to be hours, Hailey. You should go."

She nods and looks around the room. Dana hardly meets her eyes. I have no doubt Hailey got a similar earful about our relationship. But she doesn't leave. "I'll just sit over here," she says. "I won't be in the way."

She takes a seat in the corner, and reluctantly, I look down at the scrapbook. For a brief moment, I contemplate discarding it, but curiosity wins over bitterness.

As I flip through the pages, memories flood in unbidden — images of Addison and me at the aquarium, her tiny hand pressed against the glass, wonder in her eyes; snapshots of VanDusen Gardens filled with vibrant blooms and laughter. Each image is a memento of joy we shared, moments captured through Hailey's lens, a narrative of a life that once felt whole.

There's more — candid shots of Addison asleep on my chest, notes scribbled in margins, detailing her first words, her favorite foods, the days spent nestled in the sanctuary of home.

It bowls me over — the care, the love poured into these pages. The scrapbook is a reminder of all that's precious, all I've jeopardized.

"Join us," I find myself saying to Hailey. "Please."

She hesitates only for a heartbeat before moving closer. Together, we pore over the scrapbook. Even in the midst of uncertainty, this collection of memories binds us, a reminder of our shared love for Addison. I know I shouldn't have doubted that.

The moment Taylor walks through the door, I feel a familiar knot of anger in my chest. Like she has any right to be here. She doesn't.

"You shouldn't be here, Taylor," I tell her. "You don't get to waltz in now, pretending to care."

She meets my eyes with a smug smile. "Well, the hospital thought differently. They seemed to think a mother should be informed about her daughter's condition." She practically spits out the word *mother*, taunting me.

I grit my teeth. "The hospital shouldn't have called you. You gave up that right the moment you walked out on Addison and dumped her with Erica."

Taylor's smile fades slightly, but there's still that cold, calculating look in her eyes. "I love my daughter, and I will be in her life. Get used to it." She steps closer, her voice lowering to a menacing tone. "I'm ready now. And you're not going to keep me out of her life, no matter how much money you throw at me."

Her words hang in the air, and my heart goes cold. "You think I'm going to let you pretend to play the role of mother?" I hiss.

Her expression shifts, her eyes narrowing. "You have a nanny raising our daughter. The courts won't care how long I've been gone. They care about biology. And I am her mother." She crosses her arms. "You don't get to erase me."

I feel Hailey step up behind me, but I keep my focus on Taylor, the weight of her threat sinking in. She's right. She has rights. But that doesn't mean I'm going to give up. Not after everything I've done to protect Addison.

"This isn't about you," I say. "This is about Addison, what's best for her. And what's best is for you to stay the hell away."

Taylor laughs. "You think you know what's best for her? What's so scary about me being part of her life? Why can't you consider that as something good for her? Are you worried I'll take her from you and move down to LA?"

"Take her to the U.S.?" My heart pounds in my chest. "You'll never take her."

"Well, I have every right to be here," she says.

"Taylor," Hailey interrupts. "You're right. And you should be here. Take a seat and get comfortable. It's going to be a while."

Taylor wipes a tear from her eye and huffs across the room.

Hailey turns to me.

"She's not going to take Addison," I insist.

Hailey nods, her eyes searching mine. "She only wants to be part of Addison's life. I think she wants what's best for her too. You just have to work together to agree on what that is."

"But she left. She just went down to LA for a job."

"Yes, but she was suffering from postpartum depression. She could have done a lot of things, but she took care of Addison. You hated your father for leaving you for too long. Don't do the same thing to Taylor your mother did to him."

I can see the compassion in Hailey's eyes, the silent strength that's always characterized her. She's not perfect, but she's a fierce advocate for my child. And I realize I'm not perfect either. I can't cut people out the moment I feel myself losing control. I've made a huge mistake, and I'm lucky Hailey's love for Addison has brought her back here.

I pull her into an embrace, wrapping my arms around her with a need to convey everything I've failed to say before. "I'm sorry," I murmur into her hair. "When I told you to leave, I'd panicked. I was scared, and I lashed out. You deserve more than this, more than just being Addison's nanny and waiting on me."

She pulls back slightly, enough for me to see her face, read the emotion there. "Caring for Addison, for you — it was more than a job."

I nod. "I know that, and I'm so grateful. I want you to be in our lives. I want to do this together."

She smiles, and when I take her hand, she doesn't pull it away.

We sit back down together, the seconds stretching into eternities. But Hailey keeps our fingers laced together.

"Hi." Sometime later, Griffin Martin's voice cuts through the fog of worry. His arms are laden with bags. "I brought some dinner for everyone."

I manage a tight smile. "Thanks, Griffin. That's... Thank you."

"Of course, man," he says, setting the food on a nearby table. His gaze meets mine, steady and reassuring. "Davis is the best pediatric cardiologist there is. And Cordelia is right there with him. Addison's in good hands."

I know he's right, but I still worry.

"Your little girl is going to be just fine," he assures me.

I nod, trying to draw comfort from his words as I take a sandwich. We don't talk much as we wait.

Kent and Chance, doctor friends from the ED, join us soon after, slipping onto the vinyl seats with quiet solidarity. I'm not used to being on this side of a surgery, and it's awful. Going forward, I need to be quicker to give families updates on my patients and be more thoughtful in my approach.

As the hours trudge by, even my mother appears. Her eyes are wet, the lines on her face deepening as she approaches. "I'm so sorry," she says, her voice hoarse with emotion.

"Mom…" It's all I can muster, the complexities of our relationship dwarfed by the current crisis.

She takes a seat as well, and then finally, Davis emerges. He has the telltale signs of fatigue around his eyes, but his smile… His smile tells me everything before his words do.

"Addison's going to be fine," he announces, and the tension breaks.

Relief crashes over me, and I can breathe. Really breathe. "Thank God," I exhale as my family erupts into cheers and hugs. Amidst the chaos, I look for Hailey, needing her to share this joy. But she's not beside me.

I scan the room, catching just a glimpse of her slipping out the door, her eyes red-rimmed, her expression unreadable. My heart tugs, but I'm rooted to the spot, surrounded by celebrating loved ones.

"Where are you going, Hailey?" I want to call after her, but the words don't come. Instead, as soon as I have a moment, I pull out my phone.

My hands shake a little as I dial her number. It rings and rings, a sound that grows hollower with each echo. The call diverts to voicemail, and her voice—bright and cheerful—feels like a punch in the gut. "You've reached Hailey Spencer. Sorry, I can't take your call right now…"

"Hailey, it's me," I start, but then I hesitate. What do I even say? *Please come back? I need you?* Instead, I end the call, unable to put into words the turmoil that's churning inside me.

My thumb hovers over the keypad. I type out a message, delete it, and type another one. They all seem wrong. Finally, a simple text forms beneath my fingers.

Me: Can we meet? There's so much I need to say.

I hit send, watching as the message hangs in digital space, waiting for the little *Delivered* to pop up beneath it, but it doesn't. Seconds stretch into minutes, and the silence from her end is deafening. My chest tightens. She's always quick to respond, always there when Addison or I need her. The absence of her reply is an ominous void that fills the room.

"Everything okay?" Griffin claps me on the shoulder with brotherly concern.

"Fine," I lie, slipping my phone into my pocket, trying to ignore the weight of it against my thigh. "Just sending an update out to others."

As the noise of relief continues to swirl through the surgical waiting room, I'm caught in a stillness, a private purgatory of waiting for a word that doesn't come.

CHAPTER 31

Hailey

Out in the hallway, away from Christian's family, I look down at my phone, which indicates a new voice message. Addison is going to be okay, which fills me with relief. I'm so grateful to hear that.

But I need to attend to the matter at hand, whatever it may be, so I press the phone to my ear, even as it pings again. My heart thunders in my ears as the message begins to play. I don't recognize the number, but the dread settling in my gut tells me Franklin is back to harass me.

However, the voice that follows isn't the one I expect. It's firm, detached. "This is Detective Larsen from the precinct. We've arrested Franklin Richards on charges of theft and fraud and wanted to let you know. If you could call us, we'd appreciate it." He leaves a number where I can reach him.

My hand trembles uncontrollably, the phone slipping in my grip as I collapse onto a hard-plastic chair near the hospital's main entrance. *Arrested? Franklin?* How could this be real?

I look back toward the OR waiting area, but there's no need for me to be here now. I need to focus on my own life for the time being. I race back to my temporary apartment and sit on my bed to return the call from Detective Larsen.

"Thank you for returning my call," he says once I've introduced myself. "During our last interview with Franklin Richards, we learned that after leaving your residence, Mr. Richards cohabitated with another individual."

A woman—her image flits across my mind, faceless, unknowing.

"We also spoke with her, and she indicated that at one point she'd found a substantial amount of cash among his possessions."

I gasp. *A stack of cash.* My stomach churns, nausea rising. "Where did he get that money?"

"Mr. Richards claimed the money came from your grandmother." There's a pause. "He indicated he was merely safeguarding it."

I let out a humorless laugh. "Safeguarding, right."

"And—" I hear paper shuffling. "—we've determined that while you were temporarily living elsewhere—"

Christian's place, I mentally correct.

"—Mr. Richards entered your apartment and concealed the cash within a secret compartment inside an antique desk. Then recently he broke into your storage unit and found the compartment was empty."

"So, he was safeguarding it, but he hid it, and then broke in to get it from me?"

"That's what he's saying."

"The desk is my grandma's old writing desk. He's been telling me he was missing something for a while now but wouldn't tell me what it was. I searched through everything in the storage unit but didn't find anything."

The officer goes on to tell me that Franklin's food truck was all a fraud. He took my money and still has it, or he did until it went missing.

This is what he's been looking for. The money he stole from me.

I shake my head. "My grandmother left me a small insurance policy, about seventy thousand dollars, when she died. Franklin had the food truck idea and convinced me we could use it to build our future. He told me he lost everything when the truck failed, but now, you're telling me he just kept it?"

"That seems to be the case," Detective Larsen confirms. "Can we meet in the morning at your storage unit and complete a search for the missing money? If you have proof that the money was yours, it will make our case much stronger. When would you be available to meet us?"

"I'll be there. What time works for you?"

We confirm our plans, and my head is spinning. I can't believe this. Franklin lied about everything, and I believed him. What does that say about me?

When the rideshare drops me off at the storage place the next morning, Detective Larsen and another officer greet me, and I lead the way to my unit. They help me move boxes, and we free my grandmother's desk. "It has lots of little compartments and secret places, but I checked them after he told me I had something that was his," I explain. "I didn't find anything."

But now I'll try again. I stand in front of Grandma's antique desk and slide the top drawer open slowly. My fingers trace the grooves, hesitating over each familiar bump and ridge. I press, and there's a soft *click,* barely audible, but it vibrates through me. The false bottom shifts, lifting slightly. My heart stops. Slowly, I ease the panel out. "Empty," I whisper. It's like the room deflates around me, the breath I'd been holding releasing in a shaky exhale.

Detective Larsen shifts behind me, but he says nothing. I should tell him there's nothing here to find, but something holds me there, rooted to the spot. My fingers move, almost instinctively, over the smooth wood beneath the panel. *Nothing.* And then—a sliver of white catches the light. My heart lurches in my chest.

There, wedged so deeply that I almost missed it, is an envelope hidden in a corner. My hand shakes as I reach for it, my fingers struggling to grasp it well enough to tug it free. It's thicker than I expected. Heavier. The paper crackles in my hands, and for a second, I can't breathe. Slowly, I unfold the envelope, and there it is, a stack of cash, crisp and unmistakable. My stomach drops.

"Looks like you found something." Larsen's voice cuts through the silence, but I barely register it. All I can see is betrayal staring back at me, as real as the money Franklin stole.

My fingers tighten around the envelope. This is it. The proof. The final nail in the coffin of whatever trust I had left. A wave of disbelief and fury surges through my veins. I was so blind. How could I have missed this? How could I have trusted him?

"Is this...?" I start, unable to finish.

"Did your grandmother give this money to Franklin?" Detective Larsen asks.

I shake my head. "No. She left it to me."

"If you can prove that, the money's yours," the other officer confirms with a nod. "You can keep it."

I walk over to the box that holds the life insurance policy and her will and pull out the letter from the insurance company that accompanied the check. "Would you like to see the bank deposit and the name of my banker who worked with Franklin on the food truck deal?" I ask. "Her name is Ping Wu, and she helped us through the whole thing."

The detective takes her number from me and steps out. My hands tremble. Looking at all my grandmother's things, I want to live with them again. I want to keep her with me. She took me in when my parents didn't want me. She championed my dreams. And looking at the desk, I believe she made sure I found the money so I could use it the way it was intended.

Detective Larsen returns and hands me the envelope. "Ms. Wu verified your version of the events. This is your money, and it's in your storage unit. You may keep it."

My hands tremble as I clutch the envelope, feeling the weight of my grandmother's love—and her foresight. School had been a distant thought, a path I walked away from, but now, it beckons me again with newfound urgency. It's what she wanted for me, and I find it's what I want for myself.

Later, alone in the quiet of my temporary apartment, I spread out the college catalog on the tiny kitchen table. Pages filled with potential courses and career paths fan out before me, and I settle on the section for real estate studies. I'm still drawn to real estate. This could be my new beginning. I trace the requirements for the program, mentally ticking off each step I'd need to take. *I can do this.*

The phone rings. "Miss Spencer, this is the front desk. An envelope was just delivered." His tone suggests curiosity, but he doesn't pry further.

"Thank you, I'll be right down," I reply.

My pulse quickens as I make my way downstairs. *What now?*

The clerk gives me a nod as I approach, pushing the mysterious envelope across the counter toward me. It's unassuming, white and perfectly sealed, yet it feels like it weighs a ton in my hands. My name is written on the front in familiar handwriting, and my heart skips a beat. *Christian.*

I thank him and return upstairs. In the quiet apartment, I slip a finger under the flap, breaking the seal. The contents slide out, and I unfold the letter, the script dancing before my eyes.

Dear Hailey,

I've been staring at this blank page for what feels like hours, trying to find the right words. I realize now that I was wrong to push you away, to accuse you of causing the trouble with Taylor. You did not, of course, and I'm deeply sorry for the pain I've caused you. It was a terrible mistake, one I regret more than anything.

I appreciate you coming to check on Addison during her surgery. I know you care deeply for her. The house feels empty without you. I miss you, Hailey. Addison misses you too. Your absence has left a void nothing else can fill.

I was wrong to let my fears and insecurities drive you away, and you deserve so much better than the way I treated you. I can only hope that it's not too late to make things right.

I understand if you need time, if you're not ready to forgive me yet. But please know that I am truly sorry, from the bottom of my heart.

I want to make things right. I want to be the man you deserve, the man who cherishes you and stands by your side through everything.

Please, Hailey, if you can find it in your heart to forgive me, I promise to do everything I can to make up for the pain I've caused.

You are different than any woman I've ever known, and I can't imagine a future without you in it.

With all my love and much regret,
Christian

Emotions rush through me—anger, sorrow, love, and an undeniable flicker of hope. I sit back, the letter cradled in my lap. Christian's plea hangs in the balance, reaching out across the chasm his own fears carved.

CHAPTER 32

Christian

Nearly a week after Addison's surgery, I push open the familiar doors of the my father's home, the weight of the unacknowledged letter heavy in my chest. Dana has been helping me spend time with Addison just out of the hospital until I can find a new nanny, and when I arrive, Dana's sitting on the bed, skimming over a magazine. Addison is nestled against her, chubby fingers gripping a well-loved stuffed rabbit.

Addison looks up, her face brightening at the sight of me. "He he he he he," she babbles.

Dana shakes her head gently. "No, sweetheart, Hailey isn't here." She lifts her gaze to mine, her expression hardening. "I can't believe how you've screwed this up, Christian."

"I know. I know," I repeat. It feels like all I've been doing is confessing how badly I messed up, but it doesn't change anything. It doesn't bring her back. I clear my throat. "I'm trying to fix it. But she won't talk to me. I was hoping maybe you could reach out to her? See if she'll listen?" I hate how small and pathetic I sound, but I can't help it.

Dana sighs. "You can't expect me to clean up your mess. You need to figure this out. What is it you actually want?"

My heart sinks. Of course, she's right. How could I expect her to fix this for me? She warned us both. This is my mess, my failure.

But what if I can't fix it? What if it's too late? Has Hailey already decided she's done with me for good? The thought sends a fresh wave of panic through me. I can't lose her.

"Please, Dana," I say. "I just... I don't know what else to do. I have to make this right. For Addison. For me."

Dana's lips press together, and for a moment, I think she might relent. But then she shakes her head, firm and final. "This is exactly why I didn't want you to get involved with her."

Turning away, I find my father in the doorway, his arms crossed, his brow furrowed with concern. He's been standing there for how long? Watching me flounder?

He gestures for me to follow him, and even though my instincts scream to walk the other way, I find myself trailing behind him. I'm not sure I want to hear what he has to say.

"Talk to me," he says when we reach his office. "What's going on?"

"Dad, I..." My throat tightens, the words getting stuck behind a wall of pride. "I had an emotional reaction, and I screwed up," I finally admit, the words scraping out like shards of glass. "I don't know if I can fix it."

He nods. "I know what it feels like to think you're doing the right thing by pushing someone away. I always thought...it was better to let go than hurt you by fighting a war I didn't think I could win." His eyes drop to the desk between us. "But that doesn't mean it was right. I let your mother take you because I thought it would be easier on you. But all I did was leave behind what mattered most."

His eyes lift to meet mine. "I never wanted to walk away from you, Christian. And I see now that what's best is fighting for the people you love, even when you think you might fail."

This is what I've been missing, what I've been too blind to

see. I've been so afraid of failing Addison—of failing Hailey, for that matter—and of not being enough, that I pushed her away.

"So, what do I do?" I ask. "How do I fix this?"

My father leans back in his chair. "You go to her. You tell her what you just told me. That you're scared, that you're not perfect, but that you're willing to fight for her, for Addison, for your family. Make sure she knows you're not going anywhere this time."

"What if she doesn't want this?"

"You don't get to control that," Dad says. "But you have to fight for what you want. I've seen the way she looks at you and Addison. She loves you both. You need to remind her."

"Thanks, Dad," I say, feeling a new kind of weight, one that's not as crushing but still there. A responsibility. "I'll do whatever it takes."

He gives me a nod, and I see it in his eyes. I can be the man Hailey needs.

"You win by trying," he says. "Even when you don't know if you'll succeed."

I swallow hard. He's right. I've been running from this, from my own fear of failure, but running has only made things worse.

A long breath shudders out of me, and I close my eyes for a second. Maybe this is it. If I don't go to her, if I don't fight for her and the life we were creating together, I'll never forgive myself.

Dana's in the living room as I walk out, her eyes like steel, but when she sees me, something softens within them.

"I'm going to get Hailey back," I tell her. "Can you watch Addison just a bit longer?"

Dana wraps her arms around me in an unexpected embrace. "I'm sorry for being so hard on you," she whispers. "Hailey deserves someone who will fight for her, and maybe that really is you."

I nod. Her words light a fire in my chest, burning away the remnants of doubt. I say my goodbyes, and with purpose in every step, I drive to the address the private investigator gave me, Hailey's current home.

My heart hammers in my chest as I park and go inside, and it continues as I stand in front of Hailey's door in the rundown executive apartment building. I stare at the worn wood, my hand trembling slightly as I raise it to knock. *This is it.* There's no turning back now. I've rehearsed what I'll say all the way here, but it feels inadequate, too small for the enormity of what I need to tell her.

The sound of my knock echoes down the hallway, impossibly loud in the silence. I hold my breath as I wait, tense with anticipation. Fear creeps in again, whispering that I've made a mistake, that she won't want to hear what I have to say.

What if she doesn't open the door? What if she's done with me?

But before I can sink too deep into my doubts, the door swings open, and there she is — Hailey.

For a moment, everything stops. She's standing in front of me, her eyes wide with surprise, and just seeing her takes the breath from my lungs. God, I've missed her. The way her hair falls around her face, the way her eyes search mine. It hits me all over again how much I love her, how much I've lost by pushing her away.

"Christian?" Her voice is soft, hesitant. "Is Addison okay?"

"She's fine—"

"Then why are you here?"

The question is simple but so heavy. She deserves an answer, but how do I explain? My mouth feels dry, the words lodged in my throat. I try to steady myself, but there's a desperation rising inside me, a need to make this right, to make her understand how sorry I am.

"Can I come in?" I ask, the plea evident in my voice. I don't just want to be near her. I *need* to be near her. I need to see her, to explain, to beg for another chance, even if I don't deserve it.

For a moment, she just stares at me, her fingers gripping the edge of the door. I can see the hesitation in her eyes, the uncertainty, and it tears me apart.

And then, she steps back, the door opening wider. Relief

washes over me, but it's tangled with fear because, now, there's no running from this. No more walls to hide behind. This is it.

I step inside, my heart still pounding as I face her. The apartment is small and filled with cheap furniture and a faint musty smell.

Hailey crosses her arms. "What do you want?" she asks. There's no anger in her voice, no bitterness. Just exhaustion. And that's almost worse. It tells me how deeply I've hurt her, how tired she is of waiting for me to be the man she deserves.

I swallow hard. "I'm sorry," I say. "For everything. For pushing you away. For blaming you when I shouldn't have. For being too scared to let you in."

Her eyes flicker, a tiny movement, but it gives me hope. Maybe she's listening.

"I was an idiot," I continue, my chest tightening as I pour out the words I've been holding back for so long. "I thought I was protecting you by keeping you at a distance. I thought I didn't deserve you, and maybe I don't, but I can't lose you, Hailey. I love you. I've always loved you. And I'm so sorry for not showing you that when it mattered."

The silence that follows is unbearable. I watch her face, searching for any sign of what she's feeling, but her expression remains unreadable. My heart is in my throat, my pulse pounding in my ears. If she rejects me now, if she tells me it's too late… I don't know what I'll do.

Finally, after what feels like an eternity, she takes a breath. "I don't know if I can do this again. You hurt me. You blamed me for everything and threw me out like I didn't matter," she says softly.

I feel the sharp sting of regret deep in my chest. "I know," I whisper. "I know I hurt you, and I'll spend the rest of my life trying to make it up to you if you'll let me. Just…please, give me another chance. I'll be better. I'll show you I can be the man you need."

Her eyes meet mine, and for the first time, I see conflict there, the love she's still holding on to warring with the pain I caused.

"I don't know if I can trust you," she admits, her voice breaking slightly.

My chest tightens, but I force myself to speak. "I'll earn it, Hailey. Every day, I'll earn it. I'll fight for you. I'll fight for us."

The tears in her eyes finally spill over, and she wipes them away, but it's enough. It's enough to tell me there's still something between us, something worth saving.

Slowly, tentatively, she steps toward me, her arms still crossed as if to shield herself. "You don't get to break my heart again," she says, her voice quiet but firm.

I shake my head, my own eyes stinging with emotion. "I won't. I swear, I won't."

And then, in the space between heartbeats, she takes the final step, and I reach for her, pulling her into my arms. The relief, the love, the fear—it all crashes over me at once, and I hold her tight, burying my face in her hair. "I love you," I whisper, my voice cracking. "I love you so much."

Her arms slowly uncross, and I feel them wrap around me, hesitant at first, but then tighter, as if she's been waiting for this as long as I have. "I love you too," she whispers, her breath warm against my neck, and it's everything. It's everything I didn't know I needed.

Her lips find mine for a kiss that's forgiveness and longing all wrapped into one.

With eager hands and hearts, we fumble, pulling at each other's clothes, peeling away the layers between us. Each discarded garment is another step toward healing, toward becoming whole again. Her touch ignites every nerve ending, and I feel reborn under her fingertips.

I cradle her face in my hands, the warmth of her skin igniting a fire within me. Our lips part, and I taste the salt of her tears, the sweet urgency of her need. As we fall into the embrace of the bed, the world shrinks to the space where our bodies meet.

I move above her. My movements are tender, a silent promise to cherish every inch of her being, to right the wrongs with the gentlest touch.

Her fingers dig into my shoulders, her legs wrapping

around me, drawing me closer, deeper. Her breath is hot against my ear, and she shifts beneath me, a silent plea for more than this languid rhythm.

"I can't... Not like this..." Hailey gasps between ragged breaths. "I need you—hard and fast, now. We can have slow...later."

The honesty in her words strikes a chord in me, awakening a fervent cadence. I nod. This isn't just about physical release. It's a reclaiming, a fierce connection that screams of life and passion and all the turbulent love that courses between us.

With a newfound urgency, I comply, my body moving in powerful, rhythmic thrusts. The sound of our union fills the room, and she meets every drive, a perfect counterpoint to my own relentless pursuit of the release that will send us toppling into oblivion together.

"Hailey," I cry out, my voice a rough growl of devotion. In this moment, there's no holding back. It's all unleashed in the most primal of dances.

And later, when the world comes back into focus, when our breaths slow and our limbs entwine with the promise of forever, we will explore the depths of each other slowly, fully, with the reverence of a love that has been tested, broken, and forged anew. But for now, this is what we need, a fierce affirmation that we are alive and together.

CHAPTER 33

Hailey

The balloons bob against the ceiling, a rainbow of colors that Addison's wide eyes try to follow. She rests in my arms, her fingers gripping my shirt as if I'm the only anchor in this sea of faces. Today is all about her, her first birthday celebrated right on schedule. Christian has gotten it perfect, down to the last detail, even though Taylor remains a wild card, having vanished after Addison's surgery. I know he invited her today, though, and at least her absence means her case for full custody is dead.

"Can you believe she's one already?" Christian murmurs, his hand brushing over Addison's soft curls.

"Time flies," I reply.

We started over after he came to me last month. We're true partners in Addison's care this time, and I know this is where I'm meant to be — Addison's caregiver and Christian my lover.

Addison wriggles, her attention caught by the shiny foil of a balloon string within reach. I adjust her in my arms, and she immediately settles, her body molding to mine. It seems she, too, has made her preference clear, choosing the security of my embrace over the jostling group that has come to celebrate her.

In this room full of people, it's as if Addison and I exist in our own bubble. Her trust in me fills me with warmth. As Christian returns to us, I know in our own way, we're a family.

The flicker of the candle on the birthday cake catches Addison's wide-eyed gaze, and a round of "Happy Birthday" fills the room. I help her, and together we blow out the candle. Smoke wafts up, and the room erupts in applause and laughter.

I put her in her highchair and smile as Addison digs her fingers into the soft pink icing, smearing it across her cheeks in her excitement.

"Look at you two," Christian chuckles, snapping pictures. "A pair of cake monsters."

I laugh, my own hands just as sticky and smeared as Addison's. "It's a new look for us."

"Very avant garde," he teases.

Addison's giggles are contagious, but they slow down to yawns soon enough. She's had her fill of excitement, and now, the sugar crash comes calling. I carry her up to her nursery, her head resting against my shoulder, leaving a sweet, sticky mark on my skin.

Once she's settled in her crib, her breathing even and calm, I slip away to wash off the remnants of her celebration. I wipe away the frosting so at least I won't stick to our remaining guests.

"Was gonna say I'd happily volunteer to clean that off," Christian says.

His tone brings a flush to my face. "Maybe you can frost me and lick it away later tonight?" I say, grinning.

Freshened up and changed, I descend the stairs, returning to the murmur of the ongoing party. Pausing by the window, I catch sight of Taylor standing across the street next to a tree. She looks lost.

I step outside, the cool air wrapping around me as I cross the street toward her. Christian and I have talked about this. If she's in, we're in, but she's got to make the decision.

"Hey," I greet her, my voice gentle. "Addison just went

down for a nap, but you're welcome to join the party. I know Christian invited you."

Her eyes flit nervously, but I see something else there too — hope, maybe? A desire to be part of this despite everything.

"Are you sure?"

"Very sure," I confirm with a nod. "Come on."

Together, we walk back to Christian's townhouse. The door opens to a scene of casual festivity, and I feel it, the subtle shift in the room as we enter. This is a moment, a turning point. And whatever happens next, it starts here, now, with an invitation and a tentative step across the threshold.

I reach out, my hand hovering between us. It's an offering of peace in the uncertainty that surrounds Taylor. She hesitates for a mere second before she joins me inside.

Christian approaches with a smile. "Taylor, thank you for coming," he says. He takes a moment to introduce her to the cluster of family and friends gathered. "This is Addison's mother."

The words hang in the air, and Taylor nods, acknowledging the title. They all shake hands, share polite smiles.

The party resumes its gentle hum, but an hour or so later, Addison fusses through the monitor. Her schedule is nowhere to be found today. My heart tugs me upstairs, and Taylor follows. Addison's big blue eyes flicker open, still hazy from sleep. Her arms tighten around me as I lift her, hands gripping my shirt, searching for the comfort she knows. "Hey, baby girl," I murmur, brushing a kiss on her forehead. She lets out a small sigh, but I can feel the uncertainty in the way her body tenses when she notices we're not alone.

Taylor stands a few steps behind me, watching us, her hands fidgeting at her sides. "Addison," I whisper gently, "this is your mommy."

Addison's arms tighten around my neck, and my heart clenches. We have a long way to go. But I can't ignore the fact that Taylor is her mother. No matter how much I've tried to protect Addison, no matter how much I've stepped in to fill the gaps, I can't erase that.

"Happy birthday, sweet girl," Taylor says. She pulls out a stuffed bear with a pink ribbon around its neck and hands it to her.

Addison's eyes light up.

"That's for you," I reply. I shift Addison in my arms, feeling her small body press closer to mine.

Taylor's eyes are fixed on her. "Can I…" Her voice is hesitant. "Can I hold her?"

I look down at Addison, her face pressed against my shoulder, and my heart nearly explodes. I glance at Taylor again. She's here. She's showing up. That has to count for something. "It's okay," I whisper to Addison, rubbing her back. "Mommy wants to hold you."

"It's okay," Taylor repeats as I hand her over.

Addison looks up at Taylor, her wide blue eyes filled with a quiet curiosity.

Taylor lets out a shaky breath, her lips trembling as she holds Addison close. "Hi, sweetie," she whispers. "I've missed you so much." Taylor looks up at me. "Thank you," she says quietly.

I nod, swallowing the lump in my throat. "We'll figure it out."

As dusk paints the sky in shades of pink and purple, the laughter and chatter from the party dwindle, and finally, it's just the four of us left.

"I know I'm not ready to take any custody of her," Taylor admits. "I have…a lot to figure out." She looks away, her fingers absentmindedly tracing Addison's back. "The postpartum depression hit me hard, but I am seeing someone about it."

"Thank you for being honest," I say, and I mean it. There's bravery in her vulnerability.

Taylor nods. "But I'd like to be involved somehow. Babysitting, maybe? Just to start?"

Christian squeezes my shoulder, and I nod. It's a small step, but it's something, a chance for healing, for building bridges. "We can start with a night out." he offers.

"I'd like that." Taylor smiles and pats Addison. "We can have a fun night together."

Christian looks at me with an adventurous glint in his eyes. "And we can work our way up to taking off for a few days."

My heart leaps. "To wine country?" I venture.

Christian shakes his head, a smirk tugging at his lips. "I was thinking bigger than that."

I gaze at him a moment longer. We're wrapped up in each other and the anticipation of adventure, ready to work together for Addison.

EPILOGUE

Christian

Six months later

The wheels of the taxi slow to a stop, the faint screech of the brakes blending into the sounds of the city. Outside the window, Paris stretches before us, alive with a rhythm all its own in the cool evening air.

As I step out, Hailey follows, her eyes wide as she takes it all in — the flickering streetlights casting golden halos on the cobblestone.

Above us, the iconic wrought-iron balconies of the Georges V Hotel are draped in lush ivy, their black railings gleaming in the streetlamps. There's a timeless elegance to the place, as though Paris itself has been waiting for us to arrive, ready to unveil its secrets. I slip my hand into Hailey's, feeling her fingers tighten, and for a moment, we just stand there, absorbing the beauty around us.

In her wide eyes, I see the reflection of the city — the Eiffel Tower, just visible in the distance, its lights twinkling against the velvet sky, the Seine winding its way lazily through the heart of Paris, and the soft glow of cafés lining its banks. The air is cool, crisp.

Hailey leans into me. "I've always dreamed of this," she whispers, as though speaking too loudly might break the spell of the moment. "Being here with you."

I squeeze her hand. Here, in the heart of Paris, it's as if the world outside doesn't exist—only us, this city, and the promise of what's to come.

As we step through the grand entrance of the Georges V, the warmth of the lobby envelops us, a contrast to the cool night air. Crystal chandeliers hang from the ceiling, casting soft, golden light over the rich velvet drapes and marble floors. Hailey's eyes sparkle, and I can't help but smile. Paris has that effect. It makes everything seem possible.

"Can you believe we're actually here?" Hailey's voice brims with wonder as we step through the ornate doors into the hotel lobby.

I smile at her enthusiasm. And I remind myself that back in Vancouver, Addison is in good hands with Taylor, who has spent the last six months gaining strength and confidence and battling her demons. I can't believe how far we've all come. The thought brings relief, allowing me to immerse myself fully in this moment with Hailey.

Our suite is a dream, draped in lavish fabrics and adorned with golden accents, but it's the view from the balcony that steals Hailey's breath. She steps outside, her grin stretching ear to ear as the Eiffel Tower stands proudly against the skyline.

"Look at that view, Christian!" Hailey exclaims. She's already flipping through her meticulously planned itinerary on her phone. "We have to visit the Louvre, Notre Dame, Montmartre, and—"

"You've scheduled every minute," I chuckle, following her onto the balcony. Her attention to detail is one of the many things I adore about her, but I want this trip to be an exploration, not an expedition. "Are you planning to storm the Bastille? Should I start calling you Madame Tyrant?"

She swats my arm, her laughter mingling with the soft Parisian breeze. "Okay, okay, maybe I got a little carried away. But there's so much to see, and we're only here for ten days!"

"Let's take it one day at a time, and remember, whatever we don't get to is another reason to come back." I wrap my arms around her from behind, cherishing the feel of her against me. "Let's let Paris reveal itself to us, without a plan."

"Spontaneity from Mr. Has-Every-Minute-Scheduled?" Hailey teases, turning in my arms to face me. Her eyes are alight with mirth, and I lean down to capture her lips with mine.

"Only with you," I whisper against her lips.

The warmth of her body against mine is the only anchor I need. "I love you."

I slip my hand into my pocket, fingers curling around the small box that holds the key to our future. As I pull it out, Hailey's eyes widen, a gasp parting her lips.

This moment—it's everything I've been waiting for, everything I've been building up to. But now that I'm standing here, the weight of it hits me harder than I expected. It's not just about the ring or the perfect backdrop of Paris. It's about the life we've been building, the love we've fought for. The woman in front of me has been my anchor and my light, even when I didn't deserve it. She's been the constant in a world that's thrown everything at us.

I take a deep breath, my pulse racing. "There's something I need to say." I begin, my voice low, almost trembling with the weight of the moment.

I drop to one knee, and all I can see is her. "You've changed everything for me. You've brought light into my life and into Addison's life in ways I never thought possible. I was lost without you, and I don't ever want to go back to that. You've made me a better man."

I pause, my eyes searching hers. "I don't want to spend another minute without you. Not as just the woman I love, but as my wife and a mother to Addison. Will you marry me?"

The words hang in the air between us, and for a split second, everything stops—the sounds of Paris fade, the world around us blurs. All I can focus on is her, and the look in her eyes as she stares down at me.

Her lips part, but no words come out. Instead, a single tear slips down her cheek, and she presses a hand to her mouth, as if trying to contain the flood of emotions rushing through her. I wait, every nerve in my body on edge, afraid to move, afraid to breathe, afraid of what might happen next.

And then she nods.

"Yes," she whispers. "Yes, I'll marry you."

Relief crashes over me. I feel my heart swell, bigger than I ever thought possible as I slip the ring onto her finger, my hands trembling. The diamond catches the light, sparkling like the city around us, but nothing compares to the brightness in her eyes.

Hailey pulls me to my feet, her arms wrapping around me as I crush her against my chest. We stand there, holding each other, the city of love sprawling beneath us. But in this moment, it's just us. The world feels small, the future wide open.

"I love you," I whisper into her hair, my voice thick with emotion. "I love you so much."

She looks at me, her eyes glistening. "I love you too," she says, and it's enough. It's everything.

We kiss, the sweetness melting into the Parisian night, and I know without a doubt that this is exactly where we're meant to be, together, with our future stretching out in front of us, brighter than the city lights that shimmer below.

Overwhelmed by the moment, we return to the suite. My hands, steady and sure, find the hem of her dress, lifting it over her head in one fluid motion, leaving her gloriously bare before me.

With reverence, I worship her body, my mouth trailing kisses, licks, and gentle bites across the expanse of her breasts. Each touch elicits soft moans, stoking the fire that burns within us both. Her skin tastes of adventure and promise, a flavor I'm addicted to.

"Christian," she whispers, her voice thick with desire. Her hands roam over me, seeking, stroking my cock with an urgency that mirrors my own. Her pleading gaze locks onto mine, her words a sweet torment. "Please, I need you."

There's no holding back. Her plea is my command, my purpose. I'm hers, completely and irrevocably. And tonight, under the watchful eye of the Eiffel Tower, I'll show her just how much she means to me.

I lower myself between Hailey's thighs, my breath hot against her skin. The city lights cast a soft glow through the sheer curtains, but all I see is her, all I want is the taste of her. My lips find the tender bud of her clit, and she arches beneath me, a gasp escaping as I suck gently, strumming my tongue over her in a rhythm that has her hips undulating.

"Christian…" Her voice is a sweet melody, laden with desire.

One finger slips inside her, easy and smooth, followed by another, curving to find that spot that makes her legs tremble. She's wet and warm, and I stretch her slowly with three fingers, just the way she likes it. The room fills with the sound of our connection, wet noises that speak of the need between us. As I bring her to the brink, her hands clutch the sheets, her body wound tight like a spring.

"Please," she begs, her eyes wild. "I need you inside me, now."

God, how could I deny her anything? I laugh softly. "Every time you ask," I assure her, my voice husky.

Positioning myself at her entrance, I part her farther, taking in the sight of her laid bare for me. "You have the most beautiful pussy I've ever seen," I breathe.

I push inside her, and she groans, a deep, primal sound that vibrates through me. This is where I'm meant to be, nestled within her embrace, the world outside our Parisian haven fading into nothingness. I feel at home here, in the warmth of her body, as if every moment before this was just a journey leading to her.

"Christian…" Hailey's voice is heavy with desire.

"Shh," I whisper, even as I pivot inside her, holding her legs wide to delve deeper. "Just feel." My strokes are deliberate, synchronized with the rapid beat of my heart. I watch her face, the way her eyes flutter closed and lips part in silent pleasure.

"Touch yourself for me," I murmur, guiding her hands to her breasts. She complies, twisting and pulling on her nipples, the sight stoking the fire within me. I squeeze her tight, claiming her with every fiber of my being.

The rhythm builds, a crescendo of movement and sensation, and I'm getting close, so damn close. The pressure mounts, radiating from deep within. Hailey meets my gaze, vulnerability and passion intermingled in her eyes.

I want to time our climaxes perfectly, and I know we're both close. I strum her clit, staring into her eyes. As her climax reaches its peak, she clenches me.

"I love you," she breathes, the simple confession slicing through the haze of lust.

Her words detonate something inside me, and I'm lost. "Hailey!" I groan out my love as I spill into her. It's a profound surrender, the kind that only happens when two souls are irreversibly entwined.

Exhausted yet exhilarated, we collapse into the bed's embrace, our limbs tangled as we catch our breath. I'm filled with a profound sense of peace. Holding Hailey close, I press my lips to her forehead in a lingering kiss, breathing in the scent that is uniquely hers.

"Paris has so much in store for us," I tell her, my voice a low murmur against the quiet of the room. "And I'm just fine if we spend the next ten days in the room preparing to give Addison a baby brother."

"You want a boy?"

I shrug. "I want a house full."

Hailey shifts, her body still flush with mine, and she tilts her head to look at me, an impish glint in her eyes. Her tongue darts out, playfully licking the side of my face, sending a shiver down my spine.

"That sounds perfect," she says. "But right now, I have other things in mind."

I chuckle. It's all the response I need to give. Paris, with its endless treasures, will be there tomorrow, but right now, it's just Hailey and me, and whatever "other things" she has in store.

Thank you for reading *Doctor Tyrant*. If you'd like to read a scene that was deleted because it was so hot it had to be moved out. Warning! I suggest a cold glass of something and a fan to cool you down. You can download it here: https://bookhip.com/TSSLCSQ

Next up, meet the Paradise brothers.

The Paradise family vineyard was founded over a century ago by Greyson's great-great-great-great-great grandfather, and it's been the family's pride ever since. But as time passes, so do family bonds, and buried secrets have a way of coming to the surface. Each brother carries his own share of the family's history and burdens. From Greyson, the determined emergency department doctor, to Beckett, the grumpy cardiologist, to Ryker, ready to take over their mother's family practice, and Kingston, the reclusive orthopedist and inventor. The Paradise brothers struggle to protect the vineyard's legacy while finding their own paths…and love stories along the way.

I'm so excited to bring you into this world of wine, romance, and rivalry, inspired by my recent visit to the Okanagan Valley (British Columbia's wine valley). This series dives deep into the Paradise family, their legacy, and the challenges that come with running a family-owned vineyard and practicing medicine.

I'll share more details as we get closer to launch, but for now, let's raise a glass to love, legacy, and a fresh start! Below is a sneak peek, and you can watch for the series beginning in April 2025.

Greyson

I stand at the nurses' station, flipping through a chart. The morning's been dragging its feet like molasses in winter. After my shift, I'm driving to Vancouver to catch a ferry to Victoria. As I look around, I see a queasy teen clutching a bucket nearby, a victim of last night's expired takeout. Across the room, a toddler's screech pierces the air — ear infection, no doubt.

My phone is full of unread messages in the family chat. I scan through them quickly. They're mostly between my father and younger sister, Teagan, arguing over last year's frost. Teagan says the pinot grapes might not survive. Dad insists they will.

I scroll through, noting the tension in Teagan's clipped responses. Elise, her best friend and our vintner's daughter, wouldn't let her make that call lightly. She's preparing to take over when her father retires. The thought nags at me. If the grapes don't bounce back, what does that mean for the vineyard? For our family's legacy?

I shove the phone back into my pocket, the weight of responsibility lingering. Another family burden I don't have time to unpack.

"Greyson," calls Vivian Daniels, a nurse in the emergency room, snapping me from my thoughts with her velvety voice. "You're looking particularly sharp today." She leans against the counter, one eyebrow cocked playfully. I glance over the rims of my glasses, catching the playful twinkle in her eye.

Vivian and I tangled in the sheets ages ago — a mistake wrapped in tequila and poor judgment — but that ship has sailed. I don't do encores, a rule that's kept my life uncomplicated.

"Thanks, Vivian. I'm off to Vancouver this afternoon for the Breakthrough MedTalks conference."

"That's right. You're speaking at that conference. Beckett said it was a big deal."

Beckett is my younger brother and a cardiologist here in the hospital. He was excited when I was asked to speak about emergency medicine to clinicians from around the world.

I'm about to return to endless paperwork when the intercom crackles to life.

"Greyson, we've got an ambo en route," the nurse in charge announces. "Three patients, collision with farm equipment over at Dempsey Vineyards."

I fight the urge to curse. *Dempsey.* The name hits like a splinter under my skin, sharp and irritating. Memories of the last time we stood toe-to-toe at a wine council meeting flash through my mind — Dad's voice rising, mine trying to mediate, and old man Dempsey walking out in a huff. I shove it aside.

There's no room for grudges here, no space for the weight of history. These are lives in my hands, and no family feud will stop me from giving them everything I've got. Still, the name lingers like the bitter aftertaste of bad wine.

Still, the word *Dempsey* buzzes in my mind like an insect, each syllable dragging the past to the surface where I can't afford to see it.

Vivian's eyes meet mine, flirtation instantly replaced with professional resolve. No more stolen moments or playful banter; this is where we excel, where every second counts.

"Looks like our break is over," she says, her tone all business now.

"Wouldn't want it any other way," I reply. There's work to be done, and Paradise needs us ready.

I slip into a paper gown, its crinkle a prelude to urgency. With Vivian beside me, the team converges around us, a swarm of focused energy ready to combat the chaos that's about to burst through our doors.

"Let's go," I murmur, and we fall into the rhythm of preparation. Gloves snap against wrists, and my nerves crackle, an electric current of anticipation running through my veins. I hear the wail of the approaching ambulance, a siren song for the wounded.

The bay doors fly open with a clang, and we push forward, ready to receive. "What've you got?" I call, my voice cutting through the din.

Warren Sweeny, EMT and familiar face in times of crisis, emerges from the back of the ambulance. A gurney rattles out. "Thirty-seven-year-old male," Warren reports. "Hit by a dirt bike out in the vineyard. BP is ninety over sixty. Pulse one-ten." Even as he speaks, my eyes take in the scene — the pallor of the patient's skin, the crimson that stains the gurney sheets.

"Head trauma," Warren continues, pointing to a swath of bandages attempting to hold back the bleeding. "Looks like a concussion."

"Got it." My response is automatic, clinical. "On it, Warren." I motion to Will Stewart, one of the sharper tools in our shed. He's new enough to be eager, but seasoned enough to know when to ask questions—a rare mix in a trainee. 'Take the head trauma,' I instruct, meeting his steady gaze. He nods, all business, and wheels the man away to CT without hesitation. As he moves, I catch the glimmer of a surgical handbook tucked into his scrub pocket. Will never stops trying to be better, and that's exactly why he's on this team.

Will nods, all business, and wheels the man away to CT, leaving blood droplets on the shining floor.

"Let's keep moving, people," I urge, scrubbing the sight from my mind. There's more to be done, more lives hanging in the balance. The dance of emergency medicine never stops; it only changes tempo.

The ambulance bay doors shudder open again, and Warren rolls in another gurney. This one holds a kid barely into his teens, his body slack but face oddly animated. "Fourteen-year-old male," Warren barks over the clamor of the ER. "On the dirt bike. BP one-forty over one-ninety."

"Jesus, that's high," I mutter, inspecting the boy as we snip away the protective pads. The unmistakable flush of adrenaline—or something more illicit—paints his cheeks a vivid rouge. "Matthew Dempsey, right?" I lean in, trying to pierce the haze of his intoxication with my gaze.

He flails an arm, nearly clipping my jaw. "Nah, man, I ain't done nothing."

"Sure." My voice is flat, unconvinced. "Bloods, tox screen, and keep Narcan on hand." As I rattle off orders, he snickers, lost in whatever chemical joyride he's on. I don't have time for this.

Regina Prince strides over, her short frame practically buzzing with energy. Don't let her size fool you—she's the kind of doctor who commands respect from the moment she opens her mouth. 'Saline, now,' she barks, her tone sharp but calming, a paradox I've never been able to figure out. The kid flinches at her efficiency, his bravado cracking. Good. Regina will handle him, no matter what he's on.

"His parents?" I ask, already pivoting to the next crisis.

"Right behind us," someone assures me.

I leave Matthew in Regina's capable hands and turn to find Warren gesturing helplessly towards a young woman cradling her midsection. Josie Dempsey — her features twisted in pain. "She's hypotensive, same as the first guy," Warren says. "Dazed and confused after the collision."

"Josie, talk to me," I say, easing her onto a gurney. "Where does it hurt?"

"Everywhere," she breathes, her voice trembling as her hands hover protectively over her abdomen. "It was just — so fast. Enrico's mower came out of nowhere, and then Matthew on the dirt bike..." She trails off, wincing as the pain overtakes her words. Her hands clench the gurney rails. "I didn't even see Matthew."

The frustration in her voice is tinged with fear, and I quickly order Demerol to take the edge off, knowing we're only just beginning. Inspecting her, dread coils in my stomach — the way her abdomen distends isn't right. I lean down. "Josie? Are you pregnant?"

"God, no." She moans. "Unless it's immaculate conception."

I smile at her reply, but I can see she's scared and hurting. She chokes back a sob as we cut through her T-shirt.

"This was my favorite concert."

"Coldplay will be around again," I assure her, attempting a smile. I know distraction is feeble comfort when fear has its claws sunk deep.

The needle I'm handed feels like lead in my grip, but I wield it deftly, pulling fluid from her belly. It's blood — too much of it. Josie's eyes roll back, her body surrendering to unconsciousness. 'Ana!' My shout pierces the clamor, summoning the surgeon on call. Dr. Ana Blaine appears, calm and unflinching despite the blood already streaking her scrubs.

As she whisks Josie away to surgery, I take a moment to breathe. The scent of antiseptic and blood clings to the air, and the adrenaline in my veins feels both familiar and suffocating.

The name Dempsey rings in my ears. I can't help but wonder if this surgery will save her — or become another mark in our families' long history of shared tragedies. "Dammit," I whisper to no one. But there's no time to dwell. I've got more patients to see.

Blood speckles my scrubs, and the pulse of the emergency department beats around me. I take one final look at the frenzy, feeling the weight of responsibility on my shoulders, though it's almost time to disengage.

"Greyson, when are you off?" my nurse, Linda, asks, her eyes scanning for the next crisis even as she speaks to me.

I flick my wrist, the watch face glinting under harsh fluorescent lights. "Three hours ago," I admit with a rueful chuckle.

She doesn't miss a beat. "Go," she urges, already looking past me to the next task at hand. "Before we get another wave of patients."

"Will do," I promise. "And hey, I'll grab you those chocolates from Victoria if I have a chance." Her grin is brief but genuine. I've committed her favorite treat to memory.

"Thanks, Greyson. Have fun at the conference," she calls, her attention already back to the fray. "Knock 'em dead with your talk."

A nod and a half wave are all I manage before I pivot on my heel, striding to the exit. The hot spray of the hospital's staff shower does little to wash away the day. Blood speckles my mind as much as my scrubs, and my chest tightens with a cocktail of lingering adrenaline and exhaustion.

By the time I'm slipping into fresh clothes, the weight of what I'm leaving behind presses on me. Josie's pale face, the teenager's bloodshot eyes, Dad's terse messages — it's all there, a quiet storm in the background of my thoughts. I push it aside.

My Range Rover waits patiently in the parking lot like an

old friend. The drive to Victoria will be a welcome escape — an illusion of control on the open road." Slipping behind the wheel, I shake off the residue of urgency that clings like static. The engine purrs to life.

As the hospital fades in my rearview mirror, I feel a strange twinge of guilt — a whisper of everything I'm trying to leave behind for a few days in Victoria. But it's fleeting, gone with the first rush of open air through the window. *No need to worry about that now*, I tell myself. Right now, all I'll focus on is getting through this drive and finding a place where nothing feels like it's waiting for me.

We had one night. No names, no strings, no plans to ever see each other again. But fate has other ideas.

Greyson

Trinity Blaine was supposed to be a one-night and done, but now she's standing in my ER.

She's stubborn, infuriating, and always ready to argue.

She challenges every decision I make and questions everything I stand for.

And yet, I can't stay away.

Trinity says she's only here for her mother, and when her care is sorted, she'll leave.

But every heated argument, every stolen glance, every moment in my bed makes me want to keep her here longer.

I'm not supposed to feel this way. Not about her.

But the longer she's in my world, the harder it is to imagine letting her go.

Trinity

Greyson Paradise is the best ER doctor in a small-town hospital — and the biggest jerk I've ever met.

We shared a moment of passion that I can't forget. Then he ruined it by mocking my work in front of thousands.

And he doesn't even get it.

I never thought I'd have to see him again, but now my mother's in his care, and avoiding him isn't an option.

We clash over everything, but every argument seems to end the same way… in his bed.

I don't have time for messy emotions or arrogant doctors.

Greyson wants me to stay.

I just need to remember why I can't.

Dr. Greyson is a standalone romance with a happy ending. It's the first book in the Brothers Paradise series and introduces you to the Paradise family. You can read it on its own, everything you need to know is explained.

What you can expect from **Dr. Greyson**
* medical romance
* enemies to lovers
* small town
* a bet
* So hot it may melt your Kindle (with some kink and toys)
* age gap
* family saga
* a family winery

Preorders are available on Amazon.

THANK YOU

I want to give a giant shout out to Ainsley St Claire. If you haven't read her books, I encourage you to do so. She's an amazing writer and she's made the all possible for me. She's encouraged me when I wasn't sure I could do this. She helped me upload and start my social media pages. And she's ready and helped edit every single one of my books. I'm eternally grateful!

A big shout out to all of you who've read and reviewed my books. I couldn't do this without you. The more reviews, the more the algorithms show my books. Thank you for loving all my characters and for the notes of support and encouragement. They always seem to come when I need them most.

Thank you to my family. My husband, who kindly reads all my books and while we laugh that these are not autobiographical, he pretends they are. And my two boys who think kissing books are gross (how little the know!). Without their love and support I wouldn't be able to do this.

It takes a village to release a book even when we do it by ourselves. Thank you to my developmental editor, Jessica Royer Oken who makes my words shine.

Thank you to Courtnay, Linda, Iris, and Nancy who find all those pesky typos that try to burrow and stay behind. And thank you Diana for being that final set of eyes.

Thank you to Podium Audio who so kindly took a chance on me and published Mercy Medical Emergency in audio. If you haven't had a chance to check out the series, what are you waiting for?

BOOKS BY GRACE MAXWELL

Men of Mercy
Doctor of the Heart (Paisley & Davis)
Doctor of Women (Nadine & Michael)
Doctor of Sports (Eliza & Steve)
Doctor of Beauty(Laine & Jack)
Men of Mercy Box Set

Mercy Medical Emergency
Doctor Delight (Tori & Griffin)
Doctor Bossy (Amelia & Kent)
Doctor Rebel (Lucy & Chance)
Doctor Enemy (Ava & Roman)
Previously released as *A Doctor for Valentines* in "Love is in the Air, Vol 3"
Doctor Tyrant (Hailey & Christian)

Brothers Paradise
Dr. Greyson (Greyson and Trinity)
Coming April 2025

Printed in Dunstable, United Kingdom

63571505R00167